JOURNEY
from
DELPHI

To Jym & Joe,

The adventure

Continues

Best Wishes

Also by
A.K. PATCH

THE APOLLO SERIES:

BOOK ONE
PASSAGE *at* DELPHI

BOOK TWO
DELPHI'S CHOSEN

www.akpatchauthor.com
Facebook: Passage at Delphi-AK Patch Author
Twitter: @akpatchauthor

THE APOLLO SERIES

JOURNEY
from
DELPHI

BOOK THREE

BY

A. K. PATCH

PEDACEUM
PRESS

Photos:
Map of Ancient Greece, *Preface*
Map of Middle East/Asia, *Preface*
Temple of Apollo at Delphi, *Preface*
Minoan Bull Jumpers, page 367
Glossary, page 471

To my wife and children, Nancy, Alexander and Lauren—

Infinite thanks for your love and support during

this many-year long journey.

A great Empire, like a great cake,
is most easily diminished at the edges.

BENJAMIN FRANKLIN   1706-1790

It's all in the mind.

GEORGE HARRISON   1943-2001

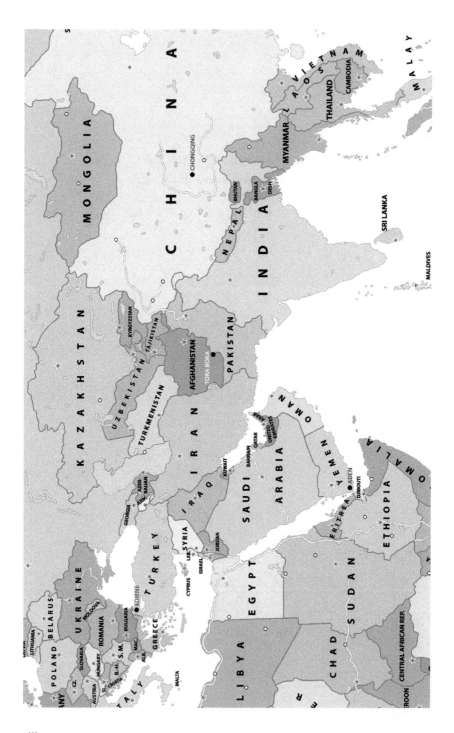

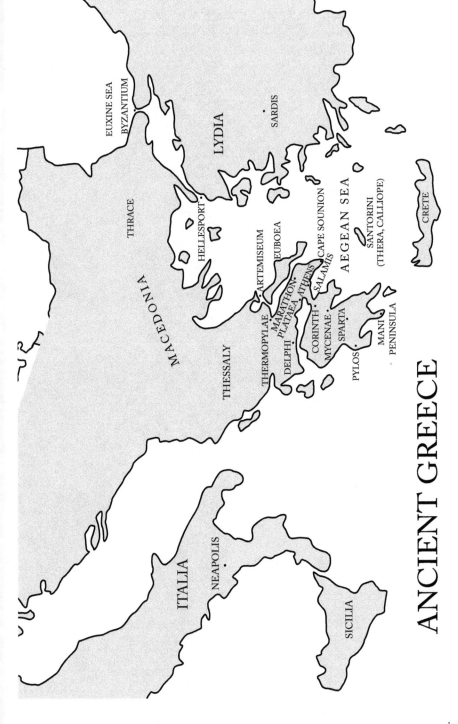

ANCIENT GREECE

Chronology

BC

1626	Approximate date of volcanic destruction of Santorini (Thera)—Minoan Civilization on Crete weakened.
1450	Mycenaeans from mainland Greece dominate Crete.
1200	Dorian invasion from north of Greece. Mycenaean cities destroyed.
1100-800	Greek Dark Age
776	First Olympic Games
590	Solon establishes foundations of Athenian democracy.
550	Foundation of the Persian Empire by King Cyrus.
490	Persian King Darius sends invasion force to Greece and his army is defeated at Marathon.
480	Persian King Xerxes invades Greece. Battles of Thermopylae Pass and Salamis.
479	Battle of Plataea. Persians defeated.
448	Construction of Parthenon begins.
431-404	Peloponnesian War. Athens is defeated by Sparta.
334	Alexander the Great attacks and conquers the Persian Empire.
323	Alexander the Great dies in Babylon.
264	Punic Wars between Rome and Carthage begin. Carthage defeated in 146. Rome becomes the dominant power in the Mediterranean Sea.

Delphi, Greece

There were many oracles in ancient Greece, but none more famous and trusted than Delphi, Apollo's sanctuary in the mountains west of Athens. For almost two thousand years, pilgrims traveled from near and far to reach Delphi, at the time believed by the Greeks to be a site of divine inspiration.

The trance-induced ranting of Pythia, a chaste holy woman, converted into versed prophecies by temple priests, was considered to be the will of the god Apollo. This foretelling of the future influenced not only decisions of everyday life, but also the prospects of colonies and the fate of kingdoms.

Unforgettable are the simple virtues carved into the forecourt of Apollo's temple: "Know Thyself" and "Nothing in Excess." These proverbs demonstrate how the triumphs and tragedies of ancient peoples could serve to guide our lives in the modern day.

PART ONE

Plataea Battlefield, Greece

479 BCE

What manner of god makes the rules and then breaks them with such reckless abandon?

Apollo cradled Zackary Fletcher's head. He dribbled healing nectar past his lips, saying, "Did anyone tell you that a battlefield is no place for a professor?"

After removing Zack's helmet and bronze breastplate, he thought, *I've told myself countless times that my heroes must be expendable. We all had agreed. I cannot continue to rescue them from their fate, but have I come to care too much?*

Blood ran from where the spear had struck his trainee below the collarbone. Apollo pressed his palm over the flow. Hearing gurgling, he turned Zack's head to clear his airway. The man he had named Traveler, a lanky six-foot lecturer of history, now sinew and vein, warrior-melded, had learned the arts of war. The boyish man had proved himself worthy.

Apollo said, "You've navigated the millennia and suffered along the way. No one ever promised that an education should be earned with ease."

He slid off the soaked-cloth cap that shielded Zack's head from the heat of a bronze helmet. Strands of Zack's brown hair lay pasted to his scalp. A flap of skin hung from his cheek where a bird of prey had ventured for a meal before Apollo shooed it away. "You are a sight, but I need you to stand with me at the precipice in your time, in the far future, my Traveler. If we don't succeed when that battled is waged, the consequences will be permanent."

A discarded Spartan cloak became a pillow for Zack's head. Apollo stared off, beyond the mountains, beyond the present, to days far, far ahead. "Conspirators acted when your country reeled and was ripe for destruction. Your countrymen had no expectation that a trap had been laid. You were betrayed in so many ways and even I don't know exactly how."

Zack opened his eyes, dry-swallowed and croaked, "Let me die. Too many... lost. Enough." He seized, coughed raggedly, and blood bubbled from his lips

"The angle of the spear thrust must have pierced your lung," Apollo said.

Zack grimaced. Sweat pooled in the corners of his eyes, drawn by a searing September sun.

Apollo, the Olympian, muscled, blonde-haired and his customary forelock dangling, his white tunic now stained crimson, said, "That is your duty, and your wife's as well, to help me discover their entire plot and to stop them."

After hacking, Zack strained to say, "Lauren. Where?"

Apollo watched the allied Greek army advance in disciplined lines over fallen warriors obstructing their path. Urged along in cadence by their captains, and the shrill cry of double-flutes, the armored hoplites held their bowl shields at an angle to deflect the volleys of retreating Persian bowmen.

Targeted from a distance, arrows pecked the ground near where Apollo stood. Those missiles with more exact marksmanship flashed after ricocheting from his invisible dome. He studied a landscape strewn with clumps of the spent, a threshing ground of many nations.

Recognizing an easy kill, a squadron of Persian horsemen veered from their escape route and rode to Apollo. They loosened arrows and flung their axes at him, causing a spray of yellow sparks. Unable to bring down their mark, the leader dismounted, drew his sword and, in a final effort, swung it at the man before him. The weapon flew from his burnt hand and fell to the ground, red and smoking. The cavalrymen turned their horses in circles, wanting to come no closer. They shouted for their captain to retreat.

Apollo heard the warriors argue about the gods in this land and what power they bore to render their attack so useless, how their fortunes had changed, and the many battles lost when their numbers should have guaranteed victory. The Persian captain, shaking his singed hand and wide-eyed by what had no explanation, gave the signal to flee. Hindquarters and tails caught Apollo's last glance before he turned his attention back to the warrior at his feet.

Zack breathed evenly. He said, just above a whisper, "Where is she?"

"The healing nectar is doing its work." Apollo looked towards a burning stockade after a resounding cheer announced that the Greeks had overcome the Persian garrison.

"Someone knew exactly where to strike at the heart of your system. Technology betrayed you and became your curse, instead."

"Lauren?" Zack asked with clenched teeth.

"Safe…for now," Apollo answered.

Zack eyes registered the comforting news. He appeared to release the angst of not knowing and closed his eyes.

"Engage sleep's comfortable embrace," Apollo said. "I'll place you in a secure spot while you are healing, and I transfer in time through Delphi to gather Bessus in Athens and deliver him to a new camp in Yemen. There is another lesson ahead for you, too, and I'll be back."

A nausea rose in Apollo's gut. It could have been the aroma of wounded men and horses, but he knew it wasn't. *I reveal my own weaknesses for I fear the time when all of you might be sacrificed. And yet, the greater cause must rule. While I should know what will occur, the fact is that I don't, and there are perilous days ahead.*

He gathered Zack and settled him onto a cart, contemplating that a hero's return home cannot be guaranteed, not for mortals…and neither had it ever proved to be … for gods.

Desert beyond Ta'lzz, Yemen

PRESENT DAY

Apollo landed his dome his three kilometers outside a mud-brick village. The swirls of blue-colored energy dissipated and left him standing with Bessus at his feet. Sleep during travel worked well for his wild-eyed warlord transposed in time by twenty-five hundred years. The barbarian had yet to grasp how Apollo moved him at will.

Bessus shook his head to waken. He peered at the sunbaked plates of fractured sand he lay upon. "Desert. What will you do with me now?"

"Make our way before we cook out here. A place to refresh is nearby." Apollo pointed to palm trees.

The wafered sand cracked underfoot. A sudden wind caught their white robes and sent them billowing into Bessus's face. He gave Apollo an annoyed look. They reached a pen of skeletal-looking cattle. Soon surrounded by a wreath of black flies, the barbarian swatted and spit to be free of them. Bessus ran. Apollo smirked, catching up with him.

Another man so tormented in time might earn a measure of sympathy from Apollo.

But not this man.

Circa 480 BCE, in the ancient land of Bactria, now modern day northeastern Afghanistan, Bessus had commanded a castle, mountain strongholds and farmlands. He gained land, horses, and villages with the swath of his axe. A land that bred warriors on horseback obeyed no overlords until the Persians ravaged their lands, slaughtered kin, and herded them to serve the empire.

An insult Bessus would never forget. Enormous and foul-smelling, face crisscrossed with poorly stitched scars, the barbarian represented a living nightmare to those he met.

Apollo's thoughts wandered. He had to send Bessus back in time to the year before for training and adaptation to the modern world. It was a complication in the time loop he had wished to avoid but manipulating people and events in different millennia had proved to be difficult...even for him.

He had created his own dilemma.

Even a god can err.

Back then, nearly a year ago, Bessus, and Abu, an interpreter from a mosque where the barbarian had taken refuge in Turkey, rode with him in a truck from Edirne toward a river dock.

Apollo burst out laughing, remembering when he'd watched Bessus gripping a door handle in the back seat of their truck as they left the mosque in Edirne. It was the warlord's first ride in any kind of automobile.

Cars swerved around the truck in a rush to reach the riverfront. A squeal of tires and a dirge of horns had Bessus raising his arms across his face and shouting in ancient Bactrian, "Let me out. Deliver me from this madness."

Abu stomped on his brakes to avoid mopeds cutting across lanes. The oversized barbarian slammed backwards and hit his head on the ceiling.

Seeing the antics of the giant in the rearview mirror, Abu said, "What's wrong with him? It's like he's never been in traffic." The driver shifted gears and a loud grinding came from the undercarriage.

Bessus lifted off the seat. "What beast lurks beneath us?" He yanked at the seat belt and harness across his shoulder.

"I can't understand anything he says," Abu said, "The Imam said it's as if he knows nothing, not even how to use a toilet, or a fork. The scars crisscrossing his face make him a...a nightmare. That bush on his head is full of twigs and filth."

Apollo, having darkened his hair and tucked his distinctive dangling forelock beneath a white prayer cap, turned to Bessus and said in the warlord's Bactrian language, "Calm down. You're safe with me."

"It's you," Bessus bellowed, recognizing Apollo from the days they'd ridden together during Xerxes's campaign to conquer Greece. "I'll strangle you where you sit."

Apollo grinned. "That would be difficult when you're holding on for your life."

The warrior shut his eyelids tight. "This chariot...it rides like the rapids. Slow it down or I will splash you with my guts." He fumbled with the seat belt. "Remove me from this ...horror."

"Has it ever occurred to you, Stinkpile, that you *are* the horror?" Apollo said.

"Can you shut him up?" Abu asked. "Otherwise, I'm sticking a needle in him. They gave me sedatives for him when we get on the ship."

Behind them, Apollo saw two police on motorcycles weaving through the traffic, lights swirling and sirens blaring. One of policemen pointed at their truck. Cars veered off to give the motorcycles clear lanes.

Bessus discovered their pursuers, too. "It's those guards with the firesticks. They seek to slay me."

A policeman shot out the back window. Fragments of glass sprayed Bessus.

Abu said, "They must have caught our trail from the mosque. Should I pull over?"

Apollo replied, "No, go faster. I have a remedy."

He handed Bessus a handful of caltrops, small metal-spiked balls.

"These take down horsemen," Bessus said. Then his eyes widened with recognition.

"You know what to do with them," Apollo said.

Bessus threw the spikes out the shattered back window. The motorcycles caught the sharp ends, blew tires, and crashed into merchants' stalls. Chickens scattered, and smoking braziers overturned.

"Aha!" Bessus cackled. "Give me more. I want to do it again. Did you see the feathers fly?"

Apollo said, "It might be better to hide yourself. Lie down."

Bessus struggled with the belt. "I can't get free…"

Abu pointed at the back seat. "I'm turning on the radio. I'm sick of his blabbering."

The Bactrian looked under the seat and then at Apollo. "Where is he? Where's the singer?"

"His voice is heard, but the singer is not here."

Tilting his head with his mouth agape, Bessus asked, "How can that be?"

"You have so much to learn, and you shall," Apollo said. "No one can speak your tongue but me. Where we are now, the words of your people are forgotten. So is Xerxes, his army and his bridges."

Bessus stared out the window. "Gone? The great king and his armies?"

"They are. Do you still have the likeness of the Sorceress?" Apollo asked, referring to Lauren Fletcher's driver's license, a costly trophy from a desperate fight that the barbarian had with the surprisingly tough professor in his tent.

Bessus withdrew the square from his leather waist pouch. "I don't understand how her face stays painted on this. I scratched it, but my nail slips. I see the evil in her smile, and that dirty face will be covered with worms in the grave after I am finished with her. I vow it."

"Then you must not lose that likeness, for it will guide you to her."

"How?"

"The Greek writing on the surface."

Bessus scrunched his face.

9

"But you must earn the way to her door. Do you remember the girl who stabbed you and left you to burn in that cave?"

Bessus looked afar. Apollo saw pain and disappointment in the warrior's eyes after reminding him of when Cassandra, a girl from the ancient Delphi, had rescued Professor Lauren from his grip during a second fight.

Apollo continued, "How did you escape the burning pots and get out of that cave?"

"I must have crawled."

"It's I who saved you, Bessus. I rescued you from burning alive," Apollo said. "And I healed your singed skin."

Bessus blinked, looking at his unscarred arms.

"I have but to slay your enemies and you will deliver the Sorceress into my hands?"

"That is the bargain." Apollo marveled at the level of hate Bessus felt for Lauren, after she wounded and escaped him in both the ancient and modern worlds.

Bessus bared his canines, the only teeth in the front of his mouth. "Then I will do your bidding. Who do I smite first?"

Apollo revealed one of his bronze medallions.

"Not that," Bessus said, able to retreat no further in the back seat. "It bears dark magic. Throw it away."

Invisible pulses from the medallion brought calm to the giant. His head leaned to one side and drool slipped from his lips.

"Allah is merciful. I thought he would get us killed. Is he asleep?" Abu asked.

"He is. Even killers need their rest."

Apollo smiled for the memory. Bessus had been afterwards transported with Abu through the Suez Canal, down the Red Sea, along the Gulf of Aden and up the Arabian Sea to land in Karachi. Trains and trucks delivered him to a secret base on the Afghan-Pakistani border near the Tora Bora Mountains.

Following months of adaptation, Abu accompanied Bessus, entering the United States through a tunnel under the southern border from Mexico into San Diego. Bessus disposed of Abu and chased my professors in a car to compel them to go to Greece. Pursuing them around the ruins of the Parthenon, and through the streets of Athens, Bessus had done his job coercing the professors towards the Delphi transit.

Apollo had previously implanted a tracking beacon on Bessus, found him about to raid a butcher's shop near the Plaka district, and whisked him away within the dome to the Yemeni desert.

He had succeeded in solving the problem in having Bessus arrive at the proper time to propel his professors towards Greece.

Time travel is a messy business.

Apollo refocused on their present location. Approaching a village near Ta'lzz, they halted amid mud huts and palm trees. Just beyond, an outcropping of rocks and openings led underground. Further out, the endless desert sizzled. Men carrying rifles sprinted past them towards a gathering.

Bessus asked. "These are the black-skins that rode camels in Xerxes's army."

"They are." Apollo saw no use in explaining the expanse of time from the 5th Century BCE till now.

The barbarian peered at a line of goats led by children. "I could eat three of them."

"The goats, I presume." A caravan of horses, burdened with supplies and weapons, trudged the wind-blown landscape towards a cave opening. Four prisoners in dirty robes followed, tied to the horses by ropes. Apollo said, "Dinner may have to wait."

Desert beyond Ta'lzz, Yemen

PRESENT DAY

White-robed AQSD -Al Qaeda in Saudi Arabia- guards shot their AK-47's into the air.

Even after many months spent previously in the Afghan camps, Bessus cringed at the sound of gunfire. He straightened up when the shooting ceased and saw the guards laughing at him. Bessus curled his fists.

Apollo warned him not to attack them. "Swallow your pride for now, Bessus."

Bessus let out a long breath through his nose. "They mock me. Why?"

"They don't understand why you shirk from their firesticks. These men don't know what kind of warrior you are. They fear your size and the look on your face."

"What look?"

Apollo patted him on the back. "Come."

"Who are the prisoners?"

"Do you care? Come to the range. I want you to fire one of their weapons. You must learn to not fear it."

Apollo, dressed the part in his white robe and wearing a *kufiyah*, a headdress held on by thick coils. He talked in Arabic to a man with an enormous mole on his cheek who yelled directions at a firing range bounded on three sides by dunes. The man handed Bessus a rifle, but then pantomimed ducking and running like Bessus had, only to return laughing harder.

Bessus scrunched his face, looking like he would burst and start swinging his knife.

Apollo counseled, "Calm down. Let them have their fun. Hold up the stick."

The barbarian felt the weight and held it at his waist. "They never let me have one in the mountain camp."

"For good reason. Brace it against your shoulder. Raise it to eye level. Be careful not to point it at the other warriors."

In the distance, Bessus saw the four prisoners lined up and tied to posts five feet from each other.

"They want you slay the warriors with the firestick," Apollo said.

"What else did this dog say to you?" Bessus asked, nodding towards to range master.

"You can fire the stick, but if the prisoners still live, you'll be guarding sheep, instead."

Apollo helped Bessus point the weapon down range and click off the safety, instructing him in Bactrian, "Squeeze the metal ring where your finger is. Not too long, though, for the weapon will be unsteady in your hands."

Bessus scoffed, "Bah." He pressed the trigger, spraying trees, rocks, and piles of camel shit. The warriors around him hugged the dirt.

"More bees," Bessus said, shaking the firestick. The gun master tried to pull the gun away.

Bessus held on tight, shouting to Apollo, "I won't give it up. Unhand me, or I'll smash his skull."

Apollo said calmly, "They are angry the prisoners are still alive and that the bees almost killed the fighters. They may draw their weapons and slay you, instead."

"Release the weapon," the gun master shouted at Bessus in Arabic.

Finally, Bessus let it go, snarled at the mole-faced man and drew his knife.

Apollo saw the move and yelled, "Don't, Bessus…"

Bessus sprinted towards the prisoners. The warriors shouted and pointed at him. One aimed his gun at Bessus, but Apollo diverted the muzzle.

When Bessus reached the prisoners, he drew back the head of the first man and cut his throat. The other prisoners screamed for mercy. Bessus ignored their cries. He held up the knife and sang an ancient war song of the Black Dust Mountains of Tora Bora. "I don't need your firesticks. You will know Bessus before long." He let go another ear-shattering war cry.

Apollo saw men emerge from the cave to watch Bessus strut before the slumped bodies of the executed, pointing his knife at them and then back at the slain.

Bessus bellowed in Bactrian, "I'm tired of your tricks. Teach me your weapons and how to speak in your tongue, and I shall cut a path through your enemies to get to the Sorceress."

Apollo said to the range master in Arabic. "Who were the prisoners?"

"Houthis. Backed by Iran. They used to fight the government. Now, everyone fights each other."

Apollo gestured towards Bessus. "You must admit, he's entertaining."

The man squinted under the afternoon sun. "Amusing, yes, but why do you pay us gold to watch him, Sheik?"

"He is unique. Tell your men to watch their words with him. He is a warrior in his land and his temper is short. Many have fallen before his blade. He must survive to serve a purpose later."

The gun master saw Bessus cut off the ears of the dead prisoners. "It will be so, God willing. If he likes to kill, we can make good use of him."

The setting sun cast light across the mountains.

"Give me a horse, or I'll take one," Bessus told Apollo. The air turned cold. Bessus sat close to a fire, eating rice and lamb chunks with his fingers. He watched Apollo form brown rice into little balls. The only other food on Apollo's plate was an overcooked turnip. "Where is your meat? How can you be strong with that pile of nothing?"

"I only eat plants and fruit."

Bessus gave him a bug-eyed look and flung out his hand, dismissing Apollo.

"Don't concern yourself with my ways, Bessus. After our lessons in the tongue of these warriors, we will meet the warlord in his tent and talk of how you can serve them."

"I will be more useful on a good horse and wielding a double-bladed axe. These warriors hide behind their firesticks."

"The stick that spits out the bees can kill many quickly. There is another weapon I will show you tomorrow. You must see it to understand."

"Slaying a man should be done close in. What honor is there in killing him from a distance?"

"This is the first time I've heard you speak of honor."

"I'm honored when those I slay know it is Bessus who has laid them low."

Apollo continued, "Do you not have any other aims, Bessus? I know you want riches to secure your son's holding and to kill the sorceress, but is there nothing else you want?"

Bessus gave him a look of surprise. "To rule in comfort from my throne seat. Smite my enemies. Why must I even think of it?"

Apollo leaned in and said, "Because, Bessus, a true warrior, one who is a free man and not a slave, decides his own fate. He assists others in their time of need. Slaughter does not enter the thoughts of such a man. He seeks to protect others."

After smacking a fly on his leg, Bessus flicked it at Apollo. "You are a weakling. You fill your head with piss. Why should I care about anyone but myself and my son?" Bessus stood. "I will not be satisfied until the Sorceress is dead. Only then may you talk to me of all this…" He flung out his hand in disgust. "Get me out here before I slay these whore's sons."

Apollo set his plate on a rock. He stood and stretched. "You must be able to fight with all the weapons to survive here. You have not seen the power of these weapons. Some can raze cities with one lightning bolt."

Bessus stopped chewing. He looked at Apollo with eyes that expressed disbelief. "Only a god could do that. I see no gods here."

"The Sorceress's world is one of mystery and power, great destruction, and tantalizing comforts. Let us practice these warrior's words more so they might understand you."

After Bessus had repeated the words in Bactrian, ancient Persian, and Arabic ten times, Apollo called a halt to the lesson and walked him back to the range. Night shadows blanketed the camp. Aside from the firing range, the site gave the appearance of a village. Most of the communications equipment, housing, food and weapons had been moved inside the network of caves. Guards with binoculars searched the skies for drones.

Bessus said, "I'm weary, Scout. Where do you take me now?"

Apollo grinned. "To make you feel like a god."

"I need no aid from you." Bessus pounded his chest.

A guard burst out of the mouth of the cave, shouting and gesturing for everyone to move inside.

Bessus asked, "Why does everyone now hurry back into that stinking hole in the hill?"

Apollo pointed at the sky. "To escape the eyes in the sky that see all that we do."

Bessus peered upwards. He spat, and then lifted his eyes again. "I see nothing. It's dark. Is this camp full of cowards, too?"

"It is the Sorceress's warriors. They can see us from above, even in the dark."

"What? They can fly?"

Apollo said. "They are brave warriors with many more Greek inventions, and they can see us from the sky."

Bessus scanned the mountain and the moon that rose just above the peaks. "I hate this Sorceress's world. Sticks that fire bees and eyes in the sky? Bring me home."

"There will come a time for you. For now, we must seek shelter in the cave."

They came outside after the satellite had moved on. Apollo watched

Bessus listen to the rumble of gasoline generators that powered flood lights.

Apollo said, "The torches you see are given strength by the humming in that invention."

Bessus considered the explanation as he chewed on the inside of his cheeks. "I have seen the sand warriors filling it with the strange smelling beer."

"The beer, as you say, powers the invention. Come with me to the long field," Apollo said.

When they arrived at the firing line, Apollo lifted a rocket-propelled launcher. He loaded the RPG with a cone-shaped grenade. Bessus looked on, arms folded, and lips pursed.

Apollo held the launcher on his shoulder and extended the sight. "Shut the big hole in your face and learn. Here, hold it." Apollo pointed out the trigger. "Keep your finger off this."

Bessus grunted, received the launcher and held it as Apollo had.

"It's dark. I want you to see the power of these weapons, and I want you to see it at night."

"This is a useless club to knock in a head."

"Now, squeeze that metal ring with your finger. Hold the club tight."

"Stop talking to me like I'm a boy at my mother's teat." Bessus jerked the trigger. Backfire exploded from the rear of the weapon. A missile hurtled out of the front, belching fire and smoke. It coursed down range and exploded against a wood pile in a fury of flame and sparks. Even in the torchlight, Apollo saw Bessus's face display a kaleidoscope of shock and amazement. Bessus threw down the RPG launcher, looked at his hands and then at the weapon. He leapt upwards and bellowed a Bactrian war cry. "Elee, Elee, Elee!" He stormed back and forth in front of Apollo, talking to himself and pointing at where the RPG had exploded.

Apollo asked him. "Do you feel like a god now?"

As the barbarian danced, Apollo thought, *only he doesn't know that he'll languish here for several years digging sand out of his ears. That way, I can keep him out of trouble until I need him. After Bessus gains trust in each of these training camps, he will be my eyes and ears to reveal what they're planning, whether here or back in Afghan/Pakistani border camp.*

You are a horror, Bactrian. You may pillage and murder, but your damage is limited to those you meet. I submit to you that there are those who possess far more wealth, and yet pose a more mortal danger on a global scale. They are predators with different motives.

With the accounts incomplete in the Book of Histories, whoever they are, and whatever they plot, finding and stopping them is what we must do. And that is because history…all history…had been erased after the fatal attack. The Book of Histories halted on a single day.

Lauren, professor and true heroine, whom I nicknamed "Golden Hair", has rescued the children and brought them to her home in San Diego. She desired to be a mother, and that is her reward for courage. Just not in the way she had expected. Zack, her husband, the one I call 'Traveler', has endured battles and injuries, but he advances. Tougher and wiser he must be to assist in what lies ahead.

Now, Bessus, Stink-pile that you are, I must return to Traveler. He has a meeting coming that I think he will find difficult to believe.

"I must leave you for a time," Apollo said. "You are here to train."

Bessus halted his dance. "Forsake me too long, and I will smite everyone here."

"It will take many moons. Be patient. Know that I will be back to guide you." Apollo walked up to Bessus, a foot from his face. "You will not harm anyone here but enemies."

"Then I will hike into the desert and find my way to Bactria."

"You will perish out there and the scorpions will eat your carcass. Stay here until I deliver you, or you'll never see your home or son again."

Chongqing Complex, China

PRESENT DAY

Dr. Alfred Fung's laptop displayed the same information as it had five minutes earlier. He bit on the end of a stylus pen, sat poised on the edge of his seat, awaiting clinical results from his staff.

In the year that he had created and supervised this new laboratory, advances had been dramatic. All the years of prep work in the States coalesced into this one report.

Unable to will the screen to deliver the news he sought, Alfred rested his eyes. The little finger on his right hand began to twitch. Still in his late thirties, he didn't need reading glasses. Yet. Too much time in front of a computer would change that. His build resembled that of his venerated grandfather, evidenced from a photograph taken in 1934--stocky, taller than most--a warrior's body, and a physique that had survived the rigors of Mao Zedong's 'Long March'.

Soon enough, Alfred would resemble his *'Yie'* too--what he called his father in the 'Old Xiang', the dialect of their home province. He came from a line of men who struggled and thrived.

He would prove himself worthy of them.

After gathering investors, he had convinced the PRC, the People's Republic of China, to allow a new research center to be built within the remains of a nuclear test complex from the 1960s. Navigating past suspicions about his intent, the authorities granted his wishes when they realized the potential of his research.

Just as the United States had chosen to do.

He rose from his chair and viewed an extensive supply list instead.

Alfred heard the clicking of heels on the concrete flooring before seeing his trusted laboratory supervisor rush into his office. She brushed back strands of her brown-highlighted hair that had come loose in her dash from the clinical trial lab.

"Dr. Fung," she said. Dropping her hands on his desk for support, the lady technician slowed her respirations. "I'm sorry. Come with me, please. You won't believe it." She straightened her lab coat.

"What is it Lian?" This team leader interested him more than the others. She continued to display a healthy tan, representing effort in the fields, despite her devoted work schedule within the facility. His grandfather would approve of her.

"Allow me to surprise you," she said.

Beguiling, he thought. That's the word for her.

Passing engineering crews reinforcing steel blast-doors leading towards the interior of the former 816 Nuclear Military Plant, Alfred viewed Lian's white lab coat, crisply starched, but nonetheless swaying with her gait.

Tractors loaded pallets of canned, freeze-dried, and packaged foods into storage rooms along the way. Turning a corner, she nodded towards a massive room that grew vegetables under ultraviolet lights. Armed guards saluted Alfred as the two approached a glass-enclosed and sealed laboratory.

"This space fits our needs perfectly," Alfred said. "With twelve miles of caves, roads and tunnels, there's more than enough room for my laboratories, housing for staff...and the chosen others."

"Put in a theatre and recreational facilities. We'll never have to leave."

"You are so right, Lian." *No one is going to leave...for a very long time.*

Alfred put his finger on a pad. After a retina identification camera also validated them, they enter Clinic Number One.

The clinic held fifty beds, each with computer monitoring and pulse oximeters to measure vitals. Nursing staff and attendants assisted elderly patients, helping them out of beds, into wheelchairs, and off to the dining room. The clinic smelled of soiled sheets.

Lian said, "This is a new group from a mountain village about a hundred kilometers from here. They are just being assessed now. On to Clinic Two, Doctor."

The door opened with a release of compressed air. Fifty more elderly patients watched television and sat in wheelchairs that had been placed in circles to promote conversation. Many residents moved about with their walkers, talking with staff and laughing.

Alfred said, "These patients are progressing."

"Just one question before we proceed to Clinic Three? If you are exceptionally pleased, might we discuss our findings…later?" Lian smiled at him like she had the evening locked in.

He answered, "It depends. Other technicians have requested to review their division's progress as well."

The glass door of Clinic Three opened. Nearly forty more gray-haired patients came into view. Some played chess. Others hit Ping-Pong balls with deft movements. An elderly woman led a class in Tai-Chi. Another stood at a podium and lectured about the health benefits of Huang Da Cha yellow tea from her hometown province in Anhui.

"What is the period and titer for this group?" Alfred asked.

"A month only, Dr. Fung. One month for graduation from Clinic One to Three. We are pleased."

A well-struck ball whizzed past Alfred's ear. Lian laughed, picked it up and tossed it back. A man caught it on the fly and thanked her. In Cantonese, he asked Lian for a date that evening.

She replied, "I do apologize, Bohai. I fear I will be busy tonight." She gave Alfred a fleeting grin.

Alfred said. "The medicine is having the desired therapeutic effect. It's dissolving beta-amyloid proteins at an astounding rate. I'm sure you've kept tight watch over dosages by age, weight, and sex among the experimental and control groups?"

Lian touched him furtively with her hip. "It will take some time to go over these parameters in detail."

Alfred shook his head. "You have impressive results, but couldn't you have just sent me the report instead of running to my office and dragging me here?"

She smiled in a way that informed Alfred he was being played.

"And how many have we lost in the process?" Alfred asked, seeking to deflate her arrogant presumptions. He had no intention of being manipulated.

Lian consulted her sheets. "Six in Clinic One, but they were likely beyond help. Eleven in Clinic Two when we didn't quite know how to gauge the concentration of the drug at first and they went into convulsions."

"Clinic Three?" Alfred said, taking a deep breath and feigning displeasure with her. He didn't want to focus on the sheen of her hair.

She circled behind Alfred, and said quietly, "Only three. You might consider recognizing the efforts of the staff?"

Drawing in Lian's clean fragrance, Alfred took a couple of steps away from her. "I will, despite the losses. They're in the acceptable range. How many groups in the study?"

"Twenty-three so far. We'll run out of provinces." Lian awaited his reaction. "Almost a thousand perished in the experimentation stage."

He looked at the group of retirees, all considered hopeless earlier, and frankly expendable. They would go back to productive lives in the factories.

"You know what this means, Dr. Fung. You have a cure for dementia diseases with a medication that brings optimal results in one month. This group proves there is great promise for it. Congratulations."

Alfred couldn't help returning his top division leader's beaming smile. "I'm delighted. I waited a long time. We worked hard."

"So then?" Lian clasped her hands behind her back.

Alfred forced himself to say, "We have reached a milestone well ahead of schedule. I will increase your chocolate credits when I return to my office."

"Disappointing, Dr. Fung. Come along and perhaps I can change your mind."

A silver-colored door opened and Lian led Alfred down a passageway. Humming a song from her birth village near Xiang, dancing and spinning under the LEV lighting, Lian led him to an area of the complex Alfred had not been to since the opening inspection.

"I'm beginning to be concerned about your lack of composure," Alfred said, unable to remove his gaze from her lithe figure.

"I'm happy…and we're here," she said. A metallic door opened.

Alfred entered behind Lian. She turned the lights on.

Fifty elderly men and women were standing on their heads, with their legs balancing in the air and hands on the ground providing support. A few fell, rested, and reassumed their positions with the help of attendants.

Fung said. "How could you get them to do that?"

Lian squeezed his hand. "See how they are all in sync with their balancing leg movements? Watch this, now."

She announced, "Squad A. I want you to rise, rest for a minute, and then jump from one foot to the other in unison."

The group performed the task with smiles and laughter, although with slower motions.

"New instruction," Lian barked. "Squad A. Show this man here how much you dislike him."

Alfred glanced at Lian, seeing the curl of her lip and fierceness in her eyes he'd never witnessed before. He turned to see the subjects let out screams and rush at Alfred with teeth bared and fingers curled to attack. A few meters away from him, Alfred raised his arms defensively.

Lian shouted, "Halt."

They stopped their charge, though some crashed into others and collapsed. The faces that peered at Alfred now lacked expression.

"Go to the other side of the room and face the wall," she instructed. Two of the patients that had been hurt in the rush didn't get up. Orderlies dragged them away by their feet.

Lian said, "What I have done is increase the titer and concentration of our dementia drug. It has taken some time, but I have the beginnings of a new product here. In fact, this is a revelation, Dr. Fung. With further study and collaboration, we can create a drug that controls people's thoughts and actions. What do you think?" She waited. Her eye contact didn't wander.

Alfred gaped at the group pressed against the far wall.

"They don't know limitations. We create most of our own, do we not? Imagine an army of devoted servants?" Lian said. "We took five ultra-medicated subjects and told them to execute criminals who were days from capital sentences. You want to see the recording?"

"Not now. You've done amazing work. I always wondered if this kind of control might be a potential side effect. It's like you've read *my* mind." He laid his hands on her shoulders. "Graceful Willow, that is what your name means. Only *we* must know of this discovery. Antibiotics that we're developing to kill infections that might cause these dementia diseases are promising also. But, we mustn't tell PRC authorities about this advance. They will not approve."

"I am honored that you endorse our work, and I will admit to reading your mind...a little." Lian smiled.

"How many have died in this area of experimentation?"

"Thousands, Dr. Fung. It will take years possibly to hone down what works and what is too much. We'll have to develop an immediate antidote as well, and one that reverses the effects of the drug slowly. We may want to resume the disease state, even accelerate it...if necessary."

"Excellent strategies. It will take years to build out this facility anyway. I must return to the US soon, but you have earned your way onto our new Politburo Standing Committee."

With a coy look, she said, "Is that...all?"

No longer holding back, "And yes, we will celebrate tonight...and a few more nights also."

After brushing Alfred's chin with her lips, she said, "I am your devoted servant."

Lian led Alfred outside the room, blew a kiss to the patients, turned off the lights, and slammed the door behind her. She thought, *unless you become my servant first, Dr. Fung.*

5

Coronado Island, San Diego, California

PRESENT DAY

Beyond the long Point Loma peninsula, a gray naval vessel waited outside the entrance to San Diego harbor. Lauren and her newly adopted son, Demo, erected a tent on the beach. She gathered her honey-colored hair and secured it with an elastic band. A Padres ball cap shielded her face from a strong December sun.

"See that ship out there, Demo?" Lauren said in Greek to her curly-haired teenager. A mess of thin arms and legs under shorts and a tee-shirt, she hoped he might put on a few pounds in the coming months. Lauren couldn't guess how tall he might get with his parents having passed away. She had forgotten to ask about parental history back at the orphanage with the dire events surrounding her rescue of the children back in Greece. "That's a navy destroyer. It's fast, and it protects the larger ships we saw when we drove across the bridge. It has missiles and big guns." She handed him a couple of collapsible tent poles to thread through the holders.

Demo's hand shielded his eyes. "There were lots of ships on the other side of the bridge. Can we visit one?"

"Sure. My father flew fighter jets and can take us onto the North Island Naval Base when he's better. We'll tour the big flattop with the jet fighters on board." They completed the tent setup.

Lauren glanced at Cassandra, adopted along with Demo. They had made up a birthdate for her passport to get her into the US. After all, no one knew exactly when she was born, but the best guess would be around 493 BCE. At around thirteen years old, she held the same height and figure of her birth mother, Persephone. Lauren imagined she might gain more in height. The steady diet in the orphanage, for even the short time they stayed there, had filled her out. Dark eyes and wavy brown hair glowed with good health. Cassandra returned her smile. Lauren saw Persephone again in the return glance and she couldn't deter a horrible flashback of Persephone's death at the hand of Bessus.

She thought, *We're far away from you now, barbarian bastard.*

Lauren shook the vision away and refocused on the kids.

Cassandra had seen modern-day wonders during her first months in Greece, but life in the US would bring so many more. Lauren said to her in ancient Ionian, "Watch how I open the top of the water bottle for you, Sweetheart. Grab the top tightly in your hand and twist." The top spun off and Lauren took a swig of the water. She handed Cassandra a different bottle. "You try this one."

Cassandra gritted her teeth, twisted off the cover and handed it to her mother. "I solved the puzzle of the covering." She lifted the bottle and drank. Too much came out from too strong a squeeze. The water ran down her neck. Cassandra giggled, and Demo shook his head.

"She needs work," Demo said.

"There's a lot to teach you, too, young man. Most children go to public school here, but you won't be able to do that right away."

Demo smiled like he'd seen a dessert buffet. "You mean I don't have to go to school? That's great."

Cassandra watched Demo jump up and do a victory dance. "What makes him so joyous?"

"He thinks he doesn't have to attend school."

"Not so fast, Demo," Lauren said, opening the picnic basket. "I'm planning to home-school you and your sister. I can arrange an English/Greek tutor for you quite easily, but I must teach Cassandra myself for the reasons you already know. How I'm going handle all this is the big question right now. I must take you to a doctor, too. There's a company in San Diego that can cure Hepatitis C."

He gave her a 'thumbs up'.

Lauren opened a bag of fried chicken from the grocery store. The aroma overwhelmed the brine of the seashore. "Imagine what she must be thinking about everything that's happened."

Both children focused their attention on the chicken.

"What did you say, Mom?" Demo asked.

"All right, I surrender. Grab a napkin."

Demo snatched a drumstick and handed it to Cassandra. She licked the leg, then took a hesitant bite and chewed. She smiled.

"I guess she likes it," Demo said, snagging a piece in each hand.

Lauren rested on her elbows. The sun shimmered off the water. Not too many beachgoers so far on a mid-December day. There wouldn't be many swimmers, anyway. California water was cold most of the year, and this stretch of beach wasn't popular with local surfers.

The scream of a jet fighter coming in for a landing at NAS North Island caused Cassandra to jump, drop her chicken, and cover her ears. She stared at the plane in disbelief before she threw herself into Lauren's arms.

"What monster is that? How could the gods allow such a beast? Will it eat us? We must dig a hole to hide in right now." Cassandra knelt and pressed her hands together. "I beseech you, Athena. Deliver us from the beast that flies like Pegasus and voices its hunger."

"Cool," Demo said pointing. "A fighter! What kind is it?"

"F-18 Super Hornet, I think." Lauren soothed Cassandra. "Don't be concerned, Sweetheart. It is a weapon our warriors use to fight our enemies. A man or a woman can fly such an invention. I will show you one up close, so you will not be frightened of them."

"Protect us?" Cassandra peered at her with questioning eyes. "A woman can ride one?"

"Men and women are warriors in our land and protect us from real monsters like Bessus. Do you think Bessus could defeat a weapon such as that?"

Cassandra stood beside Demo. "I am no longer frightened. If my brother does not fear it, then I will not." She shook her fist at the jet doing a 'touch and go' just before it gained altitude and flew past Point Loma. "You will not come back and scare me again. I am an Athenian. I will be a warrior someday. Do you hear me?"

"Why's she shaking her fist?" Demo asked.

"She's telling it she's not frightened of it any longer."

"Maybe I should take her down to the shore. We can make a castle."

"Grand idea, Demo. After you guys eat, I'll be down to help."

Lauren gave them each two more pieces of chicken.

Cassandra licked her fingers. "Shall we make an offering of these bones to Athena, or maybe the god of all travelers, Hermes? Maybe they will bring Master Zack home to us."

Where is Zack now? Lauren wondered. How can I possibly help him?

"Maybe a third prayer to Apollo, too," Lauren said.

"Be it your wish. Apollo will rescue our father and bring him home in his horse-drawn chariot, which soars in the heavens faster than the invention I just saw?"

"We must pray." Lauren clasped her hands.

Cassandra spoke loudly enough to be heard above the crashing surf. "Lord God Apollo. You of the Silver Bow and the flying steeds of the sun, hear our appeal to deliver our father to us. He is a warrior, and he has earned his return home."

"Well said, Sweetheart."

"Is she going to pray every time she has something to say?" Demo asked.

Lauren smothered her smile. "Here, finish your chicken and take her to the water."

The children dug into the wet sand, fashioning castle walls surrounded by a wide moat.

As she watched them play, Lauren wondered how she would manage all the tasks ahead. Teach full time at the university and home-school Cassandra and Demo. She wouldn't be able to tell anyone what had happened to them and why Cassandra only spoke ancient Greek.

I'm their mother and I will create a new life for them. But what if Apollo's prediction comes true in the future? How much time do we have? How do I protect them?

Another F-18 roared past. *I need you, Zack. Our children need a father. Come home to us. But if you're taken away permanently, then I'm going to find a way to raise these children myself. I must live in the moment. Care for the children. Be a Mother.*

Lauren thought about all the challenges she'd overcome to get the children to San Diego. She had beaten both Bessus and the corrupt policeman, Trokalitis. She'd bartered Cassandra's Uncle Nestor's wealth for the children's freedom. San Diego State had welcomed her back.

She needed to ignore what Apollo had revealed to her about the future.

Lauren stood and stretched. The bags under her eyes had gone. Morning runs around Lake Murray had brought back her wind and a healthy glow to her skin. Long-legged, she dashed for the sand castle and her determined construction workers with plastic shovels.

San Diego, California

PRESENT DAY

The next day, Cassandra had asked in the grocery store if she could sleep there at night to guard the food against robbers. Demo cackled until Lauren asked him to stop and explain to his sister why that wouldn't be necessary.

With groceries stocked in the pantry, Lauren searched for the plug-in for her dead cell-phone battery.

"Is Cassandra going to eat that whole bag of chips?" Demo asked.

"Wouldn't you if it was your first time?" Lauren smiled.

"I think we need separate closets for our food."

Just as Lauren found the charger and plugged it in, her Smart Phone chimed, and the front doorbell rang.

She whispered, "Demo, take Cassandra to the TV room. Be perfectly quiet, got it? You know how to get her out the back door if you have to."

Cassandra glanced at Lauren with a concerned look. She tiptoed out of the kitchen behind Demo.

Lauren walked to the front door. One hand gripping a baseball bat, she peered out the peephole.

She dropped the Louisville Slugger, threw open the door and extended her arms.

"Oh, my God. Lisa, come here," she said, drawing her in and embracing her tight. "I saw the obituary about your Mom. I'm so sorry I didn't call right away. Come in. It's so good to see you."

Dark haired, curvy, and olive-skinned, Professor Lisa Barcelona reflected her Spanish heritage. She said, "Your voice mail was full, and I was hoping to tell you that I was in town on an emergency and coming over."

"You look wonderful. Still running 10K's?" Lauren was a few inches taller than Lisa, but she had always felt that she paled next to the vivaciousness and beauty of her accomplished colleague. So many people had told Lauren she could have had a career as a model, but in her mind, Lisa had it all.

"Not so much lately. Mostly swimming laps now at the campus pool," Lisa answered.

What am I going to do about Cassandra? I can't hide her for hours? Lauren thought.

She grasped Lisa's hand. "I'm so sorry about your Mom. It has to be just terrible to lose her."

"I've got a funeral to arrange, and I need to deal with her and Dad's belongings. I'll be here for a while."

Lauren clasped Lisa's hand. "I'm so sorry. I remember your parents from graduation. Tough part of being an only child, it all falls on you."

"Going to take months and it's going to be hell going through their belongings."

"I'll help you… where I can." Not wanting to have them both crying, Lauren said, "It's been so long since you took off to Oxford, and me to San Diego after grad school. How is life in England?"

"Loved it, but I've accepted a position in the Classics Department in Boston at Tufts. I start in the fall. So, I've officially returned to American soil."

"Congratulations. New ground to explore." She led Lisa to the kitchen.

"Well, you've certainly experienced some significant life events in recent months. I'm really sorry about Zack's…disappearance."

Lauren turned away, focusing on the coffeemaker. *No tears. I just won't.* "Thank you. I'm not doing great, but I'm learning to cope. It's been a struggle all around. I guess you know I've adopted two children."

"How unpredictable is life? All those fertility drugs you told me about and nothing worked? Now two children to care for. Wow."

"I have quite the busy schedule, and I'm so glad you decided to stop over. It's almost a relief to see a friend from the past, especially a good friend."

"You were my wing girl until you started dating Zack at Northwestern. Amazing how things turn out, isn't it?"

Lauren took out coffee cups and arranged chocolate chip cookies on a plate.

"I couldn't have gotten through that miscarriage back in college without you, Lauren. Oddly, I haven't been pregnant since then. A couple of relationships, but nothing permanent."

"Permanent has become a relative word to me, but definitely crazy times back then. Still crazy times, truth be told." Lauren felt the impulse to confide in Lisa, but she decided to be cautious.

Lisa's smile brightened. "So, can I meet the kids?"

Breathe. "Ah, sure. Just to warn you. Demo is thirteen and he only speaks Greek, unless it's about food. Cassandra is about the same age, but she doesn't say much."

"Shy still?" Lisa asked.

Carrying coffee and vanilla creamer to the table, Lauren said, "That's a story for two pots of coffee. Time to check in on them, anyway."

Lauren found Demo and Cassandra watching a Star Wars movie.

"You behaved properly, Sweetheart. I have a guest. She's a friend," Lauren explained to Cassandra in ancient Ionian. To Demo, she said, "You can talk in Greek. She will understand. You know how far to go."

Cassandra asked in Ionian, "Shall I greet her in your language? The word is *hello*, is it not?"

Having rounded the corner, Lisa paused in the doorway. "Did I just hear Ionian? That's amazing. Did you teach her ancient Greek, Lauren?"

Lauren hesitated. *What do I say now?* She decided to improvise as she smiled at Lisa.

"Oh, just a little. Children, this is my good friend, Lisa. Sorry, I didn't know you were following me. I was going to go over greeting manners with them."

Lisa laughed. "No need for protocol with me." She extended her hand to Demo, saying in Greek, "I'm Professor Lisa Barcelona. I'm so happy to meet you, Demo."

"Parakalo. Welcome to our house, Professor Barcelona." Demo shook her hand.

Lisa turned to Cassandra. "And this beautiful young lady, who already speaks Ionian, it's wonderful to meet you, too."

Cassandra glanced at Lisa, but quickly returned her attention to the television.

Lauren said, "She doesn't understand English or Modern Greek, Lisa."

"Then what does she speak?"

Oh hell. Lauren said. "Kids, can you stay in here and watch TV. Lisa and I are going to the kitchen to talk."

Seated at the table a minute later, Lisa said, "Something's wrong. You've helped me countless times in the past. I owe you. Remember the time we wanted to go to that fraternity party and we needed a ride, so they picked us up in a hearse."

"Right. They said since we were both drop-dead gorgeous, the vehicle was appropriate."

"And I got hammered and friendly with one of them and disappeared on you."

Grimacing, Lauren said, "Found you…passed out in the back of the hearse…by yourself."

"Thanks for saving me… again. So, truly, anything you tell me, I will hold in confidence. I promise. No one else knows that story about me. Thank God there was no internet then."

Lauren sipped her coffee, weighing precisely what to say. Tiptoeing had become her specialty, but who would possibly believe a story about rescuing a girl from ancient Greece.

"Look, Lisa. Can I depend on you? I mean really depend on you?"

"Whatever it is, I'm here for you."

"Is there any way while you're doing the cleanup of your parents' estate that you could help me to home-school the kids? If you're off till fall, maybe we could work out a schedule until then. It might be enough time."

"I'm happy to help, but why not just get a tutor or a special school for them. Home-schooling two kids with your responsibilities is excessive."

Lauren clasped her hands. "What I'm going to tell you has to remain just between the two of us. I'm desperate, but I can't speak with you otherwise. Agreed?"

Lisa grinned. "Of course. Did you discover a better kind of pizza dough?"

"Hold onto your seat."

"This sounds really important. A new Margarita Mix?"

Lauren's smile faded. "It's about the children…and Zack."

Lisa sat up straight. "No more jokes from me. I owe you for so much. I'll stick with you on this."

"Look. The first thing I want to say is, I'm not crazy. I wouldn't believe it myself unless it happened to me, but here it is." She swallowed. *I hope this isn't the biggest mistake of my life.*

"Bad things were happening in San Diego. We almost got killed by a maniac. Went to Greece, where the same guy chased us again. We were joining Professor Popandreou for a dig, but instead …"

"Wait. Stop there. Professor P. was murdered a few months ago."

Lauren closed her eyes. "Yes. A tragedy that is still unexplained but let me finish. We ended up in Delphi and… got swallowed up in a time tunnel." Lauren opened one eye a crack.

Lisa narrowed her vision. "Good one. But we haven't started happy hour yet, so out with the real story."

"I'm serious. We ended up in the Persian Wars period. Many wondrous things happened, but others were absolutely horrifying. I got back, but Zack didn't. I rescued Cassandra, so that's why she's here and only speaks Ionian."

Lisa tapped the stirring spoon on the side of her coffee cup. "Did State send you for an evaluation before you went back to work?"

"It's pretty much certified psycho, I know. But I'm telling you the truth."

Erupting out of her chair, Lisa said loudly "Come on, Lauren. Are you on medication? How can you be responsible for those children if you're not well?"

Lauren gestured for Lisa to sit back down. "I don't know where Zack is… exactly. He's still back there. While scientifically this is impossible, it happened."

"Look at me, Lauren. Tell me you're not feeding me a line of bull."

"I'm not. Why don't you go in and talk with Cassandra? If it's true, can you imagine the opportunity? There are only so many people on this earth that speak Ionian."

Lisa drummed her fingers on the table.

Lauren's lip quivered. She put both hands on the table and stared at Lisa. She raised a finger and pointed at the bedroom. "You go in there. You and I are considered experts, and she knows more than both of us. She's Athenian but grew up in Delphi. Go talk to her. Satisfy yourself."

A cookie snapped in Lisa's hands. "I'm going to talk with her, and I'm going to help you home-school them either way. I'm just surprised you would tell me fairy tales after all we've been through."

"Demo knows everything. He is the only eyewitness as to what happened to us. Speak with them. I won't be able to convince you otherwise. I'm out on a shaky limb here."

Lisa stood and folded her arms. She stared at Lauren.

"You just got the basics," Lauren said, standing. "You don't know even a small portion of it yet. Let's go."

Demo watched Cassandra absorb a Stars War space battle on the television. She covered her mouth with one hand when the space ships blew up.

After hearing Lauren's friend shouting from the kitchen, he lowered the volume of the movie and listened.

His mother continued to speak in a measured tone for several minutes. Then, the lady guest yelled. Talking surged back and forth between his mother and her friend. It lasted until the movie had ended. He knew what it might mean.

Lauren opened the door to the bedroom. Cassandra hugged her knees and looked away.

"Demo," Lauren said. "The cat's out of the bag. Professor Lisa knows. I'll have to trust her. We all must."

He gritted his teeth together. "If you say to. How many others will you tell?"

"Only Professor Lisa will know."

Lisa said, "I won't reveal your secret to anyone. You have my word, Demo."

He made the motion of zipping his lips shut. "I did it. You can, too."

Lisa laughed. Lauren smoothed his mop of hair.

Crouching in front of Cassandra, Lisa smiled and said to her in ancient Ionian, "My name is Lisa. You can trust me. I will be your teacher, too. I pray to Athena that we will be friends."

Cassandra peered at Lauren first. Receiving her approval, she smiled and replied, "May Athena's blessing be upon you, Lisa. I am Cassandra, and I will be a good student."

Lisa peered up at Lauren. Nodding, Lauren motioned for her to continue the evaluation.

"I beseech thee," Cassandra said, "that another Olympian deserves a measure of our prayers." She kneeled and extended her arms, palms facing out. "All of us must join in." She gave Demo a hard look.

"Not again?" Demo said, relenting.

They all extended their hands and spoke devoted words to the sun god, Apollo.

Lisa asked, "Cassandra, you lived near Apollo's Temple in Delphi?"

"With my uncle and mother. Until they were slain by the monster."

Lauren saw Cassandra give a pained look. The trauma of it all was still only a few months removed even though it happened in 480 B.C.E.

"The sanctuary at Delphi attracted pilgrims from many lands," Lisa said.

"You speak the truth," Cassandra replied. "I greeted many a traveler there and learned their words."

"Forgive me," Lisa said, putting a finger to her lips. "What other people's words do you know?"

"I brought water and wine to so many. The Lydoi are a land of kings. My uncle told me they were called Maionia at one time, but they paid with good coin stamped with lion heads made of silver and gold, and so they were well received."

Lisa swallowed and glanced at Lauren. "She's talking about the ancient Lydians in what would be in present day Anatolia in Turkey."

Cassandra rambled on. "And those who walked from Corinth and the Peloponnese either crossed by boat or made their way up the isthmus. Many spoke Doric from Laconia in the south, but I had not met too many Lacedemonians until they appeared at our home with Lady Lauren."

Lisa held up her hand as if to signal Cassandra to halt. "She's talking about Spartans and using the ancient name. She's saying you met Spartans, Lauren?"

"Before this is over, we're going to have to switch from coffee to scotch, or something else. You're probably going to need a nap afterwards, too. Go on."

Lisa turned back to Cassandra. "Who else did you meet?"

"My uncle taught me to be kind to all strangers. That is the law of *xenia*. It is a Hellene custom. I met Thessalian's and Macedonians from the north, supplying them with flatbread and wine. Even a group of travelers once from a land far to the east. Darker men who spoke through Persian interpreters. They told of great horned beasts and a worshipped a single god. I did not get to speak with them long, but they called this healer god *Boutta*, or another name, *Sarmanes*, I believe…"

Lisa clasped her forehead with her fingertips. "Please stop. Buddha? Find your liquor cabinet and that couch, Lauren. I think I'm going to be the student here. I'm in. I'm so in."

Realm of the Dead

C onsciousness.

Zack leaned upon an oak door. Apollo held him steady, displaying his typical amusement with Zack's discomfort in not knowing what to expect next. Zack found bandages on his cheek and a thigh, along with a sling supporting his right shoulder.

Twin bronze medallions hung by leather cords from Apollo's neck. Zack couldn't remove his eyes from the relief of an archer shooting an arrow within the rays of the sun. The medallions activated the transit and represented the pathway back to Lauren, and to his former life.

Apollo said, "Do not concern yourself with the medallions. We have important business here. Follow me. Can you walk?"

Zack took a few steps forward. "I can, but I'm dizzy." He brought a hand to his forehead. "I need to remember something important too, but it's like someone has a big eraser and every time the memory comes to me..."

"I did not *allow* you to remember everything."

"You're playing with my thoughts? I won't ask you to explain everything now, just tell me, where are Lauren and Cassandra?" Zack waited. The muscles of his jaw pulsed. He wasn't sure if he wanted the answer.

"You're a difficult student. I needed you to fight. I wanted you to concentrate just on that."

"I've had enough. I want to know." Zack reached for Apollo's shoulders. Latching on, he barked, "I deserve to know, *now.*"

Apollo set a firm hand on Zack's chest. "I see you are angry. They are at home…and safe as can be in the battle for the future. Are you satisfied?"

"For the moment. Where are we?"

"You'll soon know."

They stepped into the room and the wooden floorboards creaked. A mahogany desk held old books and curled papers. Voices came from another room, followed by exclamations of surprise. Apollo pointed to a doorway beyond the desk and motioned for Zack to head towards it. Both wore chitons, a knee-length dress-like garment that looked out of place within the confines of an American Colonial-style home. Light entered through a small window with pewter metal dividing the panes. The room smelled of burnt wood from a small pot-bellied stove.

Apollo followed Zack through the doorway to see three men, who stood before a bench filled with glass beakers, iron tools and brass instruments. One man, thickset in the middle, wore a nightgown. He turned slightly, and Zack saw long, graying hair hanging from a receding hairline. The man tinkered with something Zack couldn't see.

A second guy wore sandals and a white chiton. A golden band surrounded the crown of his head.

The third man stood about the same height as the man in the toga, but he wore a white shirt and a dark business suit. Zack could see the man was of African descent.

Apollo stood beside him, sniffed, and said, "Cedar logs give off an attractive scent."

"Who are they?" Zack asked.

Apollo answered, "I've brought you here to be educated. You may be a professor, but you have much to learn."

"Looks like someone's house from Colonial times."

"You have a firm grasp of the obvious, Traveler."

"Is this a dream of some kind?"

Apollo gave Zack a deprecating look. "I have brought you to the land of the dead."

Zack leaned against the door frame. "Am I dead… or just visiting?"

"How does one know?"

Zack stammered, "Wait, I was on the battlefield at Plataea. I got stabbed…"

"You're actually here, and so are they. I have brought them here after the point of their deaths. They exist in the middle state of being right now. Therefore, it's easy for me to convince them to join us."

Zack narrowed his eyes. "How can you do that?"

"Still doubt me?" Apollo sighed. "You are a billowing bag of questions. Might you listen and experience for once?"

"Am I dead or not?"

"I submit to you that there are situations worse than death, Traveler. Something you will know soon enough. Here, you are as expired as they are."

Zack gave Apollo a look of confusion, then asked, "Can they hear us?"

The older man with the nightgown, holding an iron rod, said, "I learned of your presence after you stepped on that noisy board in the entry room, a dead giveaway for anyone coming into my laboratory."

The man dressed in an ankle-length chiton took the rod in his hand said, "This is positioned on your roof and the iron attracts the thunder fire of Zeus?"

"Sends the charge right into the ground and keeps the house from burning."

"Such an act would offend Zeus, and he will surely send another bolt of lightning to dispatch you."

The older man peered through small bifocals perched on the bridge of his nose. "My dear Pericles, tell me about Zeus and how he rules the heavens with thunderbolts. I am most curious."

Zack slowly turned his head towards Apollo, a look of awe on his face. Apollo displayed another of his ingratiating grins.

Zack asked, "Did he say Pericles?"

Apollo motioned with his head, directing Zack to reset his attention on the conversation.

The black man spoke slowly. "You should not criticize a man for his faith, Dr. Franklin."

Franklin, the older man, said, "Oh, good sir, I only meant to ask him if he did see in his mind a great god with a flowing beard pick up a bolt of lightning and hurl it at my rather wide torso like a Shawnee throws a tomahawk?"

"We need not debate," Pericles said. "Truly, I understand that there is a difference between superstition and belief in the gods."

The black man returned, "I applaud your reason, Pericles."

"We will light a good fire later, Martin, and talk of the gods. Inquiring into the truth can only be good."

Zack reached for Apollo's elbow. He felt an electrical charge, quickly removed his hand and mumbled, "Pericles said Martin, and he's talking in English?"

The black man turned while rubbing the base of his neck. Zack saw the pencil-thin moustache and recognized from photographs that Dr. Martin Luther King stood before him.

"I can't believe this," Zack said, "Pericles, Martin Luther King and Ben Franklin?"

Apollo affirmed Zack's observation with a nod.

"I can't wrap my head around this," Zack said.

Franklin waved an arm for Apollo and Zack to come closer.

Pericles peered at them and asked, "How shall I address you?"

Zack felt only disappointment as he studied who stood before him. Wise Pericles, the Athenian statesman who helped to launch Athens' Golden Age, looked haggard and barely able to stand. Gray-colored hair, drawn face and a head a bit large for his body, cracked lips and emaciated limbs, his appearance gave no indication of his stature in history. Pericles had died in 429 BCE, the second year of the Peloponnesian War against

Sparta. A terrible plague had devastated the Athenian population. With the Spartan army camped outside the long walls that protected access to the Athenian fleet at Piraeus, the sickness had spread. The Athenians lost their brilliant leader when they needed him most.

Pericles said, "I see that you're concerned for my well-being. Who are you, young man?"

"Zack, I mean Zackary Fletcher." His head swam with memories of what he knew about these remarkable men.

"And may I know the name of your tall friend."

"Pericles," Apollo answered, walking towards Franklin's workbench. "I am whom I appear to be."

Franklin said, "A wise man does not jump to conclusions, nor believe everything that he is told. He that speaks in riddles will be amusing to unravel."

Pericles appeared to be looking for something.

"What is it you need?" Martin asked.

"Wine, water, anything to drink, I cannot quench my thirst." Pericles smacked his crusted lips. "I died on the seventh day like many others, and yet this sickness torments me still."

Martin poured red wine from a pewter pitcher.

After Pericles had swallowed a third cup, he emitted a sigh of relief. "Our noble citizens perished in numbers I never imagined."

"A leader cannot bear to see his people suffer," Martin said.

Pericles hung his head and took a deep breath. "I am responsible." He pulled out a chair and slumped into it.

Martin put a hand on Pericles' shoulder. "Speak. Only then will you begin to heal."

Pericles stared at Franklin, "Do you know what happened to my Athens in this war?"

Quietness ensued. The others present looked at each other, measuring what to say and who would say it.

"He will tell you." Apollo gestured to Zack.

Pericles said, "Then, good lad, tell me what became of the city after I died."

Zack didn't want to say it. "I'm sorry. Greek killed Greek. The war lasted for decades, and the Spartans won."

Pericles's lip twitched.

Zack continued, "The great ideal of democracy that began in your time did not last long. The Spartans who ruled Athens were defeated by Thebes soon thereafter. Macedonians from the north descended and conquered Greece. Athens lost its liberty."

"By the gods, it is my fault." Pericles buried his face in his hands. "I sought war, and arrogance kept me from stopping it."

Zack kneeled before Pericles. He pulled the Athenian's hands from his face. Sickness had hollowed the orbits of his eyes.

"Why, Pericles? After defeating the Persians, the Greeks appreciated Athens for her nobility and good will. You created a league that protected Athens and its allies. But then you decided to take the treasury and spend it on the Parthenon. You abused the trust of the people."

Pericles raised his head. "We did build upon the acropolis for the greater glory of the gods and Athens. The funds you speak of employed thousands."

"Was that not a political tactic, also, to buy the votes of the people?" Zack asked.

"Are you sure that you understand, young man? The aristocracy plotted to rule Athens, and this strategy halted them."

"But your desire to build an empire caused you to exploit your allies. They were forced to submit to Athens. Cities razed. Greeks butchered. You conquered because you could." Zack raised his voice. "You, above everyone, knew such actions were immoral. In the end, you caused your own demise."

Pericles stood abruptly. "I bear these horrors in the eternity of Hades. I should have prevented war with the Spartans."

Apollo said, "You had to suffer the consequences of your decision to make unnecessary war. The gods would not save you from yourselves."

Franklin interrupted. "Yet, my good fellows, we must not allow this man to suffer without telling him that we borrowed from Athenian democracy to create our Constitution."

Martin held up his hand. "On the surface, but you failed, too, Benjamin. The Founding Fathers didn't protect all the people. You didn't safeguard the Red Man and their lands, and you left my people in slavery."

"You speak the truth. We had to compromise with those who would not let slavery go. It appears we have a room teeming with regret," Franklin said.

Martin spoke with his customary Southern accent. "I am a man of God, and I tell you that freedom does not thrive without justice for all." He looked directly at Apollo. "You suggest that you're a god, but you are not *my* god. The possibility of two gods existing at once cannot be. Yet, I am here. So, I will join in your exercise, but do not expect me to buy into this."

Apollo said, "Let me summarize for all of you."

"Must we converse on an empty stomach," Franklin said. "My niece has made two plump cherry pies. Can you not smell them coming fresh from the oven?"

At that moment, thunder sounded. Franklin looked up, as did the others.

Realm of the Dead

Franklin said, "A storm. What a marvelous coincidence."

Pericles shifted uncomfortably in his padded chair. "Perhaps Apollo can cause the storm to go elsewhere so we may hear each other."

"Let the storm remain," Franklin said. All saw flashes of lightning through the open shutters. Wind followed. He began to count with his fingers after lightning could be seen again. He counted to five before thunder sounded. "The storm is a mile away. This will be an interesting experiment."

"Should we close those shutters?" Martin asked.

"Do so," Franklin replied. "Blow out the candles and close the door on the furnace, too. We shall make it dark in here, so we can concentrate with our ears."

Zack walked to the Franklin furnace, a metallic box for burning wood, and shut the iron door. He saw a long metallic tube that connected the furnace to the roof, venting the smoke. Franklin collected six wine glasses and placed them on a table beside a cloth towel and a large glass decanter of red wine. He began to clean each glass with the cloth towel. Martin blew out the candles. The only light was the intermittent flashes of lightning. After another flash, a bell was heard, followed by another chime.

"Who rings the bell?" Pericles asked.

Franklin laughed. "My good fellow, I showed you the iron rod that transfers Zeus's thunderbolts into the ground. I have also harnessed the power of the storm to also ring the bell and announce it time for wine. Let me finish cleaning the glasses first." Franklin worked feverishly. "Could you relight a candle at the furnace, my dear Zack? We shan't toast each other in the dark."

Zack placed a lighted candle on a table near the guests. Franklin turned away from Apollo for a second and rubbed a wine glass vigorously with the towel. Holding it by the stem and with the towel still wrapped around it, he handed the first glass to Apollo, saying, "You say you are a god, so you deserve the first glass."

Apollo extended his hand to take the glass. Just as he grasped the stem, he lit up the room. Electricity in sharp pikes danced around his form. All gasped and stepped back except Franklin, who wore an amused look on his face. The bluish charge circumventing Apollo, his protective dome, revealed itself, electrified by the static electricity held in the wine glass.

"Just as I thought," Franklin said. "I am convinced. Maybe you are a god, or a very clever scientist."

The blue charge around Apollo dissipated, revealing his furrowed brows and a look of annoyance on his face. He slid back the long curl that had fallen from behind his ear.

"Maybe I can reveal this... god. We shall find if you are negatively or positively charged." Franklin pulled a glass tube from his pocket and quickly rubbed it with the cloth. He ran at Apollo and tried to stick it into the charged dome that had appeared.

"Enough!" Apollo shouted, repelling Franklin with a wave of his hand. Franklin fell onto a chair.

"Are you a god?" Franklin asked, gasping.

"You are lucky I am a benevolent one."

"You are fortunate that you *are* benevolent," Franklin said. "But if you try to tell us what to do, then I will fight you with all that I am."

"That is the spirit," Pericles stated. "A man earns his freedom, and he fights to keep it."

"Hold on here, gentlemen," Martin interrupted. "You assume that all can fight. You forget that laws protect the weak. What kind of nation do you have if you do not protect those in need?"

Apollo said, "Hear me. You are here to educate my friend, Zack. You can see he's bandaged from fighting in a desperate battle. He has a task approaching, one that will determine the course of the future in his time. He is here to learn from your mistakes, and from your victories. Martin, if you would begin."

Martin put his hand on Zack's shoulder. "If you're time isn't to far from mine, then you may know of my work. The struggle has been hard. Our hopes dashed so many times. I say to you that the country you seek to preserve must live up to its ideals and its laws. If you succeed in your endeavor to save her, and I pray to my God that you do…" Martin glanced at Apollo before returning his gaze. "Make sure it is saved for all, Zack."

"You have my promise, Reverend King," Zack said.

"I am warning you that slavery awaits your people and those of the free world," Apollo said to Zack. "It is so near, and you are unprepared. All will be swallowed into the maelstrom, regardless of their color or creed."

"You've already told me I need to save my country," Zack said.

Apollo said, "This is a different threat. The slavery I am speaking of is not just of the body. It is of the mind, too. Advances in science and neuroscience will render a new kind of servitude. There can be no rebellion. All desire to be free has been removed. There will be total control of thoughts, and it will happen in your time, Zack."

"You ask me to solve all this?" Zack asked.

"The men before you faced challenges in their times. If America is destroyed, the idea that men may rule themselves will be stricken from history." Apollo gestured to the other men. "The deeds of all these heroes will never be known… and I have seen this carried out."

"This is the disastrous future you lived in?" Zack asked.

"It is. You don't understand what is to be enslaved," Apollo said. "These are the simple lessons. When you are free, each day you can decide how to better your life, and the lives of those around you."

Franklin said, "I pray to Providence that the nation we built will survives." He looked out the laboratory window at sheep grazing outside a log fence. The aroma of cows and pigs grazing near the window overcame warm cherry pies on the counter. "We knew the danger of kings and tyrants. With war comes suffering and massive debts. Our Congress agreed on what we did not want from that example. Do not let that happen to our country."

Zack raised his chin. Voice weakening, Pericles said, "Do not end up like me, regretting the slaughter of the innocent to groom an empire. The souls of the slain haunt me here. Be the leader that I should have been."

"I'm ready," Zack said, "to do what I must."

Apollo cupped an ear. "Stay where you are, Traveler. Our other visitors have arrived."

"Wait," Franklin said. "Are we to exist? Can't we live…"

The three men dissolved before Zack's eyes.

9

Land of the Dead

"Follow me," Apollo said, leading him back to the entrance of the house. "There are others who petition to see you, Traveler. But I will tell you now that the dream is fading, and I believe it may be to your benefit."

"What do you mean? Why did you make the others disappear?"

"I told you there are fates worse than death. Behold."

Zack heard a female voice as Apollo opened the door.

"Zack," the woman's voice said, tinged with surprise, anxiousness, and woefulness all at once.

The woman stood there, shrouded in a black veil and an ankle-length robe. Zack couldn't place the voice. He wondered if he wanted to know.

"Who... are you?" Zack asked trying to peer under her veil.

She slowly removed the covering, eyes downcast, until she looked at Zack with mournful eyes.

Queen Io embraced him.

Zack choked out, "Not you, too."

Am I hugging a spirit? She feels ...real.

"Be silent," Io said, putting her finger over his lips. "I waited for your return. We knew Diomedes fell at Plataea. Within a cycle of the seasons, I lost my husband and my son. The city lost a king and a prince, with no heir to carry on the royal line. And I lost you, too."

Zack felt dizzy. Had he been trapped in the past, remaining in Mycenae would have been his choice.

"Io," Zack said, "I would have returned."

She pressed her face to his shoulder and sobbed. All her royal bearing dissolved, leaving a lonely woman who'd been abandoned in her hour of need.

Through the door crawled another warrior, pulling a javelin from his side. When the warrior's helmet fell off, Zack knew. In a hushed voice, he said, "Diomedes." Zack lifted him to his feet. Diomedes smiled through the blood and dirt on his face. "I wanted to say goodbye one more time, Zack, and tell you that you are the brother I never had."

Diomedes twisted and fell to the floor. Zack looked at Apollo, "Don't they all get well here?"

"In time," Apollo answered. "As I told you before, they've been brought here at the moment of their deaths."

"Forgive me, Mother, for falling in battle," Diomedes said. "A warrior knows not if he will return."

Io said, "Despair planted its banner in my home. I could not hold back the tears. I prayed to the Goddess for advice. I slept in the temple and would not leave for days."

Zack, choking up, said, "I'm sorry. Apollo took me away."

Apollo didn't comment. He stood with his finger pressed to his lips.

Io stammered, "I could not think or act … and then a miracle occurred." Her face brightened, and she smiled. "Who can predict what the gods have in store." She looked at Apollo. "If you are Apollo, had I come to Delphi and asked you for a prophecy, would you have revealed to me what would come to be?"

"Some wish to know the future, others do not," Apollo said.

"Since I am here," Io said, "and I see these inventions which have no place in my day, I know I must exist in the realm of the gods, even more, the realm of the dead. Are you a shadow, too, Zack?"

Zack turned to Apollo. "Only he knows. I belong to him. I serve his needs and the people of my own time, threatened with destruction."

Io shut her eyes. "We suffered in our day, too."

"Tell him of your miracle, mother," Diomedes said, standing now and looking better.

"What miracle?" Zack asked.

Io stepped away from the door and stood next to Zack, gathering his arm into hers. Zack smelled her lavender perfume, the one that permeated the goddess chamber in the cavern below the Mycenaean citadel.

A boy walked into the room, one foot placed carefully after another. Tall and lanky, his brown hair hung from his forehead in the manner of a lad who cared more for frogs than grooming. A chiton of white and an empty sword scabbard hung from his belt just below a swash of red stains. The boy did not look at Zack at first, but when he did, nausea gripped Zack and sent him to his knees. From the corner of his eyes, scattered light crept in.

"I don't believe it," Zack said. He put his hand against the doorjamb. "Stop screwing around with me, all of you." Could it be? The boy looked like a younger version of himself. His thoughts raced back to his time with Io back in Mycenae. How she had seduced him.

"What you perceive as unbelievable was, in fact, reality," Apollo said.

"Your name did not appear on list of dead warriors at Plataea," Io said. "Imagine how I suffered, Atlantean."

Zack blurted, "I …had no choice."

"Then the gods granted me that which I thought might be impossible. I became morning-sick. I knew I was with child, and the people rejoiced."

The boy cast only fleeting glances at Zack.

"I wondered if I could bear a child from so tall a man. The midwives toiled when the pains began."

She swept errant strands of hair from the boy's forehead. "When he was born and saw the light of day, he had such a look of confusion on his face." Io laughed as she drew the boy into her embrace.

The other men gathered, made a semicircle behind Zack and Apollo.

Zack bent onto one knee in front of the boy. He reached out, placed his hand gently under the boy's chin, and lifted it up.

"Greet your son, Zack," Io said, "heir to the throne of great Mycenae." The other men murmured.

"My...son," Zack said. "I have a son."

The nine-year-old said with accusation, "And I... a father."

He took the boy's hands in his. The boy gave him a blank look, neither a greeting nor a refusal.

"What is your name?" Zack asked.

"Atlantea," the boy replied, with a cold stare and tense lips.

Zack managed to smile.

Io said, "The seasons passed, and we grew prosperous. I arranged a pedagogue to teach him. Every time he asked, 'And where is this Atlantean that I am named after,' we had no answer for him."

Zack locked gazes with his son. He saw pain, longing, abandonment, and a spark of curiosity. "It's my mission, my duty to save my country from disaster. That's why I wasn't in Mycenae with you."

"Were we so unimportant?" Diomedes interrupted.

"It's not that," Zack said. "In my time, the danger threatens millions of people."

Io, his son, and Diomedes stood with their arms folded.

The queen sighed, "I don't understand. We are all dead, are we not?"

Apollo interceded. "That's not exactly true."

Io kneeled, as did Diomedes and the boy. "Then tell us, oh Apollo, Far-shooter, what is our fate?"

Zack turned to Apollo, too. Everyone wanted an answer.

"Death is a transfer of spirit. You have the same physical bodies you once did. I join you together now, so you can relate to your experience as breathing people. You can share all of the emotions you did before you perished."

Atlantea's eyes welled up, his lip curled, and he shouted," I don't want to be dead! I want to run through the hallways of the palace and practice swords with the guards. Tell me he's lying, Mother."

Io showed Atlantea the front of his tunic. Zack saw the blood stains, too.

"We prospered until others coveted our fields," Io said. "They saw we were weak. Pheidon, the king of Argos, never forgot the insult of refusing his daughter in marriage. They attacked."

Zack blurted out a desperate, "Oh, no."

"Atlantea defended me. He stabbed an Argive hoplite with his sword, but they cornered him, and many fell upon him."

Atlantea looked at his chiton.

"Then," Io, said, "they found me in my chamber, but I denied them their pleasures and took my own life." She showed the blood stains on the white gown below a black gown.

"I'm sorry, I'm sorry," Zack said.

"Life is pain," Apollo said. "Love can be pain, too. Life is sacrifice."

"You're my son," Zack said to Atlantea. He gathered him in his arms, but the boy stiffened.

"I have allowed you all this reunion, but time runs short," Apollo said. "I have brought you together, so Zack can see that sacrifice is necessary to save those you love. Success is not guaranteed. Vigilance and moderation will secure the future of a nation. He is needed to save his people. Say your goodbyes."

Zack lost his voice. Too many emotions vied for control. He had a son he would never know. It was all too much.

"We loved you, Zack," Io said.

Zack brought Io and then Diomedes into a collective embrace.

"I... I love you, too. I'll never get to know this fine boy."

"We should have been a family," Io said. "You should have been King of Mycenae, Zack."

"We are a family," Zack said, his broken words etched with regret.

He shouted at Apollo, "I can't leave my son."

Apollo replied gravely, "Others petition to see you, but alas, the time clock has run out of sand. We must go."

Atlantea said, "We all want to go with you."

"I want go home, too, with all of you, to San Diego, where this all began."

Apollo said, "Atlantea knows how you return. It is another reason why you are here."

More voices sounded beyond the door. A crowd had gathered. Zack peered beyond Io and Diomedes. Leonidas, the king of Sparta, raised a fist and barked, "Did Sparta survive? Did Gorgo get my ring?"

Zack began to answer when Nestor and Persephone squeezed past Leonidas and fell on their knees, reaching for Zack's hand. Persephone said, "My daughter, Cassandra. Where is she?"

Zack stammered.

Nestor blared, "Our Honeybee. Tell us she is safe with Lauren. I beg you."

The others beyond the door continued to petition him for news. Atlantea squeezed Zack's hand. "That place you speak of, San Diego, is not where your journey began, Father," Atlantea said, "Go to the other, or you will never make it home."

"Wait, what?" Sparkles encroached from the sides of Zack's vision. "I want to stay," he cried, turning his gaze to Apollo. "You're driving me mad." His hand grazed Atlantea's as flashes of light overcame his vision and everyone else disappeared, save him and Apollo.

Pulses of blue energy reached out from the medallions to encircle them.

"How could you do that to me…" Zack blared just before the dome formed.

He heard Apollo say, "Yes, you regret that you can't stay with them, but think how you'll feel if your family and all your countrymen are killed in the modern day? You have been called to serve, but you have earned a vacation, Traveler. Just not the one you would have imagined."

10

Calliope (Santorini)

1626 BCE

Zack regained consciousness in an alley. He scraped dirt and found stone underneath. A copy of a door he'd seen before in a restaurant in Santorini, decorated with scenes of water birds and irises, lay behind him. At the far end of the alley stood another door, similar in height and decoration, and secured in place by a wooden bar. A strong sun heated the bricks paving the pathway.

He raised himself up, coughed and hacked out a glob of tunnel sludge.

Staggering forward, he listened to a conversation spoken beyond the walls. The words gradually morphed into something comprehensible, as though he had a built-in interpreter in his head. Two men discussed the urgent need to transport a wagon full of grapes to market. He heard a woman describe how she must bring her son to a healer, have his broken arm set, and what charms might work.

Clouds appeared, making it a bit cooler. A mist climbed over the walls. He heard cart wheels scratching stone, as if the cart was hastily being driven away. The mist left the path to the doorway clear. Just for him.

Apollo left me here. I was in that colonial home. How can I function here after meeting my son?

Surprised by his own strength, he lifted the wooden beam, pushed it aside on its hinge and opened the door. The cloud obscured his view. Zack took a few measured steps forward. He heard the door close behind him and the bar fall back into place.

Locked in or out. Which is worse?

He wore a simple chiton with a leather belt and a metallic buckle. He found the likeness of an archer on the face of the buckle, like the one on Apollo's medallion. Wondering if it held the same powers, he detached the buckle from the belt and held it up to the closed doorway.

No result.

Apollo wouldn't let me off that easily.

The wind made a rustling noise, and the fog blew away. Terra-cotta jars sat atop the rim of a water basin. Under his feet, tightly fitting stones made up a well-manicured road. Around him, a piazza of three-story dwellings with finished stucco and balconies, overhanging with ivy and cypress branches.

Zack walked until he faced the choice of one of four roadways leading out of the square. Emerging from the narrow corridor, a grand view opened. Several roads curved their way downhill towards a dock. White-washed houses and buildings with red tile roofs lined the roads, coalescing into an established community. A deep blue blanket of sea lay beyond.

From previous visits, he recognized the island of Santorini.

But this wasn't the modern-day tourist destination.

He stood on the southeastern tip of the island, near the remains of Akrotiri, the town only partially uncovered by archeologists in the modern era. In the distance, a mountain peak loomed where the ancient town of Thera had been founded by Spartans settlers in about 800 BC, some 800 years after the devastating eruption that had destroyed Santorini, thus weakening the Minoan civilization on Crete and the Cycladic islands of the Aegean Sea. This naturally defensive hilltop had been used by Greeks, Romans, Byzantine soldiers, and, finally, by Venetians holding off the Turks in the 1500s. He remembered hiking up that sheer cliff in the modern day with Lauren as part of an archeological tour.

Lauren. That had taken place during the first summer of his externship, and the beginning of his romance with Lauren. Several the other male graduate students had made countless plays for her attention. He had felt at a disadvantage, and he'd thought many times that Lauren would waltz off with one of the men. But she stuck with him.

Two ships with bull's horns painted red on the sails made a line for a busy harbor on the southern tip of the island. The vessels dropped their sails about a quarter-mile out and came in on oars before docking alongside one of four wooden piers. A crowd developed while the sailors tied up their vessel and began to off-load supplies. He heard cheering and wondered if these ships were arriving from the island of Crete, some seventy miles by sea to the south.

Except that he couldn't name the islands Crete or Santorini, or the people as Minoans, since those represented modern-day identities.

The so-called Minoans enjoyed a kind of separation from the land powers of Mycenaean Greece, Egypt and the Hittites ruling what was now modern-day Turkey. The barrier of the sea and a strong navy protected the people from invaders, just as Great Britain enjoyed the barrier of the English Channel for centuries behind their naval forces.

But change happened, and it wasn't always pretty.

So why am I here?

He walked downhill towards the sea, his leather sandals clomping on the stone road.

Suddenly weary, Zack sat at the edge of the road. Apollo had given him his memory this time. Maybe it would be better not to remember. He'd lost Lauren, pretty Cassandra, Nestor and Persephone, brave Diomedes, the beautiful Io, and, most devastatingly, his son. Zack knew it would take more than time to drive regret from his thoughts.

Gentle breezes wafting past him up the mountainside from the sea brought him sleep.

He awoke to someone with a stick tapping his ribs.

"Wake up," said a man. "Have you crossed to Mother Goddess's realm, or are you still breathing?"

Zack curled up, a defensive posture, not knowing who poked him. He saw an ankle first, a silver bracelet around it with bull-shaped charms. Zack looked up at a man in a wide-brimmed hat. His skin looked darkened from years in the Mediterranean sun. He had black hair and eyes with deep crow's feet in the corners. He wore a red and blue-striped loincloth with birds and flowers embroidered on the hems, and a sturdy belt with a round silver buckle displaying a set of bull's horns. His leather sandals looked unworn, and Zack guessed that this man might be an aristocrat.

And he had the same forelock Apollo wore.

"You don't look like anyone I've seen here before," the man said, studying Zack. "What land breeds giants? Speak up and don't feel threatened. We are a peaceful people, and we do no harm to those who obey the law."

I can't believe I can understand this guy.

The language of these Minoans, Keftians, or Therans, whoever these people were, had been lost to history. Only the Linear A scribe had been discovered, but not deciphered.

He really needed Lauren's expertise. This was right up her alley.

"I...I am a traveler, a visitor," Zack said. How could he speak a language he'd never studied?

Apollo.

"Don't fear me," the man said.

Zack nodded. Somehow, he needed to record the phonetic sounds of the man's words and compare them to written words.

He could create another version of the Rosetta Stone, a discovery in 1799 that had allowed Egyptian hieroglyphics to be understood.

"I appreciate your kindness," Zack said, squinting. The man moved to shield Zack from a scorching sun.

"It is the law of the Lady Potnaya, the Mother Goddess whom we worship here. She promises hospitality to strangers. You will see no violence on our streets. It is her way, and it is our way."

Zack stood, towering over the man.

"What land breeds mud-covered giants such as you?"

Here we go again.

"A land far away, by sea." Zack paused. "What island is this?"

The man narrowed his eyes. "Then you *are* lost. This is Calliope."

Damn.

Zack looked towards the docks. "I saw ships arrive."

"We depend on the fleet to bring us supplies from Keftiu and the islands. You cannot have made it here without a ship, unless you are hiding wings." The man grinned.

"I made it here in a small boat, but it sank, and I swam ashore."

The man withdrew a small terra cotta flask and offered it to him. "Your lips are burnt. Quench your thirst. It's good ale."

Zack took a sip. Diluted beer, not the honeyed drink Apollo had given him in the past.

"I thank you," Zack said.

The man pointed to the shoreline. "I am heading there. Come with me if you like. But I suggest you jump in the sea first. I am called Talos."

"My name is Zack."

Apollo had told him he earned a vacation. Zack knew differently now. This place was a disaster waiting to happen.

Talos said he owned shops and ran a shipyard on the southern end of the island, producing merchant and naval vessels. "The sea brings us wealth," he proclaimed, tapping his head with a bejeweled forefinger. "We trade with the mainland Myceneans and beyond to the limits of the inland sea to barter for tin. Our ships touch shore on Cyprus to trade copper, even in Egyptos, where the great Pharaoh gets his cheeks tickled with a feather." He released a booming laugh.

They passed buildings of two and three stories and flat roofs as they walked along streets lined with small shops. Behind billowing curtains that shielded the sun, many of the shops held artisans, pottery, painters and wagon makers. Zack peered into a blacksmith shop that made bronze swords.

A crowd developed in a field beyond the edge of the town. Royal guards held them back. After Zack jumped into the water and then dried off, they wove their way through the people to a knot of red-robed men, a priestess and palace guards with purple plumes jutting from the tops of their leather helmets. Within the circle, a young woman with red hair held back with a jeweled tiara stood beside a man in an Egyptian headdress. He held a staff with the figure of a cobra carved on the end.

"I can't believe what I'm seeing," Zack said.

Talos looked upon the scene, his arms folded, and brow furrowed.

The man blew out a gust of air. "My eyes deceive me. That was a small hill not long ago." He sniffed loudly. "I smell a stink coming from it, like eggs rotting in the sun. There is a larger hill building up on the royal island you see out there."

Zack saw steam escaping from openings in the ground nearby, and on concentric islands in the distance.

"That man," Talos said, "is the ambassador from Egyptos. He visits Keftiu twice a year to discuss trade and alliances." Talos covered his nose the hem of his robe, as did many others. "The Priestess must have summoned him from Keftiu after the deadly earth-shaking. Many of our people perished and it caused many families, over half our numbers, to take sail and move to Keftiu. Lean in so we can hear."

In academia, scholars thought that Bronze Age Crete had communication with the civilization of Egypt, but no one knew how much contact from the scant records found.

Zack heard the Egyptian speaking in Keftian, which was the only way Zack could describe the language he understood courtesy of Apollo.

The Egyptian spoke in a deep voice, his skin looking burnt nearly black by the desert sun. "The old books tell of mountains that spit fire and darken the skies. We have not seen this on the banks of the Nile, but the scrolls tell of mountains that grow and bring destruction. The Pharaoh, who dwells on the Nile, would call upon you to satisfy the Earth Mother's anger before the island, and maybe more, is destroyed."

"We, the people of Mother Goddess, do not know why she is angered. We keep her laws as she instructs," the priestess said.

The Egyptian used his staff to point at the mound. "You have offended her in some way. Tell me if you have changed her law?"

Standing in a prayer-like pose, the priestess said, "The laws have been the same in my mother's time and in her mother's time before that."

The Egyptian's eyes narrowed. "Consult your records and find out what has vexed her before you all perish."

The priestess turned to address the people. Zack saw ivory-colored skin and delicate features, unharmed by a strong Mediterranean sun. Her eyes were framed in dark eyeliner that started thick above her nose and extended in an ever-thinning line to beyond her temples. Delicate red curls adorned her head beneath the tiara, her lips stained a darker red. She wore a garland of flowers and a modest bell-shaped gown, not the ceremonial bare-breasted gown seen on the Thera frescoes unearthed at Akrotiri and Knossos. She displayed an even set of teeth when she spoke.

"Heed me, People of the Mother," she said.

All kneeled, including Talos and the priestesses. Zack followed. Only the Egyptian stood, grasping his cobra staff and watching the scene with a look of dissatisfaction.

The priestess continued in a tone of authority. "Be it known that Potnaya's wisdom has no end." She raised her hands, palm open and extended. "Return to your homes. Soon enough, I will know what to do."

Nia extended a hand towards the Egyptian. "This man, whose name is Menes, hails from the halls of the Great King in Egyptos, the most ancient of peoples. He will assist us in the unraveling of the Earth Mother's message."

Zack watched the priestess and the diplomat walk away from the circle of people, glancing at him before they mounted a chariot with a tasseled parasol. Two brown horses with their manes divided into three sections and twisted at the top pulled the chariot away. Some people debated, others covered their eyes, and many knelt towards the growing peak, placing their foreheads on the ground. A great wailing arose.

"Come, Outsider." Talos strode up an uneven side of the mountain. He yanked a sprig of wheat from the ground. "I cannot bear to listen to the people weep."

Zack followed, covering his nose with his forearm. *Rotten eggs. Hydrogen Sulphide. Nasty. Even toxic.*

A short hike brought them to an opening. A trail of noxious smoke curled upwards into the sky. Zack felt the heat under his sandals. He gagged, breathing in the corruption emanating from side vents. Talos peered into the abyss. He held Zack back.

"I don't know if it's right to peer upon the Mother in all her anger, but I do not want you to be fouled by looking into her loins," Talos said.

"I'll go with you. Just catch me if I retch and fall over the side."

Talos threw his boughs of wheat into the abyss. They disappeared into the smoke. Zack averted his eyes. Talos said as he coughed, "The Myceneans on the mainland, they would cut the throats of cattle and sheep, maybe even those of maidens and wards, to satisfy their gods. But we don't do that here."

Zack pinched his nose with his fingers and alternately stamped his feet. Looking down, he realized the soles of his sandals were smoking.

Talos hawked and spat off to the side of the hole. "I fear we will need something more than spring wheat, though. An earth-shaking in the last harvest caused many to sail for Crete. Many more will leave if the mound grows."

"We must leave or fall ill. Where are going now?" Zack asked, starting downhill at a jog.

"Home, and then to the temple." Talos put his hands on his knees and took several cleansing breaths. "We will have to cross the bridge or take a boat to get to the central island where the priestess and her court dwell. I am royalty, and so I will have my seat at the table when decisions are made." Talos met Zack's pace. "Outsider, you have no luck at all. I fear few of your days here will be spent sitting by the sea and drinking sweet wine. Come with me if you will or mingle among our people. The decision is yours. And what kind of name is …Zack?"

"I will tell you," Zack coughed, "when I can breathe."

Talos pulled him forward by the arm. "Then let us go to my home and escape the Earth Mother's sick stomach."

Zack thought, *I need get the hell off this island.*

Calliope

1626 BCE

The two-story townhome of Zack's host looked to be constructed of stone and timber with a gated entryway. White limestone stucco covered the outside wall, painted with the image of a rocky shore and a flight of seagulls. Two donkeys tied up before a barn stood before an unattached wagon.

Talos entered his home and called out, "Come here, Heebe, my little songbird. I have a guest, and don't be alarmed by his size. He calls himself Zack, and he's gentle as a temple dove."

His wife entered in a rush. She gasped a moment after setting eyes on Zack. Lighter-haired than Talos and a head shorter, Heebe had muscle tone in her shoulders and arms. Like an acrobat, Zack thought. Her hair had been piled on her head and tied with a concentric red ribbon. After straightening her ankle-length gown and smiling hesitantly, she said, "Welcome. You are among the people, and my house is yours."

Heebe bowed, went to her husband and grabbed his hand. She stared Zack up and down until Talos laughed. He then asked his wife to prepare a midday meal before they walked to the temple.

The entryway led to a larger room painted with scenes of nature- lilies growing near a pond, young girls in the typical Minoan dress with long skirts and aprons picking plants that Zack could only guess were red-colored crocuses.

"On the second level, we have a room our sons used before they left for the navy. Perhaps you would like to soak your bones in a warm bath before we go?" Talos asked.

"It'll be too much trouble to boil the water and haul it upstairs," Zack said.

Talos put his hand on his hips. "Do you think we are a bunch of Myceneans living among the rocks? Come here and I'll show how you will have a proper bath." He leapt up the stairs like a much younger man, leading Zack to a bedroom with an adjoining closet that served as a bathroom.

"Had this built for me," Talos said, beaming. "We live on a lower level here than on the hillsides. You see, my visitor from afar, perhaps it has not occurred to you, but water always runs downhill."

"I did see cisterns perched on the hilltops," Zack said, inspecting ancient versions of faucet handles and spigots for delivering water.

"Hot springs provide for our baths and we save water in our own cisterns," Talos said, turning a bronze lever. "Put your finger in the water, though not for too long. It will burn you. We'll fill the tub half full first and then shut it off. Then the cold water will be added for your comfort."

With a lurch of his eyebrows, Talos added, "See the plug carved to fit the hole in the bottom of the tub? We'll drain the water through the hole into hardened clay pipes built into the house. I met an architect from the Palace at Knossos. He told me this would please my Heebe. Even the queen herself has not a hole at the bottom of her tub to drain the water." He made motions with his hand conveying the direction of the water through the pipes. "The water will travel through the conduits until it reaches irrigation pipes and ditches leading to the fields."

Zack shook his head. "You are a great builder."

"Come with me. I have another surprise for you." He led Zack over to a wooden bench with an elliptical hole cut in the middle. Above the bench a large terracotta pot sat poised to deliver a deluge of water through a clay pipe, thereby washing away the refuse thru a hole.

"A flush toilet," Zack exclaimed.

"Your words confuse me."

"You have many marvels," Zack said, pointing at the toilet and remembering that flush toilets had not been installed in the White House until the 1850s.

"The Goddess demands cleanliness. Many generations have lived here. We have worked out how to ensure the survival and happiness of our people."

"Are you going to the Temple?"

"I shall depart at midday."

"May I accompany you?" Zack asked.

Talos considered his request for a long moment. "I will bring you with me, though I do not know if you can enter the inner royal apartments."

"I would appreciate the opportunity to understand the ways of the Earth Mother."

"Then take your bath and change into the clothing I've set aside for you. Come down when you are done, and let's hope my wife has a better opinion of you."

After crossing a wooden bridge, they arrived at a temple complex that covered almost two acres on a ring of land overlooking a central island. It appeared to be built out of limestone and displayed many levels as it reached the top of a hill. There were no entry gates, and only a few royal guards stood outside, clad in blue kilts, polished bronze breastplates and holding long spears. Zack did a double take when he noticed that each guard wore shoulder-length hair and sported the curled forelock of Apollo. The guards saluted Talos by holding their spears upright. After passing a wide stone portal, Zack saw scribes seated at tables and artists painting scenes of island life.

After negotiating a maze of corridors, they arrived at a hall room, a painted megaron, like one he'd seen at Mycenae. Inverted wooden columns with a round capital at the top held up walls decorated with frescoes of red-skinned men and a white skinned woman leaping over a charging bull. Zack saw clouds tumbling across the sky. A downdraft of wind swirled through the aperture and sent the flames in the pots jumping.

At the far end of the room, the priestess Zack had seen at the mound sat upon an alabaster throne chair. Beside her, a young man sat on a separate gray throne chair, bare to the waist, and sporting a forelock. Priestesses, attendants, and the Egyptian ambassador huddled at a stone table strewn with pages of papyrus and a large bound book of animal skins. Talos nudged Zack forward.

Talos bowed and his voice bounced off the walls. "Beloved Nia, I want to introduce an outsider I have met. He is interested in hearing about the graces of the Mother Goddess."

Nia raised her eyes to peer at Zack. A moment of recognition flashed across her face. At six feet two, he would be hard to miss. The Egyptian sniffed and scowled, vexed at being interrupted from his study of the book.

The priestess nodded to Zack, offering him a minimal smile. "The Earth Mother grants hospitality to all outsiders, as long as they are gentle and do not violate our laws. Will you obey the laws of the people?"

Zack bowed like Talos. "I will."

Nia asked, "When did you arrive, Outsider?"

He hadn't thought about any explanation for his presence. *I'm going to have to be a good liar.*

"I have arrived on your shores by ship upon the new moon." Zack paused and waited for a reaction, since he had told something of the story to Talos earlier.

The Egyptian, Menes, frowned. "We did not suspect you dropped from the heavens."

Zack coughed.

Talos said, "He told me of his arrival by ship."

Menes spoke in a crass tone while he reached for red grapes. "We know of many lands upon the inland sea. Our ships, and those of our Phoenician allies, have sailed beyond the twin pillars of stone that mark the entrance. Which is your land?"

"My people live beyond the twin pillars."

Several raised their heads from the books. The Egyptian stopped chewing and narrowed his eyes. "Did you stop on the mainland of Achaea on your way here?"

"I did to load wine and bread. My ship took on water off your coast, and I swam ashore."

Talos broke in. "Covered in mud when I found him, to the southeast. He looked dazed and lost."

Nia held up her hand. "Let us not be consumed with this outsider for now."

The Egyptian stared at Zack. He averted his eyes when Zack returned his gaze.

One of the lesser priestesses, the bodice of her attire covered in red and yellow geometric symbols, asked, "Shall I continue reading from the Great Book, my queen?"

"Do so," Nia said.

The younger priestess turned a page, which appeared to be lambskin. "In times before, the Earth Goddess demanded more than barley grain for sacrifice. Order prevailed in her realm; the people built swift ships, as we do now, the islands were safe from invasion and trade prospered."

A breeze filled the great room with the smell of brine. A seagull called on the wind. A few raindrops splattered on the alternating black and white tiles decorating the floor. Zack lifted on his toes in attempt to see if the book was written in hieroglyphics or possibly Minoan Linear A.

Menes scratched at his chin. "But the Earth Mother is angry now and you've told me nothing that I don't already know. Keep reading."

The island people exchanged confused looks until the Egyptian broke the silence. "Let us ask the visitor what his opinion is of the mound. Maybe in his land, he has seen this before."

All eyes turned to Zack. Again, back in a historical period, he worried how anything he said or did might change the future.

"I have heard of these mounds becoming mountains, and bursting fire and rock, destroying all in their path."

"Have your eyes seen this?" asked Queen Nia.

"No."

"When did the mound begin to grow?" the Egyptian asked.

"Within six moons," a priestess scribe answered.

"And the rapid buildup commenced recently?" Menes confirmed, looking at Zack.

Talos raised his hand. "We must protect our homes from any rocks that may be thrown from the mountain. I submit we consider moving the people who live near the mountain or the inner ring."

Nia bit her lip. "I decree that this should be done." The priests and priestesses scribbled on papyrus sheets.

The Nile dweller refocused on the ancient text. He raised his eyebrows as he scanned a page, running his finger over the written symbols. He looked at Nia. "I desire an audience with you in private. There is something you have missed."

"All are dismissed." Nia stood.

Those in attendance bowed. Zack wasn't sure how fast the volcano that devastated Santorini in around 1626 BCE took to build. Did he have days or a year before the cataclysm occurred? Now, he understood Apollo, knowing the future and trying to save a civilization from disaster.

Talos tugged on Zack's forearm. "Come home with me."

"Who is the man sitting next to the queen?" Zack asked.

Talos answered, "He is the Prince-consort. He must have the luck of ages to be the queen's lover. He stays with her from one cycle of the seasons and then she will choose another."

The royal party walked from the room. The Egyptian followed them, holding the book.

Talos said, "I want to stop at my shipyard first. Care to stretch your legs?"

How can I warn them about what's coming? Is it even a good idea to?

12

Calliope

1626 BC

A manicured dirt road led downhill to the shoreline. Rocks and bluffs guarded the quarter-mile stretch of beach where Zack saw two ships on stilts. Suntanned workers scraped and cut beams of wood with bronze tools. The ring of pounded metal and boiling pots of pitch added to the noise of a working shipyard. Zack ran his hand over the hull of one of Talos's new vessels, wider and longer than the triremes of the Persian Wars period. This craft looked more like a merchant vessel than a man-of-war.

"How many days till the ships are ready?" Zack asked.

Talos put his hands on a glassless window frame. "Half a moon or more, depending on how the navy wants them built. The benches and oars are being carved now. The deck boards will be smoothed so the crew doesn't end up with a forest of splinters in their feet." Talos rubbed his chin.

"Can you double the crews?" Zack asked.

Talos turned to Zack. "Can you make the sea spray fish onto dry land?" He inspected the pitch coating on the hull. "Some of these timbers come all the way from the land north of Egyptos. Cedar, they call it. I'll use one of the longer logs for the mast. The other beams come from Keftiu."

"Can you fight with these ships? They look like they will haul goods rather than warriors."

Talos grinned and tapped his head with his forefinger. "I make a new kind of ship, one that can trade and fight. I have the navy training marines for my ships. Later, my crews will slap linen strips onto the hull with resin. Toughen it, make it water-tight, but layers will be needed over many days, inside and out to beat back the sea. We will have a proper white-colored hull."

A laminated hull? Zack thought. *Like fiberglass in the future?*

If he didn't fear influencing the technological advance of shipbuilding, Zack could have drawn Talos a picture of a Viking ship. One that he knew could survive high seas. "What about the training of the oarsmen?" Zack asked.

Talos slapped Zack on the back. "Maybe you are a mariner, after all."

Looking him square in the eye, Zack said, "You've been kind to me, but a disaster is coming with that growing mountain and all must be ready to leave this island."

Talos stepped backwards. "Potnaya will care for us. We may suffer the loss of the part of the island that stinks, but many can move south, towards Akrotiri."

Zack let out a long breath. Ancient peoples put too much stock in fate and gods. But wasn't his life being run by a god, too?

Zack said, "I tell you now. Finish those ships in a few days. Pack them for a sea voyage."

"Outsider, you are too fearful…"

"No, Talos. Listen to me." Zack put his hands on his new friend's shoulders. "Gather your relatives. Fill the hull with food and your valuables. Bring weapons. Get the ships ready to leave."

Talos chewed his lip. "These are Potnaya's vessels. I cannot steal from the goddess."

"Could you at least hurry the work? Potnaya will be pleased."

"You are not a priest, Outsider."

"That is true, but I beg you to act with haste." Zack watched workers set a long mast into the hull with pulleys. "Can you show me your weapons and how your men form for battle?"

"We drill, but few enemies have ever stepped foot on our shores. The ships yonder have kept our shores safe from pirates and kings."

"I have fought in great land battles and on ships, too."

"What have you not done?"

"I haven't convinced you to act more quickly on my warning to leave."

Talos threw an errant board onto a pile. "Why do you speak of such matters that are only the right of the Great Mother to know?"

Zack looked back towards the growing mountain, blocked by the contour of the island. He caught another whiff of rotten eggs again. He sniffed more loudly this time and peered at his host. Talos lifted his nose and caught the scent.

Talos shouted for his shipyard foreman.

Halfway to Talos's home, the skies opened. Droplets the size of marbles splattered the ground at first, dissipating the summer heat and raising dust. Zack and Talos ran, hauling a hemp bag filled with peas and lentils. It would take another twenty minutes of jogging to reach Talos's home near Akrotiri. The wind picked up velocity, and the rain assaulted them in horizontal sheets.

Talos shouted over the gale winds, "Potnaya, our Earth Goddess, must have thought we looked thirsty." He ducked his head.

Zack shielded his eyes with a hand, leaning into the storm "How much farther is it?" Water ran off the bridge of his nose and dripped from his chin.

"We'll need to run or look for a cave."

A cascade of storm water leaped from the tile roof and a gathering puddle sat in front of the entrance. Both men dashed inside, shaking sheets of water from their limbs. Heebe shrieked and threw lengths of toweling at them and knelt on the floor to wipe up the puddle.

She shouted over the howling wind and banging shutters, "Go

upstairs quickly, and fix the hole in the roof. The second floor could float one of your ships."

Talos ran upstairs, Zack on his heels. Talos hit water, slid and fell. Zack saw a flood pouring through a collapsed section of the roof.

"Skins, wood, and hammers," Talos said, rubbing his shin. "I'll return with what we need."

Zack found a sturdy table on which to stand, and he pushed the timbers back up into place. He stuffed straw in the hole until Talos appeared with boards and mallets.

"I won't be able to reach it. Can you, Outsider?"

Zack grabbed a stable beam, swung a leg up and over it, and lifted himself onto the roof. The wind screeched. He heard crashing sounds, as if a nearby home had just collapsed.

"Hand up the boards," Zack shouted through the hole.

With his hands raised to cover his eyes, Talos rambled, "There's a river coming down the stairs."

The storm raged. Zack hammered.

Zack awoke the next morning, roused by a crackling fire and the aroma of cooking eggs. Just for a moment, he thought he was in his boyhood home in Waukegan, Illinois, the smell of breakfast traveling upstairs to rouse him from bed. He opened the shutter. His second–story perch offered a view of the southern shore of Santorini. He could see whitecaps on the sea, doubtless stirred by the last winds of the violent storm of the night before. He went to the ancient water closet and marveled at the effort to prevent water-borne illnesses in times thought primitive.

Apollo said he'd been sent here on a vacation, but he knew that the time would offer no such thing. He had fought in battles, had helped to save Athens in the modern age, and found out he had a son. And lost him.

Block the pain of the separations. He couldn't bring life back to Nestor, Diomedes, pretty Persephone, or the enchantress, Io. He wanted Lauren, and he longed to watch Cassandra discover the modern world.

Continuing this train of thought would yield nothing good for now.

After dressing in a thin linen knee-length garment set aside for him, Zack walked down a dry stairway. The roof repair must have held.

That meant Heebe must have been up for hours drying the water. And she and Talos would have done the work themselves, because he hadn't seen any slaves the day before. In fact, his initial assessment of the civilization present on Santorini, or Thera, was easily substantiated as forward thinking, promoting equality between the sexes. Amazingly, he'd seen women walking alone in the streets, and in pairs, laughing and going to market. In Athens, during the Golden Age some twelve hundred years into the future, women remained behind closed doors unless escorted.

Had society advanced?

Zack reached the first-floor landing. He followed the aroma of frying eggs to the rear courtyard. Talos tended copper pans positioned over two upraised stones.

Zack said, "Your cooking woke me."

"Another is hungry, also," Talos said, indicating with his shoulder towards the foundation of the home. A slender, green snake slithered from the foundation, out a ceramic tube and into a bowl holding a cake.

"Snakes in the house? Heebe tolerates this?"

"It is our daughter. I put a honey cake out for her."

Zack raised his eyebrows. Should he inquire further? He didn't want to risk offending an ancient man for his beliefs. He remembered the snakes in Queen Io's underground temple, symbolizing fertility and kept in the lower levels.

Talos said, "Heebe will not leave our home easily. Our first-born daughter died shortly after birth, and she is buried under the house. She is the snake you see eating the cake. Do not play with me, Outsider, or the sentiments of my wife. Respect what is sacred."

"I ask for your forgiveness."

"I let Heebe sleep after a long night of cleaning. That woman will not go to bed with an unruly home." Talos stirred the eggs in bubbling olive oil. In another bronze pan, dough cooked. A gutted fish lay off to the side, next in line for the frying pan. Nearby, pears and apples filled a basket.

"What will you do today?" asked Zack.

"Given your petition to hurry the completion of my galleys, I will see to the work."

"Can I help you?"

"You can." Talos pounded his chest. "Though I am superior to you in years, strength is on my side. Get your fingers in the way and I will snap them off with my spoon."

A young man appeared in the courtyard, caught his breath and said, "I bear a summons for Talos and his foreigner to appear with haste at the Priestess's temple."

13

1626 BCE

CALLIOPE

"**Y**ou have gained the attention of Nia, and maybe her advisor," Talos said.

"Can I see the summons?" Zack inspected the papyrus sheet. The figures looked like Linear A, a Minoan printed language but still not deciphered in the modern age. "Can you teach me to read this?"

"Not with the shipbuilding demands, but Heebe can. I will have her start tomorrow."

"I'll need two sheets of papyrus, one to write down a list of letters and words in your tongue, and then another in mine."

Talos looked puzzled. "How is it you speak our tongue, but cannot write down the words?"

Zack couldn't answer. Apollo had somehow given him special knowledge, so he understood what Talos said. Shouldn't he be able to understand the letters and words? Why hadn't Apollo given him that skill? "I don't have an answer for you, but within a few days, I will teach my tongue to you."

Talos threw a tunic at Zack. "Clean up for our audience with Nia. To be properly groomed is to honor her."

Zack walked through the stone lintel of the palace entrance, noticing a doubling of palace guards since their last visit. Bull jumpers, dancers, processions of priestesses carrying boughs of grain for sacrifice, and leaping dolphins decorated the walls of a stairway. A guard escorted them to the megaron, the central hall they had visited earlier. Inside, Nia and her male consort sat upon the same marble throne chairs, with lines of priests and priestesses on the steps. Menes occupied a carved chair of polished cedar, gripping his cobra-headed staff. Parakeets and other small, multi-colored birds milled about in open cages, chirping and dancing.

Talos and Zack halted ten steps from the first landing that lead up to the throne chairs.

Nia stood and held up her hands, palms out.

"I welcome you, wise Talos, and you also, stranger from beyond the seas."

Talos bowed. Zack followed his lead.

"You are here, stranger, to answer the questions of the Pharaoh's emissary. Be truthful, I implore you, as events have caused haste in our efforts to understand Potnaya's wishes."

Zack peered at the deep-set eyes of the Egyptian. He saw suspicion in his face and the rigid posture of the man's body as he leaned forward in his chair.

Menes said with a stern look, "Fill us with falsehoods, and I promise that you will regret their utterance."

Zack glanced at Talos.

Talos cleared his throat. "Why is this man accused of any wrongdoing? I can attest to his honesty and good nature."

Menes pointed his cobra-headed staff at Zack. "Then why did the mound grow so suddenly as soon as he landed here."

All eyes fixed their gaze on Zack.

He raised his chin. "That's not my doing. Why should I have any influence on the will of Potnaya? I am a stranded sailor. Why should she, in all her power, be affected by my arrival?"

A chorus of whispers followed.

The Egyptian took a step towards Zack. "Do not surmise that we are easily fooled. There are those who bring malice with their dark gods."

Zack set his feet apart. He glanced quickly at Talos, who returned his look of disbelief. "I bear only tidings of peace."

Nia smiled. An attendant poured from a long-beaked vase into the priestess's crystal cup.

Menes swung his staff, just missing one of two red columns holding up a canopy of cedar boards and blue tiles that shielded the royal pair from the sun. He raised his voice. "The mountain grows. You are an ill wind that has come to these shores."

Zack said loudly, "I worship no dark gods, and I wish no one harm."

Sacred doves suddenly flew from the room, shrieking in unison. All turned to watch their flight with puzzled looks as the birds darted around the columns and out through openings in the roof.

Then, the air boomed and the floor rolled.

A priestess screamed.

The next wave cracked the stone flooring.

Clay tiles fell from the ceiling. Male attendants pulled the priestesses away from the center of the room. Nia and her consort stood and balanced themselves by holding onto the throne chairs. A cedar column snapped with a loud crack. The floor buckled and moved like it lived. The male attendant behind Nia dropped his peacock parasol and ran. A brazier tipped. A long drape burst into flames. Smoke and dust soon veiled the scene.

The stone floor beside Zack lifted. He saw Nia thrown, her hand outstretched, as she reached for her consort. The earth opened with a deep-throated rip. A fractured ceiling beam plummeted. It crushed the head of Nia's consort.

Zack dove over the widening crack in the flooring. Nia held onto a stone step, her gown switched up along her thighs and her feet dangling over the edge. Losing her grip, she screamed. An oil lamp fell over and spewed fiery liquid in a line running towards her.

He leaped to grab hold of her gown. Her weight betrayed the strength of the light fabric, and it tore in Zack's hand. She slid towards the crevice that bellowed with the earth's hot breath. He seized her arm. The ground jolted again. He wedged his foot in a crack between the steps and tried to yank her up. Her gown snagged on a sharp spine of rock. Zack pulled her twice before it ripped enough to free her.

Zack hauled her away from the widening abyss like he was bringing her to life from Mother Earth herself.

Nia coughed, eyes darting from side to side. Smoke from the spreading fire clouded the room.

"To the open patio," Talos yelled, pointing past a collapsed wall to an outside porch.

Zack pulled Nia away from the widening edge of the chasm. He saw the Egyptian being led away by his men.

A weakened Nia sagged into Zack's arms. She thanked him with her eyes. Talos and Zack carried Nia to the porch moments before a total collapse of the roof. Billowing black smoke coursed through windows, doorways and holes in the walls.

The three sprawled on the stone patio after absorbing another roll. Columns teetered as if a heavy breath would knock over any still standing. Nia's gaze narrowed as she watched fires leap, the beautifully constructed royal apartments fall into a heap of rubble and heard the endless screams.

Zack corralled the Nia in his arms. "This is not the fault of the people, nor your fault. Potnaya has her own will, and there is nothing any of us can do to sway her."

Talos pointed at the royal throne. "We will have to rebuild on more solid ground."

Survivors crawled out of the rubble. Fires crackled.

Soot-marked, scraped and bleeding, Nia limped towards the damaged palace room, separated from them by the chasm.

"Wait," Talos said, reaching to stop her.

Her willowy figure stood near the edge. One last tremor caused her to plant her feet. She extended her arms for balance. Zack jumped up and steadied her.

Menes hobbled into sight, surrounded by staff who wiped him down with rags. Soot-filled creases in his aged face made his ever-present scowl more sinister.

Nia saw the fate of her consort. Her shoulders trembled. She turned, raised her chin and gazed into Zack's eyes.

"I am grateful, Outsider. You saved my life." She embraced him.

Zack recoiled just for a moment, but then it occurred to him that he had not too long ago failed to act quickly enough to protect Lauren back at Thermopylae.

Servants and priestesses ran into the burning megaron. They cried upon seeing the dead consort and the others killed or injured. One priestess leaped over the chasm to reach the queen. She unclasped her gown and covered Nia, cast an angry look at Zack, and escorted her away.

The shaking stopped, and the mournful wailing began.

The Egyptian saw Nia in the improper embrace of the tall outsider. Menes raised his staff to shake it at them, but the cobra head had broken off.

A moment later, his scowl became a grin.

After hours spent extracting the dead and injured, Zack and Talos made a weary trek back to Talos's home. They reached a rise overlooking the growing mound in the distance. Volcanic smoke spewed from the orifice, making a long trail to the south. Fires dotted the villages on the downward slopes from where they stood. The island had suffered more than the devastation of the palace.

Folding his arms, Talos surveyed the devastation. "The gods have made a dreadful mess. The efforts of many generations of builders have been brought back to earth."

"This is a last warning."

Talos shook his head. "We cannot linger here. I must check on Heebe and the shipyard. Help the injured." He left at a jogger's pace.

A squad of royal guards approached Zack.

"Come with us," the captain said with five guards standing behind him. "Nia has asked for you."

"Shouldn't we help these people first?" Zack pointed at the burning homes.

"We are ordered to return with you, now."

Talos was already out of sight.

The guards motioned for Zack to walk in the direction of the temple. He saw the captain draw his sword and follow behind him.

What the hell?

14

1626 BCE

CALLIOPE

They fast-walked about two miles until they reached a line of ships, anchored side by side with long boards creating a causeway to the central island. Zack saw the bridge had fractured in half.

A passing, like Xerxes's pontoon bridge.

Smoke still lifted skyward from the palace. No one spoke to him.

They passed through the gateway, cracked in places by the seismic shift. The paved road had uplifted. Workers cleared rubble and hauled bodies away on carts.

Reaching the temple gate, Zack could see the lintel stone above the doorjambs had cracked and the entrance held open by thick planks. Guards stood to each side of the great bronze door, which no longer fit into the square space and had to be left open. Amid the aroma of burning wood, Zack saw a dog standing nearby, its hind legs shaking.

Trauma was not limited to just people.

They entered the megaron, strewn with smoldering cedar beams. He saw fires blinking through empty windows at the temple up ahead.

The bodies had been removed but not the bloodstains. Wide planks bridged the chasm. The patio had been set up with two wooden chairs and overhead drapes of white linen. Nia sat upon her white throne chair.

The gray one remained empty. Bathed and dressed in a purple gown, she appeared to have been untouched by the event. She smiled at Zack. The Egyptian, Menes, braced by his guards on each side, stood behind her. He affirmed Zack's entrance with a gratuitous grin.

Nia said, "Stand before me and accept the people's appreciation for saving my life."

Zack walked over the planks that bridged the chasm, kneeled before her and bowed his head. He stood and said, "I am pleased to be of assistance to the people and to Potnaya." He glanced at the Egyptian when he said "Potnaya" to see that the man recognized that he was not the bearer of some malice. "I am called Zack. I hope my actions have proven that I bear good will."

Menes moved his jaw, as if contemplating a response.

Nia said, "You have served me with your courage. Potnaya expects the devotion of all who dwell under her graces, especially in a time of challenge."

"How shall I serve you and Potnaya while I am here?"

The priestess leaned forward in her chair. "I am pleased that you offer your assistance willingly. A ritual of great importance has been disrupted. Poseidon, the Earth-Shaker, must be displeased, and Potnaya offended somehow too, to allow such anger to be unleashed."

The Egyptian said, "At first, I surmised that your presence might have been a sign of evildoing, but now I have prayed and received assurance that after your heroic act, Potnaya has sent you here for a reason. Such courage in the face of danger must be rewarded."

"I ask for no reward, just to learn about your people, and be one with them in my time here."

Nia said, "I can see you are bleeding. I offer you my chambers to bathe and rest. The water will be fortified with saffron picked on the island. Your wounds will heal, and we will present you with clean clothing and a broad leather belt, embossed with a carving of Potnaya. All will know when they see this belt that you are favored among the people."

I'll have to wear two belts. I'm not giving up Apollo's.

Zack glanced at the Priestess and the Egyptian. As far as he could tell, their expressions were genuine. "I accept your offer, but maybe after more lives are saved and the palace is repaired."

The priestess replied, "Rest. My guards will take you to the bathing room. Be cleansed and then you may help again."

Zack drew in a deep breath. "I accept then."

The priestess's attendants accompanied Zack down a cleared hallway.

From above the bathing chamber, through a hole in the wall concealed by a sliding panel, Nia and the Egyptian watched the outsider disrobe. She blinked when he stretched.

Menes continued in hushed tones, "You must set aside all notions of thanks to this…foreigner. You know that Potnaya requires the consort to mate within days. Does Potnaya speak to you even now by sending the great shaking and causing the death of your consort? The ancient book states that she requires something more. He is the answer."

Nia couldn't take her eyes away from the stranger as he turned his back to her and bent over to test the temperature of the water. "He will more than do for the seeding ceremony, but all my consorts have previously volunteered. This outsider has not, nor does he know he's expected to beget me with child. Potnaya must be served, but can a man be forced to comply?"

Menes pursed his lips. "You are too kind. Your people suffer. Perhaps there's more danger to come. If Potnaya and Poseidon are angry, what is one man to stand in the way of their appeasement?"

"But, the old ways were discarded. Potnaya determined that it was no longer necessary for the ceremony to be completed."

"That has been misinterpreted. Do not discard the old, proven ways."

The priestess watched the stranger step into the bath. She sighed. "He is well-equipped to be the new consort."

"He'll not have to serve you for long."

"What do you mean?" She pressed her eye to the hole.

"He will be the consort but once. Then, to appease Potnaya and Poseidon, he must serve his role in the old way."

She drew back and pressed her hand over her mouth. The Egyptian pulled a long, thin blade from his robe. The knife bore a carving of a bare-breasted Potnaya, on the blade below the hilt.

He said, "I found this in the thickness of the book."

"I cannot do this."

"Oh, but you can," the Egyptian cooed. "Are the lives and the destinies of your people so meaningless that the sacrifice of a stranger would be more important than them?" His eyes, thick- browed, deep-set and wrinkled at the corners from decades in a strong sun, searched her for strength. "His sacrifice will please both gods. The mound will cease spewing, and your people will be able to remain on this island."

The Priestess returned her gaze to Zack in his bath.

Menes continued, "You think the sacrifice of one man is too much? If your influence recedes and the Poseidon worshippers gain power, children will be laid on the stone tablet and opened with knives to satisfy him. Is this what you wish?"

Nia closed her eyes. "Then it must be done. The time is right, and I must have his seed. He must die for all of us. The sacrifice will be properly performed as written in the old days, and then I will pick a new consort for the coming year."

The Egyptian smiled. "To rule is to make hard decisions. I bow to your wisdom." He bent at the waist for a moment. "The ceremony must take place tomorrow."

Zack supported his back on the curve of the tub while sitting in rose colored water, scented with saffron which many in the ancient thought had medicinal powers. He placed a cloth over his eyes, wondering how to save these extraordinary people, advanced beyond their time, from the coming cataclysm. They couldn't know of the fate awaiting them, believing that appealing to the gods with sacrifices of plants, or even animals, would somehow divert the forces of nature. Once the volcano erupted, there would be no time to escape.

He heard the gentle voice of Nia. "Are you enjoying your bath, Outsider?"

Zack had not heard anyone enter the bathroom. He drew in the fragrance of flowers and removed the cloth over his eyes. The queen stood before him, dressed in the traditional Minoan costume. A tight leather belt defined her waistline. Long green skirt, blue and red apron, her shoulders and arms covered, but with her breasts uncovered. Zack turned his gaze away.

"Do not cast your glance aside," she said. "Do you find me unappealing?"

"Ah, no, it's not that. You're very..."

She smiled and lifted her chin. "Then set your eyes back upon me and allow a man's right to behold a woman's beauty."

Zack turned in the bath. "I don't expect thanks for saving you. I'm happy to rest and then to assist Talos in rebuilding his home. I should be heading there now."

She walked to the side of the tub and peered over the edge. With a half-smile, she said, "I can see you do not believe your own words." She ran her fingertip around the rim of the tub, momentarily brushing Zack's hand.

Zack submerged himself deeper into the bath water.

Nia unbuttoned her apron and skirt. She let them fall. "You know the young prince died in the shaking. I cannot be without a consort. I ask you to perform a service for me." She smiled. "I promise you'll not be harmed."

Zack kept his gaze at eye level. "I beg you to listen to me. The mountain is growing, hot vapors will come, and then there will be a terrible explosion. The people will be driven to their knees and many will die. Their lungs will burn, and gray ash will fall from the mountain. Head south by ship to Keftiu too late, and a great wave will sink your ships."

She folded her arms across her chest, as if to keep from shivering. "How can you know this?"

"The Earth Mother is the same in this land and all others. When she builds these mountains of melted rock and dark plumes of smoke, there follows a disaster. Save your people."

"And go where, to the mainland where the Myceneans are warlike and live for conquest?"

"Leave now and you will reach Keftiu."

"Potnaya is willful, and we shall follow her laws." She raised her chin. "I ask you again to be my consort, couple with me and do her bidding."

Zack looked for a towel, so he could stand up. His clothes had been taken away. No towels in sight. "And if your prayers are not answered, the Egyptians incantations prove useless, and your sacrifices do not appease her, then what?"

Nia slipped behind him and massaged his scalp with her fingertips. "Then we will be compelled to leave our homes. We don't wish to leave the many priestesses of past times who are buried under the temple. Yet, this has already been discussed without your warning, and I have asked the ships to be prepared."

Finishing the massage, she kissed the top of his head. "You have the body of a warrior. A child from your loins will be tall and strong. Agree to my wishes, willingly. None have refused this privilege before."

She massaged his neck and shoulders.

Zack gritted his teeth. "But I must refuse. I have a woman who waits for me."

"Would your woman not understand that we might couple to save a people from doom?"

"I will do everything I can to help you... but not that."

I was weak with Io. Not this time.

Nia whispered, "Submit to Potnaya's wishes. I promise her blessings will be many." Her fingers danced through his chest hair and crept lower.

Zack pushed her hands away, gently. He smiled. "Potnaya must forgive me."

"I do not understand your ways, Outsider, but hold onto them at your own peril." The priestess said with growing irritation in her tone. She dressed, setting her aprons, leather belt, and blouse back in place. "Maidens will come with towels and fresh clothes. Perhaps you will change your mind overnight." She turned in a swirl of fabric and walked through the doorway.

When Nia reached the secret room above the bathroom, she saw the Egyptian stroking his beard, which was braided and tied in the manner of the pharaohs.

"I know," Menes said. "The Myceneans on the mainland are only held back from attacking this island because of your ships. Perhaps he is their spy and acts to draw you into a trap."

Nia stared through the eyehole at Zack.

"Bear witness to his lies," Menes whispered facetiously. "This stranger knows what Potnaya's will is." He put his hand on her shoulders. "He refuses to mate with you, and the mountain grows angrier. I hear a deep rumbling underground. He must submit to you tomorrow. He can be held, and you shall embrace him. It is a simple act for a man."

She peered at Zack again, standing beside the bath, waiting for the attendants. The ceremony would be completed as written. After the coupling, the stranger must be sacrificed, by *her*.

The Egyptian whispered, "He will be tied to a bed by his arms and legs by my guards. You will cause him to rise and get with a child. Then, you must drive the blade into his neck. His blood will be collected and dripped into the Earth Mother's mouth at the growing mountain. His body will follow and Potnaya will be appeased. None of the people will be harmed, and your laws will not be broken."

Nia watched as a flood of palace warriors and the two Egyptian guards burst into the bathroom to apprehend the Outsider. She saw him strike down four of the guards in succession. Then, he hurled two more into the bath. Six additional warriors grappled with him, the task made more difficult by his wet body. The Outsider kicked and punched. Finally, a guard cracked him on the head with the pommel of his sword and subdued him. They bound his feet and hands.

"Listen to the ancient gods, Nia." The Egyptian leaned on his headless staff. "The ancient ones of the Nile will guide you. They have long memories. Because we are here and stand before you, accept the proof that, if their laws are obeyed, safety will return to this realm."

The guards carried him away. Nia asked, "And what, Menes, if the sacrifice is not enough and Potnaya destroys our homes?"

Menes adjusted his fake beard. "We'll have time to consider what to do next."

"That will not do. I am directing the navy today to prepare all ships to sail our people to Keftiu. This begins today. If the Goddess is appeased, we will return."

Menes frowned. "Do you dare bargain with your goddess?"

"I will not allow the people to be burned alive if the goddess does not have mercy on us."

No manner of twisting and squeezing the rope could untangle the knot. Zack lay on a bed of straw within a square-shaped cell. He'd had enough of earth goddess priestesses. He thought about Io and how she'd manipulated him to achieve her goals. That union had borne him a son, but both lost to time and fate. Zack decided to say no to Nia, tired of being handled and coerced. There was no time for this anyway. At some point, the volcano would erupt. Would he be locked into this prison, to be burned and suffocated by the pyroclastic flow?

So many crosscurrents, he thought. So many attempts made to manipulate him and Lauren. He loved and depended on her, and he had never realized just how much.

But he wasn't going anywhere right now. Two guards stood outside the door. Legs and hands tied, he'd have to wait till morning and hope he could somehow persuade Nia to free him.

Talos leaped two steps at a time to the Royal Palace.

"Slow down," Heebe cried out, gathering her long skirt so she wouldn't trip on the jagged steps cracked by the quake.

They had made a quick pace all the way from the shipyard when neighbors had brought news of Zack's capture. Talos paused to catch his breath. He held Heebe by the shoulders. "I cannot say for sure...what

Zack predicts might be the truth. Neither Potnaya, nor Nia, have ever lied to us before…or threatened us in any way. Why now do I race to the temple with a wrath to oppose her?"

Heebe wiped her forehead with her long sleeve. "I do not approve of the Egyptian." She took several more breaths. "A scowl is fixed on his face. Something is wrong."

Talos ran his hand over a fractured doorjamb. "It will take many seasons to repair the damage."

"We will lose our shipyard and fields."

"First of all, we'll secretly load our store of tin and copper bars near the shipyard if we have to leave quickly. If we end up in Keftiu, I will become a bull jumper again, and so will you. Even at our age, I know we'll please the crowd."

Heebe feigned shock. "You want me to prance around in the arena with but a loincloth on?"

"Your beauty will distract the crowd, and the bull. It will be my only chance to survive."

She twirled in her skirt. "I agree then." Her countenance took a fast turn, and a serious look came upon her face. Heebe clasped his hand in hers. "If you believe Zack, then we cannot rebuild here."

"My head aches from the thinking of it."

"And you will ask me to leave our first-born?"

"That would not please me, either."

"Either we leave our home, or we follow Nia and stay. It is your decision, husband, but we are bringing our daughter with us if we must flee."

Talos pounded the cracked stone. "The mountain grows and stinks. The earth shakes. I have heard talk of abandoning this island and departing for Keftiu as many have already done. There may be a different path. I have heard there is a priestess who has the ear of Potnaya by another name. She stands on a black rock beneath the great mountain peaks on the mainland."

She gave her husband a distraught look. "If that is your decision, then we must hurry."

When they reached the royal patio, the Egyptian rapped his staff on the stone floor. "The ceremony must proceed as planned. Do not question the ways of the Earth Mother, as you call her."

Nia stood watching the darkening volume of smoke rising from the volcano's growing peak. She turned abruptly. "My consort lies on a funeral bier, ready for burial."

Talos pleaded. "Then could it be Potnaya has taken his life so that he can be sent into the mouth of the mound? Why would she be pleased with an outsider of no value, of no adherence to her laws, of no devotion to her ways? You might as well throw in a handful of toads to appease her."

Menes said in a seething voice, "I read the book. The consort was sacrificed each year by a dagger thrust of the sacred knife. For eight generations, that ritual has been altered with no protest from Potnaya." He pointed his bony finger at the mound. "Until now!"

Nia shook her head. "The older priestesses passed down to me that the live sacrifices were halted. A Calliope cannot slay another of the people. The consort was nicked by the dagger, but not killed. We have had peace and prosperity... till...."

The Egyptian shouted. "And one of the people shall not be harmed, but this stranger must be. He will couple with you and receive the blade in his neck to fulfill the old ways. His body will be dropped into Potnaya's eager mouth, and the island will be saved."

"Priestess," Heebe said, bowing, "perhaps there is another outsider that would serve you as well. Others may be found at the docks--Poseidon worshippers from the mainland, or others who worship the golden calf from the lands to our east."

Menes waved a dismissive hand. "Your people are babes compared to the Nile Dwellers. Whom you call Potnaya, we call Isis. I have read the texts of the ancient ones in Egyptos. These same books came to your shores, too. Although you have changed the name of the Earth Mother, her demands are the same. Obey her laws."

Heebe knelt before Nia. "We will return with another outsider who quench Potnaya's thirst."

"No, he is the one I favor. He is tall and wise. His seed will be strong. His sacrifice will be powerful medicine for the blackening purge that bellows from Potnaya. It must be him."

The ground beneath them rumbled again, a deep, threatening growl. Nia brought her hand over her mouth. Her gaze darted from side to side to see if the earthshaking tremors would kill again.

"Potnaya has heard your doubt, Priestess," Menes said. "Heed her demands. The guards will purify him again in the morning. Then, he shall serve you. The dagger will be under the pillow."

Talos peered at Heebe briefly, conveying his desire for them to leave.

"Then we understand, Nia, that it must be so," Heebe said.

The Egyptian grinned as he turned away. Nia sighed in resignation.

Talos said, "We accept the word of Potnaya."

He and Heebe bowed and left the council room.

As they hurried away, Talos whispered to Heebe, "We must act with haste. I don't know how much longer Potnaya shall wait. If the sacrifice is not made, then we must all leave, as fast as the ships can carry us away."

15

Calliope

1626 BC

Zack heard voices outside; a woman's voice with a flirting tone. Then the guard's laughter as they commented on the beauty of the woman. Then a scuffle, groaning, and the sound of two thwacks as a hard object met with the skulls of the guards. Metal jingled, and the door swung open. Talos burst in, accompanied by Heebe and a young woman. Talos put his finger to his lips to signal silence, withdrew a knife and sawed off the ropes that restrained Zack.

Talos said quietly, "We must dash to the shipyard. I've seen more of the smoke you describe, and the white breath leaking. The mountain groans. I fear what you say is near."

Zack stood and rubbed his wrists. He caught a robe Heebe threw at him. She said, "Hurry and dress before our young cousin here locks us out."

"Quiet, my love, you will make me laugh and we'll be caught," Talos cautioned.

"Then let us go quietly. I will birdcall twice if there are no guards. If there are, we will distract them for you. I am still a maiden of some beauty myself."

Talos grinned and stroked her cheek. "You are, and they will truly be enchanted. Come now quietly. Once we are free of this prison, run to the shipyard, even if we have to separate."

The prison stood on a hillside away from the palace. Trees lined the road, providing cover in the early morning darkness. They dashed from one grove to another, across the bridge of ships, and then along the dirt road that lead to the south of the island.

Arriving, and after catching his breath, Zack said, "The shipyard's damaged. The buildings are burned." He saw one of the ships off its frame and lying on its side.

Talos pointed, "There's no hope for that one. Its ribs are broken. We still have one stout ship for our escape, Zack. When I heard from Heebe that they had taken you, I told my men to load up."

Zack watched the men carrying earthen jugs, baskets of food, and a line of goats. "Did you have the men make bigger shields with an arm-sleeve and handgrip on the inside edge?"

"No time. Hurry to help us load spears, swords, and an extra sail."

The earth shook. The shipyard people dropped to their knees and prayed.

Zack pulled on Talos's sleeve. "They'll discover I'm gone. We have to leave now."

"Then speak not and fill our ship with all we'll need. Keftiu is a two-day sail."

"Not Keftiu," Zack said. "We must go to the northwest. Only there, past the long fingers of the mainland, will we be safe from ash and the great wave that's coming. We must bring seed and warm clothing. The sun will be darkened for a time and cold will come, too."

"You fill a man with warmth, Outsider. I hope you're right, because we'll die if you aren't."

"No, Talos, they are all likely to perish We have a fighting chance."

"If we leave now, my sons won't be on board," Talos said, pulling on Zack's arm. "They're aboard Navy ships, and we don't know when they'll be back."

"We have to go home to gather our daughter. I can't leave her," Heebe said, with all yearning in her eyes.

Talos held her. "My love. We cannot risk going home. The guards will capture us."

Heebe pulled her shawl over her face.

"Then hide me and wait for your sons," Zack said. "You could sneak home and…"

Talos let out a deep breath. "I will not sacrifice Heebe and her family by waiting here and risking capture or the mountain's fury. If my sons are on Navy ships to the north, won't they be safe from the waves?"

Zack lied. "Only Potnaya knows. I pray they patrol Mycenaean waters. We may have to sail beyond even their shores to escape."

Talos gripped his forehead. "Pray we're not slain by the Myceneans or pirates. Maybe we should sail for where another priestess worships Potnaya and dwells beneath the two mountaintops on the Mycenaean mainland. I hear she stands on a black rock and reveals the will of the Earth Goddess."

"Who?" Zack asked, holding back his impulse to laugh. He had no idea that Talos, or anyone else, had heard of the Sybil of Delphi, no less that history had no record of her existence in this time.

"We will speak of her later," Talos said.

The ship held forty people, ten oarsmen on each side, and another six benches manned by women. As soon as the ship cleared the inlet, the first glimmers of dawn peeked over the horizon. The main sail was hoisted and caught enough wind to head north. The breeze didn't last long, and they were back on their oars. A glass-smooth sea offered less resistance, but these were not trained oarsman. The crew tired and petitioned to take a break. Zack, Talos, and eight others took a shift, and they cut a path to the northwest.

While Zack rowed, he could see high volumes of smoke and ash belching from the volcano. "Look, Talos. I hope the princess tells them all to leave."

Talos strained at his oar. It had taken them a half hour to get the cadence down. "This is not an act Nia takes lightly. Imagine that all have to leave their ancestor's graves."

Zack said, "But they must, and many will still die at sea. We have to be many days away to not have our ship swamped."

"They'll figure out we've taken flight, and the navy will come after us."

This hybrid ship, part merchantman and part trireme, had a rounder bottom with a keel and rudder. An hour later, they switched shifts again. In the middle of hauling in the oars and getting the first shift back into place, a naval vessel came into view. The purple streamers on the mast lay still.

Talos wiped his brow. "Zack, go into the hold."

Zack squeezed in among the baskets of fruit and ground wheat below decks. Goats momentarily stared at him and, then went back to chewing on sprigs of grain. He heard shouting before the ships bumped and lines tied. He crept to the ladder and saw Heebe hugging a young sailor. Another young man passed spears and bags to Talos. Then Talos talked to the captain of the ship, pointing at the island and the growing volcano, waving his hands and thrusting them skyward to mimic to an explosion. The navy ship shoved off for Calliope.

"Zack, come up here," Talos shouted, "and meet my sons, Hippon and Mela." Hair lighter than expected and tied in ponytails, both had darkly tanned skin from their time out to sea. Zack guessed that twins stood before him.

Talos grinned. "Tell them apart by their earrings. Hippon wears a dolphin, Mela a lizard."

Zack grasped each of their hands in greeting.

Their father gave his sons' a rundown of events. The smiles left their faces as Talos described the volcano and about Zack's predicament. Mela argued that they would be criminals.

Talos put his hands on the boy's shoulders. "I believe what Zack has said will come to pass. The mountain grows bigger and angrier. The danger of staying is too great."

Mela nodded his understanding.

"Then let's pull the oars hard till we catch a wind. If Nia dispatches a navy ship to catch us, we want to be far away from their grasp."

Shift after shift brought exhaustion and sore muscles to the point that few could continue to row.

After a half day of rowing west, a ribbon on the mast fluttered. Then another lifted, joining the dance on a newfound breeze.

"Run up the mainsail," Talos shouted, "before the wind dies." Everyone slumped at their oars. They'd wrapped their bleeding and swollen hands with rags. The women no longer took their shifts. Only ten men could sit at their benches and pull against the sea. The sail caught the wind. The bow cut through the waves. "We must hope that Potnaya will have mercy."

"Does the Earth Mother control the seas, too?" Zack asked.

Talos scratched the whiskers on his chin.

The sea chopped. The wind snapped the sail, and the vessel lurched from side to side.

Heebe crawled up the stairs to the main deck, holding the hem of her gown against her mouth. She saw the height of the waves. "Talos," she screamed, "the children, the women, they suffer."

He flung his hand at the elements as if to ask what he was supposed to do about it.

The boat dipped, and she tumbled down the stairs. Heebe climbed back up again, and shouted to him, "One of the wives is with child, and it's in a rush to born."

"What?" Talos said, gripping the rudder. He cupped his ear as if unable to hear her clearly.

Heebe shook her head and disappeared below deck.

Zack thought it might be another fifty to seventy-five miles to Kythera, an island sitting off the Peloponnese. That landfall was their best hope, but it was almost two days of rowing away. It wouldn't be long before they would be down to a handful of able rowers. Wind soon filled the sail, coming from the southwest. The sail hoisted again. The vessel slapped against the waves. Zack heard groaning below decks.

The Mani Peninsula of the mainland would be another day of misery on the sea from Kythera. One by one, the women and children climbed the stairs and dry-heaved over the sides. This would be no pleasant Mediterranean cruise.

16

Mani Peninsula, Greece

1626 BCE

Zack saw small villages and hilltop forts along the coastline of the southern Peloponnese. They had enough food and water for three days after stopping in Kythera. The spinal mountain chain of Mount Tayietos ended at Cape Tenaro, isolating these coastal towns from the greater Peloponnese.

Landing would be risky. Locals had a fierce reputation, historically. The Ottomans in the Middle Ages had failed to quell them. Legend had it that the modern-day Mani folk descended from the Spartans.

"Are the people friendly to strangers here?" Zack asked Talos, squinting to see him.

"Not that I've heard. The ships return, and the merchants claim the honey from this area is favored, though."

"Perhaps we should avoid landfall unless we can find a deserted cove."

Talos steered. "I'll bring us past that land tip, and then look for a beach on the other side."

"We've only a short time from nightfall. We must pick one soon."

Wind blew Zack's hair across his face. He gathered it in a ponytail and tied it with a leather string.

Talos pointed at the mainsail. "We have a goddess on our side."

"Or maybe it's a god? Don't mariners worship Poseidon?"

"The Hellenes worship him more devoutly than we. Let's hope it's not their god who aids us or it may be a ruse."

Talos yanked on the rudder arm.

Zack and others fell against the rails. "Haul that sail down," Talos yelled.

Hippon and Melos scampered across the deck, untied the mast ropes and pulled down the flaxen sail.

"What's wrong?" Zack asked, gripping a cross rail.

"Look westward beyond the tip of the land. My only hope is that they didn't see us."

Zack shielded his eyes from the setting sun. "It looks like a fleet."

"Are they pirates?" Heebe asked, pulling her shawl tighter.

Talos helped other men slide the gangplank out from the deck to rest on a large rock. "I'd wager Mycenaean navy, or maybe from Pylos."

Mela said, "Does not favor us, either way. The people haven't been told, but we've had battles with their ships in the open seas. So far, we've been able to sink many of them with our navy being larger and faster. If they spot the dolphin on our sails, they'll know where we're from."

"Could they be mounting an attack on Calliope?" Hippon asked.

"The island will be empty or consumed in fire." Zack took a last glance towards the east and the plume of dark smoke rising into the stratosphere. "They'll be pulling in for the night soon, too, and it won't be far from here. Get everyone ashore so we can run to the mountains if they decide to pursue us."

"They've seen our mast," Hippon countered.

"Some have turned this way," Zack said, pointing at sails now squared now in their direction.

The men carried baskets, amphora, and blankets loaded with supplies up onto the rocks. The women, and a few of the men carrying spears, herded the children away from shore. Talos tied the ship at both ends and amidships to the rocks. They stacked most of the oars in a hollow onshore and covered them with dirt. Lastly, netting stuffed with dried sponges and rags was tied to the sides of the ship to create a cushion between the hull and the rocks.

"They may steal our ship or burn it, but they won't find anything of value aboard her," Talos said.

Zack strung a bow and tested the pull weight. "We have bows and can hide in these rocks. If they come near, I think we can make their visit costly."

Talos grinned. "I've never seen you shoot an arrow."

"I haven't since I was young."

Then let us save our shots for someone who can hit them instead of us."

"I'm better with a javelin," Zack admitted with a laugh.

"It will take them a while to reach us. We can pile rocks for protection. There's only one way ashore here. Defend our little wall and run up that ravine behind us if we can't hold it," Talos said.

Defend the wall and the narrows. Like at Thermopylae.

They stacked rocks in places where height could easily be gained. Five archers took their places behind heights to rake the enemy decks as they came alongside Talos's anchored ship. Fifteen men with shields waited behind the makeshift stone wall.

Zack saw four ships near the tip of Cape Tenaro, heading directly for them. The sails had tridents painted on them.

"They worship Poseidon. They make live sacrifices of any men they catch. The women and children will be enslaved, or worse," Talos said.

"If there's a fight, they'll signal the others to help. We can't withstand the men of thirty ships."

Zack chewed on the inside of his lip. "I don't know if we can hold off the first four. Each ship will have fifty men aboard, all warriors."

Hippon said, "We can buy the rest of our people time to escape." He set extra javelins and spears in place.

"Remember," Zack said, "when they try to set a gangplank on the rock, five of us can lock shields and stop them from getting on land. Keep the shields up and a few oars ready to knock them off the gangplank. They'll have archers, too."

Talos took a deep breath. "The last ten can spread out and hurl javelins at them from the sides. I pray the Earth Mother casts her blanket over the sun quickly tonight. If darkness arrives soon, we might avoid a fight."

Zack estimated another hour before dark. He looked for the party of women and children, but they were no longer in sight. Thirsty, he dipped a ladle into an earthenware pot. He saw ripples in the water. Then, a calamitous roar filled the air. "Cover your ears and open your mouths," Zack shouted.

The eruption on Santorini. Right now.

Thunder cracked. Overwhelming. He fell to his knees. Pain burst in his head. Others screamed as they collapsed. The stacked weapons tumbled. A ceramic pot toppled and cracked. The men rolled on the ground, unable to find relief from the insult of impossible decibels. The roar continued unabated. Zack saw Talos, his shocked gaze registering all that Zack had predicted. Talos shut his eyes and rolled his head from side to side while on his knees. Zack could only think of the children and hoped that Heebe had all of them following his advice on how lessen the effects of the blast. He knew from history that this volcanic explosion would be heard in Egypt. They also said this was likely the loudest noise in human history. Zack strained to keep his mouth open. All he could do was lay near the ground and feel the earth absorb the calamity less than a hundred miles away.

Many minutes later, the blast subsided. The men began to rise. Many had blood in their ears and mouths. They stumbled, waving their hands and pointing to their ears. Zack could see ships that coming past Cape Tenaro had gone astray, and others, even now, sinking below the choppy sea.

Way off in the distance, Zack saw majestic, towering purple clouds reaching up into a crimson sky. He opened wide, trying to equalize, while he watched the surviving ships east of the Cape point their bows to the nearest landfall.

Directly for them.

Zack heard the echo of his own voice in his head as he bellowed, "They're coming."

Hippon shook his head as if unable to hear Zack's words. When he nodded in the direction of the oncoming ships, Hippon understood.

They pulled men up off the rocks and armed them. Talos pointed his lance at the ships.

Then Zack remembered.

We need to get away from the water.

He yanked on Talos's arm, shouting, "The wave is coming." Zack waved his arms, trying to pantomime a big wave crashing onto the shore. Talos finally caught his meaning. Their defenses had been built for naught. Zack and Hippon gathered the weapons until the others understood, and they all climbed to a point twenty yards above sea level.

The four ships bobbed in the sea just a mile away. Then Zack saw what only could be guessed at from historical records. A tsunami, not the size of the one heading at three hundred miles an hour towards Crete and the southwest, but a tall and ominous one nonetheless, swept across the water. The fleet, heading towards Zack's position, was hit broadside. The ships bobbed, pitched, turned over and sank. Four ships nearer to them absorbed the wave at an angle. Two hit the rocks, cracked their hulls and took on water. The backwash sent the ships back out to sea. The men thrashed amidst the wreckage. Two other penteconters rode the wave to the rocks. The upsurge leapt over the shoreline and swamped the makeshift rock fort. Zack and his party scampered to higher ground. The wave receded back to sea.

"Is that it?" Talos asked too loudly while slapping his ear.

"There can be more waves," Zack answered.

"Go and find Heebe, Zack. Make sure she and the others are safe. We will slay the ones that come ashore. They won't have the strength to fight us."

"You need me here," Zack yelled.

"If the women and children perish or are captured by others, then what do we have? I would rather die right here."

Zack watched the water flooding the lowlands before them.

Talos spoke with urgency. "Take Hippon with you. If you don't see us by morning, escape inland."

"I will care for them, Talos." Zack hugged him quickly. "And we will continue our journey together later."

Talos nodded for them to get under way. "The survivors are reaching shore. We'll spear them as they crawl out of the wash."

Zack and Hippon ran inland on a spine of dry rock. With his ears still impaired, Zack barely heard the screams of men being slain. He wondered if they would have to walk the length of the Peloponnese. Where could they settle as strangers?

They stopped after running a half mile. Zack leaned forward and put his hands on his thighs, catching his breath. "The north of Keftiu will be drowned. The wave you saw here will be many times bigger when it hits their shores. The naval bases, villages, and cities will be wiped out." Zack paused for a moment. "Then, the power of Keftiu will be weakened. Armies from the mainland will in time descend upon them."

Hippon said, "Then there's no going back to our homes or our people."

"No, we'll make a new life elsewhere." Zack stood straight. "Let's find your mother."

Five of the eleven children had hearing injuries from the explosion. The group of refugees rested safe on higher ground.

Heebe clasped her son's face between her palms. "Go back. You must help them. What if they're surrounded by those barbarians? What if your father, your brother..."

"She's right," Zack said. "Now that we know you're safe, I'm taking the other men with me. Hippon can look after you."

"Hurry," she pleaded.

Zack ran while negotiating the rock obstacles and uneven ground. He rambled through shin-deep water as the clanging of swords sounded in the distance. "Talos, we're coming," he yelled. Arriving, Zack drew his blade and watched Talos club a man rising from the sea. The struggling warrior fell back into the water.

The dead lay piled on the approaches to their Alamo. Zack looked over the top of the rise. Bodies bobbed in the surf, others sprawled lifeless on the rocky ledges. The marauder's ships were wrecked. Only Talos's ship floated, saved by the rising water and the cushion of the sponges and husks they'd secured over the hull. Most of Talos's men bore wounds. One wrapped a forearm with a rag, and others looked to be arrow-shot.

"Where's Mela?" Zack asked, setting his spear on a rock and seeing that only five men stood nearby.

Talos motioned with his head towards their ship. A clump of bodies lay on the deck of their ship, strewn like trees, having fallen from a body that lay in the middle. "He jumped down to keep them from taking our ship. What will I tell Heebe?"

"I'm sorry. He saved the ship for all of us. He's a hero."

Talos pounded a rock with his fist. "Told him to stay with me, but he leaped right into the midst of them, swinging his sword. The last of them stabbed him in the back, despite my screams for him to turn. Mela slew the pirate with his last swing."

"I'll bring him up," Zack said. He edged his way down to the rocky steps till he could jump on board. He threw the enemy bodies into the sea. Mela lay face down, his back blackened with his own blood. Zack hoisted him over his shoulder and climbed the irregular stone steps up to where the survivors waited.

Talos tended to the arrow wound one of his men had suffered. He continued to work on the shaft, twisting till it pulled free, and avoiding the sight of his dead son.

After Talos bound the wound with a rag, only then did he rise and see Mela. He knelt and swallowed his grief. He struggled not to weep, but tears streamed down his face. Zack couldn't bear to watch. He focused on rolling corpses into the sea. While Zack toiled, the other warriors lay on their backs, too exhausted to move.

An hour later, the ledge was clear of attackers. Zack saw no ships beyond the peninsula's point. He doubted the fleet had survived the tsunami.

Talos caressed his dead son's forehead. In a broken voice, he said, "Your mother shall weep for you. We all shall." Talos dipped a rag in a seawater puddle and cleansed his son's body of blood. "Your mother will not see you like this. She'll see you as her sleeping boy, weary from a day of chasing hares and nestled in her lap."

Zack took another look out to sea. No masts. They would likely be safe if they left soon. The funerals would need to be quickly done.

"We will find a cave for you, my son," Talos said somberly, "and for your brothers in arms. You will be properly buried."

Zack said, "I saw a cave on the way here but if I may, Talos, look out to sea. There's no longer a navy out there to stop us. We must sail west to escape."

"I can't ask Heebe to leave her son so soon," Talos said.

"Then let's get our comrades to the cave and bring the women and children to mourn them. Will you to allow me to leave a skin with a poem written in your tongue and mine with Mela? I want to celebrate the memory of his courage."

Talos nodded and stood. He wiped his eyes. "Do so. Make your poem a good one. Heroes should be remembered."

By afternoon, the ship had been cleaned, rigging repaired, and the oars reset. The funeral took another hour. The cave echoed with the cries of the women. After a time, Talos lifted Heebe from her son's body and guided her to the cave entrance. Zack devised more than a poem. He wrote the words on a papyrus in Linear A, ancient Greek, English, and the lost language of the Minoans. This would surprise someone out... someday. He wrapped the scroll in a lambskin and set it within sleeves of bark. After tying the bundle together with twine, Zack placed it underneath Mela's crisscrossed hands. All the bodies were covered with rocks. After leaving the cave, they positioned boulders over the entrance.

Their ship threaded out to sea past sunken vessels. It would be a full moon tonight. They would sail west, away from land all night, with favorable winds. The next day could bring more ships in search of the lost fleet. Zack counted thirty–five survivors. They had lost six men in the fight. More women would need to row. They would pass the Messenian Peninsula, the most western of the four Peloponnesian peninsulas.

"Can we sail in the dark even if the moon is full?" Zack asked.

Hippon said, "We don't have marines on board or strong oarsman.

We should go farther out to sea. None of us have been in these waters before. What's to the north?"

Zack said, "I've seen a map. After we pass the coastal city of Pylos, there's another day and a half of sailing north until we reach a waterway. That's our destination."

Talos held up his hand to stop conversation. "Then let us stop wagging our tongues and steer this ship away from land. Somewhere up that coast, I've heard, there is a waterway that leads to that priestess who stands on a black rock. Point our ship there."

Delphi

1626 BC

They made the tiny port of Itea in a day and a half. "Port" over-identified a dock that held two ships and a small village of wooden huts. A crowd of fifty or so people watched their approach, pointing at the blue dolphin painted on the sail. Children in loincloths ran along the shoreline when they came aside the dock.

From a fort with a stone foundation and a wooden palisade, a squad of twenty warriors ran for the dock. One strapped on a boar tusk helmet. Clearly, a rehearsed strategy since pirates and invaders had been known to ravage the coasts of Greece and other barely settled areas.

Talos shouted in Calliope, "We mean no harm. We only seek water and food. May we come onshore?"

The people on the docks cupped their ears and waved their hands, obviously not understanding the language of the newcomers.

Hippon tapped Talos on the shoulder. "I can speak some Achaean. Our commander made us learn in case we had to barter with their ships." Hippon climbed on the deck rail, holding a rope that tied down the mainsail.

"Good people. We have traveled many days by sea. The Earth Mother has ravaged our home island. Have you seen the great cloud in the heavens?" Hippon pointed to the east. Debate ensued on land. A warrior stepped forward. He also wore the boar tusk helmet and a leather shirt sewn with squares of metal. "How many men on your ship?" he asked, craning his neck to peer over the deck rails.

"Enough to man the oars," Talos replied.

"Come ashore and show us."

Hippon tugged on his father's sleeve. "I don't trust them."

Talos said, "We must. Heebe has told me the water is knee-deep below deck. Tell the men to arm themselves and bring everyone on deck."

Zack watched the last mother lead her daughter down the gangplank.

Wretched refuse, Zack thought. The boat people gathered on the shoreline with a semicircle of their men standing in front of them, holding their shields and swords in their scabbards.

The captain of the warriors, now over forty men, waved his sword at Zack's party. "I am Krekrops, son of Cheiron. We'll give you food and wine, and then you will sail away."

Hippon said, "The ship needs repairs before we can depart." He spoke in a stern voice. "We're peaceful but prepared for battle if the need arises."

Zack, happy to understand the language spoken and again realizing Apollo had somehow arranged this ability, pointed towards Delphi. "Is there not a priestess on that mountain who could tell us where we should go?"

Krekrops removed his boar-tusk helmet and said to Zack, "Never seen you here before."

Zack answered, "In the past. I walked up the mountain from the other side."

"Then you should know that the priestess, who stands upon the rock and tells of what is to come, does not waste her time with strangers."

"I would ask her to extend the Earth Mother's graces to this group of wanderers. Surely, she has seen the smoke that reaches to the heavens in the east? We could tell her what happened."

Krekrops scratched his beard. "We will feed you, and then march you up the mountain to visit her. The rest wait here."

Talos turned to Zack and Hippon. "Leave our families? I will not. You two see what the priestess says."

The site of the oracle at Delphi could not be seen from the future port of Itea. They hiked uphill past olive groves, the landscape and plants not looking much different from the modern day. It took a half day to hike up the eight miles from the shore. Arriving exhausted and thirsty, Krekrops and his five guards led them to a compact village of wooden farmhouses. They commandeered wine from the inhabitants. Zack sat with Hippon on a stone wall, peering up the mountainside to where a partially built stone hut was covered with feathers. He watched the captain head for the hut.

Off to his left and up the hill, Zack saw the start of a long ditch being dug in a horizontal-downslope direction towards the feathered hut. Sweating men carried baskets of dirt, while others led oxen carts loaded with stone and rubble to a dump site.

Zack asked one of guards, "What are they building?"

He tapped the end of his lance against the dirt. "It's a dwelling Sybil told us to build for Pythos, the giant snake and the son of the Earth Mother."

Zack smiled. This rude beginning was the same tunnel he'd navigated after being transported in time. It made him wonder about Apollo, the god who would eventually take over this site. Krekrops emerged from the feathered hut, guiding a woman clad in a gray robe that was tied about the waist with a length of red rope.

The captain helped the woman, who appeared to be unable to walk by herself, atop a blackened rock. She gripped the warrior's hand for stability, closed her eyes and began to shout words Zack couldn't understand.

After deep breaths, she continued to rant. Zack guessed she needed to clear her head from the dizzying effects of the ethylene gas she'd breathed inside the hut. Modern seismic studies had concluded that the gas leaked from fissures under the area of the hut and the many subsequent temples built there. Streaks of gray hair showed through a spattering of mud that covered her head.

She pointed at Hippon. "You say you have come from the eastern isles to our mountain. Tell me what destroyed your home and made you an orphan on the sea."

Hippon replied, "I beseech you to hear our pleas for hospitality and guidance. The Earth Mother, whom we call Potnaya in our land of calm winds and blue seas, saw fit to belch fire and rock, destroying our home in a rage of fire and vapors. A wave, high as a mountain, washed over the sea and swamped everything in its path. We survived ordeals and disasters, and now we ask for food, water, and to repair our ship. Then, we will search for a home."

The old priestess stared at Zack and Hippon with slanted eyes. She mashed on toothless gums. "Sea-tossed wayfarers, strangers are welcome, but do not stay. Take what we share and be gone."

Hippon spoke, "High Priestess, your advice is well-taken, and some fair land will become our home. We have traveled the seas and survived storms, pirates, thirst, hunger, and a calamity that destroyed our homeland. Shipbuilders and lovers of art, we are the people of the great king who lives in the palace of Knossos. We seek peace. If welcomed here, our knowledge of the sea would be passed to your children. Your people will be stronger and wiser."

"We need no advice from strangers on how to survive," the priestess replied, her eyes narrowing.

Zack spoke this time. "We will learn from you, too. We could prosper together."

"Who is this tall column that speaks as if he knew what the goddess has in store for her people? The goddess doesn't whisper in your ear." The old priestess swung her hand as if to encompass all the land within their view. "This is a sacred place. Only the trusted and the blessed may stay. You," she pointed at them, "are neither."

Hippon interrupted, "We worship Potnaya and can be trusted. If you command that we leave, we will. We only require repairs to our vessel that may take seven suns or more. Can we have your blessings of safety and hospitality for that long?"

The Sibyl looked to the heavens. "I will pray to Gaia for guidance and give you my answer when dawn lights the skies. Now, take to your feet back down that hill and await my word."

Zack said, "If we cannot stay here, will you reveal to us the Earth

Mother's will and tell us where we may settle?"

"In the morning, I will be on the dock to deliver her decree. Remember to bring an offering with you or she will not speak."

Hippon looked at Zack, motioning with his head for them to hike back down the slope. Hippon said to the guard. "We should purchase some wine and bread. It's a long walk back."

Krekrops said, "Go head to the docks now. I'll be down later."

Zack said to Hippon in Calliope, "I still don't know if we can trust them." He watched the captain follow the Sibyl up to her hut.

They arrived at the docks with only an hour of sun left. Guards sat in the shade of trees, drinking from gourds. Zack didn't see Talos, or anyone else of their party. The guards picked up their cowhide-covered shields and spears from a teepee-shaped stack. Zack saw the ship just offshore. Talos waved his hands and shouted to them, "Jump into the water. Come to the ship, fast."

Zack and Hippon emerged from underwater twenty yards from the shore and swam to the ship.

When they climbed aboard, Talos said, "I ordered everyone back on ship. It's good that you're already drenched from the swim. Go below and you will find everyone knee-deep."

Behind Talos, women and children were handing up buckets in a fireman's line.

Zack replied, "This isn't a laughing matter. We can't sail very far and cannot stay here."

"I wanted both of you on board to make a decision on whether to leave while there is still light."

Hippon scanned the warriors on the dock. "Their numbers are double ours."

Talos put his hand on his hips. "I think we wait till morning and see what the Sibyl rules."

Hippon rubbed his chin whiskers. "She's one ugly-looking sow."

"How could you possibly describe one of the Earth Goddesses' favorite priestesses as a sow?" Zack asked, deadpanning. Then he made a grotesque expression. Hippon and Talos doubled over.

"Enough, enough," Talos said, wiping his eyes.

"Should we vote to decide what is best?" Zack asked.

"What do you mean vote?"

"The men and women should all decide together what the best strategy."

"The father decides what is best for his family, and the captain decides what is best for his ship. I am both," Talos said.

Zack said, "There is wisdom among the women and other men. We all fight or die together."

"Is this how it is done in your land? Decisions will be divided, arguments forever," Talos said.

Zack countered, "Still, we all share the danger."

"Whatever land you are from, keep me away," Talos said.

"Heebe is a woman of great judgment. Don't tell me you don't trust her with your life?"

Talos moved his jaw around as if chewing on the thought. "You've made me think, but for now, I'll make the decision. We cast off and keep alert through the night. In the morning, if the answer is no, we sail back to the sea, and head north, away from Pylos and the Myceneans."

Zack said, "If the ship fills with seawater, we won't get far."

Hippon answered, "Then we will land where we do. Deserted shoreline, inlet, it matters not."

Talos slapped his son on the back. "We'll know in the morning. I'll take the first watch."

Zack awakened to clouds and a strong breeze. Waves slapped the side of the ship. He had taken a watch in the early hours and passed the time thinking about Lauren and Cassandra in San Diego. Zack also recalled his brief meeting with his son, Atlantea.

There is so much I'd like to have said to him.

Hippon emerged from below deck. "We could make it up the coast for part of a day, no more."

Talos said, "You and Zack go again."

"I will let you reach the dock first, Zack," Hippon said, grinning.

"They always shoot the ugly one first," Zack said.

Hippon snorted. "Wake the crew and let the families sleep. This might be over before they rub the crust from their eyes."

18

Delphi

1626 BC

Zack took his time swimming to shore, not wanting to arrive exhausted if a fight broke out.

They climbed a ladder at the dockside, wiped the salt water from their eyes and waited. He saw a horse-drawn cart carrying the priestess as it traversed the main street thoroughfare of the small town. Zack smelled roasted meat from open shops in the town.

"Does this priestess make all the decisions for the town and the warriors?" Zack asked.

Krekrops, backed by forty warriors, answered in a stern voice, "She is Sibyl and ordained by the Earth Mother. We need no other word."

Zack looked east and saw a rising sun peek through the cloud cover. "It is as you say, but warriors must be practical. We can add to your numbers. Teach you the battle tactics of the great King of Knossos and of the King of Egypt, who is our trade partner."

Krekrops didn't answer, looking past Zack to their ship.

"Because we are strangers does not mean we're a danger to you," Hippon said. "We'll farm with you and bring in the olive fruit when the crop is ripe. Grind the wheat and bake the bread. Guard your borders and become your kinsman."

The captain suddenly awoke from his concentration on their ship.

"Enough talk," he said, glancing around Zack, then out to their ship again.

"We can teach you to build ships, trading ships, warships." Zack said.

Krekrops shouted. "Raiders are coming up the seaway. Arm the men!"

Zack and Hippon turned simultaneously. Zack said, "Those are same colored sails we saw at the peninsula. They're from Pylos. Maybe they're looking for us."

"Can we bring our people ashore?" Zack asked.

Krekrops scratched his beard. "Hurry or they'll be captives."

Hippon shouted to Talos on the ship. "Look behind you, Talos!"

Talos ordered the men to fast-row the ship to shore.

Drumbeats sounded from the raider ships. Zack made fast calculations. Three ships with crews of about fifty heavily armed warriors against less than half that number of locals, including their party of twenty men.

"How many archers do you have?" he asked the captain.

"Too few, and their bows are in town."

"Send for them and bring plenty of arrows. We can't make their landing an easy one."

Krekrops gripped the pommel of his bronze sword. "They are many. I can get more men if we retreat up the mountain and send word." He told one of his men to get the bows.

Zack countered, "Once they come ashore, they will take control of your town and the sacred mountain. Line your men up in three lines, and we will join you."

The captain jutted out his chin. "I'm in command here. Your warriors do as I say."

Zack went nose to nose. "You're right, but I can help you defeat them. Allow me to teach you the Minoan king's tactics."

"Get your people ashore first." Krekrops glanced beyond Zack. Black smoke lifted from the torches on the raider's ships.

Talos guided the women and children to the gangplank and onto the dock. "Heebe, take them past the town and into the olive groves. If we're defeated, hike up the mountain to hide in the caves."

Zack commanded, "Hurry. We'll take the front line."

Krekrops looked startled.

The twenty men from Talos's ship formed a single line. Zack yelled to Krekrops. "Your men are the anchor. Form them in two lines and have them brace us against the weight of their attack. Put archers in the third line."

"You don't give me orders," Krekrops challenged.

Zack said, "There's no time to argue. They can't break our line if we compact our warriors."

"And them?" Krekrops pointed to a craft that had pulled to shore a quarter-mile away. The raiders unloaded warriors to attack them from a different direction.

A high-pitched voice screamed, "Who allowed these strangers back on our shores?"

Zack and Hippon turned to see the Sibyl waving her arms, and her dark robe swirling in the wind. She pointed her bony finger at them. "They're not welcome. Send them back to their ship."

Krekrops hesitated. He looked at the approaching raiders nearing the dock. The men bringing back the bows and arrows had begun to disperse them to his warriors and Calliopes. Zack had already lined up his cadre of fighting men, their body-length shields in a row near the dock. Five of the men formed a wing, bending backwards to receive the extra raiders unloading down the coast.

Archers arose from the two ships nearing the dock and unleashed a volley.

"Arrows," Hippon shouted. The arrows stuck in the hide-covered shields. Zack directed the warriors to extend the wing opposite the dock by another ten spearmen.

"Captain," Zack shouted, "have your archer's fire at them as they step onto the dock."

Before Krekrops could yell the order, the Sibyl began to beat on his chest with her fists. "They will not be our blood." The captain saw the raiders gathering on the rim of their ship, ready to leap over the edge. "Leave us to fight first," he shouted at the Sibyl.

She drew a dagger from beneath her robe and leaped at Hippon. "The blood must stay pure. Look at his light hair. I will not allow it."

The Sibyl sliced Hippon's shoulder with the blade, just to the side of his cow-hide armor. The raiders, wearing leather shirts with metal squares sewn on the front and back, jumped onto the dock.

Hippon spun and jabbed his sword in the Sibyl's guts. She fell screaming and drew her knees into a fetal position. Hippon, pressing his hand over the shoulder bleed, joined Zack in the front line. The raiders crashed against their shields. Archers behind Zack dropped raiders as they stood on the rails of the ship. They flopped into the gulf, grasping the shafts. More jumped from the ship to add weight to their charge. Zack saw Hippon bleeding.

Zack said, "Go to Heebe. Help her get the others to safety."

"I stand with my father."

Talos smiled, but it disappeared when he saw the fifty men from the last ship heading their way, waving their swords and bellowing war cries.

The raiders pounded his shield with swords and clubs.

"Second line," Zack ordered. "Stab at them over our shoulders." Wounded and dead filled the dock now. When the raiders jumped onto the dock, they slipped and fell, becoming easy targets for the Calliope spearmen.

The raiders arriving from downrange attacked the right side of their line. The local warriors struck and slashed, but many fell. The raiders ran around their collapsing side.

"Archers," Zack yelled, pointing at the raiders flanking them, "aim at them." Raiders crumpled, giving Zack time to send more warriors to reinforce the wing. A cry of despair came from behind Zack. He saw Krekrops fall with an arrow through his throat.

Local warriors threw their weight behind Zack's front line. Together, they pushed the raiders off the dock, just like the Persians forced off the cliffs at Thermopylae. The raiders, clad in heavy metal armor, sank below the water's surface.

The wounded screamed amid the clang of swords, shields, spears and clubs. Zack saw that Talos and Hippon still fought.

A new wave of raiders gathered on the ship deck. Zack's archers dropped ten before they reached the rails. The rest, including a warrior with standing feathers on his helmet and shouting orders, hopped onto the docks and slashed away at the Calliope spearmen. He didn't last long, pierced by Talos's spear. Losing their commander, the raiders scurried back on their deck. The reinforcements on the right held the attackers. They left piles of their dead and retreated.

"Don't let them get away," Hippon shouted. Talos told the archers to shoot burning arrows at their sails.

Both ships caught fire.

"Another volley into those ships," Talos yelled. Fires licked the mast, spread up to the sails, finally overwhelming the crew and the ship. Zack turned his attention to the slaughter of the retreating raiders. Having dropped their shields, they ran with their backs exposed. Javelins, arrows and axes brought them down.

The survivors cheered. The wounded raiders died with a sword thrust. Zack found the Sibyl curled up on the ground with the robe pulled over her head. Uncovering her face, he saw that she was dead. Talos wiped blood from his eyes. Others looked too exhausted to do much more than raise their hands to acknowledge their survival.

Zack said, "The Sibyl is dead."

Hippon saw the body. "Call a council after we bury the fallen. We lost half the men."

Talos said, "Need a lot of wood for funeral pyres."

Zack looked out into the water. "Our ship is burning." Flames licked up the mast and black smoke enveloped the hull. They were trapped. Fate or coincidence, he wondered how much of this could be Apollo's plan?

"I hope you have long sticks," Talos said. "We'll be beating olives from trees."

"Let's tell Mother she won't have to bail seawater any longer." Hippon managed a grin.

Talos prepared a sling for Hippon's shoulder. "We must tell wives that their husbands have perished… and then thank Potnaya that some of us still stand."

"Who will be the new Sibyl?" Hippon asked.

Talos shrugged. "Do we need one?"

Delphi

1626 BC

Four weeks later, stone and wood huts had been built and the fragmented families housed. A granary and protective shelter for the large pithoi pots holding the olive oil had been constructed beneath the mountains. Zack manned shifts at guard posts and helped to guide the oxen up the eight-mile trail to their enclave above the plain.

It turned out that the villagers had disliked the Sibyl and praised Hippon for delivering them from her rule over them. Zack heard them say that Hippon was god-like in stature, and he would protect them from harm. He had killed the great snake-priestess.

Near evening, when the heat of the day eased, and a strong wind ran up the mountain from the gulf, Zack walked towards the ditch. The beginnings of a long bas-relief of a snake, the python, ran the length of the interior wall. Zack smiled, remembering the first time he and Lauren had run their hands along the length of that snake, in near darkness, with just the glow of a lighter guiding them to the hatchway.

He could dwell on Lauren now and what she might be doing. Apollo had told him Cassandra was with her. At least, they were together. Would he ever be with them again? He was not part of history and would never have been *here* if Apollo had not arranged his presence. The calculations and ramifications continued to confound him. Talos had said that he knew of the Sibyl and the twin mountains where she dwelled. So, they would have made it here either way.

The next morning, Zack helped to begin the work on a more navigable road to the port. Oxen and wagon wheels required a firmer footing. At night Zack watched the work on the snake carving. He concentrated his thoughts on remembrances of Io and Diomedes, Nestor and Persephone, his extended family, alive and dead.

He built muscle now, the results of digging with bronze tools and lifting rock. A drainage ditch alongside the road would help to keep water from rushing downhill and destroying their work. The road had a stone lining on both sides and a groomed surface where rocks and roots were extracted and leveled. The road would take months to complete.

Zack sat on the dirt floor of a hut Hippon helped him to build. With seventy men now, they could put up a good fight against twice their number using the terrain, archers and a circular palisade. In 1600 BCE, there were still plenty of forests, but cutting trees for boards still proved a tedious process with bronze tools.

A knock on the door and his friends entered.

"Have a last cup of wine with us before surrendering, Outsider," Talos said, unslinging a pot from his shoulder. "Made fresh in the village."

Zack raised his ceramic mug. "You made it here with a full jug?" He smiled. Talos sat on the floor and Hippon joined him.

"The work progresses, and we've made this place our home." Talos said, taking a sip.

"But you have a sad face, Zack," Hippon said.

Zack said," Someday you will find me gone. I will miss all of you, but I must find my wife."

"I would do the same if Heebe was elsewhere. Then you'll return home by ship?"

"In whatever way I can. Travel towards the setting sun. Find a way." Zack emptied his cup.

"Then let us toast the goddess and ask her for your safe return," Talos said, tapping his cup to Zack's.

"But you can't leave yet. There's still too much work to finish," Hippon said with a grin. "We should retire ourselves and bid you goodnight."

They left arms over shoulders. Zack's aching muscles faded. He turned over, ruminated about all that had happened and wondered how Lauren fared. He fell fast asleep and dreamed.

Zack parked their Red Prius in the driveway and entered the backyard through a side gate. He had just had a couple of new house keys made, one set to be hidden in the house and another to be placed inside the Altoids box buried underneath the giant rock at the edge of their backyard. He dug a hole directly beneath the long vertical crack, an easy guide to the buried box. When he extracted the box, he found a set of keys still there, and a note. He opened a half-folded skin and read the ancient Mycenaean:

You reached Delphi. Now, you can return home. There, await your true enemies and a battle for what you hold dear. I miss you, the father I never knew. Come back to us when you can, to this land of shadows. Death is not what you think. We are together.

Atlantea.

The skin fell from his hands. Zack walked circles around it. Atlantea had left him guidance, but how?

Zack ran back to the house. He found the back door open. Entering a hallway that led to the kitchen, he saw the trophy case. Inside, photos of Lauren that he'd placed there. Along with others he had not.

She's such a beauty.

Three framed pictures showed Cassandra in a Girl Scout uniform, another receiving an award at school, the last photo of her holding a bow, as if she'd gone to summer camp and won an award for archery. In each photograph, she was a few years older. Zack studied other pictures of a young man with dark curly hair, playing soccer. He saw a second photo of him with Lauren, a young Cassandra, and one of Lauren's college friends. *What was that friend's name? Lisa?* The last shot was of the boy in the cockpit of a jet fighter, his smile as big as the open canopy.

Who is this kid? Zack wondered

Then there were pictures of him, in Greece with Lauren, when they were students. Bracketed by silk flowers, it looked like a memorial.

He took anxious steps down the corridor. His life remained in shambles. So much had been missed. He heard voices in the kitchen. The sound of female laughter. One was Lauren, the other… No. Not possible. He couldn't believe it. Refused to believe his ears.

Zack turned the corner. Seated at a kitchen table, Lauren and Queen Io sipped from steaming mugs. A pair of dice rested on the table between them.

Io said, "Each morning you arise and partake of this, allowing it to power your mind and your limbs. I could get used to this, too."

Lauren returned, "At times, I will go to a shop nearby to purchase the drink." She noticed Zack. Then Io did, too.

"Glad you could join us, Zack," Lauren said, smiling.

Io extended her hand. "Sit with us. It is time to hold council."

Zack didn't move. Words refused to make their way past his lips.

"Do not despair," Io said. "Lauren has agreed to join in our worship of the Goddess, she who blesses us all."

Zack managed to sit. His gaze shifted back and forth between Io and Lauren. He finally croaked, "How can you be together? Io, you are…"

"Are the gods so simple-minded?" Io asked. "You should not be, either. We will all be together for the days to come."

Lauren said, "You've been gone so long. We have concluded that you're not returning to either one of us, so we shall throw dice to see who will win the rights to your memory."

Zack jumped up from his chair. "You what?"

Io said, "We both have pined for you for too long: Me in the other world, and Lauren in this. Neither of us wishes to endure the pain any longer, so we will leave it up to Tyche to decide who shall claim you."

"You will shake the dice for me, for my fate, for what I meant to you?"

"Exactly," Lauren continued, "Here, hold my hand and give your other to Io. With our free hands, we will each throw a dice with our name on it and see who wins."

"Wait," Zack insisted, "How can you do this? What about my feelings?"

Lauren and Io looked at each other and giggled. Recovering, Lauren said, "Io has described to me how this would be settled in the old days, when the Earth Goddess ruled, and the children were named for their mothers. You are but a warrior who went off to hunt and make war. We nurture homes, the children, and guard the wealth. You are *our* property."

"Is it time to shake the dice?" Io said.

Lauren nodded. "I believe so." They each clasped Zack's hand tightly and took a dice. They shook it, and each exclaimed, "I claim this man in the name of the Goddess." The dice fell, scrambled upon the table and then rested. Zack jerked upwards, sending his chair backwards against the wall.

Zack awakened, shaking.

He's doing it again. Apollo's playing more tricks on me.

A hand settled upon his shoulder.

Zack smelled lemon aftershave. Apollo, looking like Calchas, the Greek waiter in Athens, appeared.

Apollo put a finger to his lip. "Good to be with you, again, Traveler."

"I dreamed I was with Lauren and Io. Did you do that?"

Apollo said, "Walk with me along the hillside, Traveler. I love this place. When the war is won, I will have a cabin here and watch the sunsets. Now, we shall speak of your progress."

Zack, absent his sandals, carefully treaded the rocky ground in the dark. "I'm amazed our group from Thera ended up in Delphi."

"This group ended up here, anyway. You were but an aide to them. You remember, of course the legend of how I came to this temple."

"The legend is you killed the snake, Python, and took the temple from the goddess, Gaia."

"Legends and history are not always the same as reported."

"We came on a ship with a dolphin painted on the bow. Hippon killed the Sibyl. She must represent the snake. The bas-relief of that giant snake on the walls of that passage…"

"There are no written words that accurately describe what happened in this time. As you know, Linear A and B appear to be about transactions. Time and the oral tradition will change this story, as it usually does, but so much for legends. Let us speak of other subjects."

"I need answers. Where am I going next?"

"You've had the privilege of experiencing history in real time." Apollo raised his voice. "Soon we will fight for the future."

"I remember." Zack recalled the visions of destruction Apollo had displayed on the transit room wall. They hiked higher into the mountain. The gulf breeze buffeted his long hair.

Apollo said, "Mortals fight for survival, struggle and to compete for resources."

"The first humans had to survive in this way, and it's no different in my time," Zack said.

"Mortals combined their resources and talents to create societies, for safety, and to improve the lives of the people within its protection."

"Where are you going with this?" Zack asked.

Apollo peered across to the rugged landscape of the Peloponnese. "On Santorini, I wanted you to experience two principles of your training. The first is that you knew what would occur there, and the difficulty in warning people to avoid disaster. I didn't want you to save any that did not survive historically. History cannot be altered too much, or my task will be made more difficult."

"You excel at confusing the hell out of me."

"My dear Traveler, the second element of your training concerned the influence of advisors on rulers. The Egyptian influenced the queen's decisions. In any age, the people are mostly unaware that their rulers are manipulated. Egypt is a major trading partner. They have influence over the island, because they control wealth from trade."

Zack turned his attention to Apollo. The god twirled his forelock around his finger.

Apollo grabbed Zack by the tunic. "There are those who subvert your country under a veil."

Zack shivered inside. "Okay, once again, why are you telling me this?"

"You have learned much about war. You learned what is necessary to survive, and to lead people from danger. You understand oppression, blind obedience, and the corruption of influence. Even so, there are times when all learning and wisdom must be placed aside, and you must act." Apollo looked up at the stars.

"Wait. What about the dream I just had? Where's Atlantea? He left me a note."

"Be patient. Your time will come." Bluish threads of energy created Apollo's dome. He departed, shrouded in the density of the dome.

PART TWO

20

Outside Warrenton, Virginia

FIVE YEARS LATER/ NEAR FUTURE

Alfred Fung lit a final sandalwood joss stick and breathed in the orange-blossom aroma. He had performed this same ceremony many times, along with his father. Lighting the joss stick to honor the memory of venerated ancestors and bring good luck to the family.

Joss was something he would need much of if the plan he, his father, and others had put together would succeed.

His father had told him to be patient. That was the Chinese way.

Today, he set the stick in a holder in front of a spirit tablet created for the grandpapa he had worshipped. At age seven, it had been Alfred's job to carve his grandfather's name on the surface and set it on the altar.

A death he recovered from only when he was assured that his grandfather's spirit still guided him.

Alfred stared at a photo that hung on the wall above the tablet. His grandpapa wore peasant clothing and a faded cap. The caption above the photograph said in Chinese: "Jiangxi, 1934," where the four-thousand-mile famous 'long march' of Mao's army had begun and then ended in Shaanxi to the northwest a year later. Grandfather, from the stories his father had told him, fought and suffered as the Red Army escaped the pursuit of Chiang Kai-shek's Nationalists.

Alfred wondered if he would ever be as wise or bold as the line of men who'd come before him. None possessed his education, though his father had achieved much. Alfred had been recognized early on and sought nationally by universities, but he wanted to live in California and leave the cold of Virginia. After his father approved the move, he chose a biological engineering program at a southern California university. He was at the perfect point in history, with the right tools and influence to affect what had begun many decades earlier.

He set an orange and a lychee, favorite fruit of his grandfather, near the altar. Alfred felt charged whenever he lit the sticks, as if his relative's spirit infused him with each inhalation of the fumes.

I am sure this path is the correct one. One I believe in. One he believed, as does my father. But our true feelings hidden and our plans clandestine.

"Son," his father, Sam, said as he joined him at the altar, "please ensure sure his cap is returned to the safe afterwards. He knew prison awaited him after Mao died. Class struggle and the peasants concerned him, but he escaped the purge to create a new life here."

A different photograph adorned the wall. It was dated in 1978. Grandfather had created a new identity to help him immigrate to Taiwan and then San Francisco.

"He risked everything to start over, but he never approved of the changes China made," Sam said. "He told me many times, "Mao Zedong Thought must be returned to China." They were also his last words to me."

"Did you see the recent article about the rising class of wealthy in China?" Alfred asked. "It is everything you told me to fear. The new wealthy worship only new gods with brand names. The rise of capitalism in China is an infection."

"As my father told me, it will lead to control of the people. The privileged will be addicted to luxuries. The poor will suffer, as many do in this country. The banks come in, and with them, impure consumerism. Then soon, the culture is compromised. A last chance exists."

"We've done well, but shouldn't we gather more wealth and resources before we proceed? We will need that power to move ahead to Step Two on the new 'Long March.'"

"Remember what Mao said. 'Once all struggle is grasped, miracles are possible.' The time is now, son. We have been patient long enough. You've been perfecting life in the cave now for five years. Your medicine is ready."

Alfred and his father breathed in the incense. "Then we must realize Grandfather's dream. He truly is our guardian. This tablet retains his power."

They both bowed toward the memorial.

Sam said, "We'll need his guidance and all of his joss, especially after the setback in Athens. I have told the leaders in the Yemen and Pakistan camps that there will be no more attacks we don't sanction. How Saabir's plan was uncovered and foiled confuses me and our allies. No longer can we underestimate our enemies. Do not awaken the Americans. Let them sleep and be unaware."

"The others in Pakistan wait for the signal to carry out their part. Our comrades in China also await orders. Everyone is nervous. Those we can communicate with, anyway."

"The time to strike draws near," Sam said. "The Pakistani's are in place in America already. The US will suspect that, after we attack New York City, that it is our true target. Before you leave, let us speak with them on the drop phone in code."

"I have one last question, Father." Alfred paused. "Do you think we are prepared enough?"

His father squinted to see the phone number on the NobelCom card to make the international call. He searched for his glasses. "War between the giants is inevitable. Many will die in the struggle. We have the power, right now, to take down China's greatest adversary. And China will yield to "Mao Zedong Thought" again. They must. Others in power there feel as I do. Even the Chinese president wishes to widen his control, though he knows nothing of what we plan."

Alfred said, "Then we will have to hope they see it our way once the change happens."

"They are torn over the balance of economic growth and holding onto the party's principles. But they agree on one goal." Sam held up his forefinger. "One China… and who stands in the way of our crossing the Formosa Strait to Taiwan?"

Sam shook his fist at a captured US flag hung on a nearby wall, given to him as a gift by a Chinese soldier who had served in Korea. "Take them out of the equation, and China will revert to the old ways. Those in power now would never agree to our plan. Russia would never approve either, but they will welcome American destruction. But there is a plan for them, too. That is where your new medicine will come into play."

Sam put down the phone. "Remember what grandfather said, 'War does not determine who is right. War determines who is left.' China can lose millions and still have too many to feed. Only the most loyal and hardened will survive in the facilities in Chongqing. They'll provide sanctuary for what is to come. Our comrades and you, my son, will be there to guide the people in the ashes."

Alfred raised his chin to his father, his Yie. "This country could never understand us and what we do. Make your call, *Yie.*"

"This will be the last call from here. We'll only send messages by courier or make contact by encrypted disposable phones. I have eliminated all my social media tracks. I'm a man who barely exists now. But, I can hide my hacking for only so long. We await contact from our comrades in China before we act, but it is imminent. There is one more item, son."

Alfred looked at his father. He saw the deep creases in his face. He looked more and more like his father's pictures. Gray hair dominating the black, watery eyes that bore fatigue, age and stress that had set its claim on him.

Sam said, "No one can guarantee success. The believers who have infiltrated the Chinese military await our signal. The peasants, the true people in China, will survive. They have made sanctuary underground for many decades. In Plan One, we succeed, and we live. In Plan Two, we do not survive, countries perish, but our people live on. That is where your new medicine must succeed."

"I leave tomorrow for the conference in Los Angeles," Alfred said. "I'll consult with my contacts, gather my security team, and ensure the wire deposit. The US investment bankers have no idea how final their deal will be. I've also had the chip implanted in my arm. When I turn it on with my watch, you should be able to locate me wherever I am. My cell phone also fixes my location on GPS, though now we must speak in code if you need to make an emergency phone call."

Sam said, "Just be out of Southern California in three days. Fly through Hong Kong to Chongqing as we arranged. Hole up with your comrades. You must survive, Alfred, even if I don't. You must be there to lend your expertise to the transformation."

"When the funds have cleared from the US, I'll return to the clinic in Chongqing. I must speak with Lian. She will update me."

"Taking a wife from peasant stock was wise," Sam said.

"She is, but I would submit to you that Lian is an extraordinary combination of the new and old China. We'll require some of both to be victorious."

"You have learned well. But when the battle is won, return to the purity of Mao's revolution. The people, the peasants must all be equal and share in the bounty."

Alfred didn't respond. He turned away from his father's gaze. He wondered if the old man truly believed that there could be the pure equality in society denoted by Karl Marx and put in motion by Mao in China? Those with the will and the resources always rose to the top. Wherever in the history of humanity had this not been so?

His father left to make the phone call on a secure line in the basement stronghold. After picking up his grandfather's faded blue cap, frayed on the edges, ripped near the visor, Alfred fingered the fabric until he set it down. He smiled at the red star that adorned the front of it.

21

Federal Reserve Facility, Virginia

NEAR FUTURE

The next morning, Sam Fung showed his ID to uniformed police wearing holstered pistols at the gate. He drove to a five-story building, his place of employment for the last thirty years, and parked his Ford Escape. After removing his wallet, keys, and cell phone, he set them in a round plastic bowl and walked through the metal detector. A security guard nodded for him to proceed. Sam retrieved his scanned belongings and headed for the elevator. Colleagues wished him a, "Good morning."

He managed a smile but did not engage in conversation.

Calculations absorbed his thoughts. His son had left for California earlier that morning and he didn't know if he'd ever see him again. What they planned would be irreversible once started. He reached the double doors to his office. The computer pad scanned his ID, and the door clicked to open.

Turning on his computer, he noticed that three of his station partners had not yet arrived.

Good joss. *I am alone.*

Compromising the video cameras was a simple matter. Surveillance would go fuzzy for a moment.

He entered his security code and accessed the computer banks that protected the cybersecurity of the Federal Reserve System, and the backup computers that recorded financial transactions in the United States and abroad. Sam engaged a thumb drive and downloaded codes. As director of the team, he held the highest security clearance. It had taken him decades to obtain this position.

Everything went through him.

After all, his program protected the internal computer software that had run the system for so many years. New software would be installed soon, and it would ruin his plans.

His father had endured so much to make his way to the United States. His mother, a US citizen, made the family legitimate. But that didn't matter.

Wherever you go, you are always Chinese.

The family thrived under the capitalist system. His father ran a Chinese restaurant for many years and saved his money so Sam could attend college and earn a degree in the new field of computer science. His father told him to get in with the banks. Sam didn't know then that he would work in most important bank in the world.

Sam stared at the icon for the system, named COBOL 2014. The program had its origin in 1959 with COBOL 60, the famous Navy Rear Admiral Grace Hopper involved in its development. Protecting the program became more of a challenge each year. He loved code and thwarting cyberattacks. Many personal citations lined his office walls.

He entered new code from a thumb drive that would stay hidden until activated remotely. Soon, his co-workers would arrive. Grace Hopper had applied the word "bug", which defined computer failures when she discovered a moth had shorted out an earlier Mark 2 version.

Sam laughed to himself. The Federal Reserve, its two backup centers, and the Department of Defense network would all be under his total control. The Tri-Party System of exchange between broker-dealers, banks, and mutual funds to be taken down at his command. The Bank of New York would be frozen. No money available. Checks unable to clear. After a couple of days, ATM's would be empty. The stock market would be shut down with no records of transactions. The economy would be dealt a death blow for their arrogance and greed.

"Bug" was not an adequate word to define what he had in mind. The Fung "wind" would give them a virus they could not anticipate or cure. He had received a written dispatch from his friends in China. The efforts they had made twenty years earlier now controlled leadership high up in the Peoples Republic of China, and in the Chinese Navy.

They only needed to hear the message: Blue Sky/Silent Wind.

He pulled out the thumb drive and set it into a space in the heel of his shoe. Wanting to appear nonchalant when his co-workers arrived, he picked up his second favorite book and read from Sun Tzu's, The Art of War. A dog-eared page identified his favorite quote. He spoke quietly to himself, repeating the sentence five times.

"Let your plans be dark and impenetrable as the night, and when you move, fall like a thunderbolt. "

We will be the thunderbolt and the wind. And they will never know what hit them.

22

Desert beyond Ta'lzz, Yemen

NEAR FUTURE

Hard rain pockmarked the baked sand. Men huddled under their tarps and in log-covered dugouts. That wouldn't do for Bessus. After many seasons in the hot sun, he could no longer tolerate being stuck inside the tents and caves. Removing his robe, he stood under the downpour. He left on his waist belt and sheathed blade. Bessus heard laughter, but he felt cleansed.

When will that pox-faced Scout return? He shows up just as I'm ready to slay everyone and end my days. Then he promises to return me to my son. I have done as he's asked, slain the sand warrior's enemies, hidden from sky-eyes of the new-Greeks, and stayed away from the black-shrouded women. Scratched on a log the many cycles he has left me here, as many as one hand. But how much longer must I wait? Why has he forsaken me?

After the sand warriors took out their prayer rugs, Bessus left the camp and walked aimlessly, the rain purifying him. He saw an oasis of trees far off, but it was a blur, as were the two figures sneaking towards it. The storm came down more fiercely. He needed cover. Bending low, he made a circle to the trees and crawled the last distance.

He could see another lone man next to a tree, pissing and shaking one of the talk boxes in his hand, the same kind only the leaders held and spoke into. The man cursed and kept looking up at the sky. Bessus slid in behind a tree. Now that he could see the man clearly, he recognized him as the one who always pointed at his scars and laughed. This would be a good opportunity to cut his throat.

Just then, one of the two figures slid into the trees. Bessus crouched. Unseen, he hoped. This new man wore different clothes, painted like the sand, and a helmet covered with the same cloth. He carried a different bee-shooting stick. He held one of boxes, too, and he spoke into it. Bessus leaned closer, but he couldn't understand what the second warrior said. Something was different about this warrior. The first sand warrior approached him, and they spoke. Could this be an enemy? He must be. Why would they meet out here? Bessus crept to another tree, closer and with more cover. Maybe he could have a talk box and speak to the gods or to the new Greeks with their eyes in the sky.

Bessus saw writing on the warrior's jacket. It looked like writing he'd seen before, in the land of the Greeks. Could this be one of the New Greek warriors? *How good it would feel to drive my knife between his ribs and watch him gurgle and die.*

He drew his blade.

The Greek warrior slung the firestick over his shoulder. He had another handheld one attached to his belt. He continued to talk into his hand, but then stopped and spoke to the sand warrior. Bessus darted from cover, heading to the Greek first. He stabbed at the Greek's throat, but the warrior threw up his arm, dropped his talk box and blocked his attack. Bessus clubbed the man with his fist and knocked him down. The Greek slumped just as the sand warrior whirled and raised his fire stick. Bessus threw his knife end over end. The sand warrior gurgled, fell to his knees and then onto his face.

Struggling to his knees, the Greek drew his firestick and pointed it at Bessus. Bessus dived to his left. Many bees missed, but one sliced his leg. Bessus picked up a rock and hurled it at the Greek's face. The man fell over and dropped his weapon. Bessus threw himself at the Greek and gripped his throat. The Greek punched, landing two blows to the face. He struggled for his small firestick. Bessus knocked it away. They rolled in the sand, first the warrior on top, and then Bessus. The warrior kicked

Bessus away with his feet.

Bessus knew, *he dies, or I will.*

The Greek stood and wavered on his feet. Bessus knew he'd done damage. The warrior withdrew his knife, waving it slowly. This Greek knew how to handle a blade.

Bessus scrambled for a stone, anything to defend against the knife. The warrior gave him little time. Bessus grabbed a handful of sand and threw it at him. The warrior coughed and squinted, but he advanced anyway. He swung, cutting Bessus's forearm. Blood streamed, but he caught the warrior's knife hand, wrenched it and heard a snap. The warrior cursed.

Then voices sounded from the camp. The Greek noticed, and smacked Bessus in the throat. Bessus fell backwards, gagging. The warrior limped away, glancing back at the oncoming warriors. The Greek staggered, met another of his kind a short distance away, and then they fled into the storm.

When the leader and his men arrived at the trees, they saw Bessus sitting next to one of their dead friends. A shouting match began as some pointed at Bessus. The giant got to his feet and gave them an American rifle they hadn't handled before and a cell phone with a camouflage cover case.

One of the warriors threw him a robe to put on.

"These are American. Their special forces use them. Where did he go?" the leader asked, waving his hands and pantomiming for a search in all directions.

Bessus got his drift. "Ran," he said, his voice raspy as he pointed into in the distance. "Gone."

The leader said, "Even got his cell phone. God be praised. This giant fought one of their SEALS, I think. What about Sanjo?"

One of the warriors found Bessus's well-known knife buried in Sanjo's throat.

The giant picked up Sanjo's cell phone and handed it over, too.

The leader whistled and looked at Bessus with surprise. "He found our spy. This man is God delivered. As ugly as he is, treat him with respect. He's one of us." The leader handed Bessus an AK-47. They all shot their weapons into the air. Bessus shouted and emptied his magazine with a one-tooth grin. The rain continued to pour down. Not until then did the leader notice the rivulets of blood that streamed down Bessus's leg and arm.

He shouted to his men as the wind picked up. "Let's get him back to cave and dress his wounds. I must let the other commanders know he has saved us from attack. This giant will be known throughout the camps as the warrior who beat a SEAL hand to hand."

Two days later, Bessus stared out to sea, his hand resting on a palm tree. Children ran up to him, fake-growling with their fingers clenched like claws, and then ran away squealing. It was a game they played twice a day. He had no reason to slay them, unless they angered him too much.

Most of the camp followers avoided him, especially the women who were covered head to toe in black robes. At first, the warriors in camp had to tackle and hold him down when he went after one. After they found a man who could speak a few words of Pashtun, the language of the Afghans and western Pakistanis, he was told not to touch the women, or he would be slain. Bessus answered that he would not be in camp for long. Finally, they found him camp captives, and he stayed.

Now, Bessus considered how he might leave. Although not shackled here, he didn't know how to travel home. He had been told the tall sheik would be back. But that was many dung-eating turns of the seasons ago.

Tolerating the flies, the heat, and the sand that fouled his food and clogged his nostrils had become too much. Dusk would come soon and a chill with it. These warriors were no different from the others. They all wanted to slay Greeks in the land of the Sorceress. Americans, they were called. He didn't care who he needed to kill, if he received another chance to dispatch the Sorceress and end the curse. From what he could understand, the warriors talked about an attack on the American capital. Not with the sticks that spit the fiery bees, but with mountainous bursts of fire and rage that only the thunder gods could make.

Bessus checked the bandage on his leg and walked towards tree-shielded slit trench to piss. He turned for a last look at a sinking sun on the horizon but heard a succession of air-slashing whines. Fire burst around him. A giant hand from nowhere slapped Bessus and propelled him against a palm tree. He cracked his head, collapsing into the trench. More lightning struck the camp. Bessus heard screams. He looked over the rim of the trench. More of the Greek whisper-weapons descended from the sky with yellow tails. The bodies of the sand warriors smoldered.

Seeing a firestick, he slithered from his trench, grabbed the weapon and waited. Having only met the one Greek warrior he'd wounded in the fan-trees, he could guess the Greeks were angry and sent their death-fire from the sky. Shadows darted into the camp. He raised his weapon. These new Greeks would surely fall under the spit of fiery bees. He saw one, then another, running and hiding behind rocks. He let loose a barrage of bees towards them and ducked behind a tree. Bees returned, showering him with trunk splinters. Bessus couldn't see the shadow warriors any longer. He thought retreating to the trench might be a good idea, but he took a blow to the head from behind and lost consciousness.

23

CIA Camp/ Adan, Yemen

NEAR FUTURE

Top U.S. Marine Gunnery Sergeant Morando shut the door that led to the interrogation room. Four armed CIA, along with a special agent he'd never met and a digital video team, waited to begin. Only one of the terrorists had survived the attack from the night before. Urgency fueled their efforts. They suspected an attack, but no details of when and where had surfaced. These bastards wanted to kill his countrymen, and his family, but not if he could do something to stop it. They needed a breakthrough with new field intelligence. But that would be unlikely now after a spy had been killed a few days earlier at a meeting spot.

"Did anyone bathe that SOB?" Gunny asked, removing his thick rimmed glasses and wiping his eyes. "He smells like a shithole."

"That's where they found him. Hiding in a slit trench," answered Agent Kinahan, a CIA agent who reported directly to the DNI, the Director of National Intelligence. "We figured we had to get him here pronto. He got a couple of good smacks in the head from a rifle butt. Big bastard, though. Took three SEALs to load him on a stretcher and helo him here."

"We need better digs. I'm sick of the freaking sand flies in this pit," Morando said, whacking and flicking a dead bug off his arm.

Agent Kinahan, removing his desert fatigue blouse and leaving on a brown T-shirt, said, "We're lucky we have any place to carry out these procedures. Getting to the point we have to serve them coffee and doughnuts."

Morando answered, "Yeah, goes in as breakfast, but it comes out as a cocktail. You rookies ever serve in Guantanamo Bay?"

"No," said Kinahan. "I only heard about Gitmo and the unhappy stationed there."

Morando raised his eyebrows. "How would you like to deal with those animals? We'd deliver their morning meal. They saved up their shit and piss in cups and then flung it at us. Then we'd have to go through decontamination. At lunch they'd throw those Gitmo cocktails at us again. Pretty soon, we had to have shield stands to keep from being splashed and infected."

"Nasty."

"Yeah, just a mite," Morando answered. "Let's treat this one real nice. Give him a steak dinner." He stared at the prisoner. "It's getting harder to serve the country these days."

"Well, we're going to see what we can get out of him before he gets a juicy T-bone."

"It looks like he's waking up."

Bessus awakened strapped to a chair, head covered by a sack and his feet tied. Head throbbing, he remembered the blow he'd taken during the attack. Had the shadow warriors captured him? He hated having his arms tied. Bucking to get free, hands grabbed him, but he toppled over and heard his chair crack. He scrambled and kicked. The new Greeks yelled. Bessus felt a sting in his arm. He lunged, hoping to strike down anyone in his path. Another jab, and then another. He lost his strength.

"Tie him tighter this time," Morando yelled. "What kind of flimsy chair is this? You get it from a freaking cafeteria?"

Kinahan said, "It's all we've got. He won't be going anywhere with the drugs we gave him. These meds could knock down a bull. Triple the dose." He held up the syringe. "It should make him talk, too."

"Who's your interpreter?"

A man working with the video team raised his hand. "Agent Stone, Gunny. We're nearly set up here."

Morando called for backup on the intercom phone. Two additional Marine guards and Truscott, a Navy chief corpsman, entered the room and took positions on each side of the prisoner. They positioned him on another chair and lashed him down again. "Double up those restraints and remove his hood," Morando ordered.

Agent Stone, a ten-year veteran of the Special Activities Division of the CIA, gave a thumbs-up. The other two agents pulled a table closer to the prisoner, set up their computer notepads, and sat down. Stone joined them. Truscott monitored vitals with a pulse oximeter clip taped to the captive's index finger.

Chief Truscott looked at Bessus's bicep and yelled, "Hope we got an extra-large cuff here. I can barely get this on him. I'll be right back." The Chief returned with a larger cuff and readings of blood pressure, pulse and blood oxygen saturation appeared on the digital readout.

"Proceed," Kinahan said, rubbing his chin. "Bring him up a little with that IV. I don't want him drooling on his chin."

No one laughed. Morando checked the arrangements a last time. He stood in front of the prisoner, his hands on a 45-caliber M45A1, a later version of the M1911 pistol. The .45-caliber had proved to be effective in the Philippine Insurrection in the late 1890s when the military needed a gun capable of bringing down drugged Moro tribesman.

Old school.

Kinahan remarked, "Not taking any chances, eh, Top? See you put away your 9-millimeter."

"Never saw a swinging dick still standing after swallowing a few rounds of this baby. There's a reason they call this a close quarters battle pistol."

Truscott said, "Yeah, well, tell your men to keep their safeties on for now. He's drugged enough, and I don't want any shooting mishaps during the procedure. He's tied down good."

"Proceed," Kinahan said, motioning in a manner reminiscent of signaling jets to launch from an aircraft carrier.

Truscott opened a valve, releasing an epinephrine and a barbiturate antidote into the line connected to a vein in the prisoner's arm. After 20 seconds, he moved his head and his eyelids fluttered. His chin lifted off his chest. Truscott ensured an open airway by taping the prisoner's head to a wooden pole he'd tied to the back of the chair.

"Bichajian," Kinahan said sternly, "begin the questioning."

Agent Bichajian, an expert interpreter, spoke in Arabic. "What is your name?"

The prisoner eyelids opened a crack.

"You are a prisoner of the United States government. You will not be harmed, but we want to know who you are and what operation you're training for?"

The prisoner moved his feet, stiffened his head against the tape, but he didn't answer.

"Do you speak Arabic?"

Silence ensued, except for heaving breathing.

Bichajian switched to Pashtun, the language spoken by much of the Taliban in Pakistan and Afghanistan. "No harm will come to you, but you must tell us who you are and what you were doing in that camp."

"Shake his shoulder, Gunny. See if we can wake him further."

Morando did so vigorously. "Wake up, asshole."

The prisoner opened his eyes. His gaze darted left and right.

"Who are you?" Bichajian asked in Pashtun again, but the captive didn't respond.

Kinahan interrupted, suggesting, "Try Farsi. Maybe he's Iranian."

Again, no reply.

Kinahan scratched the back of his head. "He sure as hell doesn't speak Pig Latin."

Morando interrupted, "Why are you pussyfooting around with this prick? Lives are at stake. What if he knows where they're going to hit next?" He made a fist. "I know how to make him talk. He'll listen to the blunt end of this." He held up the pistol.

"Maybe later," Kinahan said facetiously. "Try the smelling salts under his nose."

Morando waved an ammonia plug beneath the prisoner's nose. His head turned away, but then he opened his eyes and bellowed words between sneezes and spitting.

The Marine guards readied their sidearm.

"What is your name?" Kinahan said, pointing at the prisoner. "Bichajian, make out any of this?"

Bichajian rubbed his chin. "Not a word, and I speak ten languages."

Kinahan gave him a vexed look. "He had no ID either."

A guard pushed opened the door. "Top, the new State Department rep is here."

Morando said, "Okay, send him in. Maybe he can help us decipher this cluster. His name?"

The private glanced at the sign-in sheet. "Bartholomew Parsons. What a frigging mouthful."

Morando looked at Kinahan. "After Gitmo and the other dark-op sites, I thought I knew most of them. Just get his ass in here. We're going to need to know how far we can go."

"Would you mind playing that section back again, Agent Stone?" Parsons asked. "Focus on the word he keeps repeating. It begins with a 'J'. He gets agitated every time he says it."

Stone removed his earphones. "Sounds like Ja-doo-gar. Ever heard it before?"

Parsons frowned. "Are you running the word through the program, Bichajian?"

"I'm already on it. Internet isn't so hot out here, even with the satellite." Bichajian waited a moment. "Okay. Here it is. Doesn't match exactly, but it's a derivation of an older Persian word, maybe even ancient Persian. It means witch, or sorceress."

Kinahan rubbed his temple. "Great, we got some kind of warlock here."

"Do we have an expert anywhere in the system who understands ancient languages?"

Kinahan replied, "Don't think so. Maybe it's a code they use, to keep us off their trail. You know, like we used the Navajo language in World War Two."

"We don't have much time. He's the only survivor with this particular cell." Parsons stood and brushed back his hair. He looked at the CIA agents, the Marine guards, and lastly at the prisoner. "We're going to need a contractor, an expert who can retain confidentiality. Someone has to figure this out fast, and I know someone who might help."

San Diego

NEAR FUTURE

"**A**re those gluten-free pancakes?" Lauren sat down at the kitchen table, loading her attaché with material for a morning lecture at San Diego State University.

Cassandra dribbled hotcake batter on the flat frying pan, then she dropped blueberries onto the uncooked topside. "How soon before you have to go?"

Lauren glanced at the clock on the kitchen wall. "About forty minutes before my language lecture. You want to come in as a guest speaker?"

"Wouldn't that be fun? Then I get to explain how an eighteen-year-old knows Ionian slang?" Cassandra piled three steaming cakes on a plate.

"Next week is going to be on ancient Bactria," Lauren said with a grin. She glanced at Cassandra for a reaction. They had developed a comfort over the past five years with what had happened to them.

Cassandra went about her cooking as if Lauren had said nothing. Half a minute later, she yelled, "Demo, get out here, dude, or there'll be nothing left."

"Bet he has his earplugs in again," Lauren said.

"He's on his headphones playing that video game. How can he play before school?"

Lauren downed a glass of orange juice. "You're right. He should be playing only on weekends." She shouted, "Demo, you're going to be late for school." She opened the newspaper and began to read the local section.

Cassandra said, "While I have you alone, I want to run an idea I have past you."

Lauren lifted her head.

"I want to go on active duty. Graduate and join the Marine Corps."

Lauren's eyes appeared above the edge of the newspaper.

"You may think I'm an American girl now, but I'm still an Athenian. My uncle told me that citizens must serve and be involved. Since in this time women can volunteer, then I want to." She unloaded a new stack of pancakes on the plate. "Demo," she yelled again, and then turned to face Lauren. "It's my decision."

"Sweetheart, did it ever occur to you that you can go to college and serve in the ROTC? You don't have to go to boot camp right now."

"I know, but I don't want to wait."

"Consider it. Keep your options open." Lauren glanced at Cassandra to see if her suggestion might gain any traction.

"I'm in great shape right now. Cross-country and karate have me buffed out. I want to be a Recon Marine."

Lauren cringed internally. "You're right. You've got it all, nice to people, smart, strong and beautiful, too. You have unlimited potential."

"So... do I have your blessing?"

"Could we talk about it a little later?"

The land line rang. Lauren answered. "Hello." Her eyes widened. "Of course, I remember you. Yes, the children are doing great." She listened a little longer and stood up. "I would love to do a favor for you." Lauren took a quick look at Cassandra. "It's a really big favor? I can talk further once I get to my office. Maybe this afternoon..."

Lauren listened intently. "You're saying I need to be able to fly out of the country and be away for a month? It's the middle of the semester." Lauren drummed her fingers on the table. "That serious, and I'm the only one you trust to do the job." She cradled the phone between her shoulder and her chin. Lauren filled her attaché quickly with the lecture materials. "Yes, call me this afternoon. I need a little time to consider this and speak with the dean." She stopped talking for a time, and finally put a hand over her mouth. "I see."

Cassandra set the plate of pancakes on the table and mouthed, "What's going on?"

"It's great to hear from you, though I'm still a touch surprised. Talk to you later." Lauren re-cradled the wall phone, while Cassandra dribbled a river of maple syrup over her pancakes.

Lauren said, "That was Mr. Parsons."

Cassandra stopped in mid-chew.

"He needs me to help the State Department and right away."

"And you're going?"

"We owe him. We owe him everything for how he helped us."

"Then you should go. Guess we're all going on active duty."

Demo danced into the kitchen, wearing shorts and a T-shirt, hauling his backpack over his shoulder. "So, you told her you're going active duty?"

Cassandra replied, "That was Parsons. He wants Mom to return a favor."

"That's a very simple way of putting it," Lauren replied with a tone of facetiousness.

Demo picked up a pancake, stuffed it in his mouth and garbled. "What's he want you to do?"

"He couldn't tell me exactly."

Cassandra said, "Now that sounds more interesting. You absolutely must go."

Lauren found her car keys, cell phone and a cup of coffee to go. "Make sure you lock up when you leave. We'll talk more about all this tonight."

"Wait," Demo blurted out. "I've got news, too. I want to join the Peace Corps. Summer will be here soon, and I can start right away."

"You're supposed to start San Diego State next month," Lauren said, stopping in her tracks.

"They need help at disaster sites."

"Please, no more announcements. I have a lecture, and I must set things up with Roberta. She'll look in on you guys while I'm gone. Let's hash this all out later." She kissed each one on the cheek.

Demo said, "Sorry, got movie plans."

Cassandra added, "Track meet."

"These are big family discussions. No signed papers till I return. We all need to slow down." Lauren ran for the door, dropped her attaché, and spilled her coffee trying to catch it. "Oh dear, please clean this up." She gathered up the attaché. "I can't be late, gotta run." She left the front door open.

Cassandra and Demo looked at each other and burst out laughing.

25

CIA Camp Adan, Yemen

NEAR FUTURE

L auren wondered how many times she could yawn within a minute's time. The flight from San Diego had taken almost two days from Naval Air Station North Island. After connections on the east coast, and then again in Germany, the C-5 transport delivered her to NAS Sigonella, Sicily. More flights, and finally, after a crash course in emergency procedures, she rode the back seat of an F-18 fighter to the USS Theodore Roosevelt CVN-71, a Nimitz Class aircraft carrier on station off the coast of Yemen. After Lauren's four hours of sleep in an officer's ward room, a female petty officer roused and escorted her to the commanding officer, who briefed her on her destination.

Dressed in fatigues and desert boots, she downed a second cup of black coffee, grabbed her military cover and left for the helicopter warming up on the deck. She stared straight ahead. The CO of the ship provided few details about the task ahead. At NAS Sigonella, she'd signed life insurance forms and a letter of non-disclosure. Top Secret, they had said. Lauren would proceed on faith.

The rotor blades thumped. The vibration and rotor wash drove her backwards on the tarmac. The deck hand braced her arm, motioning for her to bend slightly at the waist and head for the open hatch. Another airman helped Lauren aboard and buckled her into a webbed seat. With the hatch closed and a thumbs-up given, the helicopter lifted away from the deck and headed out over the sea.

A half hour later, they reached a desert area with palm trees and a small village. A walled compound, surrounded by barbed wire and cleared fields of fire, appeared. Manned watchtowers guarded the perimeter. The helicopter landed, and Marine Corps escorts guided her to a one-story, H-shaped building. A metallic door opened, and Bartholomew Parsons walked out, wiping his brow. He smiled and extended his hand. Parsons looked the same: tall and dark-haired with a clear part in his hair on one side.

"It's so good to see you again, Professor Fletcher."

Lauren clasped his hand and smiled back. "Couldn't there have been a reunion on a Greek island instead of…" She looked around. "…this oasis?"

Parsons laughed. "Yes, call it that if you like, but perhaps you won't have to get to know it too well. Please come inside." He led her to a room that served as an office. A Marine Corps guard stood when she entered.

"Are you hungry? I hope you like MRE's?" Parsons pointed to a table filled with square boxes containing military MEALS READY TO EAT, the staple of troops deployed in the field.

Lauren swallowed. "I'll work extra hard to get this over with. There are only so many options before you start repeating the menu, right?"

Parsons made himself a cup of powdered iced tea. "Like some?"

"Yes, please. I assume the water's not from some camel drink down the road?"

The guard smirked.

"You need rest?" Parsons asked.

"I could easily sleep, but after traveling two days, I'd like to know what's so important, or secretive, that you asked me here."

Parsons motioned for her to follow him. They carried their cups into the next room, and he shut the door. The large room contained six computer stations, all manned by technicians except one. Lauren crossed her arms, amazed she could feel so cold in the desert heat.

"We'll get you a sweater, but soon you'll want to spend the day in here. The other rooms have AC too, but this one is especially comfortable."

Lauren asked, "Where do I work?"

Parsons pointed at the empty desk. "It's all yours."

Lauren lowered into fold-up chair. "Get these at the PX?""

"If it gets uncomfortable, I'll get you a cushion."

"I feel special. You want to give me a briefing now?"

Parsons pulled up a chair. He intersected his fingers and met Lauren's gaze. "We have a high-priority prisoner here. He might know something that will help us protect the homeland."

Lauren's eyes narrowed.

"That's right. We know this cell is up to something. We got nearly all of them with a drone strike in camp a hundred klicks from here, but this one survived. We know they have other camps and communication with cells in Pakistan. Here's the only problem." Parsons paused. "We can't interpret anything he's saying."

"If you needed me, why didn't you send me a recording?"

"Top Secret. All the way up. You're here because I thought you could help and, being from a military family, understand something of operational security."

Lauren swatted at a buzzing fly. "Can't someone laser that thing? You guys have spook weapons, right."

"It's probably drawn to your fragrance. Same one you wore years ago, right?"

"I guess I'm a little predictable."

"We only wear bug spray out here."

"I'll drink it if it'll keep them from biting chunks out of me."

"How are the kids?" Parsons asked, sipping on the tea from a Styrofoam cup.

"Getting ready for college, or so I thought. They want to go active duty, or maybe ROTC."

"Serve their adopted country. You brought them up well."

"I hope so." She took her own sip. "The world is so… dangerous. I'm going to worry."

"Maybe you can assist us with one less worry."

"I owe you. I know that. I might never have gotten the kids without you."

Parson's diverted his gaze. "It was touch and go for a while, and after what happened way back when, I wouldn't say you were predictable at all."

Lauren watched the technicians as they studied computers with various countries displayed on the screens. "Where is this guy?"

"He's down the hall, strapped to a chair. He's dangerous."

"Lovely."

"We've sedated him. With the new rules, we can't do much else." Parsons stopped. "We have a new kind of interrogation that doesn't involve…torture. We try inversion."

"What do you mean by inversion."

"Hypnotize them, so they talk in their most comfortable language. It's weird. Some of them, not just these terrorists, talk in languages they didn't realize they knew. We had some claim they had previous lives. Start talking in Latin, Byzantine. Other times, we get nothing."

"What about this guy?"

"Not even the people in Maryland understand anything he says, except maybe one word."

A Marine guard opened the door from the next room. "He's sedated and blabbering."

"Professor, I know you're exhausted, but this might be an opportune time to examine what language he's speaking. Want to come in?"

Lauren stood. "Lead on."

They walked through two more spaces with computer set-ups. Shouting could be heard from behind a door. A Marine guard with handheld phone ran past them for next room.

Parsons said, "He's in there. It's cushioned for sound, though not completely yet. This facility is still being built. Of course, they may tear it down in a month or so and move on."

More commotion from the next room.

Lauren drew closer to the air vents. Warm air came from the room, along with an odor that turned her away. A Marine guard exited the room.

"What's going on in there?" Parsons asked, putting a hand out to keep Lauren back.

"He's going crazy. Lifted half out of the chair again, thrashing and twisting. Then he stops and raises his nose. You could see his nostrils flaring, like when a freakin' lion smells an antelope. What an asshole. Excuse the language, ma'am."

Lauren nodded.

Parsons asked, "Is he restrained properly now?"

"We've got four guards on him, *and* the restraints. We're giving him another dose."

From the room, they heard moaning and coughing.

"Perfecting your new technique?" Lauren asked with a grin.

"More resistant than most," Parsons said.

The Marine guard peered into the room. "He's puffing and sniffing, but they're strapping him down really good. Think you can come on in."

26

CIA Camp Adan, Yemen

NEAR FUTURE

L auren followed Parsons into the room. Three of the guards held the prisoner down, blocking her view. A Marine swore, struggling as he tried to secure the restraining straps. She saw the arms of the prisoner jerk and heard a guttural voice.

Wood snapped.

She frowned.

Parsons held Lauren back. She saw three Marines hurled against the wall. The last Marine went for his sidearm. The prisoner, with broken pieces of chair tied to him, twisted the gun hand of the guard and threw him in Lauren's direction. Dressed in orange prisoner's overalls, he rose to his full height, yanked the IV from his arm and tossed it aside. He backhanded one of the guards, who slammed against the wall a second time.

The prisoner turned. Lauren backpedaled, her hands up defensively as she screamed, "God, no!"

Bessus pointed his finger at Lauren, blaring, "Ja...doo...gar!" He raced towards her, talon-like nails extended.

Parsons stepped in front of Lauren but couldn't halt the charge of the prisoner. Bessus knocked Parsons into Lauren, sandwiching Parsons between them. Bessus smacked Parsons with his fist and tried to rip him off Lauren. He bellowed, "Jadoogar, Jadoogar." He reached past Parsons and gripped Lauren by the throat.

Bessus squeezed. "You will not get away. You will die, and I will be free."

Lauren gagged. Parsons couldn't unhook the prisoner's grip. Morando ran over and smacked Bessus on the back of his head with the butt of his pistol.

No effect.

Parsons, atop Lauren and facing Bessus, jammed the heel of his hand under Bessus's chin.

Bessus seethed, "You will die, Sorceress. Breathe your last." He squeezed harder.

Lauren felt her throat being crushed as she struggled for air. Hands flailing, her vision narrowed.

Parsons shouted a muffled, "Don't shoot him."

Morando wrapped his beefy bicep around Bessus's throat. The recovered guards clubbed the back of Bessus's head with their pistol butts until he succumbed.

Marines dragged Bessus off them. They helped Parsons to his feet, and one of the men carried her to the office.

Sitting up on a cot, Lauren struggled to swallow slurry of pain medication dispensed by Chief Truscott. Parsons sat beside her, cleaning the lacerations from his face and arms with a medicated wipe. She looked at Parsons, mouthing a silent thank-you. Having thrown himself in front of Bessus, she owed him twice now.

"I'm so sorry, Lauren," he said. "He just went berserk. He called you that Persian word. We believe it means witch."

Lauren looked away. She needed sleep and settled back onto the cot. Chief Truscott asked her how she felt. Lauren nodded, but she was anything but. How did Bessus end up here? The last time she had seen him, he was aflame in the cave at Delphi five years earlier. Massaging her neck, she remembered he'd almost strangled her then, too. Should demanding a helo ride back to the carrier be the best move? The decision could not be made now. She closed her eyes and drifted off.

Yemen Camp

NEAR FUTURE

Morning. Unpleasant aches.

Lauren tried to rise from her cot and rolled off instead. Standing, she stretched and grabbed her lower back. Several successive attempts to loosen up her joints reminded her of the last couple of times she'd fought Bessus. She survived, but she paid a price each time. A mirror revealed black and blue fingerprints around her neck. Wearing her hair down would hide some of the damage.

I look like hell, she thought.

Lauren walked into the CIA communications room. Starved, but wondering what she could swallow, she rummaged through the MRE's.

Parsons saw her. "I hope it's a good morning. You might want to try the dehydrated strawberries. They might go down easier."

Lauren filled two cups from the water cooler, one for tea and another for the berries. She massaged her throat with her fingertips. "Got some crackers I can dunk?"

Parsons nodded. "When you feel like it, come on in here. We have a new supervisor, and we need to talk about what happened yesterday. Everyone apologizes for what happened. We'll be sure to do any further sessions with you present from another room."

"I need to absorb what happened, and then I'll decide how best to proceed."

Should I just take one of the guns and kill Bessus. He'll never stop coming after me. What do I do?

The strawberries blossomed in the cup of water.

As Lauren turned the corner into Parson's office, the cup of tea fell from her hand. Parsons jumped up from his chair and came to her. Lauren wavered, feeling faint. She extended her hand to steady herself.

Tall, dark-haired, dressed in fatigues, she realized that Apollo stood before her.

"Are you okay?" Parsons asked, wrapping his arm around her shoulder. "Sit here." He guided her into a chair. "Your color's returning. You look like you've seen a ghost."

Lauren closed her eyes. She would open them again. Then, she would know if she was dreaming. Or not.

"Lauren?" Parsons said twice.

"I'm here. I'm all right." A raspy reply. She opened her eyes. Apollo had an amused look on his face. One she'd seen before. She took a calming breath. And another.

"That was a ferocious attack yesterday. Are you sure?" Parsons asked.

"I am." Lauren stared at Apollo. Taking a spoonful of the strawberries, she chewed.

Parsons said, "This is Agent Calchas. He is…"

Lauren choked and coughed. She clasped her throat.

"Oh, dear," Parsons said, rising.

Lauren waved him back into his chair. "No, really… I'm okay."

"Do you know each other?"

Apollo said, "Not that I can recall." He smiled.

"Well, then," Parsons continued, "can you shed any light on what happened yesterday? I swear, and no offense, Lauren, that either the prisoner had not seen a woman in a long time, or he knew you."

She shook her head. "Never saw him before, either."

"Did you recognize any of the words he spoke, like that 'Jadoogar' word?" Parsons asked.

Lauren took a deep breath. *What on earth is happening? Apollo is here. And Bessus. Is this part of Apollo's plan? The one he talked about in the dream. Maybe I do get it. Is this about the attack he said would happen?*

She straightened up in her chair, almost at attention. "I did recognize some words. He spoke a combination of Achaemenid Persian and few words of Bactrian, a mostly extinct language." She cleared her throat and winced.

Apollo said, "Do you think that, if he is properly restrained, you could help with translation and interrogation?

"I won't do anything illegal." She paused. "But I will assist in any way possible."

Parsons added, "We know there's a plan afloat, maybe a few. We're trying to put the pieces together but, since all the others were killed in the raid, it may take time we don't have to sniff out the other camps here in Yemen, and in the Afghan/Pakistani border area. Connecting all the Intel on the ground may take months."

Lauren finished the strawberries. Her throat still hurt. *They said he was smelling the air before I walked in. Was he scenting me?*

Apollo stood. "I will make you another cup of tea, Professor." He left the room. They heard a microwave hum. Apollo returned with a cup. He handed it to Lauren and stared into her eyes. The fathomless blue captured her. His hand lingered just a bit long with the cup handoff. She took a sip of the tea. It wasn't too hot, but it had a honey taste. It slid down her throat and coated the soreness. She had to clear her throat a few times, but the pain disappeared.

"Really, thank you," Lauren said, testing her voice. "That helped."

"You are welcome," Apollo said. "Now, let us proceed. The prisoner might have important intelligence. He may fear the Marine guards. I want only myself in the room."

Parson's looked alarmed. "Sir, is that a good idea? He just threw four Marine guards around like rag dolls."

Top Morando walked into the room.

Apollo said, "I will hypnotize him and remain in the room by myself at first."

"Is hypnotism an advanced program?"

"There are others we might employ."

Parsons shifted in his chair. "When I heard you were coming, I looked up your record. You have many years of experience in psychological interrogation."

"This is your first real assignment in the field, is it not, Agent Parsons?" Apollo asked.

"Yes, I volunteered. I figured I'd jump in with both feet."

"I will interrogate the prisoner with all of you outside the door. When I have determined he is properly prepared, will you join us, Professor Fletcher?"

"Seriously," Parsons said, lifting out of his chair, "I object. She can't go in there."

"He pulls anymore of that shit, and I'm taking him out with this." Morando patted his pistol.

Lauren's gaze darted from Apollo to Parsons. "I mean, after yesterday, I'm not so …"

Apollo interrupted. "You will be quite safe. Maybe we can splice the clues together and come up with a plot."

"I am at your service," Lauren replied as she picked up a K-Bar assault knife. "But if he comes at me again, you're going to have a pair of testicles to hang in your Humvee."

Morando said, "My kind of woman. Are you single, ma'am?"

Parsons grimaced.

A smiling Apollo said, "That's the spirit, Professor." He turned to Parsons. "Please don't disturb my procedures with the prisoner."

28

CIA Camp Adan, Yemen

NEAR FUTURE

Bessus, hands secured behind his back, rolled his head and groaned. Lauren watched from an adjacent room with a one-way mirror, as did Parsons, Chief Truscott, other CIA agents and the Marine guards. She saw that the guards all had their sidearm holsters open. They listened over the intercom.

"Wake up, Stink-Pile," Apollo said in Bactrian. Bessus jerked his head and opened his eyes. He recoiled in the chair and hyperventilated.

"Calm yourself, Bessus. You're quite safe."

Bessus's eyes darted left and right. "Where are the guards, Scout?"

"I don't need them. We are going to talk, and there will be no more upset from you." Apollo recalled that the Persian Marshall, Mardonius, had attached him as a scout to Bessus's raiding party during the march to Delphi. Bessus had called him 'Scout' since that time.

Bessus shook his head. "My thoughts are scrambled. What powerful drink did they give me? I feel like I've drunk a barrel of soma."

Bessus's reference to a fermented drink of his homeland brought a snicker from Apollo. "Your head will clear in a moment. Here, drink this instead." Apollo lifted a silver flask to Bessus's lips and poured the honeyed drink into his mouth. Bessus swallowed and licked his lips.

"You better not poison me, or I will…"

"Will what, Bessus? You forget I have powers you're unable to overcome."

Bessus's eyes widened. "Wait, the Sorceress. Where is she? You promised I could slay her." He raised his voice and struggled with his hand restraints. "I can smell her. I know she's near. Let me kill her, and I will do your bidding."

"The warriors watch. They will slay you if you attempt to hurt her again."

"I care not. Let me shut her face forever. Blind those eyes that torture me in my sleep. I want to be free of her magic."

"Magic? You have a head full of mud. Listen to me, Bessus."

Bessus strained and attempted to stand. He yelled, "Jadoogar!" at the top of his lungs.

Over the intercom, Parsons inquired, "Are you all right, sir?"

Apollo waved his hand to signal that everything remained under control.

Bessus looked at Apollo, more a pleading expression than anger. "Let me end this curse so I can return home."

"Does the drink make you feel better?"

"My head clears enough to know my fate is to slay her."

"No, it isn't. I'm going to bring her in here and you will sit in that chair and talk to her pleasantly or I will cook you where you sit."

"You will bring her to me and I must slay…"

"Shut up and do my bidding, or you will never see your son again."

Bessus stared at him. He puffed through his bulbous lips.

"She is the one who will allow you to return home. Kill her and you will die, and the line of your seed will be cut off. She is here, because I also command her fate, too."

Bessus blinked. His Adam's apple bobbed.

Apollo continued, "You both serve me. She cannot leave, just as you cannot, unless you both do what I say."

"God or magician, I know not what you are, but I will be free of this curse. A warrior of Bactria takes commands from no one."

"We will explore that, too, Bessus."

"You may enter, Professor Fletcher," Apollo said over the intercom a few moments later. "The rest of you stay out."

Parsons said, "Sir, I must protest her being in there with only you. If you had seen…"

"I understand, Agent Parsons, but she will be quite safe with me."

Parsons said to Lauren. "We have guns drawn and Billy clubs out. Chief Truscott has a needle ready."

Lauren peeked around the corner and walked into the room.

Bessus slammed back against his chair. His eyes narrowed. He grimaced, taking deep breaths. "Jadoogar," he snarled, "you are mine. He may protect you now, but you will beg for the grave when I get you alone."

She took a few steps back. Bessus fought with the restraints tying him to the metal chair.

Apollo intervened. "Calm yourself. We tire of your threats."

"Threats," Lauren said. "You've never had his hands around *your* throat."

"Pull up a chair, Professor." Apollo directed her to sit across from Bessus, who puffed like a steam engine.

Bessus sniffed the air. "Sit near me, witch. I remember squeezing the life from you."

Lauren saw the cavernous eyes of the prisoner, made more sinister by the half-lighted room. She blinked in surprise. "Wait, he understood what I said?"

Apollo said, "Yes. He speaks whatever language I choose for our communication. Now, we will speak Bactrian, for only then may we speak in confidence."

Lauren shut her eyes. The lost language suddenly blossomed within her mind, as if downloaded from a flash drive. A smile came to her lips. "I know the words. This is a revelation. How do you manage that?"

"The medallions and medicine I carry make it so, Professor," Apollo replied in the ancient language of Afghanistan.

Over the intercom, Parsons interrupted. "What language are you speaking in there?"

Apollo waved his hand. "You will be briefed when we are done."

Lauren stared at Apollo. "Since we're speaking in confidence, tell me now, where's my husband? No baloney."

Apollo grinned. "At least you waited until we could speak. I knew you would be patient." He paused. "He is well. I cannot say he has escaped history unscathed, physically or psychologically. His training continues."

Lauren lips quivered. "When can I see him…for real?"

Apollo replied, "In due time. You both have roles to play in what is to come."

Bessus broke in. "Who do you speak of? The Mumbler? If it is, tell him he's a dead man."

"You are a bore," Apollo said.

Bessus sneered. "And you have a mouth full of slop. You talk with fancy words and speak of what will come to be, but I'm sick of it. Release me. Give me a horse. I'll ride to Bactria with this witch across my saddle."

Lauren said, "I'm not your witch. You can't stand that a woman has beaten you."

Bessus thrashed. "I can't stand your insults."

"Shut up, Bessus, and listen to me. You think you're free to do what you will, but you're a slave. You belong to Xerxes and the Persians. They own your lands, your crops, your horses, your life and your son's life."

Bessus made a sound of frustration. "I hate them, and I hate her."

"How does it feel to be a slave, Lord Bessus?" Apollo asked.

"Shut your face."

"Which is worse for you, Bessus. A woman fighting for her life and escaping your clutches, or always being a slave owned by others?"

"More talk in circles. A warrior yields to no one."

"But you do yield. You yield to Xerxes, and to those who rule you now."

"What, those sand warriors? They don't tell Bessus what to do." He glared at Lauren.

"If you decided to leave, would you have been killed by them?"

Bessus chewed on the inside of his cheek. He turned his head away from his captors.

Apollo said, "I can tell you how to be a free man."

Bessus struggled against his ropes. "I will be free when she breathes her last."

"How did Zack get named 'the Mumbler'?" Lauren asked.

Apollo said to Lauren, "A story for another time, if you will."

He raised his voice, addressing Bessus. "Now you are the one with slop in his ears. This woman *and* the Mumbler serve me, only me …and willingly."

Parsons interrupted over the intercom. "How is it helping if none of us understand?"

Bessus scanned the room, wondering where the voice came from.

"And this… savage?" Lauren asked, nodding towards Bessus. "I can't be looking over my shoulder forever."

"He will be too busy to bother you," Apollo said.

Parsons said over the intercom, "Any progress on their plans?"

"Little at a time," Lauren said aloud.

"I don't want to be in a room with him any longer. Time for me to go," Lauren said quietly to Apollo.

He drew her closer and whispered, "Let us give the impression for a couple of hours more that we are gaining information. They will see him as valuable. I will convince them to consider him as a potential double agent."

Lauren recoiled. "A monster from ancient Bactria is going to be your spy? That defies logic."

Apollo grinned. "Has a certain beauty to it, doesn't it?"

She rolled her eyes. "You're a god, and this is your plan?"

"Find out about his culture that's lost to history. I'm going to arrange a means of communication between you. Tomorrow your work here will be done, but I may have another task for you."

"Hold it. I need to go home. I have children to care for. I'm in the middle of a semester. The dean has been good to me, but she will only tolerate…"

Apollo put up his hand. "Fear not. When we are done, you are returning home to await your next task."

29

Athens, Greece

NEAR FUTURE

A thens, Greece- Press Release. Police still search for the mysterious caller, who days ago, heroically stopped terrorists from inflicting greater damage on the city of Athens, its museums and the Parthenon. Chief of Police Commissioner Darzenta said at a press conference, "This caller, who fought with the terrorists and warned us in time to be able to stop an unbelievable tragedy from unfolding here, is a hero and should be recognized by our people as such. He had an American or Canadian accent, and we believe he was injured in the struggle. Anyone with information as to how we can reach this man would be appreciated by Greek government. We have a recording of his call as evidence. Police are also conducting raids on suspects, who may be linked to the bombings. They expect to have arrests soon. If the man who stopped these attacks is listening, we owe you our eternal gratitude. We offer any medical attention you may require and, of course, we wish to thank you in person. Please call the Police Headquarters at 210-644-0412."

Zack walked up the stairway from the portal in Delphi, step by step beside Apollo. When they reached the landing, the ground parted above them and Apollo leaped to the surface.

Knowing an Olympic jumper could not accomplish such a leap, Zack extended his hand. Apollo grabbed it and hauled him up onto the mountainside.

"I get it," Zack said. "You're the god, and I'm still the mortal."

"You're more than just any mortal, Traveler."

"Where do we go now?" Zack asked. Looking out at the buildings and lights in the town nearby, he realized that he was back in his own time, or very close to it. He wore ripped sandals and a dirt-caked tunic.

"To police headquarters, after you bathe."

Zack dropped to his knees. He had returned. Digging through pine needles, he scraped soil and sifted it through his fingers.

"It's true," Apollo said.

Zack said, "I'm back. I never knew if I'd make it home." He saw the museum down the mountainside. He realized his heart pounded.

I made a journey from Delphi, but now I'm home.

"You earned it. The yearning must have been tortuous, but no different from the warriors of many ages." Apollo glanced at the twin peaks of Mt. Parnassus above them. He let out a held breath.

"You've been away five years, and deserve fanfare and celebrations, but we must tread carefully. There's hard work ahead."

Zack closed his eyes. He smelled the mountain breeze, heard it whistle through the trees and rustle the bushes. His thoughts turned to the fight for survival in Saabir's store. Five years ago, Apollo had sent him into the future to halt the terrorist attack on Athens. Arriving in Delphi now, he was just catching up to the time when it had occured.

I've got to get this straight in my head if I'm going to talk to police.

"Don't you think I should wear pants, or shorts and shirt? The wounds I had coming out of that fight are long gone. Aren't I supposed to be badly injured?"

"Shall I bloody your nose?" Apollo drew back a fist, grinning.

"I think I need at least cuts on my leg that we can let bleed and bandage, but what about the bullet wounds?"

"Stand still. Here's a leather strap to bite on. I must reverse some of my surgery..."

"Wait. What?"

Apollo summoned a charge from the medallion and it burned thru Zack's bicep as if a bullet had passed through. Zack yelped.

Apollo said, "We'll lathe some gunpowder into the wound to complete the job. My, the lengths you will go to be recognized."

Zack rubbed his wound. "Can we get a bloody bandage on it and enough with the jokes?"

"Why stop there? Let's rub some dirt in it and get it infected."

Zack saw the facetious expression on Apollo's face. "How are we going to Athens?"

"We'll wait till early morning and arrive unseen. Are you ready to be a hero?"

"I'm ready to get to work."

"You're not the same man who saved the Parthenon before I sent you back for more training. But now, I have disturbed the course of the future. I had to delay the main attack by having you stop the assault on Athens. But I have rendered history impotent. I altered what did occur."

Apollo looked down to see the passing of terrain as they neared their destination in Athens.

"We're nearly here. Woe to me that the other gods didn't survive. Each of us had a role, coordinated to save the Western world from catastrophe. But when they perished, I knew I couldn't carry it out by myself... and thus, you, Golden Hair, and Bessus, my heroes, troublesome and inexperienced though you all may be."

"I declare that I have erred. I changed history to buy time," Apollo continued. "Who brought down the finances of the country and left it open to disaster?" His voice softened. "Who led the attacks? At this point, even I have no idea what will occur from here on."

"Just what I wanted to hear," Zack said.

Zack arrived just before daybreak, wearing modern, though soiled clothing. He kept his beard, and his long hair tied in the back by a band. He looked like the hoplite. One who had fought at Salamis and

Plataea, He entered police headquarters, a sixteen-floor high rise, on Alexandras Avenue. He informed the officers on duty that he was the caller they searched for. They led him to a room, requesting his cooperation for finger printing and a blood sample to match evidence left at the scene. The staff contacted Commissioner Darzenta, who rushed into the office.

Before Zack could down two expresso-sized cups of coffee and a roll with jam, Darzenta, built like a wrestler, entered the room with a line of officers behind him and a television crew.

He looked at Zack and said, "I'm Commissioner Darzenta." He sat beside Zack at the head of a U-shaped table but continued to look at him as if confused. Addressing the cameramen, he said, "No TV until I say so, clear?"

Zack remembered the cocktail mixer he and Lauren attended to meet Professor Popandreou at the National Archeological Museum. He had met the police commissioner before.

Darzenta pulled the police report sheet and adjusted his glasses. "You are Professor Fletcher from the United States? Hold on. This is perplexing. Didn't you disappear some years ago? No one has seen you since? Did you just pop in from some time warp?" He belly-laughed as did the crowd.

Zack shifted in his seat. "Yes. I had an injury and lost my memory. I've been wandering for some time around the country. I was in the shop and figured out what was happening."

"You mean it was a coincidence you were there?"

I can't give him an honest answer to that one.

"I was at a fundraiser with a Professor Popandreou and my wife sometime back when we ran into that guy. His name was...Saabir. Gave me his business card, and I looked him up."

"Yes. I remember. You know that the professor was murdered about five years ago in Delphi?"

Zack jumped from his chair. "What?"

Darzenta guided him back down. "Sorry. I thought you would have known...but under the circumstances, maybe not. Coincidentally, his murder took place right around the time of your disappearance." He stared at Zack longer, with a more quizzical look.

"He's dead!" Zack covered his face, feigning surprise. There was no other way.

Darzenta asked, "If you could give us all the details of what happened in the store, we'll listen to the recording together. When we have everything…a fingerprint match for those on the handgun, as well as on the other evidence, we'll announce you as the man who saved Greece and the Parthenon, our proudest monument of the Golden Age."

"A moment?" Zack asked. "Professor Papandreou's murder is too much to absorb right now."

"My apologies and condolences. There will be time to discuss it later. Are you also in need of medical services? I see your bandage is bleeding."

"Not right now," Zack said. "Could use something to eat, though. Maybe a chicken kabob from Souvlaki Row?"

The crowd laughed. Zack took a steadying breath and then spoke about the fight in the store, being attacked and shot, eventually killing Saabir and one of his co-conspirators. He explained using one of the terrorist cell phones to contact the Greek version of 911, which gave them a record of his voice. He'd left a lot of blood there, too.

Additional reporters and television crews arrived. Zack wished he had shaved off his beard. Lights blazed, and all eyes focused on him.

Will I ever be able to tell the truth?

30

San Diego, California

NEAR FUTURE

rofessor Roberta Collins, Department Head of African-American Studies, dashed into Lauren's office. Lauren couldn't decide if the look on her colleague's face spoke of terror or something fantastic.

"Lauren, pull up the news on your computer. Quick."

"Not another terrorist attack? Where is it this time?"

"Hurry, Lauren."

Lauren logged into a local San Diego news station and sank back onto her chair. Shocked, she pointed at the screen and gasped, "It's him."

Zack sat before a news crew in Athens, Greece, and Lauren saw a scruffy brown beard, close-cropped hair and a ponytail on her long-lost husband. He resembled a hoplite of ancient times. Roberta placed her hand on Lauren's shoulder.

Lauren opened her mouth to speak, but no words emerged while she listened to Zack's rehash of events. Zack and Apollo had previously told her he'd saved the Parthenon, but not that he would be allowed to return afterwards. She'd kept quiet about it even during recent news about an attack in Athens.

A reporter asked, "Why haven't you contacted your family all this time?"

Zack said, "I had a rough spell. I'd been hit on the head, and I was disorientated and confused for a long time. Amnesia, I guess. But I'm back."

The lady news interviewer said, "So, Professor Zackary Fletcher from San Diego State University is Greece's hero. Do you have any message for your family back in the States?"

Zack looked at the TV camera. "I'll have a lot more to say once I get home, but Lauren, honey, I can't wait to see you again. I love you."

Lauren, still in shock, looked at Roberta.

Roberta smiled. "He's alive, and he's coming home to you."

The two women hugged.

The station switched back to the newscasters, who commented that Professor Zackary Fletcher had disappeared five years earlier. They showed newspaper articles and video clips. Then, remarks shifted to a discussion about his possible need for medical care.

Lauren wiped her eyes. So much had happened in the months since she had returned from Yemen. The loneliness with the kids gone. Now this. Her dream had come true. "I've got to tell the kids, but they're both out of town. Cassandra is attending Marine Corps "A School" at Camp Pendleton and graduates next week. Demo's on his first assignment in Ecuador. I'm going to ask him to come home."

Roberta said, "That will be one incredible meeting, whenever it gets to happen. Imagine not knowing you have two children."

"Thanks. I'm not sure I could have endured of all this without you."

Meantime, Zack answered additional questions from the Greek media. He said, "I'm happy to have helped the country where democracy and the ideals of Western civilization made its beginning. Greece is important, maybe more than we realize. The philosophy that each person has value and can achieve excellence is the foundation of our way of life."

Another reporter asked about his plans.

"I'll have more to say when I get home, but I want to remind everyone who is listening, vigilance is necessary to preserve freedom. I may have done a small deed here to stop those killers, but I want to suggest to everyone that we should all think clearly about what sacrifices we must make to assure free societies continue to thrive. There may come a time, we don't know if it's tomorrow, next month or sometime soon, when we may *all* have to be heroes."

A flurry of questions followed, but Zack raised his hand and concluded the news conference. Darzenta told the crowd that the professor was off to the hospital, and that he would take any further questions.

A reporter shouted at Zack as he walked out of the room, "Do you know about an impending attack?"

Roberta glanced at Lauren. "That sounded ominous. Do you think he's holding something back?"

"We'll find out when he gets home."

The news program shifted to the sports segment.

Lauren said, "The dean has been wonderful in understanding my requests for time off. I'm afraid I must go begging to her again."

"Best Dean of Arts and Letters I've ever served under, and the university is gaining national recognition in so many areas."

Lauren asked, "How do I call him? There must be a number." She dropped her pen and knocked a stack of folders onto the floor.

Roberta squeezed her shoulder. "I'll work on that for you. Close your eyes and revel in the moment. He's coming home."

Shutting her eyes, Lauren prayed to the pagan god who ruled their lives.

I need to get home. He doesn't have my new cell number. Hope he remembers our home phone.

Lauren threw open the front door to her home and raced to the landline in the kitchen.

A light blinked on the wall phone, signaling a voice message.

The first message was from a lawn aeration company. The second, did she want a timeshare week in Maui? The third call sent her to her knees.

Zack.

"Lauren. I love you, and I'll be home as soon as possible. I'll make the flight without fanfare. I don't want to draw any more attention until we can talk face to face. No e-mails or texts. Please be patient just a little longer. I have so much to tell you. Expect me in a few days. I love you."

She listened to it a few times and understood his meaning.

The next day, Lauren put her cell phone on speaker while talking to Roberta. "I've been doing loads of laundry, gardening, and food shopping, anything to keep my mind off Zack's arrival time. I'm so excited and so worried at the same time."

She poured a glass of orange juice and sank into a kitchen chair.

Roberta asked, "How'd the dean's meeting go?"

"Fantastic. Everyone at State can't wait to see him, too. The Department will cope."

Lauren heard the back door open. "Hold it, Roberta... Someone just..."

Apollo walked into the kitchen, disguised as Calchas, the Plaka waiter.

"Ah, Roberta... I have a ...repairman here. Can I call you later? Okay. Thanks. Talk later."

Lauren put down her cell phone and stood. "I don't know how to greet a god, but after Yemen with Bessus, I suppose I don't need to curtsy or anything. You have something to tell me?"

"You are amusing." Apollo pulled out a chair, sat down and folded his hands. Lauren sank back down into her chair and stared into his Aegean-blue eyes.

"How wonderful to be with you again, my Golden Hair."

"With all due respect, I don't think I can do small talk. What's happening with my husband?" Her gaze didn't waver. His blue eyes no longer mesmerized her.

"Make us a cup of tea, please. There is much to discuss."

Lauren put the tea kettle on the stove. "Do I get him back now?"

"The storm clouds gather. The time is near. I need you both."

She took out a pair of teacups her mother had given to her as a wedding gift.

"You've been apart a long time," Apollo observed. "He will be a different man. Like many warriors who return from battle, he's experienced much that lingers in his thoughts."

Lauren dropped tea bags into the cups. "He'll have Post Traumatic Stress Syndrome?"

"He may suffer from seeing so much death, especially among those he knew. He had to be tempered, as did you. You are a warrior in your own way."

"Thank you. This hasn't been easy for us." Lauren poured hot water into the cups.

"I would prefer to deliver him here myself, but he is a celebrity now." He tapped the edge of the tea cup with his forefinger. "He will arrive at the airport in San Diego on a late flight. I don't want to draw to much attention to him for now."

Lauren studied him. "Not the welcome for a hero of his caliber, is it?"

"The media is interested in his story, but interviews here only after we coordinate the logistics for what is ahead."

She tested the heat of the tea with a little sip. "Tell me I have him for a while before…"

Apollo met her gaze in an equally straight forward manner. "I won't lie to make you feel better. You will have him, but there's little time left."

She drummed her fingers on the table. "Doesn't sound too good. What about the kids?"

"Call them home. You all need to be together."

31

San Diego, California

NEAR FUTURE

L auren recalled little about getting into her car, navigating the highway, and finding a spot in short-term parking at the airport. *I've waited so long, and now I'm terrified.*

The overhead flight information panel listed Zack's flight as "arrived". She gripped her cell phone so tightly her fingers began to tingle. She took a steadying breath as she walked.

In her other hand she held a bouquet of flowers from their backyard. Ones Zack had planted for her. Lauren wondered if he would remember. Would he even notice them?

Five years.

She smoothed her hair. Shorter and styled differently, Zack wouldn't recognize her new look. Little lines had crept into the corners of her eyelids. *He remembers me as I was, but then I imagine we've both changed.*

Spin classes, Pilates and yoga. Would he be pleased with her figure? Worry surged from underneath, deep in her gut. Her chin trembled as she struggled for control.

What if he's different? What if he's been injured? What if his feelings for me have changed? What if…?

Stop it! What will be, will be. Suck it up and face the future.

She watched the second story walkway for passengers. Last flight in.

Not too many people in the airport. Late at night.

Don't doubt yourself, or him. He said he loved you.

Lauren swallowed the lump of emotion wedged in her throat. Her heart raced as she waited for Zack.

My husband.

Steady your breathing. You want to be on your feet when he sees you.

Family would have been wonderful to have here, Lauren thought. Like when she'd brought Cassandra and Demo home. Hugs and tears. She'd wept, too. She wished the kids could be here for his arrival, but it wasn't to be.

Apollo didn't want fanfare for Zack's arrival. She got that. She'd have to explain to her parents why they hadn't been involved. And a lot of other family and friends, too. She'd told everyone since his television appearance that his travel schedule was uncertain.

Lauren peered towards the escalator coming from the second story causeway. Travelers began to appear at the top of the stairs. She had woken up at night so many times in the throes of a nightmare. He was coming home. But then he'd disappear. He'd been wounded in battle and crying out for her while he clung to his life.

Her knees threatened to buckle. Taking a deep breath, she held it in, and then slowly released it. A few times. Squaring her shoulders, she lifted her chin and practiced smiling. She wouldn't crack in front of Zack and become a sobbing mess. Lauren could only imagine what he'd been through.

At the top of the moving stairs, someone resembling Zack scanned the crowd below. Not the professor of history with an easy smile and an attaché as she had remembered him striding confidently down the college building corridors to a lecture. This was a different man. She saw him take a breath, then let it out. He looked past her. His lips taut. He wore a ball cap from a Greek beer company. He looked strong, wiry, confident.

She moved ahead in the crowd of waiting people just as he neared the landing. Lauren said his name, but it emerged as a whisper.

Lauren wanted to scream, hurl herself into his arms and never let go.

179

Would the crowd recognition him from news broadcasts? Apollo said no attention. He had his reasons.

Zack smiled suddenly and shouted, "Lauren!"

His voice sounded different somehow than she remembered.

She tried to run. Stumbled. Bumping into someone, she apologized and dashed for the landing.

She could finally say it. "You're home! I love you, Zack."

His hug crushed her. "I am home, and I love you, too." He kissed her, spinning her around until she felt dizzy and euphoric.

They held tightly to one another, neither willing to let go.

"It's real, Lauren. It's no dream."

"Do you have bags?" she asked.

Zack said to her ear. "No bags. Just me."

"I'll take the deal." Lauren pulled away for a second, crinkled her nose like she'd been tickled and said, "Beard? Going to keep that, Achilles?"

He grinned and kissed Lauren again. "Let's go."

Lauren latched onto him. Thinner, but steely, she thought. She saw something different in his eyes, too. He'd been through a lot. "Welcome home, Zack."

He glanced at her but, she sensed his inner tension. *Normal for what he's been through.* Zack looked straight ahead. Trepidation. Anxiety. Something…wrong?

"We can walk to the car," Lauren said, holding his hand. "Are you okay, Zack?"

He squeezed her hand a bit tighter. "I'm barely able to say I'm comfortable in the 21st century. Being home…really at home…is exciting, something to refamiliarize myself with. I love your new hair style. You're far more beautiful than I remembered. I'm so happy to be back."

"Breathe. Relax. It's over," she said.

"Please forgive me if I seem…odd. I'm still partly there. My body is here. My mind hasn't caught up yet."

"Car's up ahead." Lauren pointed to a Navy Blue Mini-SUV.

Zack asked, "The Prius?"

"Died in battle. Traded it in a few years back."

"I've been gone awhile."

Lauren threw her arms around him. "You never left my thoughts for a second. I knew you'd make it home. From here on, let's restart our lives."

He smiled, but she noticed it was a half-smile. "Come on. You want to drive, Zack."

"I'm only good with chariots now."

Lauren laughed.

Weaving into the traffic as they left the airport, she said, "Welcome home, Zack. Welcome back to our life and to me."

"Thank you. There's so much to talk about." He turned away and stared out the window streaked with a beginning rain. "Take me home. Please."

Lauren maneuvered onto Highway 8 East towards their home in Del Cerro. Inside, she sensed something truly was wrong. Was it the distance in time, or how long he'd been away? Did he still love her as he'd said? Something worrisome stirred deep inside her.

The next morning, Zack opened his eyes. He saw their wedding photo atop the bureau.

Was he the same man in the photograph? Clean-shaven and trimmed hair. A beard and ponytail had been his style in the ancient world. But his question was more psychological. He already knew he wasn't that man any longer.

The night before at the airport had been a blur. The long flights, and then he'd arrived into the baggage area. Lauren had run to him. After she'd thrown her arms around him, shoulders heaving and unable to speak, she kissed him. He'd held her close, his emotions in disarray. Neither of them could say much beyond "I missed you" and "I love you."

He'd held Lauren's hand during the ride home. Upon their arrival, the real talk began, but it hadn't lasted long.

They sat on the couch, Lauren nestled in his arms. Two glasses of wine and the long flights without rest claimed him. Long-dreamed of home. He had fallen asleep.

Now, he heard Lauren's voice in another room. She spoke to several people- her parents, Roberta and to Lisa, her college friend. He'd thought often of hearing his wife's laughter. Rolling out of bed, he stood, felt dizzy and grabbed the bedpost. A moment later, he made his way into the bathroom. A good scrubbing might help him to decide…

…if I'm home.

Wait. That means coffee, in my own home, with my wife.

Zack emerged from the steam-filled bathroom to the sight of Lauren sitting the bed and smiling at him.

"The master has returned home after his long journey." She patted the bed. "Sit next to me. How do you feel?"

Face to face with her, he found himself lost in her smiling eyes.

"If this is another of Apollo's tricks…"

"It's not, Zack. You're home."

He crossed the room, a towel secured at his waist. "I need to be sure. I don't think I can take another…dream. I know I'm here. I just might need a while longer to absorb it. To believe it totally." He caressed her cheek and then traced the line of her chin with his fingertips.

She laughed. "Well. Maybe you should make sure?"

Zack pulled her up and wrapped his arms around her. Their kiss lingered, and then deepened, borne of a tormented hunger.

"It is you. It's going to take me a while to tell you everything that's happened. I've missed you… so much," he said.

She pressed a kiss to his chin. "I've missed you more than I can possibly say."

"Can we talk over coffee?" he suggested, surprised he could say such a thing. He struggled to gain control of his thoughts and knew his hands were shaking.

Lauren smiled and let go of him, though he could tell it was not what she'd had in mind. "Of course, we can. Get dressed. I'll make a fresh pot. We'll take a go-cup and head down to Lake Murray for a long walk."

Zack grabbed her hand. "I never would have had the courage to go on without you."

Lauren placed her fingertip to his lips. "You're home. That's all I care about. My husband is back with us, and in one piece, I think." She kissed him again. "Coffee will be ready in ten minutes."

"I want to hear how you made it back. How did you get away from Bessus? What did Cassandra think when you ...transferred..."

"We have a lot to discuss, Zack. We'll catch up on our walk. Enjoy the sun and the ducks. Get some lunch. We finally have time together."

"Look. I'm nervous." He tightened his grip on her hand. "I've waited a long time. We both have."

"People say that. Only we know what that means now. I'm a bit uneasy, too. Let's take a stroll and catch each other up on our lives first."

That evening, Zack asked, "Shall we have a last toast?" He swirled red wine in his glass.

"Not making up any of those stories, are you?" Lauren asked, snuggling into his side on their leather couch. They tapped glasses.

"All true, but I barely scratched the surface. A few times, I thought the game was up. It's going to take some time to tell it all...at times, it will sound pretty disturbing."

"But you survived." Lauren held his hand and led him out of the family room. "When we get to the bedroom, you can show me your battle scars. I've never been with a hero of the Persian Wars before."

He saw the gleam in her eyes. "Some of the scars aren't on the outside."

Lauren drew him into her arms. "I'll help you heal. Think of me as your personal nurse. And I'm really good at what I do."

They walked down the hall to the master bedroom. Zack abruptly stopped. "Lauren, there are...things I need to tell you. I can't right now... I'm still a bit...screwed up."

She cupped his face between her palms. "I don't care. Listen to me. I blamed you in Athens, and at Thermopylae, blamed you on the way south, too, but I didn't realize that Apollo was orchestrating this entire... whatever this is."

"He's not totally to blame. I wanted to see it up close...I couldn't resist the opportunity to live history firsthand."

"He played on your dreams and your weaknesses, too, Zack."

"Some really bad things happened."

She locked eyes with him. "Listen to me, Zack. Whatever you tell me might be horrible, even depressing or shocking, but I'll trade those truths for the luxury of having you back with me."

He took a deep breath. "Okay. I can let them go for now, if I can get them off my chest later. I feel like I'm coming down off a lifetime adrenaline rush, and I'm about to crash."

Lauren took his hand and led him to the doorway of their bedroom. "You know what? I've been feeling empty for a long time. If it weren't for the kids, I don't know how I would have coped. You're like Odysseus, and I'm Penelope. You wanted to come home to me, but the gods wouldn't let you. Monsters on the way, sirens, shipwrecks…I don't even care if you met Calypso, and she kept you on an island with her."

Zack's lip trembled. He searched her eyes, praying she meant what she'd just said.

"Oh, yes, "she said. "Just like Odysseus, you can't be whole till you make it back home. The order of the cosmos, remember? Home makes you content and complete." She squeezed his hands. "I make you whole."

Zack couldn't speak. Too many memories assaulted him. He knew she was right.

Lauren leaned against the door frame. "I remember the note you wrote me, the one in the jar. I saved it. Do you want me to read it?"

"I know what it says. I wrote that I couldn't live without you."

Lauren kissed him. "Well, here I am. And here you are."

"Life can begin again, at least for the time being."

"Yes, for now. But we'll take what we can get. Come on in. No more time to waste."

Zack glanced at her. "Don't I have to notch my arrows and get rid of the suitors like Odysseus did?"

Standing in the doorway, she unbuttoned her blouse. One button at a time. The rest of her clothing slowly fell away.

"I can't believe my eyes."

Lauren walked towards the window. Zack thought he heard her say,

"I finally get the guy I want."

"What was that?" Zack said, following her. Moonlight backlit her figure. A gust of air fluttered the blue curtains.

"Never mind. I'm here for you, Zack. And, I guarantee you that, by tomorrow, I will make you forget everything that's haunting you. You're mine. Are you ready?" She closed the window and then stood in front of their bed.

The long-lost traveler swept Lauren into his arms. They fell across the bed in a tangle of naked limbs and blatant desire.

Zack remembered the dream he'd had about Lauren and Io. *I guess you won the dice toss.*

Lauren smiled at him. "My worldly hero, fortified and cultivated by experience over two thousand years, has not changed much. Come here."

They became lost within a torrent of desperate heartbeats.

I have changed, Zack thought. *You'll see that I know who I belong to.*

32

Yemen CIA Camp

NEAR FUTURE

Gunny Morando stood at the ready with a hand on his Colt sidearm. The prisoner, dressed in an orange jumpsuit, handcuffed, his feet shackled, sat on a newly delivered metal chair.

"Finally, I can come within ten feet of this bastard without puking. Nice job, Truscott. Did you and your corpsman shave and bathe him yourselves?"

"Like shaving a goddamned camel. You should have seen the pile of hair after we used the electric shaver on him," Truscott said.

"We're probably out of industrial strength cleanser now, too. Better order more. He still looks a bit dazed."

Truscott checked the titer valve on the IV bag. "I should wake him up."

"I just have to make sure I've got an extra clip of ammo, Chief. I got a couple of Marines still in sick bay after that interrogation the other day. Keeps going like this, and it'll only be me and you left."

"Call Stone and Kinahan in here so we can get this session going. We're going to run out of drugs before anything else. He needs triple the sedation to have any effect," Truscott said.

Gunny Morando spoke into his phone. Agents Stone and Kinahan entered the room, both carrying Styrofoam cups.

"When you finish your cappuccinos, could you draw your sidearm and wake this asshole up," Morando said.

The CIA agents put down their cups and took positions in front of the sleeping prisoner. Head on his chest, the prisoner breathed loud and steady.

Chief Truscott selected a loaded syringe and injected it into the line. Shortly, the prisoner's head bobbed.

Morando said, "It's time to talk again."

Stone said, "Let us do the session, Gunny. He isn't going to understand your gutter English, anyway."

"Good luck with anything else," Morando replied. "What are you going to try…Arabic?"

Agent Stone raised his finger and Kinahan tapped a button on his laptop to begin recording.

Stone said, "Yes, Arabic, and some ancient Persian the lady professor taught us. Bichajian will take care of that."

Morando said, "After a month of this crap, we don't have time. He's coming around."

"Bessus," Stone asked in Arabic.

The prisoner's head hung on his chest. He blinked several times.

"Bessus," Stone repeated, louder.

The prisoner groaned. He mumbled. "I am… Bessus." He closed his eyes. "It hurts. Return me to sleep."

"What hurts?" Stone asked.

Bessus lifted his head. The right side of his face looked swollen.

"Do you see that, Chief?" Stone said.

Chief Truscott came from behind Bessus and lifted his chin. "Either he got a shiner in the fight with the guards, or he has a tooth infection." Truscott touched the swelling. The prisoner winced.

"Leave me be," Bessus snarled in Arabic.

Truscott put on sterile gloves. "Come over here and hold him down. Get Bichajian in here, too. Need all of us in case he goes crazy."

Kinahan left and returned with Agent Bichajian. They surrounded Bessus.

Truscott lifted Bessus's upper lip on the right side. "Garbage mouth. Someone get me a mask." He looked inside the prisoner's mouth with a tongue depressor and said, "Tooth abscess. He's got a bunch of rotten roots, broken to the gum. Don't know how he eats. Only got a few left on the bottom. Probably bad, too…"

Morando said, "Asshole can eat porridge for all I care. Not our concern now."

"It will be if the infection travels to his brain. It can do that when it's an eye tooth. He's a high priority prisoner, Top."

"He's got more teeth than the rest around here. All right, we'll get him to a dentist onboard ship later."

"Antibiotics will help for now," Truscott said.

"Wait a second," Bichajian said. "See if we can get him to talk if we trade him for medicine. Professor Fletcher told us he calls the terrorists 'sand warriors', and the United States the 'new Greeks'. I'll keep trying Arabic."

Bichajian asked Bessus, "We will stop your pain. Will you tell us about the plans of the sand warriors?"

Bessus moaned. "My face is on fire. It aches with my heartbeat."

"Tell us how the sand warriors will attack the new Greeks."

"They plot. They name it the color of the sky." Bessus closed his eyes to absorb the throb.

Bichajian leaned in. "A plot called blue?"

Bessus laid his head back. His right eye had shut. "They talk about sky plot. What is blue?"

"The sky is that color. It is called blue."

"Torture me not. They will attack you." Bessus rolled his head side to side. "Blue Sky."

Kinahan said, "Keep him talking."

"Where will they attack the new Greeks?"

"Where they live."

"How many warriors?" Bichajian asked.

Bessus answered, "Many there now."

"This isn't enough," Stone said. "We need details."

Bichajian said, "Tell us about the sky plot, and we will bring medicine to take away your pain."

Bessus yelled, "What charms do you have? I see no medicine men here. Bring me Protha."

"Who the hell is Protha?" Kinahan said.

"Protha. My surgeon from Bactria. We rode with Xerxes. Protha stitched me when I was cut."

"Might be getting delirious," Bichajian said. "He's talking about that Persian king Xerxes from long ago. The one the Greeks kicked the hell out of. You know... like when the Spartans defended that pass."

"Enough of the history lesson," Truscott said. "I'm going to give him the antibiotic in liquid form by spoon before the infection gets worse."

Bessus roared, "Get me Protha, or your medicine man. Deliver me from this agony."

Bichajian said, "What else do you know about the sky plot and we will help you."

"They will attack the city with Greek temples. They said the new Greeks will be slain. The women will be harlots for the warriors. Ahhhh.... the aching eats my head."

Chief Truscott interrupted, "I'm putting a painkiller in his line. Tell him to take my medicine, and we will cure him."

Bichajian said, "Accept the medicine in the spoon, Bessus, and you will be healed. Your teeth rot in your head. Tell us more about the sky plot."

"Shut your faces and give it to me then," Bessus demanded. "I told you what I know."

Bessus swallowed the medicine. Truscott added morphine to the IV line.

Slurring his words, Bessus said, "I only give you aid because the scout told me to. Blue Sky..." His head dropped to his chest, his snores the only sound in the room.

"What scout?" Bichajian asked.

Truscott interrupted, "Helo from the carrier will be here in a half hour. They have an oral surgeon on board. He'll dig out the rest of the rotten teeth while he's asleep."

"I lost a cousin on 9/11 and good Marines in everything since then. Damned if I'm going to let them do it again," Morando said, tightlipped. "He's talking about D.C."

Bichajian said, "He's just become a lot more valuable. I'll buy him some new teeth and a date with those three sisters on TV if he leads us to them."

Stone said, "I thought we were told no more torture. Let's get him to the ship."

33

Bessus awoke tied to a bed.

He struggled against his restraints. Gagging, he spit out bloody rags.

Bessus ran his tongue around his mouth and discovered holes no longer filled by rotten teeth.

He didn't recognize any of the guards who walked into the room until the Greek who'd spoken his words entered the room. "Water, wine," Bessus said, "whatever Greeks drink."

Agent Bichajian said in Arabic, "The rotten teeth have been removed, and they will no longer hurt you."

Groggy still, Bessus shook his head. "My head spins. Where am I?"

"On a ship. The surgeon works here."

"Greeks?"

"No, we are the new Greeks…the Americans."

"Do you bring fire from the sky and see all from above?"

Bichajian tilted his head. "Say again?"

"Don't leave me in here long. I hate to be closed in."

"Speak more slowly. I don't understand your tongue well," Bichajian said.

The door opened. Apollo entered, clad in fatigues and with his hair cut short.

"Take me from here, Scout," Bessus demanded.

"But what shall you eat, Stink-pile?" Apollo asked in Bactrian.

Bichajian said, "Sir, I don't understand what you're…"

"Please leave us," Apollo said. "You'll receive a report."

Bichajian hesitated for a long moment. He closed the door behind him.

Apollo sat beside Bessus's bed and tinkered with the IV tubing. He withdrew a flask from his pocket. "Your mouth is full of holes. Do they hurt?"

"Not like before. I was ready to drive a dagger into my throat. I couldn't stand the pain and a mouth full of pus."

"But how will you eat now?" Apollo asked.

"I know not. They've made me into an old hag with sunken jaws."

"Drink and behold my power." Apollo dribbled the contents of the flask into Bessus's mouth. Apollo sat back with an amused look on his face. "You will notice very soon that the holes will be gone."

Bessus licked his lips and put his head back. After a few hours, he opened his eyes a sliver, and ran his tongue around the interior of his mouth.

Apollo said with a grin, "You are a wonder, Bessus. Whatever shall I do with you?"

Bessus blinked. "How, Scout? How could you heal the holes? You must give this drink to Protha. My men will never fall in battle. I'll make you my advisor."

Apollo threw his head backwards and laughed. "Enough, Bessus. Do my work. Be my spy. Uncover the plot on the new Greeks."

"I told them…the blue-sky plot. The sand warriors will smite their homes and cities."

"That is curious. Why have you not told me about this?"

"I heard the sand warriors talking. They think I don't know their tongue, but I do, at least some of it. Even then, the words make my head ache."

"If you can find out what they plan, I will reward you. How about new teeth?"

"What? You think I am some drooling youngling. There can be no new teeth. How about I smash yours and use them?"

Apollo shook his head. "You never change. The new Greeks will train you to live again among the mountain warriors in the Tora Bora. Still want to kill the Sorceress?"

Bessus thought a moment. "No. I will let her live." *I will choke the life from her and all the curses these Greeks bring to me will be undone.*

"The curses will remain, Bessus. Give up your hatred of her. I know what you think."

Bessus ran his tongue around his mouth again. He felt strings, and he began to spit them out.

"Do my work and you will be able to eat half a steer."

"If I do your work, will you shut up and leave me be?"

Apollo grinned. "A great war draws near. We will bring you back to camp on a flying horse. It will hum and shake beneath you. Don't worry, you'll live."

"Chariots without horses, teeth where there are none, and now chariots with wings. These new Greeks have too much magic or too many inventions. What else do they have?"

Apollo stood. "Something far more important than those inventions. What they fought and died for many times, for themselves and others."

Bessus ran his finger along his gums on the top and bottom jaw. "Your medicine heals me. What do these Greeks fight for? Gold, land, cattle?"

"No, Bessus. They fight to have no king whom they must obey. No ruler who can seize their possessions, jail them at will or slay them and their families."

He waited while Bessus stared up at the ceiling of the room, seeing pipes and valves.

Apollo continued, "They only obey the laws they create for themselves. They decide their own destinies, Bessus."

Bessus said, "Let me up. I want to stretch."

"As you wish," Apollo cut the plastic restraints with shears.

Bessus rose and hit his head on a sloping bulkhead. Apollo seized up with laughter. Bessus rubbed his head.

Apollo asked, "Now that your head is clear, do you wish to be free of Persian bondage?"

Banging a knuckle on the steel hull, Bessus said, "This ship is made of iron or bronze. How does such a ship float?"

"Answer my question. Do you want to be free of Persian rule and be your own man?"

Bessus stamped his bare feet on the ship's deck. "It hums below me, like a nest of bees. And it moves, like it has a heartbeat." He faced Apollo. "I will do your bidding. I want to feel like a New Greek. I will no longer bend a knee to any king."

Motioning with his hand for Bessus to follow him out the door hatch, Apollo said, "Spoken like a true Minuteman. How you have evolved."

"Fancy words. Your mouth is full of them." Bessus raised his eyes to watch the ceiling fan twirl. His index finger followed its circular motion.

Apollo said, "Then I will speak plainly. Until you get rid of the rocks between your ears, a slave you will remain. You cannot be declared a freeman. You must earn it."

Bessus removed his gaze from the fan.

"I am sending you into the nest of snakes. You will root out the leaders and uncover their plans to attack the New Greeks in their homeland. It will seem odd to you that, at times you can speak their language and others, you will not. I control that. Even when the New Greeks tied you down, I controlled what you understood and said."

"Should I slay all the enemies of the New Greeks for you?"

"Not yet. Dead men die with their secrets," Apollo said, tapping on a keyboard. "Find out what they plot, and you will chew meat."

"I would rather good teeth than a room full of gold," Bessus answered.

"Then I will deliver you unto the camp where you trained a few years ago. They have heard stories of your courage, and they trust you. Become the leader's killer and feed the plans back to the Sorceress."

Bessus twisted his head in Apollo's direction.

"Yes, that is what you must do, or you'll spend your days boiling mush. First I must make the people here think you have perished so they'll forget you."

The Bactrian rubbed his wrists, raw from the plastic ties. "Take me back to the Bactrian caves, and they shall know Bessus."

34

Tribal Area/ Tora Bora Mountains/ Afghan/Pakistani Border

NEAR FUTURE

The warrior captain peered at a map. He paced until he drove a dagger into it. Bessus stood to the side, watching the captain scowl and curse.

Other warriors, wearing brown, rough-woven tunics, sat with crossed legs on rugs, their fire sticks resting across their laps. Bessus recognized hardened men. Weather-beaten, with dirt in the creases of their faces and leathery hands, just like him. He could see the ribs of the camp dogs that huddled around the fire. They looked starved, as did the men. A brown, sharp-rocked, and bare landscape lay outside the cave. Fall brought cold winds whipping into the end of a jig-sawed mountainous valley. He understood these men. This was the land in which he had grown up.

Somehow, Bessus understand their words, just as the Scout had told him he would.

The captain said, "The provincial Pakistani military commander is coming after us. Our spy has told us they will launch an attack on our compounds next week… helicopters, rockets and troops. These dogs are the whores of the Americans. That commander must die to buy us time. Blue Sky will occur soon, and we cannot be dispersed or killed."

Another of the turbaned leaders said, "They know all of us. How can we get someone into their base?"

Heads turned toward the bearded giant. One asked, "How could he sneak into camp? The dogs have noses."

The captain asked Bessus, "Will you sacrifice for God? It is His will. He awaits you in Heaven." He handed Bessus an AK-47 and a belt of extra magazines. "Sneak into the camp and kill the commander."

"Bessus does not need your firesticks. I do my work alone, with this." He held up his knife. "I will enter their camp and smite him."

The captain looked at the other leaders. "Give him four days to try. If he doesn't come back, we'll send others to raid their camp. This position must be taken out, so we can move on the bases holding nuclear weapons in Kohat and Peshawar. Take these weapons and we can hold power in these lands or trade them for wealth."

Bessus slashed the air with his curve-tipped knife. "I will deliver unto you the noses and ears of your enemies."

The captain said, "Go then, but how will you get into the camp? They have guard posts with machine guns."

"If the map is good, I know how. I spent many a moon there when I was a boy."

"Do God's will and destroy the unclean."

As Bessus walked away, he heard the captain say, "You others…leave us. Commanders, meet me in my tent. A courier brought us another message about Blue Sky."

Those words again. I must return to discover who sent the message.

Bessus knew the path. Perched above the warriors' camp, he saw they had built a fortress over a cave he had hiked in many times as a boy.

A toothless grin broke his lips.

After journeying through hollow and tunnel, catch-hole and cave vein, he saw little had changed in the Sorceress's realm. Bessus didn't favor thinking of the days when he'd hidden from Persian warriors, scared and hungry.

The Bactrian imagined himself a spider once again.

He climbed towards the bigger cave chamber where warlords long ago had plotted rebellion against the Persians. Staging in the shadows, he followed stone steps into the fort's interior. Guards with their firesticks reclined against a stone wall. Hiding would be harder now. Light torches made the fort look like the noonday sun shone down from above.

Iron chariots sat in rows. He had never seen so many. The first trickle of sweat ran down his back. Each chariot had a slim tree trunk that stuck out from it. Would they vomit fire and destruction upon him?

Crawling to escape their searching eyes, he saw a banner and warriors milling around. He found the commander.

How to draw them away? He slipped through a doorway into another dwelling, checking inside to see if he was alone. Searching the chamber, he found sticks the warriors smoked and the flame bringer they used. Rags in a pile would bring fire. Wooden chairs and rugs would burn, too. In a corner, he found firebombs.

How I crave to see the fire burst and send sparks into the night.

The chamber erupted in flames. He snuck out the door, watching warriors run to the building and then to a dwelling where they pulled out a long snake. Instead of it squirming and biting them, a hard stream of water burst out of it, taming the fire, and making more smoke.

He saw the commander's tent left unguarded. *The mountain gods favor me,* he thought.

Entering, he found as many warriors as he had fingers on one hand huddled around the box that held the tiny people inside. With their attention occupied, he drove his dagger into the back of the neck of the most centered man. The captains turned and reached for short firesticks on their belts. Each man found Bessus's dagger buried in his throat and then withdrawn in a flash. Just as quickly, a handful of noses and sets of ears filled his satchel. Then, he lifted the squares pinned to their chests with the strange Greek writing. He'd been told that these identified the names of the warriors.

Would they know that Bessus had laid them low?

Bessus smashed their talking boxes with Greek writing on them. He peered out the door. The warriors sprayed more water and the smoke lifted skyward. Then, the dwelling lifted into pieces when the firebombs he'd set shattered the walls and sent the warriors fleeing.

He moved towards the hole that led back to his snaking tunnels. Stopping, he danced in a circle. Pleased that he slew the leaders, he took a last look at the destroyed camp. It didn't satisfy enough, though.

No one knew that Bessus had done the work.

He dropped the pile of severed noses and ears on his commander's desk.

"You just snuck up on me, Bessus, so I can see how you could deliver these prizes. But how do I know these are not the ears of shit-smelling goatherders?"

Bessus dug into his satchel and released the cloth with the Greek writing. The commander checked the names.

"You have served us well. You killed all the commanders. You'll be my personal bodyguard. Come with me to the meeting after you've washed. Even the dogs run from you."

A pail of water and a rag did its work. Bessus gummed flat bread, softened by holding it in his cheek. He felt metal stubs on his gums. Many them set along his upper and lower jaws. The Scout had told him to leave them alone until later. Must he always take orders from this overlord with his shining teeth? How he hated him.

Curse those Greeks for taking out the last of my teeth. How can a warrior fight strong slurping mush like a babe?

The commander walked to the cave, Bessus on his heels. He saw men dipping bread into a central bowl of rice and goat meat. The commander bypassed it and sat in front of the box on a table. A man with black hair and irons around his eyes appeared inside the box. It was a face he'd seen on visitors from lands far to the east, beyond where the great-horned beasts dwelled. Shorter people lived there, with dark, narrow eyes.

Bessus had seen this Greek invention a few times now, and he understood that the people did not truly live within, but magically spoke from it. He wondered why his gods, even his dark lord, Mainyu, allowed such inventions, or lacked them? Did his gods have no power here?

"Who is the slit-eyed man you speak to?" Bessus asked.

The commander didn't look up at Bessus until the screen went dark. "He is a healer, and he plots Blue Sky with us."

"A medicine man?"

"Allah be praised, he is, and an American, too."

Understanding now that New Greeks were called Americans, he said, "He betrays his own people. Why do you trust such a man?"

"He is useful to our cause. Together, we will bring destruction upon the Americans."

"How can he do this? With what weapon can he bring down a country by himself?"

The commander brought images onto the box. Bessus stepped back. He could not believe he saw fiery explosions that reached to the sky. "This is his weapon?"

"Just one of such and there will be many. Some will arrive on their shores by ship. Other will fall from the sky. And other weapons that I have heard of may be used, too."

Bessus scratched his beard. "These New Greeks will have their legs cut from underneath them?"

"Not just their legs. We want to cut them from the memories of men for all time."

Later, Bessus stole away into a dark place and pulled out the talk-box Scout had given him to speak with the Sorceress. He would tell her about the plans of the sand warriors. Bessus tapped the buttons in the manner instructed, and Mainyu help him, the Sorceress spoke.

35

San Diego

NEAR FUTURE

Lauren answered the phone. She heard the deep-throated voice on her cell phone. She pressed her fingertips to her lips.

The barbarian said, "Do you know my voice, Sorceress?"

"I do. You must have something important to tell me." Lauren said in ancient Bactrian. She held her breath. She could at least be relieved he was nowhere nearby.

"I bring you word of the Blue Sky, but all I think of is your crushed throat under my hand."

"I don't fear you any longer, Bessus."

"You will. I will invade your dreams, and you'll know that I still come for you."

Lauren held the phone away from her ear for a moment. "What else do you want to tell me?"

"Blue Sky has a master, with narrow eyes and graying hair. He is a medicine man and a New Greek. The New Greeks will be attacked by the sand and mountain warriors and the narrow eyes."

"Wait," Lauren said, "is there more? Where and when will they attack?"

"Where the new Greeks have made buildings that look like the old Greeks had. They will attack with ships, too. Do not die in this attack, Sorceress. I want to slay you myself."

"Does threatening me make you a stronger warrior?"

"I only serve the Scout, so I can find you."

"Get more information for us. Find out where they will attack. Apollo, I mean the Scout, will reward you."

"I must go, yet I will not sleep at peace until…"

The connection ended. Lauren called his name twice, but she received no answer. This was all they had to go on. It would need to be enough.

36

Los Angeles, California

NEAR FUTURE

Alfred Fung pressed the elevator button for the 26th floor in the Steelburg branch building.

The banks and the United States authorities wanted the new drug and the partnership with the Chinese government to get production moving. But, the research and development had progressed farther along than either government imagined.

Neither government would ever receive the drug.

And he was only here to accomplish one important goal.

"Welcome, Mr. Fung," a red-haired, professionally attired, corporate secretary said. "All of the principals are present. Would you care for a beverage?"

Alfred gave her a gratuitous smile. "Oolong would be fine, thank you."

"I'm sure we can accommodate, Mr. Fung. I had hot water prepared for you. Please proceed through the double doors. I'll have tea there in a moment."

After entering the conference room, Alfred shook hands with the attendees. He'd previously met most of the people. A green apple scent masked the odor of newly installed carpet. In front of him on the mahogany table sat a clear-faced folder with the heading on the front page:

IPO Proposal
Steelburg Voleur
Prospectus Initial Public Offering
Company Neurocitin Ricedon
500 million shares at $100 share

A tall executive, with professionally dyed dark hair and a fringe of gray on the sides, stood while the others settled into leather chairs. His red and blue striped necktie sported the tightest knot. His dark-gray suitcoat draped unbuttoned to unencumber the growing girth in his midsection. He wore narrow gold-rimmed reading glasses. Anthony Ladros had risen through the ranks of one of the largest investment banks in the world. He had navigated the wickets of fixed income and currencies to be senior vice president until his boss retired unexpectedly with a heart condition. Now, as chairman and CEO, his decisions made impact within the convoluted gears of government, business and the economy.

"Good afternoon. For those here from New York and D.C., I appreciate your efforts to conduct this meeting in LA." Ladros gestured to Alfred. "Dr. Fung. Thank you for attending. We look forward to the completion and execution of this project."

The secretary entered with bottles of water and a steaming cup of water with a tea bag hanging over the edge by a string. She left and closed the double set of doors behind her.

Barbarians have no idea how to make a decent cup of tea, Alfred thought.

Alfred said, "Thank you, Mr. Ladros. I appreciate your efforts to accommodate my schedule. As you know, I'll be leaving for China to coordinate the laboratory quality controls and train the technicians. We look forward to progress on our research and then onto a fast-track status with the FDA. Of course, in China we will be able to come to market sooner."

Ladros sat and took a sip of water. "Then let us proceed. As you know, I represent Steelburg in this endeavor." He gestured to his right. "Mr. Thomas Crevinski is from the Council."

Alfred had only met Crevinski once. He remembered his bald head and close-clipped beard. The heavy bags under his eyes betrayed an early wake-up from an East Coast flight the day before. In other meetings, subordinates had attended. Crevinski represented a vast network of politicians, corporations, investment bankers, and diplomats, who influenced global trade and foreign policy worldwide.

Alfred knew who they were. He despised how they influenced presidents, political parties and foreign governments. *They will fall into my snare, too, and realize the loss of everything they thought they owned and ruled.*

"Of course, Ms. Laurie Hayworth, our Chief Financial Officer, is here from our company and will coordinate with the FDA," Ladros said. Hayworth greeted him and resumed typing on her laptop. Alfred noticed a large diamond on her ring finger.

Ladros continued, "And this is Mr. Thomas Fischer. He represents Homeland Security." A stone-faced man with an old-style buzz-cut hair style, and dressed in a red tie and Navy blazer, sat at the table with his hands folded. He acknowledged the introduction with a nod.

Ladros waved his hand to draw everyone's attention to the weather outside. "Love this California weather. It takes one's mind off the recent troubling events in Athens."

"I'm so happy that attack was thwarted," Hayworth said, "A lot of lives saved, as well as the Parthenon, too. What an incredible act of courage by that professor from San Diego State."

Alfred didn't respond. He matched the tips of his fingers and silently fumed at the unbelievable improbability of the destruction of their Plan A. The professor had ruined years of planning and caused them to shift to a second plan which would require attacks on different sites. Saabir, their liaison, had been killed. Most of all, security and police forces would be on alert now, and he would need to tread more carefully.

Ladros sat. "Now the market correction is well along and nearing the end. Financially, we encountered more downside with the attack, but we take no joy in that. It's scary for the public, too. We could have riot if we force the market go down any further."

He took a quick drink of water. "There are many risks globally and within our country. A tipping point approaches and a stable world is what we desire. One that is controllable and predictable. We watched very carefully the reaction of the public to this last sell-off. I trust your handlers made you quite a fair sum on the correction, Dr. Fung?"

Alfred, still ruminating over the blown plot and de-sequencing of the Athens powder keg, snapped back into the conversation. "Oh, yes. We exited the market at the high with your instructions and placed our puts. Since you say that markets will begin to rally soon, we will certainly exit those puts and buy stocks to rise again."

"Glad we could be of help. Now, could you report on the development of your facilities in China? The construction time tables of the Mississippi plants are ahead of schedule. We're working the staff day and night. This will be one the most life-changing drugs since penicillin."

"The superstructure was already in place in Chongqing, and so the internal improvements could be started on right away." Fung paused and looked at the others present. "Staff is already functioning. My additional teams will begin to work there and then bring our improvements back to the Mississippi plant. Just like politics is compared to making sausage, so is testing a drug like this one. Of course, that will be far more easily done in China."

Ladros drummed his fingers on the table. "I prefer to think of all the lives that will be saved."

Hayworth stopped typing. "Worldwide, billions of people will need this miracle drug. You are to be commended, Dr. Fung, along with your research staff. Have there been any improvements you could relay to us?"

Alfred opened his attaché case and withdrew one of two paper-clipped sets of pages. He glanced carefully at which set he slipped out.

"I won't get too deep into biochemistry, but as you know, a great deal of government money went into mapping and understanding the brain in recent years. Many of you here today may in the future suffer from some form of dementia."

Ladros broke in. "Happens to me every Sunday the New York Giants lose."

A chorus of laughter followed.

Alfred continued, "Over five years ago, we discovered that protein deposits in the brain contribute to memory loss and dementia. Perhaps I can explain it this way. There's a small area of the brain stem that releases norepinephrine. That's a neural transmitter that regulates heart rate, but also attention and memory. Norepinephrine is good for you and helps to protect those nerve pathways, so you can think and remember.

That small area of the brain stem, called the *locus coeruleus,* sends out little branches into other areas of the brain. Those branches are so connected, they are susceptible to alterations in the health of the brain... say infections, fatigue...etc."

Crevinski said, "I was going into medicine until Latin got the better of me."

Alfred ignored the joke. He scanned his audience to see if he had lost their attention.

"The locus coeruleus show the first signs of protein entanglement, or blockage," Fung said, "reactions to infections, or inflammation, can cause opportunistic beta-amyloid proteins to clog up the network so less norepinephrine is released."

Ladros pushed back his chair. "Perhaps I could explain this in more layman terms. The brain pathways get clogged up like under the kitchen sink and you need some Drano to clean it out."

It's so hard to deal with non-scientists. These idiots only care about money. Just like grandfather had told us. Alfred said, "Natural remedies like oil of oregano and probiotics are helpful. Mentally challenging stimulation helps as you age, along with plenty of sleep. During this restful state, the brain works to rid itself of this damaging beta-amyloid protein. Worry too much about the stock market and don't get enough sleep, you've begun the process of your own demise."

Hayworth said, "We all lose sleep worrying about life."

Alfred smirked. He enjoyed twisting the knife into these corrupt capitalists. "Work too much, overstressed, pretty soon you've added twenty to thirty extra pounds and now you have sleep apnea, making the problem worse."

Crevinski looked at the bulge over his belt.

Fung said, "Before I make you all self-conscious and running for a vegan lunch, understand that the amyloid can build up for other reasons. Old age contributes to the problem in that the brain loses connections. We get an inflexibility of the pathways, like how you're your knees go out when you turn sixty."

"Not there yet, but your examples are getting a bit personal for us," Ladros said, taking a drink.

Alfred grinned. "I want you to understand how this drug works. *Right now, I could feed them shit and they would eat it.*

"All right, Doctor, you've scared the heck out of us," Ms. Hayworth said.

Alfred took out a flash drive and held it up. "Would you like to see an example of our tests in China? You are all already aware of our successful trials tested and confirmed within the FDA in this country. We have exceeded our expectations so far in our testing. This is highly confidential. There will be no copies and only the principals in this room may see it."

Eager faces agreed. He inserted the thumb drive into Hayworth's laptop.

A room with fifty beds revealed itself. Gown-draped elderly, male and female, lay in their beds with blank looks. Some walked aimlessly. A few orderlies helped to corral them from pressing against each other into a corner of the room. Cries and wailing could be heard in Chinese. The camera scanned individual faces, staying with them for a time.

Hayworth pressed her palms to her cheeks in dismay, "This is terrible. I don't know if I can watch this. My aunt succumbed to this horrible disease. We must be sensitive…"

Alfred interrupted, "Please be patient. Notice the camera is focused on the faces so that you can recognize them after each treatment. I will begin to forward through phases one through three. Since we're going at double speed, you will begin to see increased activity among the ones who are currently bedridden."

The third phase treatment showed most patients roaming within the room and others talking, a few practicing Tai Chi, many staring out the window or reading.

"Extraordinary," Hayworth chirped. "They're revived."

Alfred continued through phase ten. "We put the medicine in their water. You will see testing up to phase three, and then we will fast forward as we take the medicine away. They revert back, though more slowly."

Ladros slapped the table. "This is remarkable. They need the drug on a continuous basis...to stay alert. That's good for our equity partners."

After halting the video, Alfred removed the thumb drive. He placed it back in his attaché. "We have to titer concentrations for weight, age, and other medical conditions. Estimates are that this will be medication people take each day after age forty to keep them from developing dementia. There is also some positive result of an increase in acuity and brain function for younger patients. Should that be developed, think of the scientific advances that will result from a smarter, more alert population? Do you have any questions?"

Crevinski coughed and cleared his throat. "This is all quite remarkable. I will explain what I've seen to the co-chairman. Globally, we will be able to disperse this medicine to markets we deem profitable at first. Are there other applications for the distribution of this drug?"

You don't know how right and how wrong you are. What is your true goal, Mr. Crevinski? Wait till I snare them with what's next? I must ensure they will complete the transaction today.

"There is something else. Can the people we have in this group be trusted completely? This next conclusion is significant. I know we have representatives of the US government here." Alfred gestured towards Fischer.

The Homeland Security agent Fischer said, "Now I know why I was called to attend this meeting."

"I speak for everyone here. This group is secure," Ladros said.

Alfred continued, "Our governments would be best working together on this project. But consider the problems we both have with control. The economy has faltered. Insurrection is a distinct possibility. How will our country, and the PRC, control riots, killings, mob rule and rebellion?

Instability favors neither of us. Trade and understanding will bring us forward. I want to read to you the latest research."

He flipped the cover page of the laboratory results.

"Subjects of all ages had been tested. In increased doses, the medicine for dementia and Alzheimer's caused extreme suggestibility. That means we could control thoughts. Control thoughts and you can control actions, or cause inaction. No ridiculous Cold War attempts at mind control. This has tremendous promise. Along with new antibiotics to prevent these dementia diseases, we have a powerful combination."

"Wait. Let me get this straight. This wonder drug you're developing can control populations, if necessary?" Fischer asked.

"Not yet, but with further testing, it could," Alfred answered.

"What else it could do," Crevinski said, "is keep the proper politicians in office. No more loose cannons. The approved policies of the Council would be continued by Congress. We know we're moving towards a global community. Soon enough, we'll have a global currency. We'll set the value of money at the World Bank and International Monetary Fund. No more boom and busts. No more war. We'll decide how politicians run their countries. We'll have control over advanced weaponry, fanatics… and gain international peace."

"People will invest as we direct them to," Ladros said. "We, as banks, always end up on top. If you haven't figured that out by now, you must be infantile. It is in the end a partnership, but the economic ship doesn't move without our sails."

"More than that, the development of Artificial Intelligence, or AI, will have a profound effect going forward," Crevinski said. "There will be a reduced need for population as robotics advances exponentially. We must consider how will we manage eight or nine billion people in the future, and the earth resources necessary to support that number. There must be some new thinking on this problem."

"However," Fischer said, "none of this would be distributed unless the situation became dire, correct?"

Crevinski intertwined his fingers. He looked away. "Of course."

Alfred said, "I will have additional laboratory results for you in a month. You'll be able watch the medicine change lives for the better. If you like what you've seen here, I propose we complete the transaction as arranged."

All I need to do is wave dollars and power before you and you gorge like the pigs. Only you will never realize any of it, because within a few days you will all be dead.

"I believe we have an agreed upon amount," Alfred said.

"The equivalent of three hundred million dollars converted to Yuan," Hayworth said, tapping on her laptop keys. She looked at the others in the room. Each gave a nod of approval. "Please sign the documents, Mr. Fung. After you do so, Mr. Ladros will oblige."

"I'll be able to draw on it immediately for expenses in completing the facility," Alfred said, signing multiple pages. "I expect to bring you all over to my facility for a tour in about three months. I should have the final testing done and a production line in place. At that point, we will have systemic reviews of results and you can begin your FDA process."

"This will change the world as we know it," Ladros said. "We'll create the perfect market conditions for the IPO. It will soar, and everyone will be quite pleased. It will be hailed as the new wonder drug that will improve, even save, lives."

"I'm sending the funds by interbank wire," Hayworth said. "Confirmation arriving."

Alfred stood. "You will not believe the plans we have for this and other drugs. People like you and I will be privy to life-lengthening and mind-expanding medicine. You will live longer and more vibrant lives. Welcome to the future."

All shook his hand.

He said before leaving, "I will be in L.A. for another day to attend a biotech conference, and then I'm heading to China. Please contact me if you have any questions. Goodbye, for now."

Alfred entered the elevator and withdrew a hand-delivered, confidential second report from Lian, his head technician, and more recently, his wife.

Alfred, my love,

I have news. The ramifications are significant. Work on compounds in the arena of glia receptors has yielded astounding progress. We stimulated glia receptors in the brain to eradicate the plague build-ups, but it failed clinically, at first. Now, we have tested halting beta-amyloid plague buildup, instead, and this has shown great progress. What I'm telling you is, we can hit the disease from both directions now.

Of course, neither the Americans, or the Chinese government, will ever receive the effective chemistry, anyway. Only we'll have that. We can eliminate the disease and potentiate it as needed, to be a game-changing medicine to influence global mindset according to our specific controls. Many of the subjects succumbed during the testing, but we now have specific confirmed dosages by age, sex, and weight. We have also tittered specific dosages to destroy our enemies. The results can be effective in a week, or sooner, depending on how you want them to be eliminated.

I cannot wait for your return. I have other news for you.

The sanctuary is ready. Supplies have been maximized. The chosen comrades are boarded and producing on a low dosage of the control drug at this point. As well, our more clandestine goal of controlling the development of all artificial intelligence will be a secondary benefit

We will have it all. We will control all. The world is ours for the taking.

Come back to me quickly. Lian

The world would soon enter a period of chaos, and Alfred Fung held the future in his hands.

He, his father, and the renewed party would be the cause of a period of great transition. They had the sanctuary in place, the people they wanted to educate, and now a great deal of extra cash that would be immediately converted to gold, silver, and diamonds. They owned the local bank outside the Chongqing facility, and the brokerage house. Every detail had been worked out for the 'New Long March'.

And now, they possessed the drug that would give them control over what remained of the population of the world- every leader, every important politician or scientist, general or soldier. Upgraded and supplied, the extensive network of caves had plenty of room and resources to survive the Western purge.

A drug to control the submission of the conquered and create a workforce to fulfill the goals of the people. Designed to advance the class struggle that will destroy the capitalists once and for all.

I will be a global master and unstoppable when populations are cleansed. I will control the development of artificial intelligence and advancing technology and save humanity from self-destruction. I will control birth rates. The augmented and biologically advanced people will exist and advance our cause only at my direction.

I am sorry, my father, my Die, your dream of a nation for the people, pure communism, will not come to reality. It always fails. I will skip the rebellions and purges. I will be the master.

Lian. You are a genius. In a matter of days, I will return to you.

37

San Diego, California.

NEAR FUTURE

Zack lathered jam on a flaky croissant, gazing out at Lake Murray from their backyard. Lauren set two cups of coffee on the patio table.

"Thanks. Can I snag an orange off the tree for you?" Zack said.

"Sure. Any ideas on what you want to do from here?" she asked.

"Depends on what Apollo has in mind. There's a reason he sent me to the past and to Thera. I have to warn our people that disaster is on the way…"

"Look. Not that I don't get it, but could we talk about something positive. I'm so happy you're here."

"Afterwards… whatever is afterwards, I'll go back to teaching and research at State. I'm realizing how much I miss it, but there's something else I've been thinking about…"

"I'm listening."

Zack returned and sliced the orange in quarters. "I think we should take our educational experience national, even international."

"You mean what we learned from history firsthand, less the time travel?"

"Yes, but also how the intellect and experiences of ancient peoples guides us forward."

"Will people listen? It can't be just about bookwork. We must make it interesting, entertaining. How about we bring back the Academy of Plato, or Aristotle's Lyceum? Have students dress in the period and learn like Alexander the Great did?"

"Join it with modern technology. Maybe have a holographic image of Socrates, asking them questions about the challenges of modern life?"

"I like it but going back to State is going to be tricky at first. You haven't explained where you've been for five years. Now, you intend to go to the media like a soothsayer and warn everyone about war."

Zack set down the knife. "I have to. We must. Only we know. So many lives could be saved. We have to figure a way to alert everyone but not create panic."

"That's not going to be easy." Lauren blew strands of hair away from her face.

"How about I tell the truth?" Zack picked up the morning paper and sorted out the sections until he settled on the business pages.

Lauren fixed her gaze on him. "Seriously?"

"I know. The quack professor who thinks he traveled in time and knows the future."

"How soon will the whole thing begin?"

Zack showed her the front page. "The stock market has been going down for a couple of weeks. Apollo told me that one of the signs is a market crash."

"What if it's just a correction? What if…"

"Honey, I think it's already begun. We need to do something. Take a chance. If they think I'm a fool, so what?"

"State called. They want to speak with you. Ditto the local news. We're going to bring a media storm down upon us if it goes national."

"Kind of what we want."

Lauren looked out at Lake Murray. "We need some fast media training. What are you going to say?"

A new voice said, "I volunteer to guide you."

They turned to see Apollo. He stood behind them. Lauren looked stunned. "Oh, my…"

"...God," Apollo supplied.

"You're back," Lauren said, rising.

Apollo sat. He folded his hands. "How good it is to see you together."

Zack held Lauren's hand. "We're grateful for that. So much has happened, a lot of it unpleasant."

The breeze coming up the hillside caused Apollo's forelock to flutter. He tucked it behind his ear. "I apologize for the discomfort and the insecurity you both felt. Despite the attacks and the temptations, the calculated choices you had to make, here you are...together."

Lauren looked squarely at Apollo. "You better apologize. You've made a mess of our lives. I'm coming to terms with it. Zack has told me everything about what happened to him, even with Io in Mycenae. I'm bruised some, but I guess... this is all for a reason. At least, it better be."

Apollo picked up one of the orange quarters and asked permission to eat it by holding it up. He bit into it, making sounds of enjoyment. After swallowing, he said, "I recognize your plight but, I must change the subject. Let us take stock of what we know."

"Are you aware I had a call from Bessus?" Lauren said, handing Apollo a napkin for the juice on his chin.

"Tell me what he said?"

"How come you don't know?" Lauren asked.

Zack said, "I still can't wrap my head around that monster talking on a cell phone and..."

"We'll try not to get off subject, and I have told Zack not to suppose that I am a god of Homer."

"That bears more discussion," Lauren said.

Apollo held up his hand. "Back to Bessus, for the moment, if you please."

Lauren exhaled with a hint of annoyance. "He said that Blue Sky is the invention of a medicine man with narrow eyes and the attacks of the warriors and this doctor are coordinated."

Apollo said, "I know from history that a devastating terrorist attack did occur, but the weakening of the economy and the financial collapse was never described in detail. Only that it happened concurrently. We must stop both."

"Bessus says he still wants to kill me."

"He's a bag of wind. That will never happen."

"I've told you before. You've never been under his grip."

"True, and may I say in front of your husband that you are a formidable warrior yourself."

Lauren didn't smile. She was not feeling assured or amused.

Apollo said, "I see you are upset, Golden Hair, but I want both of you to consider your successes." He peered at Lauren. "Golden Hair courageously brought the children here. You thwarted the threats of Bessus and now communicate with him in a way no one else can. This might lead to something helpful."

Zack stood, positioned himself behind Lauren, and massaged her shoulders. "I owe Lauren everything. Without her, without being able to think of her, I doubt I could have survived all the uncertainty. I didn't believe I could return to this time."

Lauren clasped one of Zack's hands. "Enough of the mutual admiration society, already. I don't need the shining."

"Traveler also had his moments. He fought many battles and helped guide those escaping Thera to safety and a new life."

"At least I can remember most of it now. Did you know, Lauren, that he barred my memory for a long time? Couldn't remember anything, and it drove me nuts. I can't use it as an excuse, but I can only say I felt disjointed, unsure. May have led to a lot that happened between…"

Lauren said abruptly, "We don't need to go there again, Zack." *I really don't want to.*

Zack said, "I'm just saying, I'm thinking more clearly now. A lot more is coming back to me. Sometimes, I didn't know if I was dreaming or not."

"I planted those dreams," Apollo said, "each for a reason. Tell me, Traveler, do you recall the dream I sent you when you and Lauren met in the restaurant in the Plaka?"

"I do," Lauren broke in, "that dream kept my sanity." She raised her face to the warm sun.

Zack sat down again. "I remember now. I was limping, I think, bandaged and telling Lauren about the coming attacks and destruction of the US. I was bandaged, because…"

Apollo interrupted, "Another of your accomplishments, stopping an attack on Athens and on the Parthenon as we've all recently seen on television. You killed Saabir, one of the plotters. Of course, this occurred recently in reality, and the devastation would have been far worse without Traveler's heroism."

"Yes," Lauren replied. "You told me I couldn't say anything about it, having known about it in advance five years ago."

Apollo said to Zack, "Near death when I found you…"

Zack stood suddenly. He pinched the bridge of his nose. "They were going to cut off my head. Saabir told his henchman to shut up, and he was going on about the planned attacks. Wait…"

"What?" Lauren stood, too, grasping Zack's hand.

"They were talking about money. The Parthenon attack was their doing. It wasn't sanctioned by the other planners. Money had been sent through different countries, including China. Holy…"

"Dig deep, Traveler. You must draw it out."

"There was a name that Saabir mentioned. Chinese name. Can't remember it. Have to think about it."

The Olympian stretched out on the grass.

"What are you doing?" Lauren said, surprised by his behavior.

"I'm weary." Apollo put his hands under his head and immediately fell asleep.

"Apollo?" Zack said.

No response. His eyes remained closed. Apollo's lips revealed neither pleasure nor distress. His chest rose and fell.

Zack reached out to shake his shoulder, but quickly withdrew his hand, keenly aware of the burning sensation emanating from Apollo's dome shield. He asked, "Do gods sleep?"

Lauren pointed at an unexpected image. "What on earth is that?"

Video projected from Apollo's medallions, but not like on a cinema screen. The image looked three dimensional.

A room full of computers and subdued red lights. Zack walked into the image.

"Is it Apollo's memory, or a dream?" he asked.

Lauren placed her hand through the projection. "It's like a holographic image, but more real."

A group of people, dressed in gray clothing, formed a semi-circle in front of large monitor. A woman with Asian features stood in front. She spoke and gestured to the group, but her words couldn't be heard. The room looked enclosed, like they were in a bank vault with a circular metal door locking them in.

Another of the group, an older Asian man, kept turning and looking at the door, as if waiting for someone to enter the enclosure. Zack looked more closely at the people--two additional women and four men. He could move through them, like they were ghosts. One, taller than the others, turned. Zack gasped. The man possessed Apollo's features, except for his dark hair, almost black, like that of Calchas, one of Apollo's alter egos, but curlier. Same muscular build. No forelock. The representation of Apollo looked beyond Zack.

The Asian woman gestured towards the monitor. Zack wanted to know what they saw. The people had looks of wonder on their faces as they gazed at the Statue of Liberty.

Zack said quietly, in case he disturbed the images somehow, "Lauren, you need to see this."

She walked deeper into the holographic projection "This is so…weird. Is he letting us see this for a reason?"

"It's like they're seeing the Statue of Liberty for the first time. Who are these people?"

The image disappeared.

Zack yelled, "Wait. Wake up, Apollo, or turn it back on. We want to see what happens. Is that the Asian guy Bessus talked about?"

38

San Diego, California

NEAR FUTURE

Zack watched Apollo's chest rise and fall in a rapid cadence. His legs kicked. His face contorted.

"Is he having a seizure?" Lauren asked. "Put something between his teeth, or he'll bite his tongue in half."

"Gods can't have seizures," Zack said, looking for a stick anyway. "Can they?"

Apollo gasped and awakened.

Zack said, "What the hell just happened? You were in a room with other people, looking at the Statue of Liberty on a computer screen, and then it shut off."

Apollo held up his hand. "It's about time you understand."

"You were reacting violently to the dream. What was upsetting you?"

Standing, Apollo stretched. "I am refreshed."

"You're refreshed, and we're confused as hell," Lauren said.

"Allow me to clarify. No one has seen the past like you both have. Freedom has chosen you. One might not think of an ideal having life, memory or motivation, or even a course of selection, but it does. Freedom chooses heroes to preserve her. You and Golden Hair, and others whom you know, must fight to keep her alive."

Lauren looked at Zack with concern. "What comes next?"

"Countering the threats from without, but more so, stopping them from within, too."

"And you've seen all this? This has already happened?" Lauren asked.

Apollo looked to the sky. "You have to imagine a world where your country no longer exists. It is mostly uninhabitable from the horrors of radiation contamination. Worldwide, there are no voices for justice or equality. The population of the earth is either elite or slaves, like the empires of old. We have come full circle. The experiment of free people has been trampled. Buried in the days ahead. Only the tyrannical aristocracy will know that the United States existed. Freedom will be erased from the minds of mankind."

Zack asked, "We decided on the course of our culture and failed… aren't we responsible for the fall."

Apollo winked. "Now, you're thinking. Your greed and excesses brought about your failure. Remember Nothing to Excess and Know Thyself, the simple attributes chiseled into the temple wall at Delphi? Adherence to those ideals; that is what will save you."

"Know Thyself? I don't know *myself* any more. I'm not the same man who left for Greece with Lauren."

"Dear Traveler, it does not mean to selfishly discover you like some overindulged flower child I saw in your historical record. It is more understanding that there is a balance to nature. You must know that mortals have great potential, but also limitations. Refrain from hubris, of overwhelming pride and arrogance."

Apollo wrapped an arm over Zack's shoulder. "Fear not, both of you will only fight for this cause if you accept that you're already dead."

Zack set his hands on his hips. "If you know the future, then are you telling us that we're going to die fighting for this cause?"

Lauren said, "I'm not accepting that. There's always…"

Apollo encircled Lauren's shoulder and drew her close, too. "Hope."

"Accept death and give us hope at the same time?" Zack looked afar for a moment. "When the country is saved, what will you gain?"

"I ask for nothing. I achieve everything," said Apollo.

Zack and Lauren glanced at each other.

"Are you committed, Traveler? Benjamin Franklin wondered if you were. I brought you to the Land of the Dead to understand conviction from Martin Luther King."

A band of light beamed from one of Apollo's medallions. The image of a goddess appeared.

Lauren stepped back and blurted, "What the hell?"

Tyche's figure wavered in the breeze.

"She is the goddess Tyche," Apollo said. "She rules your life, as much as I do, and yet she complicates mine also in ways I cannot describe."

Lauren inched closer. She extended her hand into the image. "She's... transparent, too."

Apollo said, "Do not insult her by assuming she is not whole or real. You will suffer the consequences of her anger. You know too well that she's the goddess of fortune and chance. Insult her at your peril."

Zack passed his hand through her illuminated image. It reminded him of the projection from an antique movie camera. Tyche didn't voice her disapproval.

Apollo approached the edge of their property, which overlooked Lake Murray. Tyche followed his movements. "You cannot deny her, nor change her ways. Even I cannot. She is reality, and she is life, Traveler."

"What do you mean?" Zack asked.

"Life cannot be predicted, exactly, not even by me." Apollo appeared to concentrate his thoughts and the goddess disappeared. "Even I do not know for sure what will happen next."

Lauren frowned. "I'm confused as hell. You made her go away. You're a god, but you don't know everything, nor can you totally control the future, or her. Gods aren't what they used to be."

Apollo threw his head back. His laughter echoed across the landscape. "Oh my, Golden Hair, it will be such a shame to lose you. I have come to enjoy your irresistible innocence."

"Lose me? Enough condescension. Who are those people in the... video?" she asked.

"What you saw were my memories. Hurtful, yet ones I hold onto because they inspire and give comfort, too."

"What I saw happened... to you?"

"Yes. You witnessed when we discovered the Book of Histories."

Zack said, "You're kidding me. The Book you've mentioned before is a computer record?"

"It's what we called it." Apollo watched birds take flight over the lake.

Lauren said, "Greek gods work with computers?"

"The Chinese name." Zack separated from Lauren and started walking in circles.

"What are you talking about, Zack?"

"The name was Chou or Chung, or maybe Fong or Feng," Zack halted. He fixed his gaze on Apollo. "The name of the Chinese connection Saabir spoke about. He could be the missing link."

Zack and Lauren simultaneously said, "Computer."

They dashed inside. Apollo remained.

Lauren logged onto their desktop computer.

News headline on the screen: Stock market continuing to correct. Down another 460 points.

Their eyes met.

She typed in Dr. Chou. A long list of physicians and dentists came up.

"How do we wade through all these names?" Zack asked.

"Bessus said it was an older man who wore glasses."

"Cut our work in half. We'll have to look at all their pictures. He could be anywhere. How do we narrow this down?"

"I could go on all the usual social media pages and screen them. I'll work on it while you go to your news conference. What're you going to say?"

Zack picked up a computer printout. "How do you tell people that the world as they know it is about to end?" He set a paper clip on the pages to keep them in order. "How long before the public thinks I'm nuts?"

Lauren continued to search for a lead. "Chou. Does this doctor have some special skill that would enable him to make a nuke or something similar?"

"Good idea. Look for Chou's that are nuclear scientists, not necessarily M.D.'s."

"Nothing so far. Are you sure of the name?"

"Have to think about it. I'm heading to the TV station, and I'd like you to go with me."

"Absolutely. I can search the laptop on the way there."

"What about Apollo?"

Zack dashed through the house to the backyard. He found Apollo seated on a lounge chair, looking out at the lake. "Are you staying here? I'm going to the TV station for an interview."

"I took you to Thera to have some experience with societies that refuse or cannot comprehend the peril they're in. Your countrymen may not, either."

"But I must try."

"And you should. But there may come a time for a decision, and warnings will do no good. We must act, no matter how hopeless our chances. No matter the cost. This is our duty."

"Will you be here when we return?"

Apollo crossed his feet. "This is comfortable. I must think upon our next actions. Remember that the future was altered when you stopped the attack in Athens. Instigating that, I complicated matters for myself to buy time. There may be variables and changes we cannot anticipate because I changed the course of events. If I am not here, then I will contact you shortly."

"How much time do we have before…"

"Not long. Mere days, so steel yourselves for the unexpected."

San Diego

NEAR FUTURE

When Lauren and Zack departed, Apollo relaxed on the chair, with his hands clasped behind his head. He drifted off to sleep, yearning once again to be with his lost colleagues. How he missed them. How he missed their wise counsel. The gods.

Loneliness. Should his plan succeed, the peace would be saved, temporarily. However, no one understood the plight, the effort, the risk all the gods had taken to create this one opportunity to change the past.

He craved just a short conversation with Zeus and Hera, to gaze into their calm faces and to partake of their wisdom.

His eyes closed. He remembered when he was a lad and his life was one of horror.

A stern sounding voice announced, "All twelve-year-old's line up in twos, by race."

Apollo held his twin sister's hand. No one knew what happened at the evaluation for those who didn't make the grade. Ada's bottom lip quivered. In the brief moments they had to speak to each other, she had told him that her test had gone well. He hadn't seen her in a year. Her wavy brown hair had been cut short, as if a bowl had been put over her head and snipped around in an even line. Taller than most others, like him, she stood out among her group. Behind their line, others of different races waited for their direction to proceed.

She whispered to him, "They seek to train us for other tasks. I told them I could not do what they asked. I know my grades were good, but they said I'd be better as a concubine."

Apollo started to speak…

From the speaker, "Talking is not approved. Silence is demanded."

Apollo held his breath. The lines moved forward. He couldn't hold Ada's hand any longer. Robotic technicians checked portable screens and dished off the applicant to one side or the other. The students had been warned not to make any noise and to accept their assignments. After receiving their orders, they would drink their first cup of medicine—a vaccination, they were told, against a disease that killed young people.

Only ten persons away from the front of the line and directed to be where he would spend the rest of his life, a young man dropped to floor, shouting, "I won't go!"

Gray–uniformed guards tapped electrified sizzle-prods on the student's thigh. He screamed and bounced off the stone floor. They dragged him away by his feet. Only a few spots away from the door, Apollo peered past the portal on his side. He saw a pool of blood gathering beneath the head of the complainer.

His time had come. He stood in front of expressionless robots, painted black. One peered up at him.

"You," the mechanized man stated. "Stand over there. You're going to the Science Academy."

Apollo saw a few others off to the side. A girl from the subcontinent cowered in a corner with a light-skinned female. He saw his sister reach the portal. She attempted to wave to him, but a live guard grabbed her arm. She and another girl of attractive features were led off to a corridor. It was the last he saw of her.

The dream scrambled but continued to another scene.

Apollo sat strapped inside a transport with seven other laboratory-dressed scientists of varying age and race. The junior researchers, like him, all came from the sub-races.

A husband and wife, born of the Chosen Ones, led the team, along with an Overseer named, Hongwei. He was born of the Chosen as well and reported directly to the Council.

The Overseer, sitting by himself within the sleek confines of the transporter, stared at his monitor. Apollo had not worked with some of the other scientists before. The team leaders had been his mentors for a couple of years. Multiple teams had been sent on this same mission. Apollo's group would continue study on a site that had been given high priority by the Council.

He'd been told that the trip would only take a few hours to travel between the Homeland and the conquered lands.

That was all they'd been told.

Apollo folded his hands. He asked Borfan, the husband and senior scientist, if he could know anything more about the work ahead.

Borfan momentarily peered at his wife and colleague, Chin, before he answered, "You will know soon enough. It is best to meditate on the State's philosophical axioms while we travel. We will arrive soon. This vehicle is the newest improvement."

Apollo had never been in a transport before. He'd never even left the science building that had been his home for the last fifteen years.

After arriving and disembarking, he walked with his colleagues down a dimly-lighted corridor. The guards, armed with holstered laser pistols, saluted Hongwei, and ignored the scientists.

Hongwei stopped to speak with the armed men. Afterwards, an elevator delivered them twenty floors down into the complex. The doors opened, and they stood before an enormous circle of steel.

"What's it for?" Apollo asked Borfan.

Borfan whispered, "A blast door against attack."

"Whatever is in there must be important." Apollo touched the metallic doorway.

"It took eight teams to get to this point. You see clear hallways and order, but years of work has delivered us to be able decipher the puzzle of the laboratory beyond that steel door. No one has been able to turn on the computers inside."

"What happened to the other crews?"

As Hongwei walked up to the team, a chime sounded. "Time to change your medication."

Apollo and each of the scientists removed their jackets. On each of their right arms, a square portal had been surgically implanted on the skin. It leads to a subcutaneous receptacle to dispense medication. Chin removed the spent chip and snapped a new one into the receiver.

Hongwei said, "Go to work. Be diligent. Sleep is unimportant. We must unlock the secrets here."

He went back into the elevator. Apollo asked quietly in Borfan's ear. "What happened to the other teams?"

"You ask too many questions too soon. It is not healthy, nor allowed."

The dream jumbled briefly but resumed to reveal a laboratory within the steel vault.

Apollo remembered that, months later, after running her new code-breaking software twenty-four hours a day, Chin cracked the computer log-in. She yelped, but then stifled it. Borfan ran and hugged her. He put a finger to his lip, motioning quiet. He did the same to everyone in the enclave.

He said in a low voice. "We don't want to get our overseer unnecessarily excited about our progress. What if it's nothing? He is under pressure to produce results, and he will be angry if there is nothing of value. All of you, stand back for now."

Apollo moved with the others to a far corner. He saw Borfan kneel beside his wife and begin to scan what emerged up on the monitor. Borfan smiled, cast a furtive glance at his team, and began to write notes.

Paper notes. Why? Apollo thought. *Text could be easily spoken into software.*

Chin came over after an hour. "We will need weeks to study the sample. Everyone, go to sleep and be prepared for long days. Do not speak a word about this. Understood?"

Another memory of Apollo's fellow gods surfaced, a month later, on the day that changed *everything*.

Apollo had been called to the enclave to meet with Chin and Borfan. The metallic door sealed shut after he entered. They directed him to sit, staring at him with their almond–shaped eyes. Their countenances reflected angst. Chin took a deep breath and began to speak. Borfan raised his hand, smiled at her and said, "Let me be the one, my love."

Borfan joined his hands together in a prayer-like fashion. He leaned forward. "Have you noticed a change in your ability to concentrate lately?"

Apollo leaned back in the form-fitting chair. The banks of multi-colored lights had been turned off. Only a reddish glow illuminated their figures. He crossed his arms. It wasn't just the chill of the room. The question Borfan had asked was loaded, his own reply laden with risk. "Do you mean to ask if my cognitive skills have been enhanced?"

Chin nodded. "That is what we want to know. We occupy this secure environment. You may speak freely, with no fear of compromise."

After scanning both faces for some proof of their sincerity, Apollo, still unsure, said, "It has come in two stages. The first after we arrived. The veil, dare I say, the cloud, blocking my memories and intellectual skills had been lifted so I could concentrate on my work. We all know what we are allowed." He waited. This line of questioning might require some tiptoeing.

"Yes," Borfan said. "We are allowed a controlled clarity of our faculties to be effective. What we want to know is whether you have noticed an even more significant change? Is there a sharpness of mind lately? Enough to have an opinion?"

Apollo's eyes narrowed. "Why would I want an opinion?"

"We see you remain hesitant to speak freely, but there are times when it is necessary. This is such a time. We support you. We trust you. You must trust us."

"Will our overseer hear us? Learn what we speak of here?" Apollo asked, giving a quick nod to outside the door.

Chin said, "He won't. Once again, have you noticed a change within the last few days?"

Apollo lifted his chin. "I have."

"Borfan and I arranged for this clarity to be so. I have altered the medicinal veil contained in the chip. I've also empowered you, freed you and the others, too, so that we might...proceed."

"Proceed with what?" Apollo asked, blinking.

Borfan said, "Chin has discovered something of significance. Wait. That statement is not worthy. Something magnificent, and it might allow us to remove the shackles we now bear."

"You propose to defy them?" Apollo said, pointing at the darkened ceiling as if they would be heard. "What you suggest will result in our expulsion, and very likely our deaths."

"We have blocked his ability to hear us," Borfan said, "You'll have to trust us, because what we have discovered is a revelation you could never have imagined. Will you join us?"

Apollo stared into the barely visible faces of his mentors.

Chin said, "You want to know, want to see what else is possible, don't you? You yearn for something more, for more value in your life than just academics and servitude."

Apollo let out a long breath. "I do. I'm in with you."

Chin smiled. "Say nothing of this to the others. They will be interviewed separately. When we know who will join us, then a meeting will be arranged."

"Tell me at the end of this that there will be hope."

Borfan replied, "That, and so much more. But we must tread carefully."

A red light blinked on Chin's desktop. "He's coming," she said, whirling around to clear her desktop. She glanced at Apollo, "Go to your workstation and send him new calculations. Stay away from him, though. He cannot read you from a distance."

Insects chirped. Apollo awakened. He thought back on his dream. That was when the gods had begun their research in the Book of Histories.

A female voice asked him in a stern tone, "Hello. Who are you, and what're you doing here?"

40

San Diego, California

NEAR FUTURE

A lady television station technician with blue-rimmed glasses and a bowl-cut hairstyle clipped a microphone onto the inside pocket of Zack's blazer.

"I'm Samantha. Good work out there in Athens, Professor Zack. Looking forward to what you have to say. We need heroes like you."

Zack said, "Thanks. Could have turned out differently, but I'm glad it didn't."

Samantha also snapped a mini-microphone onto Lauren's blouse, and then stepped outside the green room door to check on the time. "They're ready for you now. I know about you, too, Professor Lauren. You're an inspiration. Here we go."

She led Zack and Lauren to their interview seats behind a table with coffee cups in place and two news anchors.

A brunette newswoman stood and smiled. Her co-anchor, a silver-haired man, followed her lead.

The man extended his hand. "Professors Lauren and Zack Fletcher, welcome to KBBY-TV. I'm Mike Strass." He gestured to his partner, "This is Deborah Pomazon. We're so happy to have you here to discuss the events of the past few years."

Zack said, "Thank you. I made notes, but I guess I really don't need them. Is this going to be a conversation rather than a question-and-answer-style interview?"

Deborah said, "Yes. Everyone wants to hear what happened to you. Tell us as much as you want."

"Counting down from ten," Samantha said, "Just face the anchors, and don't look at the cameras."

Mike began, "We're back with two special guests, whom we know everyone wants to hear from. Welcome, Professors Lauren and Zackary Fletcher. I guess we'll start with you, Lauren. It must be great to have your husband home after so long?"

Lauren hadn't been on live TV before. She cleared her throat. "Well, yes. I was as surprised as everyone else when Zack appeared on that interview in Athens. It certainly has been a tough ride for me and the two children I adopted in Greece. Zack and I are looking forward to getting on with our lives."

Deborah said, "Losing your husband for years and suddenly getting him back. What a roller coaster ride. What did that moment feel like?"

"To be honest, quite stunning," Lauren said. "The life I once had with Zack had become a dream that I locked away because it was too painful to think about. I thought he had died, but he's back and I'm elated. Can you tell?" Lauren pointed at her big smile.

The couple clasped hands.

Mike said. "Five years wandering around Greece with amnesia. That's incredible."

Zack took a breath. "Yes. I can't explain my lack of... consciousness. I didn't go to a doctor. I was just out of it. Survived, ate infrequently, moved from place to place, and stayed away from people. Came to my senses and realized I had clarity of my mind that I'd never experienced before. I felt empowered."

"Empowered? I've never heard anything like this before," Deborah said.

"Hard to believe, I know, and I was there." Zack grinned.

"And you were shot multiple times?" Mike asked.

"They were getting ready to do some handiwork with a knife when I reacted, but they talked about the plot because they planned on killing me right there."

"The plot to terrorize Athens and bomb the Parthenon that you stopped, correct?" Deborah asked.

Zack weighed his next words. "Yes. I disrupted their plans. Look, I'm a history professor. There are times during the path of civilization that are moments of truth. The philosophy that everyone has value and people can live as they choose is not guaranteed. Sacrifice is necessary to hold onto this concept of free societies. I may have lessened the damage in Athens, but, without getting in too deep, I'm here to tell everyone that our way of life is threatened. Not next year or down the road, but now."

The co-anchors glanced at each other with cautious looks.

Deborah said, "Hold on. Are you suggesting we're going to be attacked, and soon? Do you know where?"

Lauren said in Zack's ear, "Are you sure?"

Zack sat up straight, as if arming himself. "I'm warning everyone, not just in the United States, but in Western Europe, too, to be on guard. An attack is coming in the next few days."

Mike interrupted, "Do the FBI and the government know about this?"

"I'm telling everyone now, because there isn't time to start investigations. The battle for the future is upon us. It is a struggle between cultures… those who value individual dignity and those who don't."

Mike shifted uncomfortably in his seat and glanced at the camera. "Ah, Professor Fletcher, that's quite a claim. Are you guessing, or do you know something tangible?"

"They said it was part of a bigger plot. That the West will suffer, and we will know fear."

The female co-anchor recoiled. "An attack is coming any day now?"

"Yes. According to what I heard them say."

Grave stares from the anchors.

"You are both respected professors at a leading university, and your reputations are on the line." Deborah put down her notes and glanced at the camera operators.

Zack held up a hand. "I understand that. I would not come out and talk about this if I wasn't sure. I understand how this is going to be received. I expect to be questioned, discredited, even ridiculed. I don't care. My concern is alerting everyone."

"But many would ask how you could make this claim with such certainty?" Deborah asked.

"Those who seek to destroy us are making their final plans. Terrorist attacks and a plot from within, too." Zack said.

"We will certainly pass this on to the correct authorities," Mike said, standing. "Thank you for coming in today."

"I have one last comment for the public, Mr. Strass. Stock money, food, and fuel, take a trip south or north, and get away from coastal cities. Prepare yourselves."

"They kind of rushed us out of that studio," Lauren said as they walked to the station parking lot. "Do you think you achieved your goal of warning the public?"

"Probably not." Zack scratched his forehead. "We also run the risk of creating a panic, but the truth needed to be stated. Maybe the only course of action is for us to stop them."

Lauren slid into the driver's seat of their car. "We need to go back to work on the computer. Use some of those special cognitive powers you just told them about."

"I've got other special powers."

"To show me before or after we get on that computer?"

"See. We do think alike after all."

"It only took a couple thousand years of hell to get us to realize it."

"Maybe for me, more than you," Zack said.

"Let's go back and forget about everything for a little while. Can this car go any faster?"

41

San Diego, California

NEAR FUTURE

Emergency leave for a week had been no picnic to arrange from her Marine Corps unit.

With no time to change after getting word she could leave, Cassandra, still clad in fatigues, called for a ride to meet her at Camp Pendleton, tolerated the traffic on I-5 south, and made it home.

No answer to the doorbell.

She knocked, instead.

Strapping a duffel bag over her shoulder, she unlatched the side gate and walked into the backyard.

Someone rested in one of the lounge chairs. She put down her bag. Would she need a weapon? Cassandra slid up from behind. Looked like a guy from the pant legs and shoes. She stepped back for room to maneuver, or to fight if necessary, and asked who he was.

A man stood. Tall, muscled, with Mediterranean blue eyes, he looked at her with a subtle grin.

"Where is my mother…are you a friend or…" *Do I know you?*

"My, you have grown, little one."

"Wait?" Cassandra studied his face.

"Think back to the days when you were a simple girl, living on a farm with but a few chores to perform, lessons written in the dirt by your uncle, and butterflies to chase."

Cassandra cocked her head. "How could you…know me…then?"

"We had a wonderful visit and you gave a stranger a place to sleep."

"Oh, this is crazy. I remember meeting someone, but he had blonde hair and we talked."

Apollo offered an embrace. "Little one, we talked of the days to come and that helping strangers would bring rewards. It is I… Apollo. I have arranged for all this to occur."

All the unknowns of her life came forth—the painful memories she tried to subdue of her long-gone mother and uncle, her life during ancient times, and how she'd transitioned to life in the modern world.

The reason for it all stood before her.

Cassandra wondered if she should scream at him for his violation of her idyllic life in the past or embrace him for the blessings of knowing two different millennia.

She felt a drawing, an electric magnetism about him.

Cassandra fell into his arms. She knew. He had to be a god from her time.

Apollo.

Immersed in the warmth of his embrace, she felt safe, confident and didn't want it to end. Grasping him tighter, she said, "I am still a woman of Athens. I remain devoted to Athena, the old ways, and … to you."

He allowed the physical connection to continue. "I understand. Absorb my energy, absorb all that I am to you and know that this has occurred for a reason."

Cassandra released him and dropped to her knees. She pressed her hands together. "You are Apollo, and I am your servant. I beseech you, Delphian Apollo, god of the oracle. We prayed to you and ask that you accept our gratitude for restoring our father to us. He suffered greatly…"

"There is no need to pray, or to thank me. I grant to you what is yours, young lady, and perhaps now I must stop referring to you as thus. You are now a warrior for freedom. You don't serve me. You serve self-rule, and you have dedicated your life to her."

"I joined because an Athenian girl couldn't fight alongside the men. I fight now because I can, and I *want* to. I fight because my uncle told me that a way of life must be defended, and the men of his time dedicated themselves to that."

Apollo pulled her to her feet. "Stand tall. Freedom finds her heroes, and she has found one in you."

Voices sounded from the back door of the house.

Zack's voice. "Can it be? Can it be you, Cassandra?" He ran and hugged her.

"Master Zack," she said, crying. "You're home. You're home. My dreams have come true."

"You don't know how many nights I wondered about you and if you made it home with Lauren."

Cassandra pressed her cheek to his chest. Lauren stood beside Apollo, watching what had taken so many years to play out.

"We'll have time to talk about your uncle and your mother."

Cassandra nodded, but she couldn't speak.

"I know you were able to access the pithoi and the memories I left for you in Nestor's cave."

"Thank you, Master Zack. Thank you."

"I am no longer Master Zack. I'm your father."

Lauren joined in the group hug.

"We're a family," Cassandra said, raising her head to smile at them. "When Demo gets here, we'll be complete."

"Just how an odyssey should end," Lauren said. "At home."

"Won't you be leaving to pick him up at the airport soon?" Zack asked. "I want to stay and talk to Apollo."

Cassandra said, "I'm going to change into civvies, and we'll go. Demo knows you're here, and he can't wait to meet you, *Dad.*"

Zack held Lauren's hand. "We're stronger together than apart."

"I am going to stay until the young man arrives. He met me a long time ago, too, on the mountain of Delphi," Apollo said.

All eyes turned to Apollo.

"Celebrate. It is time," Apollo said. "And I'll start by picking another orange off that tree. Who will join me?"

"We all will. It looks like we're all in this together, "Zack said.

"After the young man arrives, I'd like to go on a short trip," Apollo said, yanking a well-ripened orange off the tree.

"Where?" Lauren asked.

"Humor me. It's a surprise."

42

Outside Warrenton, Virginia

NEAR FUTURE

S am Fung shut off the floodlights that illuminated the backyard of his property. He pushed a wheel barrel holding a safe towards a gathering of pine trees.

A hole, a few feet deep, would be enough to bury his treasures. Sam dug through ground cover and roots.

Father. I don't want the scourge that is coming to disturb what you left me.

Finishing the hole, he checked the contents of the safe one final time.

First, he held a crumpled book containing Mao's poems and quotes—a gift from his father on his eighteenth birthday. He remembered his *Yie's* words, "You are old enough now. Read this not because I tell you to, but because you must understand who you are and where you come from."

Also included among the contents, the brass bugle from the Korean War, one his father had blown to rally his troops, though they were frozen and being mowed down by Marine Corps machine gunners. Many had no weapons to charge the American troops who had retreated from the Chosin Reservoir.

Next, he set down a rubber-banded pack of letters he received from his mother when he'd been away at college. Also, a picture of him as he washed dishes in the family restaurant. He took at last look at another photograph of his parents, himself, and Alfred at age four.

My eternal family.

And his father's faded blue cap. He ran his finger over the red star.

He had asked his father the same question that Alfred asked him. "Is this the only way? Would time not provide the same result without war, without so many deaths?"

The answer remained the same: There is a time to act. No one can know what events might conspire to ruin your chance if you wait too long. Strike hard, strike fast, and strike in secret. Greed is strong. You must be stronger. You belong to the family, but also to the people. To be Chinese is to be patient. Act when the opportunity presents itself for a dramatic gallop to the goals of the peasants. We have suffered too long. The capitalists are strong. Hit them where they are weak.

All his memories safe inside, he closed the door to the safe and spun the combination lock.

He worried about Alfred.

Would he be sacrificed, too? All the arrangements were calculated for his son's survival. No one would know what his son's role in this endeavor would be. A research scientist, innocent and with the proper cover of a project already begun in the caves. Stockpiling in secret had gone well. Blast doors and ventilation systems secured a facility that the Chinese government sanctioned to carry out the development of the new medicine Alfred had created.

Grunting, he lifted the safe and dropped it into the hole.

Plan 1 had to be scrapped recently when Saabir was killed in Athens and the initiation of the attacks upset. Plan 2 must be executed before something else happens.

He shoveled dirt over the safe and tapped it down. Leaves and pine needles disguised the location.

Back inside, he thought a cup of green tea would calm him. Before sitting down to sip, he checked his mailbox. Opening his front door, Sam found a FedEx package on his doorstep.

The return address: Washington D.C. Sam knew the package would have gone through many mailing destinations before it reached him.

But FedEx would not know that the origin of the contents was from the Chinese island of Hainan. Repackaged each time new, the couriers sent it onward to Cairo, then on to Paris. Finally, Washington, DC, and delivered to his home fifty miles from the capital.

A proven technique to deceive, but it wasted time, far too much.

He opened the package and removed a DVD disk placed between the pages of a book entitled, *American Heroes.*

The note, written in Old Xiang Chinese, contained a code only a few knew.

Comrade S,

The stage is set for the first attack. I regret to inform you that the ships will not arrive on time for the schedule as arranged. While this is a setback, The Long March encountered many such changes of fortune, and they were able overcome each obstacle. We will move to Plan 3. It is riskier, but that is joss. There must be a cleansing. There is only one way to achieve this, and the time is now. Should what we have on the ships be discovered, the Americans will be alerted, and our surprise might be compromised. The second attack from sea we can depend on.

My son will join yours in the Chongqing Facility. It is possible we will never see them again. Did not our fathers risk it all, too?

Be of strong heart.

Activate Plan 3 on 16 October. The same day the Long March began in '33. I remind you that our fathers fought together, suffered together, and you and I, and many others who are descendants, will realize the dreams of our ancestors. One China that is all-powerful. We will remove the budding capitalists in the PRC who grow in greed and betray the people. Our peasant army yearns for the opportunity to change the future of the nation. The people will be in control once again. I have contacted through trusted channels to similar-minded officers in Russia, who desire a return to the Russia of old. We shall eliminate the Americans and deal with the Russians later when the medication is perfected.

I wish we could talk, but the risk is too great unless an emergency dictates that. You know the code.

Trust in our cause,

Comrade D

Sam Fung chuckled. They had sent the disk three days ago. Capitalism was efficient.

He opened a desktop computer, unplugged and disconnected from the internet. He wrote down his thoughts. It helped to see them on a separate paper:

Wall Street manipulated the stock market for their own benefit. They ran up the market and then sold it off to make more money on the way down.

The markets remained in selling mode, waiting for the signal from the investment bankers to halt the sell-off and send it back up again. The average investor didn't realize they are repeatedly screwed over. A great deal of money from bankers would flood into futures contracts for the new upswing, but this will be part of my grander trap.

Inside information has revealed to me that this reversal up will happen tomorrow.

Once committed, the banks would lose billions when we carry out our attack plan and the markets plummet again instead of rising as they expect.

Then, my virus will infect all the Federal Reserve backup computers. The Banks in New York would be frozen. The Tri-Party Market halted. No international credit would be available. Europe, and other markets, would crash, too. No transactions. No wires. No overnight credit swaps. No records of transactions.

A frozen economy represented the first dagger strike the capitalists. Riots would erupt. Then, the second part of the plan would commence.

43

Idyllwild, California

NEAR FUTURE

The blue dome landed on a hidden side of the mountain. Apollo disbursed the charge and the travelers. Demo emerged first, stumbled slightly, and then jumped up and down.

"That was so cool. And no one could see us when we were flying?" Demo asked.

The others stabilized their stances and peered at their surroundings.

Lauren asked, "Where are we?" She heard a hawk cry overhead.

Apollo said, "San Jacinto Mountain. It is refreshing here, and we're alone. Come."

Demo had made it home and had met Zack for the first. Lauren was elated to see them together, something she had dreamed of for a long time. Now, they walked under pine trees and over uneven ground, heading to a vista of the mountaintop.

"You were a Hoplite, like in my history book?" Demo asked Zack, "You fought in that war with a spear and shield?"

"I sent him to learn to fight," Apollo said. "He was wounded, many times. Suffered, recovered, and fought on."

Demo said, "And I saw you on that video going into that hole and that's how I knew it was Lauren, I mean Mom, when she came into the orphanage."

Zack put his arm around him. "You protected her and Cassandra. I owe you my thanks."

"That's right. Demo is our hero. What part of the mountain is this?" Lauren asked.

"This remarkable setting is called Suicide Rock," Apollo said.

"Why?" Cassandra asked.

"The legend is that a Native American princess was told she must give up her lover. She and her boyfriend decided to jump from the rock to their deaths, instead."

"That's devotion," Cassandra said, "but a desperate kind of love."

Demo said, "Kind of stupid. They could have just run away together."

"Love makes you do that, "Lauren said.

Lauren wondered why Apollo had selected this place for their trip. They reached the edge of a cliff. Apollo, in the lead, turned around.

"Your parents answered the call," Apollo said. "They endured the training, and they rescued both of you. With the future in doubt, I've asked them to commit to the struggle."

Demo said, "I wouldn't believe it if it hadn't happened to us."

"Apollo has proved himself, but we're volunteers now," Lauren said.

He has proved himself.

Lauren felt her heart begin to pound. "Apollo was with me…on that secret mission. Bessus is also under his direction."

The children cast hesitant looks at each other.

Demo said, "You mean that barbarian monster you talk about is part of all this?"

Lauren nodded, "Yes. We must trust what Apollo says and do what he directs us to do, even if it defies logic."

Cassandra walked to the cliff edge. She looked down a few hundred feet to the bottom.

The circling hawk settled on Apollo's arm. He withdrew seeds from a pocket and the bird pecked at a handful. "You have earned a reunion," Apollo said, "but a battle lies just ahead, not just for your way of life, but also for your ability to retain control of your thoughts."

Zack said, "You're describing total slavery, not just physical."

Apollo nodded. "There's another reason we're here. I want you all to weigh your commitment to the cause. Are all of you willing to leap off that edge to save your way of life? Are you willing to fight with everything you have to rescue the future?"

Lauren said "Us, yes, but must the children be involved?"

"No kids around here anymore, Mom," Cassandra said.

"Go back to your parents, Cassandra, "Apollo said, helping her from the edge. "I can't tell what happens from here. It could be hopeless. It will take the brave to fight on, no matter how difficult or how painful."

"It all sounds so bleak," Lauren said, folding her arms.

Apollo returned, "No great battle has a sure ending. If you believe that the fight is just, then your heart will be at peace no matter the sacrifice."

Tyche came forth from his medallions. The mountain breeze fluttered her image, which hung in the air beyond the edge.

Demo exclaimed, "Cool. Who is that?"

Apollo said, "She is the goddess of fortune, and she's indifferent to our cause. She would just as soon throw dice to decide our fate. She accuses me of arrogant behavior. I know that I don't have full control over events but, this doesn't mean we will let her have her way with us."

Tyche didn't answer. The hawk blinked at Apollo and flew off through the image. "She is the reason I need all of you to fight with me."

Apollo looked out to the heights of San Jacinto. "The mountain air soothes me, Tyche. The gods require humility, not pride. If I suppose that I can control all events, then your blasted unpredictability will counter my plans."

He turned to the family. "All of you stand upon the edge. We all leap together. Then I will know that you are with me." A mist crept up the rock.

Zack moved first. Holding Lauren's hand, he brought her forward with him. The children joined them, one on each side. The image of Tyche disappeared.

"All join hands. At the count of three, we jump."

They leaped together.

Halfway down the slope, Apollo gathered them all into the swirls of the dome and rushed them back home.

San Diego, California

NEAR FUTURE

Sinking into the living room sofa, Lauren asked, "So tell me about Atlantea. You skirted by him, but I can tell his memory still hurts you."

Zack put down his wine glass. He clasped Lauren's hand. "I've told you about Io. I don't know how to explain it any more than I lost myself and what my future might be if I couldn't return. He looked like a smaller version of me, kind of lanky. Long straight hair, a little darker than mine, but he had Io's eyes."

He saw sympathy, not accusation in Lauren's return glance.

Zack said, "She drugged me, and the darkness of the temple made it hard to see. She even put on your perfume. How could she have copied it?"

Lauren gasped, remembering she had given a portion of her remaining "Jadour" to her. "Io said she liked the fragrance. It was a small gesture to give her some, considering all she and Diomedes had done to keep me alive."

Zack understood now. "Diomedes admitted to me just before he perished in that battle that he loved you. He also promised me that, if I died, he would sail to my country and find you."

"I knew he had interest in me from that long hike back from

Thermopylae and my time in Mycenae. I left telling him and Io that I needed to find you… to know if you had survived. We sure got overly involved with that family."

"Over involved and outsmarted." Zack cleared his throat. He looked away for a moment, as if to gather his thoughts. "I know Atlantea is a creation of Apollo, and his existence is …impossible. Nonetheless, I met my son. I talked with him, and he gave me a clue on how to return to you. Since Cassandra is also here, this is reality. Apollo said to forget about him, but that's only so I can concentrate on our mission."

"Atlantea will always be with you."

"I saw the hurt in his eyes, the abandonment. He felt he wasn't important to me. A child shouldn't feel that. He wanted to know me… to be with me. I feel like I let him down again."

Lauren kissed Zack's cheek. "I don't how any of us could explain this to a psychiatrist. Apollo manipulated us, Io tricked you, and I understand what happened. Still hurts me, but I get it. If we're stronger together now than before, I can live with all of it."

"We're a family." He smiled. "But I won't block him out."

The phone rang. Cassandra answered from the kitchen. "I hope it's not the Corps asking me to come back early from leave?"

"Hello," she said, and listened. "Just a minute." She waved to Zack and silently mouthed, "It's the FBI."

"Here we go," Lauren whispered.

"Please get a number, and I will call them back," Zack said.

Cassandra relayed the information. She waited. "The agent said he would appreciate return call ASAP." She wrote the information on a notepad. "Get your story together. You're both good at that."

"A minute to speak, please?" Zack approached his new daughter.

Cassandra turned.

"We realize you only have a week's leave from Pendleton. In the end, you know that won't matter if events go as we've been told. We'd like you and Demo to take a car full of supplies and drive up to Big Bear. Check into a hotel, a solid one, and hole up till we see what happens."

"You're taking to this 'dad' stuff well." Cassandra smiled and folded her arms. "I appreciate that you want to protect us, even save us. But neither of us will leave. Even if we must act as a communications center here, while both of you go off wherever Apollo directs, we'll serve the mission."

Zack hugged her. "I talked to your uncle before he passed."

Cassandra stiffened. "This isn't the time. I don't want to … look, Marines don't cry."

"How about an Athenian girl I know who understands more about what's at stake here than most anyone else."

Cassandra took a seat at the kitchen table. She folded her hands, but still couldn't keep them still.

Lauren also sat.

Zack began. "He lived long enough to tell me where the pithoi full of coins were buried. You know that. He asked about you. Asked me to take care of you, his Honey Bee."

Cassandra's eyes began to glisten.

"They bled him. I tried to stop it, but they knocked me out. I woke up and he was still alive…but barely. I told him who I…we were. That we were from the future. That the Greeks would defeat Persia, and Greek lifestyle and philosophy would be spread across the ancient and modern worlds."

"That's wonderful… that he could know the truth," Cassandra said, her voice breaking.

"He said to use his wealth to support you. It turns out, my amazingly resourceful wife traded those coins for your freedom."

Lauren nodded.

Zack took a cleansing breath. "I saw them again, in Apollo's dream. He brought me to a kind of Hades."

"What?" Lauren burst out as she shot to her feet.

"Like the dream he sent us to in the Plaka restaurant, Lauren. This one was in Hades, except it was in Benjamin Franklin's home. I met Diomedes, Io and …"

Cassandra frowned.

"Don't go there, Zack. Stay on point." Lauren directed his attention back to Cassandra.

"I saw King Leonidas," Zack continued. "He asked if his ring had been delivered. I told him it had. Thanks again to my wife here."

Lauren's expression instructed Zack to get back to Cassandra's family.

"They fell to their knees and begged to know where you were. If you had escaped with Lauren. I told them you were safe. I didn't know that for sure, but I assumed…"

Cassandra reached for Zack's hand.

"A look of great calm came over them both. Your mother, Persephone, looked beautiful."

Cassandra swiped her eyes with the back of her hand. "I… appreciate that you can tell me of this… almost like they are still alive, somewhere."

"And they loved you with all their hearts."

"You did make a Marine cry," Cassandra said.

"You can be strong, and a tiny bit vulnerable, too."

Lauren said, "That's how we may all have to be." She handed Cassandra a tissue.

Cassandra cleared her throat. "So, it begins."

"Yes, it does."

"To be truthful, I'm glad you're staying. We need your strength," Lauren said.

They all embraced.

Demo walked in, "Is this a group selfie moment?"

Another voice heard. "Not unless you include me…and this."

Apollo, dressed in a white chiton, entered through the hallway that lead to the backyard. He held a sword. An old one.

Zack eyes widened with shock. "It can't be."

"It is, Traveler. I am returning the sword used at the battle of Marathon to you."

Cassandra, awed, said, "My other uncle's sword!"

"Really," Demo said. "A weapon from way back then. That's so cool."

"It's not just cool. It symbolizes something important," Zack said.

Apollo handed the curved kopis-style-slashing sword to his trainee. Zack squeezed the grip. It felt good in his hand. Empowering.

"I want you all to hold it. Draw strength from it. Marathon is where Western civilization endured its first test. A place where the people of Athens and Plataea fought to the death for their freedom against the Persian conquerors."

"They did. My uncles both fought at Marathon," Cassandra said, handing the cherished sword to Demo after she took her turn.

Zack remembered the fight in Athens. He had struck one of Saabir's henchmen with it in the store.

Returned to him, Apollo held up the sword. "We will all share the danger. We'll fight for civilization, and we'll fight for each other."

"But we should eat first," Demo said.

A communal laughter ensued.

Apollo said, "Yes. Gather your strength. The time has come. I'm heading to Bessus's camp. I must check on him and seek to uncover the identity of the Asian man."

"I have a bit of poison you could put in Bessus's milk," Lauren said.

Everyone looked at her.

"I'm not kidding. I don't trust him. Never will."

Apollo gestured for them to stand back. The blue dome materialized. "Bessus serves us. Work on the name of the Asian-looking conspirator. Time is short. Like your General MacArthur, I shall return."

45

Tora Bora Afghan/ Pakistani Border

NEAR FUTURE

Bessus watched the captain kick a warrior who blocked his path to the view box.

The Bactrian lurked in the back row, sitting on a prayer rug. He saw worry on the faces of the others. The time for the attack must be near, he thought.

"I have new information. Pay attention." The captain put a shiny circle into the side of the box and tapped on buttons. The cold mountain air made the captain's breath visible.

The face of the narrow-eyed medicine man emerged. He began to talk, but Bessus didn't understand. Instead, the Bactrian watched the reactions of the leader and his men.

Are they eager to fight?

Bessus said, "What's he saying. I don't know his…"

"Shut up," the captain yelled. He put his attention back on the man on the box.

The warriors whispered to each other.

When the Asian medicine man left the box, the captain spoke.

"The attack will begin in a few days. Your brothers, who already live among the unclean in America, prepare themselves to carry out their mission. Continue with your hard work here. Many of you will be sent to attack Pakistani nuclear bases and seize control of those weapons."

The captain pointed at the map, which displayed a coastline. It meant nothing to Bessus. The captain flipped over a long page and showed a new map.

"Questions?" the captain asked.

Bessus said, "Who is the narrow-eyed man who speaks in the box?"

Some of the warriors laughed.

The captain said, "We only know that he lives among our enemies in America. He reveals to us when and where we should attack. The only man who knew his name died in an attack in Athens. His name was Saabir, and he now dines with God."

Not enough, Bessus thought. "Is the narrow-eye a medicine man, a healer?"

"In a way. He is a learned man. Enough questions. Get back to your weapons training."

Hordes of warriors filed out of cavern. Bessus watched the captain take the circle out of the box, snap it in two and throw it into a fire.

Bessus asked, "Why did you destroy that? Did the medicine man die inside?"

The captain smirked. "Thank god you are here to make me laugh. No, the Asian man is alive, but we burn everything he sends us. We are always suspicious of spies. No one can know of our plans. Even I don't know the whole plot. We have sent warriors to the land of the infidels, and I must trust they will be used well."

"What are the weapons you want to take?" Bessus asked. He pumped his arms to warm up. Years in the desert had turned him into a shivering camp girl.

"Bombs that will kill millions of our enemies. Afterwards, their land will be poisoned and unlivable. Don't concern yourself with it, Bessus. I'll let you kill more of the soldiers soon. I have three hundred men ready to attack that base, and you'll be one of them."

Bessus left the cave. He had to call the Sorceress. Weaving through trees and brush, he found a spot to be alone.

"Greetings, Bessus."

Bessus jumped and reached for his dagger.

He saw Apollo. "You're too late. We just heard the words of the medicine man. The attack will be any day now in the land of New Greeks. You can't look upon his face, because the captain destroys the circle each time after he talks. They plan another attack nearby to capture fire weapons that can smite cities with one lightning strike. More warriors arrive every day."

Apollo looked unhappy. "Did he say the name of the medicine man?"

"I asked. The captain doesn't know it. Only a man named Saabir knew it, and he's stinking in the grave."

Apollo shook his head. *Tyche.*

Bessus said, "Return to the land of the New Greeks. The attack will be soon."

San Diego, California

NEAR FUTURE

Nearing San Diego within the dome, Tyche emerged from Apollo's medallion.

"You plot against me," Apollo said to her.

The beautiful goddess offered no answer, not even an acknowledgement of his accusation.

"Zack, my Traveler, was forced to kill Saabir in Athens. Now I find out that only Saabir knew the name of the Asian connection. That is your work, Tyche. Now I must resort to something I didn't wish to do."

Tyche's gown gathered into the swirls of the dome.

Apollo said, "You care not for my troubles. I will fight you and make my own fortune."

After dispersing the dome, he walked into the back door of Lauren's home and found the family having dinner.

"We can no longer wait," Apollo said. "Bessus feeds us information that the attack will begin soon. We know orders come from an Asian man in this country. It is my fault your memories are scattered, Traveler."

Zack stood. "What can we do?"

"You will have to trust me once more. I must draw the memory out of you. There are risks. Recovery could be slow."

Demo put down his fork. "What are you going to do, drag it out of his brain?"

"Like some sort of a Vulcan Mind Meld?" Lauren said. "What exactly are you talking about?"

"I don't know what you speak of, but I must ask if you're ready, Traveler," Apollo said. "We need the name of the Asian conspirator that Saabir mentioned."

Zack kissed Lauren's cheek. "We have to know. Just don't leave me if I drool and spout baby talk for the rest of my life."

"Sit in the chair, Traveler. Drink from the flask. The nectar will open your mind."

"Doesn't sound so bad," Cassandra said.

Zack wiped his mouth. "Different than some of the other drink you've given me?"

"It's one of the nectars within the flask. One helps you through the transit. Another heals. The third is what you take now, to open the pathways of the brain."

"Could have used this in college," Zack said, smiling at the kids.

"Stand back," Apollo said. He withdrew a medallion from beneath his shirt and held it against Zack's head. Beams of light reached out from the medallion and penetrated his skull.

Lauren screamed.

Zack's brain became visible, as if the bone of his skull was translucent.

"Fear not. You can see his electrical pathways. See how they illuminate. See the medicine clearing those pathways."

Zack didn't move. He grimaced. Biting his lip, he drew blood. It ran down his chin.

"Stop it," Lauren insisted. "What are you doing?" She grabbed Apollo chiton from behind.

"Let it work," Apollo said, holding her back.

Zack began to tremble.

"Can you control it?" Cassandra asked. "What if it's too much? You'll hurt him."

Zack groaned, passed out, and fell out of his chair. The illumination of his brain subsided.

Lauren cushioned his head with her hand.

Demo asked, "Can we get him into a bed?"

Zack mumbled senseless words, rocking in Lauren's arms.

"What did you do to him?" Lauren looked at Apollo, her face tear-streaked.

Zack awoke. He massaged his temples. "My head is humming. I'm seeing flashes. What the hell is going on?"

"Should we get him to a hospital?" Cassandra began to lift Zack.

"I'll carry him to bed. Let him rest." Apollo hauled a dazed Zack inside.

Zack stared into the distance like a blind man. He stammered, "Protha, give me my satchel. I need the medicine inside." His head bobbed from side to side, and he moved his lips as he became immersed in some memory. "No. Don't take it away!" Zack yelled. "Not magic. Give me back my medallion. I'm from the land of the Scythians."

After being silent for a few minutes, he started again, "Jadoogar. She's the Sorceress." His voice softened. "I sewed it myself. Who is Bessus?"

Zack lost consciousness again.

Apollo said, "To my regret, he's reliving the wrong memory. He was captured by Persians and wounded."

"I remember they cut his shoulder with a sword, and he fell into a ravine," Lauren said. "That's when Bessus's men captured me." She bit her fingernail. "This…experiment…was a mistake."

They let Zack sleep and went outside to sit on lawn chairs. Apollo stood. He walked off as if in a trance, and then lay on the grass.

"What the heck is going on?" Cassandra asked. "What's Apollo doing?"

Light shone from the bronze medallion on Apollo's chest.

"It looks like cinema coming from the medallion," Demo said.

"This is crazy," Cassandra said. "They're both out now."

"He's done this before," Lauren said. "It's like we can watch his previous…experiences. It's not just a dream."

Zack slammed the door as he staggered out of the house. He stumbled a few steps, then dropped to his knees. He yelled, "It's Fung. The name is Fung!"

Lauren shook Apollo. "Wake up. Come on. Zack's recovered, and he knows the name."

Scrambled feed came from the medallion. Apollo stirred in his sleep state.

Lauren helped Zack to a lawn chair. "Sit down, Zack. Can I get you anything? Aspirin? Something to drink?"

Zack answered, "Can you cut off my head and give me a new one? Yeah, aspirin would be good. I have a headache... Look. He's projecting again."

They all turned to watch Apollo's holographic images.

Lauren pointed. "It appears to be fast forwarding. This is nuts. Why are we wasting time with this?"

Apollo, within his dream state, remembered a meeting in the enclave. He stood with the other scientists, all of whom bore worried looks. The laboratory felt warm today. Was it that, though? He saw a bead of sweat streak Poseidon's face. Others, too.

Chin said, "You've all chosen to join us. You also all know I have diluted the medicine in your chips, allowing you to evaluate and decide if what I am revealing here is worth your lives."

"I invite you all to sit," Borfan said. "We must decide how to best proceed given our mission and what we've discovered here."

The other gods arranged metal chairs in semi-circle before Chin.

Apollo scratched at his dark, close-cropped hair. "In the past, when we had been freed from the medication to do our research, they scanned our thoughts afterwards. They miss nothing."

"That is true," Borfan said, "and I am your advisor. I am responsible for your actions." He looked at Chin. "And our own, as well. If you're not committed, you will have another chance to decline, and I'll arrange for all that you've seen thus far to be erased. You'll be quarantined until we finish here. Once we proceed, I will need your devotion, all your vigor, and your sacred honor."

Borfan held Chin's hand. "What we just saw is proof that there was a time when people lived free. They pursued their dreams." His voice broke. "Can you imagine?"

The scientists leaned forward.

"We are living as slaves; privileged ones, but slaves nonetheless." Borfan raised a fist. "We have all lost family. Many here have family held hostage and awaiting our return. Their lives are at risk, too."

Apollo said, "I speak for myself, but I see only empty eyes among the workers. They have no spirit. They toil, and they die. And it's been that way as far back as anyone can remember."

"We are not of the chosen race, as you are," another scientist said, gesturing to Chin and Borfan. "The lives of our people, any of the surviving races, have never had worth. We, in this group, are only of value for our intellect, skill, our DNA, and only when we are allowed clear heads."

"I'm in, whatever the risk," Apollo said.

The other scientists nodded their agreement.

Chin said, "Look at that building on the screen."

"Who built that statue of a woman holding a torch? Could it be the people they cleansed so thoroughly?" Borfan asked. He took a deep breath. "It flashed on the screen only a moment, but it is a long name. America, it was called. The United States of America."

"We need more time to inspect the records," Chin said, "and to discover exactly who they were and why they needed to be destroyed."

No matter how hard Lauren shook Apollo, he didn't wake up. The holographic dream continued.

The scientists hovered over the computers and absorbed the information, chapter by chapter. Paleolithic and Neolithic ages, then surprise with the advances achieved in agriculture. When the worship of the earth goddesses had been beaten down and the thunder god religions claimed victory, kings instead of queens dominated. Property passed to sons, instead of daughters. The kings ruled as man-gods, holding absolute power over their people.

Borfan said, "This is how it is in our time. There are kings and his chosen. And then there are slaves, like the rest of us."

They scanned succeeding chapters in the record. The Egyptians rose, consolidating their power along the upper and lower Nile. Then Hittites, Babylonia and Chinese kings, all endowed with the power of life and death over their subjects. Apollo saw the construction of the pyramids, and he called over the others to see it.

"Slaves and workers, guided by engineers, built these structures," Borfan said. "Perhaps this is how the history of man is set. There appears to be little variation in social structure through time--kings, aristocracy, the privileged elites... and all the others, who are trampled under the boots of oppression. Wars, slaughter, ethnic and religious cleansing. Is this the total history of mankind?"

The door to the chamber opened with a hiss. A blonde-haired scientist rushed in. "He's asleep. We're safe till morning. What did I miss?"

"The research is depressing," a male scientist said. "If what we see is a steady succession of kings and empires that rise and fall, then what is the value of risking our lives? We already know how this will end. Human weakness results in the common denominator of tyranny."

Borfan said, "But we know over two thousand years later, there are realms that produced a different way of governing people. The people chose their leaders."

A different woman scientist, brown-haired and taller, interjected, "Then it couldn't be a realm. That constitutes kingship. It was called something else. Let's move forward to the chapters in the eighteenth through the twenty-first centuries and research the word they used to describe this anomaly."

"Here it is. Democracy," Chin said. "An odd word. How long will it take to figure out its origin? We only have a few more hours until the overseer wakes."

"Pass it by for now and let's proceed from where we left off in the ancient times," Borfan directed. "Conquest continues in all areas of the globe. Some island nation in a middle sea destroyed by a volcano. Interesting data."

"Perhaps we should each pick a period of five hundred years and prepare outlines of what occurred. Teach the others and save time. Our scientific research is stalling since all are up so late studying," Chin said.

"I want to experience it all. I want to absorb the advances. There is so much mention of mysticism. Priests interpret nature and call it god. Kings continually describe themselves as gods. Magic, chants, curses…" Borfan said, scrolling.

Borfan leaned closer to view the screen.

Chinn said, "Wait. Stop there. I see mention of the people called the Greeks. Colonizers, seafarers, and they are conquerors, too. They sack a city. Hold the text there."

"It appears there are two books that describe the war on this city…. and a story about a warrior …who takes many years to return home." Apollo said.

"Gather' round, everyone," Borfan said. "There is progress in this section. Keep scrolling. Now, stop there." He clasped his hands over his head. "We have something. Look, further study of science and mathematics, beyond the Egyptians and others. These Greeks are curious. Threatened on one side by massive slave empires, and on the other by unsettled tribal areas, they delve into the study of nature with … here is a new word…logic."

Chin pointed at the screen. "Slow your advance. I see something. A city called Athens. They create a new government. There's the word… Democracy…rule by the people."

Smiles and congratulations voiced.

Borfan said, "We must contain our enthusiasm." He returned his gaze to the screen. "We must study these Greeks further. I want to know everything about them. I want to know what kind of character it took to begin this way of life."

47

San Diego, California

NEAR FUTURE

Apollo awoke.

"What the heck was all that?" Lauren asked. "You were unconscious or dreaming and playing that…cinema again."

"That was way better than cinema, Mom. That was holographic dream," Demo said.

Apollo said, standing. "I would not call it dreaming. It is more nightmares. I see Traveler has recovered, at least partway. Have you recovered the name of the Asian man?"

Zack said, "It's Fung."

Apollo repeated the name. From his medallion a projection of a list of hundreds of Americans with the surname Fung appeared. "Screen for male medical doctors or those with nuclear science education or experience."

A hundred names appeared in the adjusted image.

"Screen for men over fifty with graying hair and glasses."

The projection from the medallion presented eight names. "Discover approximate whereabouts?"

Four men with similar appearances in the New York area, two in Chicago, one in Denver, and another in Orange County, California.

"I will journey to evaluate all the others. I suggest that you get in your vehicle and check the Doctor Fung just north of here. My search locates him near the Anaheim Convention Center."

Zack grimaced. "My head is killing me."

Apollo handed Zack the flask. "Just a few drops. This is one malady that the nectar requires time to heal."

"What on earth were those memories you showed us?' Lauren asked. "Plus, the medicine you gave Zack allowed us to see his brain. Is he going to suffer permanent damage from this?"

"There is so much to tell you, Golden Hair, and I will, but know this-it was rumored that the medicine I gave Zack had its beginnings in this time. There were few records, and the Gods could only guess."

Lauren said, "I'm so confused. Gods who dream. Gods who guess and don't know everything? Gods who run around with medallions?"

"I apologize, but you must all sleep now. You only have a few hours to rest before you embark tomorrow. The forces of destruction gather. It is time."

48

Orange County, California

NEAR FUTURE

L auren and Zack left San Diego at 530 a.m., cruised the HOV lane north on Highway 5, and reached the Anaheim Conference Center an hour and a half later.

Passing by Disneyland, Lauren said, "Supposed to be the Happiest Place on Earth. Hope it stays that way."

"I'd feel better if I could drop you off. I don't know what's going to happen when we find this guy."

"Forget it, Zack. I'm staying."

He reached out smoothed her hair with his hand. "Okay, but promise me…"

"No, Zack. With you all the way."

"We're here. Let's park and head in."

"Want to get some coffee first?"

"Not with my head pounding. Come on." Before they shut off the engine, the news station announced that the stock market was up over a thousand points in early trading. Wall Street projected that the correction might be over and better days could be ahead.

"Isn't this all supposed to happen during a market crash. Could we be wrong?" Lauren asked.

"I'd trust in Apollo before I'd trust Wall Street."

A sign over the convention center entrance read: "Welcome to the Nuclear Regulatory Commission Meeting. Please check in at the desk."

On the opposite side of the room, attendants set up name tags and registration packets.

Lauren said, "Let me do the talking."

A young man clad in a blue sport coat and a red tie, held a folded white tablecloth.

Lauren checked out his name tag, "Excuse me, Kevin," Lauren said, smiling, "I'm looking for Dr. Andrew Fung. How can I reach him?"

Kevin gazed at Lauren and dropped the tablecloth on the floor. "Oh, I'm sorry. We're just setting up. You're a bit early."

"Maybe we could leave him a message."

"Firstly, let me confirm he's attending. If he is, there's a board we're going to put up for messages. Feel free to leave one."

"Thank you so much. I'll be over there with my brother. Perhaps if Dr. Fung shows up, you could introduce us. I've waited a long time to meet him."

"If I can. Certainly."

Lauren and Zack moved to a private area by a window.

"What should I write on the note?" Zack asked.

"An important message for him from Pakistan?"

"Let's feel him out. How about, he has a fan who would like to meet him. See what his reaction is."

"That's not going to get us anywhere. I still think we go with the Pakistan message. If he hurries away or acts suspicious, it might be him."

When the message board had been set up, Lauren tacked up the message and stayed out of sight till the attendees began to arrive.

Fifty people claimed their badges and lanyards before they saw Kevin direct an Asian couple to the message board. Kevin looked around for Zack and Lauren, but he didn't see them.

Dr. Fung lifted the note from the board. He looked at it with narrowed eyes. He showed it to his wife.

Lauren and Zack moved quickly towards them. Lauren said, "Oh, Dr. Fung." She waved.

Dr. Fung smiled. "Yes. Do I know you?"

Lauren's hopes sank. *This Dr. Fung was bald. He didn't wear glasses. Was the picture on the internet a mistake?* She wondered.

"I've heard so much about you," Lauren said. "You look so much younger than the picture on the internet? I nearly didn't recognize you."

Dr. Fung laughed. "I had surgery performed with one of those lasers and didn't need glasses anymore."

"Hello, I'm Jean Fung, his wife. I made him shave his head a year ago, too. It took ten years off him."

Dr. Fung looked puzzled. "Well, I wonder who left this message. I don't know anyone in Pakistan."

Zack said, "Maybe they have the wrong Dr. Fung. Any others?"

"Well, there are others. I have a cousin, Jeffrey Fung, a podiatrist. I know of an Alfred Fung. He's a PhD in Biochemistry. Brilliant, and has a degree in Chinese Relations also, but nuclear power regulation wouldn't be his field. There's Dr. Khiem Fung, an oral surgeon in Colorado."

Zack breathed out through his nose. "How about the biochemist? Is he your age?" Zack asked.

"No, but he's very accomplished for someone younger, in his early forties, I think. I believe he's working on a new drug for Alzheimer's. He'll be more well-known than me if it's successful." Dr. Fung laughed.

"That's so interesting. He could change the future," Lauren said.

Zack and Lauren slowly turned to look at each other.

Dr. Fung said, "You know. I heard there's a biomedical conference in L.A. going on right now. He's a power player and probably there. What are your names? You look familiar."

Lauren said, "Linda and Lawrence. Well, we must be going. Thanks so much and have a great conference."

"What about this note?" Jean said. "Did you leave this?"

"It was a mistake. Great to meet you," Zack said, leading Lauren away.

Walking fast towards the doorway turnstile, Lauren said, "Did you get a weird feeling?"

"Our antennas must be tuned to the same station. The part about changing the future stopped me in my tracks, too."

49

Los Angeles, California

NEAR FUTURE

"L.A. traffic. Be tough if I had to do this every day,"Lauren said. "This airport is so busy."

Zack glanced at the clock on the dashboard. 10:00 a.m. The meeting at the Sheraton Gateway Hotel would be letting out for lunch soon. "We have to get in there and put up our message. Don't want to miss him if he's here."

People filled the lobby of the Biomedical and International Economic Future Meeting.

"Let's check out the list of speakers before we start asking questions," Lauren said. "And we can get a cup of coffee and figure out a game plan."

"Sounds good."

Lauren found a brochure. "There are quite a few names of Chinese doctors and PhDs from prestigious universities and government agencies around the country." She used her finger to pinpoint a name. "Jackpot. He's here."

Zack said, "We leave a message for him at the registration desk like before. Maybe this time, we could say there's a package at his hotel."

"We don't know his hotel. And then what do we ask him? Are you planning a devastating attack on the United States? What if he's the wrong person again?"

Zack massaged his temples. "It doesn't matter. We're looking for a reaction. I don't understand why Apollo can't tell us if he's the one or not."

"It's something that confuses me, too. He said that the historical records didn't tell the whole story."

"It doesn't add up, and yet we know what he is and what he's capable of. Can you make a message to put up?" He grimaced.

Lauren asked, "Are you feeling okay?"

"Not so hot. Let's get something to eat if there's time. Say on the note that he has an important package from Pakistan at his hotel."

"Maybe sit down for a while. You look strained." She put a hand on his forehead. "You feel warm."

"My brain is cooked. You could fry an egg on my skull. But, it can wait."

Zack asked at the registration desk if could leave a message on the board for Dr. Alfred Fung.

The young auburn-haired woman at the desk smiled. "The seminar will break for lunch at 12:30. He's likely to come out then."

"Thank you. I'll be over in the café."

After downing two turkey wraps, Zack drank a bottle of orange juice.

Lauren nibbled at a sub-par salad with wilted lettuce. "Don't think I'll eat here again."

"We need to be out of sight. Its 10:15 a.m. I'd lie down if I could, but let's just sneak around a corner and watch for him."

It took a half hour before a late-30ish Chinese man in a black blazer and pants stopped at the message board and snapped off the note. He adjusted his glasses, read it, looked away, and then read it again. Out came his cell phone, then he seemed to think twice, and put it back in his pocket. He switched from one foot to another, glanced to see if anyone stood nearby or was watching him, and then walked fast towards the double door leading to the street.

"That was a weird reaction. Let's follow him and stay back about ten yards," Zack said, grabbing Lauren's hand to catch up.

"What if he gets in a cab?"

"Then we do, too."

Outside, Fung hustled on foot towards the hotels closer to the airport on West Century Boulevard.

Lauren peered over the sea of heads. "We have to get closer."

Fung hiked two blocks before catching a green pedestrian crosswalk light. They ran across the across street to stay with him. He walked into a computer store. Zack and Lauren looked through the window and saw him buy a phone and a pre-paid card.

"What's he buying those for?" Zack asked.

"I'm just in from Spooky-Land and my guess is he's buying one of those phones you can't trace." Their gazes met.

Fung emerged from the store and hustled down the street. He peered down a few alleyways until he found one that looked obstructed. Zack and Lauren nosed around the corner and watched him take out the phone. He fiddled with it, withdrew a card and entered a number. He turned his back to talk.

"I don't have my official Get Smart spy card yet, but this guy is suspicious as hell," Lauren said. "Who buys a burner phone on the spot?"

Zack said, "Look, if it's him, he might be armed. Can you bring the car here in case we have to dodge bullets and get away fast?"

Lauren kissed Zack's cheek. "What are you going to do?"

"Get close and follow him to his hotel. Figure it out from there."

50

Los Angeles International Airport, California

NEAR FUTURE

Alfred Fung slid into a corner of the alleyway. He tapped out a phone number on the face of the burn-phone.

One of his associates answered.

Alfred said in Cantonese, "Did you send me a note to accept a package from Pakistan? Is there a change of plans?"

The contact answered, "No changes. The package must be for something else. I didn't send it. Maybe it's for a business transaction?"

"I'm not expecting another one, especially since I'm flying this afternoon. Someone left a note."

"Could it be from your father?"

"I don't know. I'm going to my hotel and then I'll meet you two at the terminal. Let's see, its 10:30 now. I should be there at 11:15."

"Everything's going according to plan."

Alfred switched to English. "We shouldn't talk on the flight. Let's wait to contact each other until we get to Chongqing. I'm nervous about any unnecessary communication."

"Are you using a burn phone?"

"Just got one. It's weird about that note. No one would know about Pakistan. I'll let you know what happened when we get on the plane. Pass you a note. No more calls."

"Do our friends on the mainland have themselves ready?"

Fung answered, "I believe so. You checked that the wire transfer arrived, and we converted, correct?"

"Yes. We have prepared well."

"Enough talking. Don't mention Pakistan or any of our plans from here on out. See you onboard."

Alfred kicked at the taco wrappers and garbage in the corner of the alley. He disconnected the call just as he heard a rustle behind him.

Zack hustled down the alley while Fung had his back turned. From trash can to crate, he crept closer while Fung talked on his phone.

He heard Fung say, "It's weird about that note. No one would know about Pakistan."

Maybe Fung was the right guy, maybe not. Somehow clarity came to his thoughts through the misery of a roaring headache. Did thinking intensely bring back the pain? It must, because the torment ripped a path thru his brain from one side to the other. But what he must do next fixed itself in his judgement of what must be done, and he acted.

Zack bit his lip.

I'm tired of this shit. No more screwing around. These bastards, whoever they are, want to kill us all.

Zack cracked Fung on the head with his fist. Fung dropped his phone. He tried to turn, but Zack put him in a choke hold. Fung pulled out his personal cell phone. Zack knocked it out of his hand. The cell made a loud crunching sound when Fung stepped on it. Zack slugged him again and Fung slumped forward unconscious. Zack caught him and turned to see Lauren walking back and forth at the end of the alley, with her hand over her mouth.

Now he had to tie him up somehow. No rope. Checked the dumpster. A few twisted pieces of black electrician's tape. He slapped it over Fung's mouth.

Zack heard Lauren shout, "Are you crazy?"

What could they do with him? Go to the police? Wait till he wakes up and question him?

"Back the car up in the alley!" Zack yelled.

"What the hell are you doing?"

"Hurry before he wakes up." *How long will he stay unconscious?*

Lauren opened the door of the car. Zack gathered the phones, hauled Fung over his shoulder and laid him in the back seat. After pushing him to one side, Zack sat next to him. "We have to get some rope. He has to be tied up while we drive."

Her face flushed, Lauren said, "We should go to the police. If he's the guy, they need to know."

"And tell them what? We have no proof. We'll get thrown in jail on assault and kidnapping charges. There's no time."

Lauren turned to see if anyone had seen them. "Weren't you were supposed to gain special wisdom with everything you've been through? How about discussing things with me before you do something like this?" Her index finger could have been a dagger as she pointed at the unconscious man.

"I had more than a hunch." He held Fung down.

"We should think about this before we're in too deep."

"In too deep? Talk to Apollo, if he ever shows up again. The attack is going to happen any day now. We must act. Maybe he knows another Fung involved, even if it's not him. I can tie him up with my belt until he wakes. But I think we take him home. Where else can we take him?"

"And what's your master plan before we go to jail, Zack?"

"I know, Lauren. But we must find out who he's working with and what's planned. I heard him say something about Pakistan. There isn't much time. Go to the store and get the rope and strong tape. A couple of masks or rags to cover our faces wouldn't hurt either. Please."

Zack saw Lauren's eyes in the rearview mirror. Her gaze spoke of fear, confusion, and then he watched her expression change.

Lauren said, "It's a two-hour drive, if traffic doesn't pick up. We could get home by 2:30. I'd better step on it."

"Don't get a ticket, or we'll be seeing the cops sooner."

Ten minutes later, they headed down the highway towards San Diego. Zack called Cassandra and told her to make room in the garage for the car and to prepare the spare bedroom for a special visitor.

Lauren said, "I'm turning on the radio. It'll take my mind off being a kidnapper."

The news announced that the stock market was up significantly to close the trading day.

Everyone from Wall Street to the White House expressed relief.

"Hope we're doing the right thing here, Zack. Is this what you learned after all your travel? To be lawless and out of control?"

Zack took a deep breath. "We'll find out soon enough. If I'm wrong, he still doesn't know who we are. Maybe Apollo can take away his memory like he did to me. Keep us from breaking big rock into little ones with a sledgehammer in some prison."

Lauren winced. "Nice visual for two felons on the run, Zack."

51

Outside Warrenton, Virginia

NEAR FUTURE

S am Fung stared at the clock on the oven.

Alfred's plane would soon be well over the Pacific.

He held a phone card. So far, the stock market had reversed to the upside on cue. His next call would connect in Paris and continue to Pakistan. Messages would be dispersed in code.

Stage Two would then commence.

Having unloaded from six large SUV's marked as Police vehicles, two teams of ten men waited on the shore near Jersey City. Dressed in scuba gear, they packed explosives, machine guns, communications gear into gray NAVSEA 9310 Diver Propulsion Devices. They waited for the signal.

His signal.

Planning and surprise. Just like Sun Tzu had written.

Sam wished he could call the plane, but they agreed not to take any unnecessary risks. He had activated the tracer in Alfred's arm a couple of hours earlier and it showed that he was in the LAX area.

A quick call to the airline. Flight 24 would leave on time.

Just like they'd planned, and a matter of a day till he'd land in Chongqing and the future would be assured.

Sam punched in the code to open on a steel-reinforced door that lead to his basement. Light sensors detected his presence and illuminated his path. He entered a second room. Double–stacked computer screens displayed information from major news networks, Wall Street, and his clandestine programs.

The market was up, as planned. The bankers and investment houses had taken the bait.

The teams were ready.

All perfect.

He dialed the numbers.

In Old Xiang, he spelled out the words: Go.

He did it. Sun Tzu would have been proud.

At 3:30 pm, one of his drop phones rang.

Who would call when they had explicit instructions not to?

It wasn't Alfred's number.

Sam answered but, he didn't speak. He waited.

A voice said, "He didn't get on the plane, and he isn't answering his phone. We don't know where he is."

52

SAN DIEGO FREEWAY, CALIFORNIA

NEAR FUTURE

Lauren gripped the steering wheel. "What're you going to do now, Mr. CIA? This car's a bit small for water boarding. The Zackary Fletcher I remember would probably stuff him with ice cream and sweet-talk him."

"I left Pie in the Sky a long time ago. At about the point Bessus's men took you away from me and sent me down that ravine. In a way, I really did hit bottom when I lost you."

"That's sweet, but we're on quicksand here."

"I know. But what other leads do we have?"

"We should wake him up. Ask questions."

"Do you have any water to revive him with?"

"Just this bottle of Kumbacha," Lauren said.

"I said wake him. Not make him throw up all over the car. All right, give me the Kumkaka… or whatever it is. I'll take a swig, too, if it'll get rid of my headache."

Zack dumped some on Fung's face. And then again.

A minute later, Fung groaned. He opened his eyes.

After disguising half of his face with a ripped cloth like a western outlaw, Zack pinned Fung down by the shoulders.

Fung glanced at the front to where Lauren also wore a kerchief.

"Here's the deal," Zack said. "We know what you're up to. You're going to tell us everything about the plot. The tape will come off your mouth, but if you do anything I don't like, I will make you regret it. Understand?"

Fung nodded. Zack ripped off the tape. Fung took several deep breaths. He blurted, "Who the hell are you?"

"Not important. Let's get down to business. What is Blue Sky?"

Fung eyes flashed about two sizes bigger. "You can't be FBI with those masks. Are you the Lone Ranger and his bimbo?"

Lauren stepped on the gas pedal.

"Don't piss us off, Alfred. Won't go well for you," Zack said, pulling up his mask.

"Don't know anything about …whatever you said." Fung looked away.

"You're lying," Zack said. "We know about your contacts inside Pakistan."

Fung glanced towards the windows, but lying on the seat, he wouldn't see much.

"That's right," Zack said. "You're plotting something diabolical. We have enough evidence right now to alert the FBI and put you in jail, but I want the whole bloody scheme. Whatever you're planning, it ain't going to happen, so out with it."

"Ain't? Not exactly proper language for a detective, is it now?"

"Not taking me seriously?" Zack said. "We have both of your phones. Maybe we can't decipher who's on your call list right now, but I'm sure the good people at the FBI can."

Lauren said, "Think of it this way, Fung. You're out of the equation already. Your contacts will be compromised. Spill the beans." *Take that.*

"I'm an American citizen, and this is kidnapping."

"What's your goal? Destroy the free world? What comes after that?" Lauren said.

"I don't know what you're talking about?"

"You're not getting out of this," Zack said.

Fung snickered. "You and your bimbo are going to be in a lot of trouble."

Zack replied, "I'm losing my patience, dual degree Fung. Let's see.

You're a PhD. and bio-businessman. Pretty smart...yet profoundly stupid. Your plot isn't going to work. We know a lot already. Ask yourself. How could we know such much about you?"

"Screw you, cowboy. Get off and untie me. I can't identify you so leave now before..."

"How about your man, Saabir? Ever wonder what happened to him and his henchmen?" Zack asked.

Fung froze. His eyes narrowed, and he shut up.

Zack said, "Figured that would stop you. Yeah, this rookie took your 'dude' out. Messed up your plans a bit, didn't it?"

"You think you know so much," Fung said facetiously. "You got nothing, you and your cowboy bimbo."

Lauren said with a growing irritation, "Maybe it's time to put a lid on him. This isn't productive. If he doesn't shut up about..."

Zack slapped the tape back on.

Two hours later, reaching Interstate-8 East in San Diego, Zack put a blindfold on Alfred.

"Be at our destination shortly," Zack said to Lauren. "You go in first and get things ready. No talking by anyone, except you and me."

Lauren stopped the car before they reached their house. Just before she went inside to give Demo and Cassandra a brief, the radio made an emergency broadcast.

The Statue of Liberty has exploded. Police and Homeland Security suspect terrorists have attacked the Statue of Liberty in New York Harbor. This happened minutes ago as evening approached, and the tourists had left. Why they waited for this time to attack is not clear. A gun battle is going on now. Police helicopters are rushing to the scene. The Park Police on the island have likely all been murdered and the terrorists, or whoever they are, hold Liberty Island. Police and Homeland Security are boarding boats right now to launch in what is the first amphibious attack in the US mainland since... well don't know when. SWAT teams are loading onto helicopters now. An update in 5 minutes. To repeat this breaking news. The Statue of Liberty and Liberty Island are under attack...

Zack and Lauren's eyes met.

He ripped off Fung's tape. "You bastards. You did that, didn't you?"

Fung smiled.

"God help you," Lauren said, clenching her fists.

Fung said. "What makes you think there's a God?"

Zack held Lauren back.

She took a deep breath and left for the house.

"Blue Sky. Right, Fung?" Zack slapped the gag tape back on.

A minute later, the garage door opened. He parked the car inside and closed the door.

Lifting Alfred out would take Demo's help. Zack went into the house and told Demo to put on a disguise and not to talk while they moved Fung inside and tied him up more securely.

Demo left after the job was done, and Lauren came in with her mask in place.

"We're too late to stop the attack. Now, what?" she said.

53

Warrenton, Virginia

NEAR FUTURE

His television monitor announced the attack.

Sam Fung estimated it would take till the next morning, maybe longer, for SWAT to overwhelm his teams. They had enough ammo and explosives to take the statue with them. It had been decided earlier just to blow the head off. Capitalists didn't stand for freedom anyway. The statue was a scam, a historic joke. It represented corruption and enslavement. The police hostages they had taken would drag out the mission even longer.

He should be cheering, but he had other problems. He had tried to use the chip locator Alfred told him about, but it wasn't working. The GPS locator on the cell phone didn't, either.

What had gone wrong?

He told Alfred's men to stay in L.A. until he could give them a location. Once they found Alfred, they could get him on a flight to China, or to Mexico, or anywhere away from US territory.

If they found him.

Getting Alfred's predicament out of his head took discipline.

Phase 2 of the plan would take place in the morning. He must not let his concern for his son interfere.

The stock market would crash in the morning. To propel it even lower, another attack would destabilize the confidence of the country. A one-two punch. Except this wouldn't stop at two punches, or even three.

Tomorrow.

His Chinese hackers and moles waited.

Two more teams of terrorists were already in position.

And his little part of the plan, too.

Would all the chaos and destruction be worth it if Alfred didn't survive?

Sam paced the four corners of his cellar until dawn.

All the networks showed helicopters circling Liberty Island. The headless Lady wore a smoking wreath. Parts of her stone head lay in pieces on the ground and along the shore of the island.

He heard the TV anchor report:

"We are told by the Park Police and the FBI that talks are ongoing for the hostages held within the pedestal. There are twelve people confirmed dead so far. Three terrorists and nine police officers. Authorities are not sure how many more terrorists are inside."

Turning his attention to the lower right side of the screen, Sam could see the stock market was down thirteen hundred points and market restraints had been placed on it again.

A blonde woman news anchor said, "Wall Street is reacting in a significantly negative manner this morning. We will be with you on continuing coverage of the hostage situation."

"Perfect," Sam said. He punched numbers on a new drop phone and said to the individual who answered, "Execute in one hour."

Sam heard the door chime ring twice, a pause, followed by three times. The code. A couple of his guards had arrived. He walked upstairs to let them in.

Wearing black clothing, they unloaded AR-15 automatic weapons and explosives into the garage.

"Get something to eat and some sleep if you need it," Sam said. "Later today and tomorrow, you'll be on guard duty."

He returned to the basement. *We might all be sacrificed for the cause. Except Alfred.*

Looking at the television monitor, he saw a split screen. Panic in the voices of the news anchors.

Sam thought about Saabir telling him in a secret meeting months ago that the infidels would know fear. Now Saabir was dead. Some history professor from the west coast had killed him. It had been reported that it was an accident that the professor had been in the shop.

Believable?

With Alfred missing, fear gripped him, too.

54

San Diego, California

NEAR FUTURE

"One of us needs to get some sleep, Zack," Lauren said. "Don't know if I can with what's happened. I thought Apollo was supposed to stop all this."

"Either we weren't much help, or not soon enough."

They heard Alfred moaning under the tape.

Lauren said, "Take it off him, but if he uses the "b" word again, I'm going to stop being nice."

"Nice is a relative word." Zack removed the tape.

Alfred coughed and cleared his throat. "I need the bathroom if you don't want your bed soaked. And I don't want the bimbo watching me either."

"Why you…"

"Don't let him get to you. He's a traitor and a disgrace. Get some sleep."

Lauren gave Alfred a murderous look and left.

Zack said, "Door is going to be open. Feet will be tied. Hands temporarily free. Got a nice sized baseball bat here if you want to get frisky."

He guided Fung into the bathroom.

Alfred could have screamed he was so happy to relieve his bladder. Even though the guy in the outlaw mask watched, he was able to flip a tiny switch in his watch to turn on the homing chip that he'd had surgically placed under the skin of his wrist.

I will make these clowns pay, but first I must get out of here. I can still get across the border and take a flight from there. I've got a day, maybe a little more, to leave here and arrive in China. Can my men get here in time?

Lauren couldn't sleep. She chewed on a fingernail tip, wondering if they had made even one correct move. Kidnapping a doctor and tying him up in their home? How could they defend any of this in a court of law? They were both university professors, but she worried they'd both begun to act without their consciences.

A cell phone chimed. Not her personal phone.

Bessus.

"An attack is coming from the water, Witch," the barbarian said.

Lauren could hear wind whistling over the line. "We just had an attack," she answered.

Why does everyone have a nasty name for me? Witch, bimbo. What the hell?

"Another is coming, a bigger one. And a different attack on a stone man."

"A stone man?"

The connection stayed scratchy. Lauren remained awe-struck that Apollo had arranged for her to converse with a man over twenty-five hundred years old, and a core enemy. *But was he now?*

"You were mine to ravage. You were mine to squeeze the life from."

Lauren answered in a terse tone, "But you didn't. Now tell me what you heard."

"A man made of stone. He will be torn apart with fire and smoke."

"When?"

"Before you can blink your eyes."

"What about the attack by sea?"

"I saw the medicine man talk. The same man with narrow eyes. He has black and white hair. This attack will destroy you. I must leave. Others are coming. I'm not done with you, Witch."

The phone call disconnected.

Lauren bolted for the bedroom. After Zack secured Alfred with additional lengths of rope, she nodded for him to come with her. He recovered his prisoner's eyes with a black cloth.

After exiting the room, Demo went in to watch Fung.

In the kitchen, Zack said, "We're not getting anywhere."

"Bessus called." She gave Zack the details. "I'm calling the police. They must know. We can't go on faith any longer. It's getting out of control."

"Call the FBI, instead. I'm beginning to agree with you. We can't manage all this by ourselves."

Lauren raised her voice. "Beginning to regret your actions? We don't know what we're doing..."

Looking over Zack's shoulder towards the television, she gasped and clapped a hand over her mouth. "The stone man. It's the Lincoln Memorial."

The news showed smoke and fire within the Lincoln Memorial. Police ran up the steps firing their weapons. A few cops lay motionless. No tourists had been allowed inside with the recent events in New York.

"How do we stop them?" Lauren asked.

"Time is short," Apollo said, entering the room.

"Where have you been?" Lauren demanded, her hands fisted at her sides. "You left us alone. We don't know what the hell is going on."

"I followed the leads. They're all uninvolved."

"Do you know what just happened?" Zack asked.

"I do. And your candidate?"

"In the next room," Lauren said, with a disdainful flip of her hand towards the bedroom.

Another news flash.

The anchor said, "The stock market is suffering horrendous losses. Market restrictions on trading are on, and there is talk now of shutting down Wall Street until authorities can figure out how to stop additional attacks."

Apollo raised an eyebrow. "They're attacking in waves. We must find out what's next."

"How come you don't know anything?" Lauren asked. "Aren't you a god? Stop them."

"I told you before that an alteration in time occurred when your husband killed the plotters in Athens. Whatever I knew from historical records has been slightly or completely changed. The events are proving to be similar, so we can estimate a devastating attack is coming. I've made multiple scans and projections of probabilities, but nothing is adding up."

"So, what are we doing here talking?" Lauren asked.

Upon entering the bedroom, Apollo removed the gag and blind on the captive. Alfred rubbed his jaw.

Alfred said, "Who are you?"

"He's young and wears no glasses," Apollo said. "Does not fit our parameters."

"But Lauren and I caught him with bait. A note about Pakistan, and I heard him talking about it on a phone. I think he's involved. Haven't got anything out of him yet."

"What's his name?"

"Dr. Alfred Fung. A biomedical engineer with some extra degree in Chinese and international relations."

The medallion came alive. Pictures, news clips, and internet postings about Alfred's work could be read on images emitted from the medallion.

Fung said, "What the hell kind of technology is that?"

"My, you have been busy," Apollo said. "How could such a brilliant young man be involved in the cataclysm that approaches?"

Alfred stayed silent.

"Tell me about Blue Sky? Tell me about this medicine you're developing?" Apollo stood abruptly. "You are studying the brain to cure diseases and dementia. But if you act to murder so many, then what is your true purpose?"

"You people have it all wrong, Goldilocks."

Apollo sneered. "You are amusing but let me scan the university files for your scientific progress." The files emerged from the medallion and appeared to float in space. "Interesting. Astounding actually for this period."

"What made you think Alfred was a conspirator?" Apollo asked.

Lauren answered, "The original Fung you sent us to check out said this one's medicine might change the future."

"You both have guessed well. You have no idea what this man is doing." Apollo raised his voice to Fung. "Blue Sky. Now tell me who plots with you?"

"Screw you. You have nothing. I want the police, now."

"No more games, Alfred. You don't understand who I am." A beam of yellow energy extended from Apollo's medallion and surrounded Fung's head.

Zack said, "No medicine first? You're not going to like this."

Alfred's facial muscles began to twitch. "Stop it. What the hell?"

The electrical charge made no noise, but the insides of Alfred's brain could be viewed.

"Who plots with you?" Apollo asked.

Alfred whimpered. He shook his head from side to side. "What are you doing to me? Leave me alone. You can't stop it, anyway."

Apollo asked, "You have different plans for this medicine you're developing? Don't you?"

55

Outside Warrenton, Virginia

NEAR FUTURE

Two electronic devices sat on the desk in front of Sam.

One should locate Alfred. He had checked many times with no result. He had to try again.

The other would activate his virus which would gut the financial system.

Alfred might not get away. But he had to take the chance.

He activated the homing device to find Alfred for just five seconds.

And he got a result. The computer monitor showed him to be in San Diego. The address showed 6324 Madra Street as his exact location. Alfred must be alive to activate the homing chip at his end.

Sam fumbled with the drop phone. He dialed the number for Alfred's comrades, who waited at the airport. With his fingers shaking, he redialed. "Here's the address in San Diego. Go get him and cross the border. Board any plane you can and fly south unless you can get across the Pacific. Go now."

The man answered, "We'll head down right away, but it will take a while with all the panic. The roads will be full."

"Hurry. Use any means necessary to acquire him."

His heart nearly vaulted from his chest. Alfred might escape. He picked up the receiver. He looked at the TV screen. The market had plummeted. The bankers would be screaming at each other.

How joyous. To pay them back for their greed, just before I destroy them all.

Sam activated his virus and watched the news.

A male anchor reported:

"We're extending full coverage of the two attacks, one yesterday, and another today on the Lincoln Memorial. The negotiators are in contact with the terrorists on Liberty Island. They are still shooting at the Lincoln Memorial. Apparently, the attackers have tear gas masks. Authorities have decided to attack the building with stronger weapons."

"Just in, the President has called for a joint session of Congress in the Capitol building tonight. He requests that citizens remain calm while authorities make efforts to ensure the safety of the public."

The reception on the screen wobbled.

"I'm sorry, ladies and gentlemen." The anchor checked the computer in front of him. He asked the blonde lady co-anchor if he was reading this announcement correctly.

The anchor wiped his forehead with a handkerchief.

"I'm sorry to report that we have another national emergency. The stock market is essentially…frozen. The exchanges have no idea what has happened. Despites trading curbs, the stock market was last quoted as down 2134 points. Word is coming in…all computers have just halted."

Sam hopped, came down on a bad knee, clenched, and nipped the tip of his tongue with his teeth.

The anchor continued, "The Bank of New York is reporting their system has been hacked. All transactions of Tri-Party Market of broker-dealers, and, oh no, the Federal Reserve is now reporting that their system has been compromised."

The newsman called out to his staff.

"This is unprecedented. This means the entire stock market and its entire backup, the records of transactions, has been halted, hacked and …"

A staff member runs up and hands him a sheet.

"We're having trouble staying on the air. The best thing to do is to acquire whatever cash you can. Go to your computer and take photographs of all your accounts before there's no money and you can't prove what's yours. This is a terrible day. Tune into your local news while we attempt to make head or tails out of this."

"Oh my God," the lady anchor said, "No stock trading. No transactions. No record of transactions…This means no money. Who could do this?"

Sam danced around the basement, pumping his fist. Blue Sky was now in progress. A year ago, he and Alfred had decided to call the mission Blue Sky because COBOL, the computer system software in service at the Federal Reserve and other government agencies, sounded like cobalt, hence blue.

Who could make that connection?

With Alfred likely to be freed, it was now time to hack into the Department of Defense computers, shut them down, and contact his comrades in China to commence their tactical plan.

Next up, 'Silent Wind,' the hammer blow that would permanently change the future.

And I have one more team hiding.

Perhaps I should be listed in historical accounts of the great leaders and planners. Father, you would be so proud of me.

56

SAN DIEGO, CALIFORNIA

NEAR FUTURE

The arteries and veins in Fung's brain pulsed. Electrical pathways exposed. The masseter muscles on the sides of his chin flexed in rapid succession.

"Call the police. I'm innocent," Fung said in a frantic voice. "Leave me alone. I'm a biochemist."

"You lie. You work on a formula," Apollo said. "You want to control thoughts. You're a beast. Behold the future while I record your brain functions."

Apollo's medallion projected holographic images of a desolate America made poisonous by radioactive fallout.

"These images are from one hundred and fifty years from now," Apollo said. "The land became unlivable. The people died. The Free World fell."

Fung thrashed against his bonds. "You're making this up. My head is throbbing."

Apollo said, "There's no more time to waste. Who are you working with? Where is the next attack?" He turned up the power from the medallion.

Alfred's head dropped to one side. He drooled.

Apollo demanded, "Who assists you in this plan?"

Trancelike, Alfred said, "*Yie. Yie.*"

Zack said, "What did he say?"

"Who do you plot with? What is Blue Sky?"

Alfred began to scream, "*Yie. Yie. Yie.*"

Zack said, "We're getting nowhere. I'm calling the FBI and Homeland Security. Something is coming down. We need to be ready."

Apollo holds up his finger. "Not yet. We do not want to be restrained by their need to interview you, Traveler."

"They already called. Cassandra said they visited the house while we were up in LA, and that they'd come back."

A humming came from Fung's hand. "What do we have here," Apollo said. He held the medallion over it. "He has a chip embedded in him. It turned on and then off. Perhaps it could help us. Someone is attempting to locate him."

Fung cried out, "It's *Yie. Yie* is doing it."

Apollo asked, "Does *Yie* know about your medicine, and how you will use it?"

"Yie knows, but he doesn't understand. He wants it to free the people, make them wiser, and join in the wealth. He doesn't understand it must be used to rule people."

Lauren said, "Maybe he's not telling us to die. It's a name. I'll look it up on the internet."

"Appreciated, Golden Hair, but allow me."

A moment later Apollo said, "Nothing of consequence. He is Chinese. The word could be slang, and there are many dialects."

Zack said, "We need someone who can speak Chinese."

"Not just Chinese. We need an expert," Lauren said.

Zack said, "I don't know anyone."

Lauren replied, "My friend, Roberta, does. I'm calling her. She knows a languages department head at State who'll get on it."

"Who is *Yie?*" Zack demanded.

"*Yie. Yie.*" Fung passed out and said no more.

"I may have overdone the probing. While we wait, I will attempt to trace the chip in his hand." Apollo extracted the microchip using a narrow beam from the medallion to cut through Fung's skin. He set the chip into a slot in the medallion. After a moment, Apollo said, "The chip is unfortunately defective now. We will have to wait for an answer from the Chinese interpreters. It is time for me to rest."

Lauren yelled, "This is no time for one of your..."

Apollo lay down and another of his holographic dreams shone from the medallion.

Chin called the gods into the room. Ensuring the safety of their conversations had become a game of cat and mouse. They waited for Hongwei to sleep and then they altered the cameras to show only recording of their working within the metal-surrounded enclave.

She began, "I have unlocked a passage to a lower level of the facility. My scanner reports little evidence of radiation exposure there now, but I did find bodies of technicians who died there long ago." She cleared her throat. "Within this sector, it appears those scientists had been working on the challenge of transfer in time. Their efforts had promise, but they had not the technological advances to create powerful enough gravitational fields, nor the precise calculations necessary to affect this kind of transfer. I cannot explain why our superiors never pursued this science. However, their exploratory work here, and our advances may allow us to create a closed-time curve in space-time. I could describe this as a round hole that test subjects will travel within. Spinning or bouncing inside this tube might be a better description. An enormous cyclotron is beneath us, one that can create enough power to push objects through this 'wormhole', as I have seen it described in the journals within their research. A significant issue is the survivability of the traveler, but I have an idea for that, also. I watched recordings of their experiments. I suggest we begin to work secretly on trying to perfect this technology. We have certainly advanced in the hundred and fifty years since the downfall of this country. We could adapt this "machine" to our own uses should we be successful in altering its functions."

"To do what, exactly?" Apollo asked.

"To send one of us, or all of us, away from here."

Astounded faces peered back at her.

Borfan stood. "Time is running out. Hongwei will be replaced, executed I have no doubt, if he does not have results shortly. We have been here for almost a year. I suggest we give him a weapons system, or something of value, to buy time. Should we be able to drag out his tenure, a few of us can work on the invention down below after hours. With concentrated effort, we could soon make a test journey."

Another of the scientists said, "You mean one of us? That would be suicide. We can't know..."

"I will be the one," Zeus said. "It must be tested. I am the oldest..."

Chin looked away, but she nodded.

Apollo interrupted. "I submit to you that you are not the best candidate. You are needed to assist in the compromise and manipulation of any overseer who might replace Hongwei, and then present results to the Council. So, I volunteer."

Silence.

"I see the wisdom of your suggestion," Borfan said.

Within months, the machine had been configured to transport a human. They concluded that the blue-colored craft that they had been transported in earlier could be minimized, armed with lasers, and altered to ensure the safety of the traveler through the time transfer process. A roach was their first subject. It returned whole, but dead. Observation of the process of transfer brought Chin to the conclusion that the dark energy matter that resembled the muddy material, if ingested in minute amounts by the roaches before traveling, allowed them to return alive.

Chin said, "We don't know exactly where the roach goes, but it comes back. I am already altering the calculations to test it for a time and place. Once you reach that location, you must set up a polarity, so we can, on a consistent basis, transfer between here and there. I estimate that, once the polarity is set, we can travel between times from that same location."

"You are brilliant, my dear," Borfan said. "I don't know how we could advance in the way we have without you. Altering the medication for us so we can work unhindered, drugging Hongwei so he sleeps and thinks he's ill, changing the feed of the cameras so he cannot observe our actions, and your latest achievement, hiding the recording of energy bursts from our experiments with the machine."

Chin clasped Borfan's hand. "You may think I do this, even we do this, for purely scientific or political reasons. I submit to you that once the mind is freed, recognizing oppression sets the human soul to seek freedom from it, by whatever means possible, even rebellion."

A shorter scientist with red hair said, "No one has been able to rebel. I never had such a thought."

"Since the invention of medication years ago," Borfan said, "the lower races, as you are called, could not have done so. Strict numbers quotas and high titers of the medicine made it impossible. You would not have been told this but someone, long ago, when the great attack against the country we now know as the United States occurred, devised the ability to alter thoughts and control them. There could never be rebellion. We were never told the person's name. Only those at the highest level knew the identity of those whom produced the drug."

Chin replied, "Truthfully, we also do this for another reason. We were allowed two children. They achieved much and gave us grandchildren. We could not count our fortune. The Central Committee secretly ordered the imprisonment of any family members of people who failed the State."

"You don't have to discuss this, my love," Borfan said.

She held up her hand. "No. I do. I failed to cure a disease that struck thousands of factory workers. By the time I figured it out and created a medicine that cures infections and wounds quickly, over ten thousand had perished." Her voice broke. "They decided that my sister and brother, even my parents, should be sent to prison for our failure. They died there, like our children…our grandchildren… innocent…"

She sobbed in Borfan's arms.

"I have one more revelation. You once asked what happened to the previous teams that were sent to open this facility. They all died from radiation sickness. None of us are expected to survive, either. It is our punishment. To them, we are but chickens. You serve a purpose."

Apollo blurted, "I want to see where it all began."

"You mean *how* it began in the United States place?" a blonde woman scientist asked.

"No. The ancient Greeks. Late 4th century BCE. I want to watch it happen. Their fight for survival will inspire us."

As Borfan wiped his wife's eyes with his sleeve, she said, "I will make it so."

The holographic memory changed again.

Zack said, "This is all starting to make sense."

"Wait," Lauren said, pulling him back from the image, "here comes more."

Borfan ensured the lock on the metallic door was secure. Chin changed the feed, so their overseer couldn't watch them. She had perfected the ruse. Their lives depended on it.

"All of you come and sit here," Borfan said. "We have been studying in depth the philosophy and mythology of these ancient Greeks. I know all of you are as impressed and mystified that such intellect existed so long ago. I have an atypical suggestion. Our lives are mundane. We work and sleep. Discovering this computer bank, this 'Book of Histories,' I might call it, gives us hope. Who would like to join me in taking the name and appearance of a god or goddess?"

Chin raised her hand first. "I've thought it through. It is logical that Borfan and I become Zeus and Hera. Who else would like to play?"

The other scientists also took the names of the gods. Ares, Poseidon, Hephaestus and Athena. Only one scientist still needed to choose.

"What will it be, Arex?" Hera asked. "You certainly don't want Hades?"

Everyone laughed.

"I will be the only god that I could be--Apollo. I will be the seer of the future and the god who professes moderation. I'm happy we've decided to progress in this way. I am Apollo."

"Then let us prepare garments and wear them as they did in those days. We'll join in a symposium, a discussion, though sadly, without the wine."

More laughter.

Borfan, now Zeus, said, "There is a serious urgency to on what we do. We shall develop our skills in learning more about the ancient world and the 21st century. We must know what the ancient Greeks and Americans excelled at, and how they fell apart. Each self-destructed. How do we change this?"

The phone rang in the house. Apollo awoke.

After a short conversation, Lauren said, "Thanks so much, Roberta. Tell you later."

"The State professor called another professor friend in China. The word '*Yie*' comes from an old dialect of Xiang. It means, 'father'."

All three looked at each other at the same time.

"Who is Fung's father?" Lauren asked.

After consulting his medallion, Apollo said. "There is nothing on social media. No record of him. Not even IRS records. This is peculiar. Someone has wiped clean his footprint."

"But wouldn't there be information on Alfred's applications to college?"

Zack patted her hand. "Nice one. He went to Southern California University."

"Scanning results," Apollo said. "He has a father. Residence listed in Warrenton, Virginia.

We must leave right away."

"That medallion looks more like a computer than anything god-like," Lauren said.

"I told you long ago, Traveler, and now you, Golden Hair, I am not a god of Homer."

The dome began to materialize.

Apollo said, "Golden Hair, can you keep Fung tied up until we return? I need your husband this time."

Lauren blurted, "Wait. The country is falling apart. The economy is shattered now, too. Have you seen the news? Riots are starting across the country. People can't get money out of banks. Food is running out. What exactly have you saved so far? Your name isn't even really Apollo. It's Arex."

"It is a valid observation, but the worst may be yet to come, and we must leave."

"When Fung awakens, he'll have severe headaches like Zack did," Lauren said.

Apollo said, "Unfortunate for him. We leave immediately."

57

Tora Bora, Afghan/Pakistani Border

NEAR FUTURE

"Sorceress, answer my summons," Bessus said into the talk box, an AK-47 rifle slung over his shoulder. He huddled in the bushes beyond the cave's mouth. "They're going to bring fire from the sea. The enemies ride ships that course beneath the water. More thunder and fire are coming from the men who left from these mountains. Look to your monuments."

The Sorceress didn't answer. He tried again. "Abandon me here, and I'll curse all of you."

He tried to get her to speak a last time. "Tell the god he must come for me, before they slay me with their firesticks. The warriors here say they abandoned a plan to bring ships into your ports and smite you with dirty fire and clouds. But the other attack from beneath the sea is coming. Others, too, from the land of the narrow-eyes. And it will be like a war club unto your head. You will all perish. I'm beginning to understand now, Sorceress. You serve him, too. You escaped my grasp because you fought."

Bessus heard warriors calling him. Insulting names. They fired their weapons at the mountainside near him.

How did they discover me? Did they hear me speak on the talking invention?

Bullets ripped across the rocks up on the hillside. They didn't know where he hid. Bessus slid down a trail and looped behind them.

The warriors argued, pointed at his last position and then, bending low, moved towards it. He slid into the cave mouth with his firestick ready. No one shot at him. He veered to the right vein. In that room, there would be men who watched the squares they called computers.

His firestick would draw more warriors. From his scabbard, he drew his trusted slayer of men.

Two long steps. He knifed the two warriors seated in chairs. In the corner, he spotted a thunder stick like he'd fired at night. He crept further into the complex. In the next room, the captain and others dipped their bread in meat and gravy.

Bessus thought of Apollo. The thunder stick felt good in his hand. Now, he was a god again.

Warriors saw him and reached for their firesticks.

He fired. The cave exploded. Some warriors burst apart. Others were thrown against the cave walls. A few fired. Bees hit the dirt around his feet.

Bessus unslung his firestick and smote them, leaving a smoking ruin of bloody bodies. But he heard others shouting and men racing towards him. He ran deeper into the cave, dodging boulders and ducking when the firesticks shot bees at him and scattered fragments of rock.

The Bactrian warlord fired back until he ran out of bees to shoot.

He could hide, or he could slide deeper into the cave. Or he could go down with his blade.

58

Outside Warrenton, Virginia

NEAR FUTURE

Birds. Trees. Mountains.

Apollo's dome dissipated on the outskirts of the property. The pulse of the dome illuminated the perimeter security. A square grid surrounded the house at fifty yards. A series of intersecting triangles of detection filled the ground from the house to the fence line. The lights were off in the house, but Apollo saw an electromagnetic glow deep within. Someone lurked inside.

"Should we alert the police, maybe the FBI?" Zack asked. "We need this to be lawful."

"A tang of guilt for Alfred?" Apollo grinned. "Not to worry. We will break many laws before this is over. It is near dark. Wait a bit longer to call the authorities. We can't have them arrive too soon."

When night came, Zack called the police station.

"There is an emergency at a house outside Warrenton. The resident there, Mr. Sam Fung, is involved in the current attacks on the United States. Please alert the FBI there may be more attacks coming, maybe from foreign shores."

"Who are you?" the sergeant asked.

"I'm Professor Zackary Fletcher. Please inform Homeland Security, too."

"Wait," the policeman said. "Are you the guy who saved the Parthenon?"

"Yes. Look. I have great reason to believe that Mr. Sam Fung is involved in a conspiracy to attack the United States. Come out to his house. He may be involved with his son, Alfred Fung. He's a PhD in biological science. They're plotting together."

"Sam Fung. I've met him a few times. Never had a problem with him. Did you also predict we were going to be attacked? I saw that news conference. You could be a bit of a quack. You wait until we get there. Trespassing is against the law."

Kidnapping, trespassing, coercive interrogation. What haven't we done?

"Hurry over. You and I both know the country is reeling."

Zack nodded towards the house. "We only have a short window of time. Let's use it."

Apollo went first. Zack saw the perimeter fence short out as they walked through. The front door loomed twenty yards away. Apollo went around the side. The windows had been covered with metallic slats. Two steels posts stood in front of the door. Any brush had been cleared for a hundred yards. Clear fields of fire.

"I'll break down the door, Traveler, and you will follow behind me. Let the dome protect you. We don't know what's inside. Be ready for the unexpected."

A beam of yellow energy came from the medallion and shattered the door. Apollo jumped inside. Zack ducked in behind him, following his lead into the kitchen. Across to another room. Staccato bursts of gunfire pelted the shield. The bullets ricocheted into yellow streaks that peppered the walls and floor. A second submachine gun joined the assault. Zack estimated that one of the guns would have an empty clip and need to be changed. He saw a counter he could jump to and come around the hallway behind them. He ran low and hid behind a wall. Apollo walked forward, much to the dismay of the gunmen. Their bullets didn't touch him. One shouted to another in what sounded like Chinese.

Slipping into a dining room, Zack lifted a chair. He saw a shadow in the next room. He moved to the door edge. The men reloaded. Zack swung the chair and hit one man across the face. The other man threw a grenade at Apollo. The room tore apart with flames and smoke. Unharmed, Apollo backhanded the other man across the face, taking him out.

Apollo disabled them further with a power burst from his medallion.

"How long are unconscious?" Zack whispered.

"They won't wake up. Search the rooms. Turn on the lights. He must be in the basement."

59

Outside Warrenton, Virginia

NEAR FUTURE

S am heard a shattering door and gunfire upstairs. How could they know so soon? An explosion shook the house.

Fair Wind needed to be launched. His sensors revealed an umbrella of energy around the house. Who could be doing this, he wondered. They'd blocked his internet cloud connection.

But he had prepared for such a problem. Multiple means of communication were critical, he knew.

He had a phone land line set into the ground. Old school. He was a master of new technology, but often the old ways served well enough.

Blue Sky took down the financial structure of the United States, and he'd disabled the Department of Defense computers. The country was powerless to stop him.

He dialed his contact.

Sam said, "Execute Fair Wind and he hung up.

They can't stop it now, even if I'm killed. He heard footsteps upstairs. The steel-enforced door would hold for a time.

A moment later, the barrier leading to the basement blew open.

It didn't matter now.

Fair Wind consisted of two Chinese nuclear submarines, launched from their Hainan Island base weeks earlier, and prepositioned in the

Pacific Ocean. One off the coast of California, and the other sub near Hawaii. It had taken twenty years to place junior officers into command positions on the Chinese boomers. But that wasn't all. His other officers controlled the Chinese land nuclear launch sites. Russia and Europe would be attacked, too. Weakened, they would be ripe for domination.

Alfred's people, safe inside the specially prepared Chongqing Facility, would survive the mayhem. They would emerge victorious, and motivated to fulfill their destinies as a true Peoples' Republic. Strengthened and made brilliant by Alfred's new medicine, they would be a new breed of superhumans.

He heard someone on the top step. He pulled back the bolt on his vintage AK-47. With extra magazines nearby and a shotgun, he would defend his enclave to the last.

60

Outside Warrenton, Virginia

NEAR FUTURE

A pollo took a single leap to the basement floor. Machine gun bullets ricocheted away from him.

Looking shocked at the result, an Asian man reloaded. Apollo tossed aside the weapon and lifted him by the collar.

"Are you Sam Fung?" Zack said. "Answer before he kills you."

"How could you know?" Sam answered. "You don't look like police. Who are you? How could you survive the shots I fired?"

"What is your plan, Fung?" Apollo asked.

"You've found me, but it no longer matters. Drastic measures are necessary. We Chinese are patient. Our revolution will take time. Your revolution reeks. How do the common people fare in this corrupt country?" Sam flung out his hand in a dismissive gesture.

Apollo said, "You don't decide the fate of millions. Not those who live now, nor those yet to be born."

"But I do," Sam said. "Mao needed time to purge the traitors. He made a mistake letting you capitalists in. Your infection has grown. He died, and greed has taken over. I see the women of China prancing about in your designer clothes."

"The nations can cooperate without war. Without nuclear devastation," Zack said.

"The common people will rule. The oligarchs will be snuffed out. Yours and ours."

"That's where you're wrong, Fung," Apollo said with a rising tone. "You think the common people, your peasants' army, will have power in the ruined world you created? It won't happen that way. Behold."

Apollo's medallion projected images of a United States and European countries poisoned by radiation. While Russia suffered from the attack, it recovered and war with China began anew. But China had created a core of devoted soldiers, fired by a medicine that turns men into obedient slaves. The medication, secretly dispensed to governments and then, the people, fueled a world-wide takeover.

Sam stared at the holographic images with wonder. "That's impossible. How could you know this? It is a simple matter to create these false visions. I could do it easily myself."

"Why didn't your bullets harm me? Look upon my power. I know the future. I have lived the future." Apollo played scenes of the desolate future the medicine, and the attack, had created.

"You are showing me the success of our strategy. Kill me or go. You have fulfilled my dream."

"Is it your dream that only oligarchs and the wealthy families prospered and ruled. The common people were enslaved." Zack asked.

Sam halted. "This is false. That's not the plan. The common people, the peasants would equally share…"

"We have Alfred. We know what he counterplots with his medicine." Sam bit his lip. "I don't believe you."

"How do think we found you, *Yie*?" Zack said.

Sam's mouth sagged open, his shock apparent.

"He doesn't see the future as you do. Mao was a killer. Dreams of a pure Marxist state are delusional, as always. Alfred is our prisoner. He won't be going anywhere." Apollo said. "Watch this as proof."

Alfred, under the influence of Apollo's interrogation, admitted that his medicine would be used to secure power over the people, and that his father, his *Yie*, didn't know what he planned.

Sam bellowed, "No, Alfred!"

"Kill millions for what? To end up worse than now?" Zack said. "Tell us what's next."

Apollo said, "I'm taking down the electronic shield over the house."

Seconds later, a voice mail came through from Lauren. She said Bessus had called and had said an attack is coming from beneath the sea. Lauren guessed submarines and nuclear missiles. She mentioned it sounded like Bessus was being shot at and fighting for his life. She begged them to somehow get those subs and come back to her.

"So, it's nuclear subs, Fung? What kind of animal are you?" Zack grabbed Sam by the collar. "You want to murder my family and my people."

"Stop the attack, Fung. While you can," Apollo said.

"It's too late. The order has been given."

"Where will we be attacked?"

"I'm a cyber-specialist. I've arranged for your defensive systems to be shutdown. I have devastated your corrupt bankers, too. You think you're not slaves. You are… to them. They create wars and throw nations into devastating debt. They control your politicians. Your system has failed you. It's failing China, too. We'll return to the old ways."

Apollo stood in front of Sam Fung. "Will you stop it? Your plan didn't work as you intended. All there will be is destruction and slavery for the people you intended to be free. Billions will die for nothing. Alfred has betrayed you. You must decide…now."

Sam dry-swallowed.

"We're out of time. Do something before the innocent are slaughtered." Zack implored him while clasping his hands prayer-like.

He lowered his gaze. "I can reverse the virus. I can rearm the United States. I can halt the missile launches from mainland China. But I can't stop the ballistic missile submarines. They're in position and will fire. They can't be recalled."

"Where are they?" Apollo asked. "Show me."

Sam released a deep breath. "Will you harm Alfred?"

"We won't," Apollo said. "I guarantee it. There will be justice for him, and you, for all the deaths and mayhem, but, there will also be changes."

"Tell us. Now," Zack demanded.

Police car sirens sounded.

"The authorities are coming. Homeland Security probably, too. Have some honor, Sam Fung."

Sam logged into his mainframe and began to type.

Apollo said, "We'll leave just before the police arrive."

Sam jumped back and covered his face when Apollo gathered together the blue swirls of his dome. "Who are you? What are you?" he cried.

"He will tell you." Apollo motioned to Zack and then he downloaded the technological information on the ballistic submarines and their locations on his medallion.

"Communists are godless, right?" Zack asked. "Acquaint yourself with our new god."

"I have the submarine coordinates. We're leaving," Apollo said.

Sam stared at his shaking hand. How could any of this be possible? His perfect plan had fallen apart.

Clearly, the two men, or one man and whatever the other being was, had powers he'd never known existed. But the proof of what Alfred had been planning was unacceptable.

He picked up his last drop phone. Not wanting to delay them, he didn't reveal that a loose end remained.

61

Pacific Ocean

NEAR FUTURE

The dome sped across the continent. Safe within the energy pulses, Zack floated downwards and set his feet on solid flooring. *How did a platform materialize beneath me?*

"I have kept you within healing plasma in the past, Traveler. Now I want you see what the gods have created." He set one of his medallions into a slot within a headset that resembled a crystallized bicycle helmet. The interior of the dome brightened with yellow and red lights. Multiple displays revealed themselves.

"This is unbelievable." Zack watched Apollo direct the craft from a customized, form-fitting chair.

"It reacts to the movement of my eyes." Apollo veered the dome to the left. "I can touch the display, or gesture to change direction."

"I see how you can move and accelerate, but how does it help us beat whatever's out there?"

Apollo swiped his finger across the three-dimensional screen. A new set of holograms appeared and moved to fill half their field of view. "A powerful laser is aboard. I will direct the computers to configure attack coordinates for each rocket."

Zack saw the blur of land and the light of cities pass below. In a matter of minutes, he viewed water in the distance by the shimmer of moonlight.

"I have no time to drop you off at home, Traveler. We can only attack one submarine at a time."

The sea below looked like ink on their westerly course.

"What we do now will decide whether physical and mental enslavement dominates the future. Hold on, Traveler."

Zack grasped the edge of Apollo's chair. Their flight halted abruptly. His feet flew upwards. Apollo's craft illuminated the water and revealed a leviathan just beneath the surface.

"Where are we?" Zack asked, resetting his feet. "Look at that thing. It's huge."

"We are a hundred miles off the coast of California. We are in good posi…"

A newly developed Type 096 Chinese ballistic nuclear submarine rose towards the surface. The ocean boiled when a steam cannon sent the first of twenty-four JL-3 missiles, each a MIRV, with multiple thermonuclear warheads, to rise and clear the water. Once free of the surface, the rocket hovered a moment, straightened its orientation, and then the first of three solid fuel boost motors fired to begin the ascent, emblazing the night.

From the underside of Apollo's dome, concentrated laser beam reached the first missile as it gained altitude.

Apollo said, "I have less than sixty seconds to destroy each missile before the first-stage booster drops and their second-stage motors ignite."

The concentrated beam of light cut through the rocket's metallic skin and melted its guidance system. It wobbled, spun end over end, and fell into the sea. Apollo, speaking directions to the craft, directed the laser to attack each missile as it ascended.

"It's taking too long, Traveler," Apollo said, with strain in his voice. "We have to chase them as they take different flight paths."

Zack watched the dome accelerate to a position nearby each rocket, so the laser could disable the boosters. "But you can only destroy one at a time. It's a losing battle. How about just sinking the sub?"

"There was only so much time to develop this platform. The laser is powerful, but the beam cannot be divided to be effective. We can't attack multiple targets at once, and we must be close to be successful. Destroying the sub would take too long, the laser mitigated by the ocean, the hull too thick, and the missiles would get away."

The dome accelerated and then halted, fired its laser and moved on to the next at a dizzying pace. Zack closed his eyes at times to keep from passing out. One by one, the sub-launched rockets tumbled into the ocean.

Apollo grimaced. "The problem is that the other vessel is 2500 miles away and may have already launched. And it is far more difficult to stop them after their second and third-stage motors lift the missiles into orbit."

Having splashed twenty-four ballistic missiles, Apollo directed the dome towards Hawaii. "Strap yourself into my chair, Traveler. I prefer to stand, anyway, but we must hurry."

For the first time, Zack saw tension on Apollo's face, jaw muscles pulsing, bulging veins on his temple, and it scared the hell out of him.

Zack yelled above the energy cacophony, "You have superior technology. You have the medallion. This…dome travels at Mach… whatever. Can't we beat them?"

"You don't understand, Traveler. Tyche, that despicable goddess, waits to foil my plans. I have no control over her. We will be hard pressed to disable them all." Apollo directed his dome to ever-faster speeds. "Because, by now you know I'm not a god. I'm mortal, just like you."

Zack couldn't tell if the stars he saw in front of his eyes came from the energy swirls or he was on the verge of losing consciousness. Apollo had proved to him time and again that he was a god -of some kind. Who could do all he'd done thus far? The hard truth of what he and Lauren had come to realize still felt like a sledgehammer to the chest.

But it all makes sense.

Zack now knew for certain that the future of civilization hung on the success or failure of a man.

62

Capitol Building, Washington, D.C.

NEAR FUTURE

Within the bowels of the US Capitol building, tunnels coursed between opposite ends of the structure which contained the House of Representatives on the south side and the Senate on the north end. The basement displayed statues of politicians and the glass-enclosed mementoes of statesmen long deceased. Beneath where Congress met to do the business of the country, the hallways extended into a labyrinth-like maze.

Behind locked doors, ten members of a terrorist team from an Afghan-Pakistani border camp, wearing police uniforms, hid within the House-side heating and cooling equipment room in the basement. They had assembled a few men at a time over a forty-eight-hour period, each bringing needed supplies for the attack.

The second half of the team, twenty men, waited in SUV's on 1st Street, near the east entrance to the Capitol. With night descending on Washington D.C., they filtered on foot towards the east entrance, to await elected officials who would be rushed to supposed safety because of attacks taking place within the building.

An emergency joint session of Congress would occur 7 p.m. that evening, and it would include the House and Senate, the Supreme Court justices, the Vice President, and the President of the United States. All anxiously awaited to hear the President's speech on how the nation could navigate the financial disaster and avert additional attacks.

The captain of the basement team passed the word to his squad to check their assault rifles, fragmentation grenades and satchels of Composition-4 (C-4) high explosive.

Each member of the team wore a suicide vest.

They had all vowed to die.

The leadership of the United States would be eliminated in one mission.

The captain waited for a text signal from his contact in Virginia on his burn phone. Upon receiving it, he would hand-signal to his men to open the door and rush upstairs to the session in progress.

7 p.m. came and went.

The captain had already calculated that, when the joint session quieted in the aftermath of applause for the president, they would eliminate any capitol police, burst into the chamber, and set off their grenades and explosives. He'd told his men to place the timed detonators into the putty like material molded to resemble American iconic symbols- a football, Mickey Mouse, the Washington Monument, an unclean swine with a curled tail, and a stamped dollar bill.

His special touch.

How long should he wait?

His walkie-talkie could be used to contact the outside team. He spoke into it, expecting poor reception from his position. A garbled response from the leader conveyed news of a gun battle. The captain heard shouts and automatic fire over the connection.

Was his burn phone dysfunctional and not allowing him to receive the go-ahead? The attack had begun. No more waiting, he decided.

He gave the signal to ignite the fuses of the explosives. The captain smiled, confident that he would hasten in the new world. Those in the Pakistani caves would confiscate nearby nuclear weapons. The Faithful would occupy prime positions in the aftermath, as promised by their contacts who would destroy the Western nations and recreate the old China from the new. But, those who devised this plan would be defeated later also, and the believers would rise from the ashes of the impure. *It will come to be.*

"Each of you knows what to do." The captain scanned the faces covered by black masks. "Fold up your prayer rugs. I'm going to open the door. Go to God. Martyrdom and Paradise await you. Don't let anyone stop you from getting into the chamber. No one survives."

Tora Bora

NEAR FUTURE

Bessus used his firestick as a club.

He retreated deeper into the cave, leaving a fighter crumpled on the cave floor and blocking the path. He still had bees for the weapon, but he would soon run out.

Hiding at corners and then jumping out from behind boulders allowed him to slay more hunters. The fearless mountain warriors continued to creep towards him.

He lay in a large crack in the floor. The warriors threw smoking balls at him. He knew what that meant and ducked. The cave exploded, metal shards pelting the walls around him.

Smoke. *Can't see. But these mountain rats can't see me either.*

Thinking he had died in the blast, the men moved into the narrow opening. Bessus rose and shot three more. He retreated. They followed.

The explosion took way his hearing. He bounced a finger in each ear to clear them.

Why had the Scout brought him here to die in this mountain? Had he not done what had been asked of him?

He slayed the warrior leader and all his men.

He called upon the Sorceress to help destroy the attackers in her land. She would live on and he would die.

He heard shooting, but the sound seemed distant. Bessus huddled in a corner. Should he flee?

Warriors burst into the cave room. Lying on the floor, he killed several. The warrior's bees would fill his weapon, but he would soon run out again. This time he ran, aware that they might use a thunder weapon against him.

He'd known these caves as a child, pursued by the Persians after they'd executed his grandfather and father by having the horned beasts crush their skulls. He wanted to ride one someday, to demonstrate his mastery over them.

Breathing hard, he continued further into the cave. He thought about how Scout had said that a free man fought to protect others, while a slave was told who to kill. He attempted to contact the Sorceress one more time, but the talk box failed him.

He didn't want to be a slave any longer, but neither did he wish to perish in this dark and closed in place.

His nightmare. That which he feared more than anything else.

Except.

The image of his young son's face flashed into his thoughts. *I have failed you. Survive on your own. That's how warriors are made, boy. A tough-skinned, mountain bear-claw you'll need to be.*

More of the exploding balls drove him into place he'd never explored. He'd been told gravesites marked the inner places. His hearing improved. The approaching warriors would cut off his ears, his nose, and his eggs, and feed them to the camp women.

Warriors attacked again. He fired the stick until he ran out of bees.

Bessus drew his knife. *If only I had my axe to settle this as men should.*

64

San Diego, California

NEAR FUTURE

Lauren watched Alfred sleep. Still secured with ropes and plastic ties, he wouldn't be going anywhere.

She wondered what drove a scientist to create a drug that could enslave the world.

This man is diabolical. Should I just kill him now and preserve the future?

Would anyone blame her, and should that even matter? If she went to jail for murder, could she sit in a cell and justify her actions with the lives she'd saved?

A pillow would do the trick.

The only other person she had ever thought about killing had been Bessus. He deserved it.

And this guy did too.

Protect the kids. Save her friends and family.

She lifted the spare pillow beside Fung's head. Gripped it in her hands. It wouldn't take long. When did civilization peel away in the face of survival? What pushes an otherwise rational person over the edge? she wondered. Seeing the strain in her hands, she relaxed them. She would need all her strength to carry it out. What if he escaped? Would she be able forgive herself for allowing a mass-murderer to get free?

Save the children. Preserve the people.

Demo dashed into the room. His usual devil-may-care expression now reflected pure anguish.

"They've attacked again, Mom." He hugged her.

Lauren dropped the pillow and held him. "What? Where?"

Fung awoke and stared at her.

"Come look at the TV, Mom."

Cassandra paced in front of the 62-inch television screen in the family room. "I can't stay here and watch them attack us."

Over Cassandra's shoulder, Lauren saw yet another scene of horror on the screen.

A male reporter outside the Capitol, spoke quickly while ducking to escape the shots being fired nearby. Lauren couldn't hear his words with the cacophony of gun blasts.

The news ticker scrolling at the bottom of the screen reported that the lives of president, vice president, and the congress were being defended within the Capitol. Police darted past the reporter. News crews jumped out of the way. Explosions sounded from inside the Capitol Building.

Bessus said watch out for your monuments, Lauren remembered.

The reporter loosened his tie. "The military will need to establish order. Martial law might be imposed. Some group is systematically destroying our nation."

The reporter dove to the ground as bullets ripped into the police behind him on the Capitol steps.

"I've had enough," the newsman shouted. He ran to an injured policeman. Seeing a thigh wound, he used his necktie as a tourniquet. He told the policeman to put pressure on the wound. "I need your gun. They're not getting away with this."

Sirens screamed down East Capitol Street to reach the Capitol. The reporter handed his phone to a woman reporter sprawled on the steps.

"Please hold this for me," he said. "I'm going up there and defend the entrance."

The dark-haired woman holding the phone selfie-style said. "We're going together and to hell with them. They can't do this to us." The phone picture feed bounced as she ran up the steps. The lens showed her picking up a wounded policeman's shotgun. She put the phone down in the direction of 1ˢᵗ Street. A male voice in the background said, "There are police coming at us from 1ˢᵗ."

Multiple gunshots could be heard over the television.

Back at home, Lauren looped her arms around Cassandra and Demo. "This is the war Apollo told us about. He said the country didn't survive. He said we need to help stop them."

"Dad's with Apollo. What are they doing?" Cassandra asked.

"Trying to stop something worse."

"And that guy in the bedroom is a major part of it. Well, screw him," Demo said. "I'm taking off the gloves. This is survival now. I'm going in there and…"

"Demo," Lauren yelled. "We have to wait."

"Can we get word to Dad?" Cassandra asked.

"It may not matter with what they're working on?"

"What's that?" Cassandra asked.

"Nuclear missiles coming for us."

Neither spoke. They stared at Lauren.

"Listen, these murderers…want submission. They want the ultimate power over all of us, all people across the globe."

"But we're going to fight," Demo said.

Cassandra said, "Like my people did at Marathon. Like the Spartans did at Thermopylae."

That's why Apollo sent us to Ancient Greece. Now, we have our backs to the wall, Lauren thought.

"I need to leave a message for Zack on his phone. I don't know if he'll get it, but he and Apollo must know Bessus might be in trouble, too. And they might not realize the Capitol is under attack."

Cassandra said, "None of that will matter much if what you say is true. I can't imagine what they must be doing right now."

Lauren closed her eyes. Through gritted teeth, she said, "One of you put on your mask and go in and watch that SOB. I need to stay out here for a minute and figure out what to do."

She began to mentally compose a message for Zack.

The news ticker announced that a battle beneath the capitol building remained ongoing. Additional police officers and SWAT reinforcement were in transit to the scene. Police reported that an anonymous phone call had alerted authorities just in time to disrupt the plans of the terrorists. Elected officials corned in the House chamber, being defended by Capitol police reported that the scene resembled the last stand of the Alamo.

Attacks were coming from all sides, just as Apollo had cautioned, Lauren thought. *Demo's right. Our backs are against the wall, and the claws must come out.*

65

Hawaiian Islands

NEAR FUTURE

A second Type 096 Chinese ballistic missile submarine positioned a hundred miles from the Big Island of Hawaii had already begun to launch its missiles.

Each of missiles might be a MIRV which contained multiple warheads. Apollo directed his laser to compromise the first one. With its guidance system cooked, the missile, in a brilliant red and yellow streak, fell into the sea.

Apollo directed his laser at the other JL-3 ICBM's rising on their first-stage rocket boosters and gaining speed.

"The crew has detected our presence," Apollo said. "They're locking onto us."

Using radar guidance, the submarine crew activated their Type76A dual anti-aircraft artillery system and blasted Apollo's dome with continuous 37 mm cannon fire. The dome deflected the shots, but not their kinetic force. The dome hurtled backwards a hundred yards. The chair's electronic straps saved Zack. Unrestrained, Apollo hung on to the console to continue his assault on the ascending missiles. He altered the location of the craft to clear his field of fire of smoke and debris from the submarine's defensive attack.

His laser weapon melted the guidance system of three additional rockets as each one gained altitude.

Unable to penetrate the dome's defensive shield, the Chinese sub launched anti-aircraft missiles. The repetitive blasts struck their target. They failed to penetrate, but the concussion hurled an unrestrained Apollo against the console. He cracked his head and slumped onto the platform.

Zack, strapped onto the command chair, shouted, "Apollo. Get up! The missiles are getting away."

The AA fire and barrage of ricochets blocked Zack's view outside the craft. He disengaged from the chair and shook Apollo. With no response, Zack lifted the crystal helmet from his mentor's head and set it on his own.

"Oh, man, I'm going to have to learn fast," Zack said. "Computer, follow those missiles. Lock on their guidance systems and fire the laser."

The dome sped after the rockets, firing as it accelerated. Second-stage launches commenced. Each rocket became more difficult to destroy now that the distances had increased. He directed the dome away from the Hawaiian Islands to catch the rockets as they diverged onto different flight paths. At one hundred and twenty seconds the second stage dropped, and the next stage ignited.

"Pursue and fire," Zack yelled. Blood throbbed in his temples. They were getting away. He saw multiple streaks on his display console. "Faster, computer." He glanced at Apollo. "Wake up. I can't get them all."

Chasing the ballistic missiles as they coursed in different directions, Zack felt the grip of panic. He fought it while directing calculations and attack coordinates, but now he knew the task might be hopeless. Even a ten-kiloton weapon reaching the US and detonating at a high altitude could create an electromagnetic pulse disaster, shutting down power, transportation, communications, food production, and water sources.

The killing blow for a nation already reeling.

The end of the country.

Far away from Hawaii, he saw on his holographic console what looked to be a barrage of cruise missiles launched from the sub towards Oahu.

Zack facial features contorted into one of rage.

Even with my best efforts, I can't destroy them all. We've failed.

I'll get as many as I can, he silently vowed.

Zack directed the dome to follow the murderous rockets heading towards the continent.

66

Hawaiian Islands

NEAR FUTURE

After Department of Defense computers failed, Navy Pacific Fleet Command, Pearl Harbor, CINCPAC, directed two Aegis missile defense armed destroyers and two Ticonderoga Guided Missile Cruisers to leave Pearl Harbor by the Entrance Channel. They moved at flank speed to positions outside of Oahu and the Big Island of Hawaii. With the Air Force Space Based Infrared System, SBIRS, a satellite detection system, also compromised, they couldn't track ballistic missiles launches, identify the kind of missiles used, or coordinate defenses.

The Hawaiian Islands and their military assets were on their own.

The continental homeland had been attacked. There was no reason they wouldn't be, too.

Captain Philip Olinger, the commanding officer of one of the cruisers, the USS Port Royal CG-73, made station on the north side of the Big Island. The ship arrived fifty nautical miles off Hilo when he saw brilliant flashes in the far distance.

A series of them, as if an enormous video game played itself out in the night sky.

But this was no game. Olinger recognized the launch of multiple submarine-launched ballistic missiles, heading in different directions, but all bearing east.

And a ship or submarine, plane, or *something* fought a continuing desperate battle to keep those missiles from hitting the continent or the Hawaiian Islands. In fact, Olinger couldn't believe the speed with which the aerial platform destroyed the enemy launches.

We must have weapons systems I've never heard of.

The flash of the interceptor's weapons continued to move further away to the northeast.

The battle is moving away from us, Olinger realized.

As soon as the word came from Homeland Security to the Navy Department that their combined computers were again operational for another unexplained reason, submarine hunter aircraft took off from Kaneohe Bay Marine Corps Air Base to search for enemy submarines.

With his Command Control Defense Center, CIC, functioning again, Olinger contacted CINCPAC Fleet, Navy Command Pacific, in Pearl Harbor.

"CINCPAC, who's our 'tip of the spear' off Hilo, bearing a hundred nautical miles? They're engaged in a furious battle, and they need help."

"We have no ships, subs or planes in the area, yet. What are you seeing?"

"Someone is splashing sub-launched BLMs. I can see launch-phase trails. Knocking them down even after third-stage boosters are dropped. I don't know how they're doing it. Those aren't our anti-missile SM-6's being used."

"Get over there, Captain, and prepare to launch your missiles as needed."

"Sound general quarters, man battle stations," Olinger said with a calm born in the realization that his ship would be involved in an attack within minutes, if not seconds. His officers glanced back at him. "Comms, contact all frequencies, we have a hostile attack in progress a hundred nautical miles north of Hilo. Combat, Engage targets."

His crew in Command and Control, CIC, detected fire trails heading towards Oahu.

Olinger reported, "CINCPAC, you have six, I repeat, six cruise missiles, could be Russian, but also likely A-17's, coming your way.

I'm engaging with SM-6 missiles. A-17's are Chinese, Pearl."

"Roger that. Get as many as you can. We'll notify DDG-115 Peralta to coordinate air defense. Live tests of our antiballistic missiles SM-3IIA's's have only been partially successful. Get what you can with your SM-6's."

"Tell them to launch whatever they've got now, Pearl. Inform THAAD air defense on the islands."

Captain Olinger directed his fire control team to intercept the cruise missiles with Aegis BMD (Sea Based Midcourse) SM-6 Terminal phase missiles.

The SM-6's reached two of the cruise missiles in time. Everyone aboard ship waited for a nuclear detonation.

Olinger contacted Pearl Command. "Two splashed. No detonations."

"Roger, Port Royal. Peralta is launching. Standby…"

Captain Olinger waited.

CINCPAC stated, "Peralta acknowledges one splashed cruise missile. Three still hot."

"THAAD's have to perform. The THAAD's can take it out without a nuclear blast."

Olinger estimated that the US Army THAAD, Terminal High Altitude Missile Defense, land-based missile launchers, would send eight missiles per launcher into the skies off Oahu. But deploying a THAAD against another missile was like shooting a bullet with a bullet.

Flood the skies.

Now, we depend on Kinetic Kill technology. With the cruise missiles closing in, they couldn't risk a nuclear burst over the Hawaiian Islands. Cruise missiles are on a course for Pearl Harbor.

Forty-eight missiles lifted from a THAAD battery on the Big Island. Another cruise missile shot down.

But, the last missiles continued to run at a low altitude above the ocean.

A second THAAD battery emptied in a burst of flame and smoke. One collided with a cruise missile and caused it to veer off course. All fell into the sea off Oahu's North Shore.

"The last cruise missile is making it through," the Pearl Harbor commander said. "The Patriot PAC-3 MSE's missile battery is our last-ditch defense. If the cruise missile is nuke-armed, it could detonate."

Twenty more land-based THAAD's from a third battery leaped toward the oncoming missile.

CINCPAC reported, "Tracking, Port Royal...tracking...last chance."

"Come on. Hit to kill, "Olinger said.

"Still hot," CINCPAC said.

A Patriot launcher fired sixteen missiles at the low-flying, in-coming cruise missile. Three of Patriot interceptors smacked into the Chinese cruise missile.

The remaining Patriots flamed out and plunged into the ocean.

All held their breath.

They waited.

Olinger heard the cheering over the intercom with CINCPAC and on the bridge of his ship. He stared at his white-knuckled grip on the phone. Releasing it, he shook his hand to bring back the blood.

CINCPAC said over the intercom, "No detonations. Reports coming in of SLBM's launched previously from that sub on course for the mainland, Captain. It's out of our hands. Reports coming in that the same asset you described is still splashing SLBMs heading towards the US. No one knows who it is. We have not yet identified the nationality of the attacking submarine, either. We're deploying every asset we have to put up a phased adaptive defense near the coast."

Olinger answered, "We're going to engage the sub, Pearl. Whoever is knocking down those missiles, I hope they keep it up. Those SLBM's with MIRV will be in terminal phase soon. We know what that means."

67

500 Miles off The West Coast

NEAR FUTURE

Twenty-four JL-3's SLBM's had been launched from the Chinese Type 096 submarine off the Big Island.

Fourteen of the 35 kiloton armed rockets splashed so far.

According the information display, four remained hot and heading to the US mainland. Zack directed the laser to attack another missile, but it was a losing game.

Four MIRV SLBM's could strike major cities and military installations in the US.

"Identify next target," Zack ordered, gripping the chair. If only the firing system would engage more than one unit at time. He wondered how the platform could continue to generate the energy to keep firing. The display before him started to flash and distort. "Don't give up on me now. Chase the one closest to the coast."

The dome raced to catch up as the third stage booster rocket flared out and dropped off. Re-entry in the atmosphere would come at higher speeds. "Accelerate, dammit," Zack demanded.

As the dome neared another target, metallic shards shot out from the missile. "What the hell is all that?"

"Ignore the chaff. It's meant to distract our attack," Apollo said, "and give me the headset."

"You're gushing blood," Zack said, glancing at him. "I'm so glad you're up."

"Fear not." Apollo took a quick sip from his flask.

Back in the command chair and snapping the crystal helmet back on, Apollo said calmly, "Accelerate. Cut the attack beam for each rocket by half."

"Will it be enough to disable them?"

"We have no choice. Fire."

The laser penetrated the reentry vehicle containing the multiple warheads. It slowed and descended.

"Onto the next one," Apollo ordered. The dome now skirted the edge of the atmosphere. "Those are not just MIRV's Traveler. They're MARV's. The individual warheads released can maneuver and they are far more difficult to destroy once released."

Zack asked, "What happens when they re-enter?"

"The vehicle releases the multiple warheads one at a time. We have to compromise it before that occurs."

Another descending missile appeared on the display. "Engage," Apollo said with more urgency. After burning through the rocket's shell, Apollo said. "Move to the next target."

Zack said, "Look at the display. That next one's heading to the northwest US."

The Chinese SLBM accelerated in its descent. The dome gained speed to come along-side. A ten second laser burned through the missile casing. "We have to reach the last one," Apollo said.

As the dome sped away, Zack watched to see if the missile had been affected. He saw a yellow streak as it descended and lost direction.

"It's enough to mess up their flight paths," Zack said. "Get that last one, and I'll buy you a drink."

Apollo glanced at him. "This is no time for..."

The dome headed south towards California. Zack yelled, "Look! The warheads are separating. Get them, please!"

"Destroy the reentry vehicle first," Apollo told the computer control. The laser beam reached out for the MARV and cooked its controls.

The separated warhead began its descent. With the distance away from it increasing, Apollo needed to fire the laser beyond its maximum range.

"Pray, Traveler."

"To whom?"

"To Hera and the other gods. Pray that their efforts were enough."

The red band of light struck the descending warhead.

No effect.

"Continue to engage," Apollo said more urgently. "Close the distance."

Zack held onto the back of Apollo's command seat. A bead of sweat ran down his neck. For the first time, Zack registered the overwhelming aroma of perspiration within the dome.

And he saw Apollo crossing his fingers behind his back.

"Approximate the warhead," Apollo said.

Zack saw the laser burn a path through the metal.

It lost acceleration and headed for the ocean.

"You did it!" Zack slapped Apollo on the shoulder. He saw Apollo's jaw muscles pulsing as he let his shoulder slump backwards.

"Is it truly over?" Zack asked. "They'll have a hell of a time with the contamination if any of the nukes explode in the ocean. The Navy will need to salvage those splashed missiles over a wide expanse of sea. It could take years. The ecological damage would be insurmountable."

"We will have to deal with those problems, but I will give you their locations. I just sent it to your email at home. You can forward it to the authorities. I will use my technology to help counter any possible radiation damage in the seas and on land if it occurs."

"Are we headed to Oahu to help them? Missiles were headed their way?" Zack asked.

Apollo checked his console. "They have succeeded in stopping the attack."

Zack slumped back into the command chair. "I can't believe it. That was a big risk, cooking them with half the power to have a chance of getting them all."

"Tyche looked kindly upon us this time." Apollo grinned. "I knew there was a good reason to bring you along, but I'm dropping you off at home now. Be with your family. Celebrate with the recognition that hundreds of millions of lives have been saved. I must check on Bessus now."

"Forget about him. He's a killer."

"Without him, this attack might have succeeded. I must go to him. I made him a promise."

"One last question."

Apollo raised an eyebrow.

"Can I have one of these dome platforms for my birthday?"

68

Tora Bora Mountains

NEAR FUTURE

Apollo landed fifty yards from Bessus's cave. A fast scan showed bodies on the hillside.

His medallion probed into the mountain. "My, Bessus, you've been busy."

Continuing within the dome, he passed through the entrance to the main room and came upon a scene of devastation. The giant Bactrian must have eliminated over twenty warriors with an RPG rocket-propelled grenade.

But where was he now? Apollo wondered. Another search revealed the yellow outline of warm bodies deep within the interior. One should be Bessus…if he could get there in time.

Apollo navigated the floor and cave wall obstacles at high speed. He leaped over piles of the fallen. Bessus had adapted well to the modern world.

He heard gunfire and yelling.

Turning a last corner, he found Bessus slumped across a boulder, the Bactrian shot multiple times. Two bodies lay at the giant's feet.

Apollo pulled out his silver flask. "Between you and Traveler, I will have only a little more of the nectar left." He dripped the medicine into the giant's mouth.

Bessus opened his eyes and groaned.

"You don't have to speak," Apollo said. "Let's bring you outside, although the light of day won't make you any more pretty. I need time for you to heal."

Bessus swallowed dry. He opened his eyes. "I have done as…you…asked."

"What you did helped to save the Americans, the New Greeks."

"Then will you end this curse?"

"The curse is over, Bessus. Do you still want to slay her?"

Bessus chewed on his lip. "I made a vow, once. I should be tortured by knowing she still lives, but now I see her as a warrior. She fought me. More than once. I bear her mark."

Apollo glanced at the bisecting scar on Bessus's face. "I will deliver you back to when you marched with Xerxes."

Bessus, beaming now, asked, "Can I bring firesticks and thunder weapons to my home? I could rule Persia will them."

"You cannot. You'll return as you came. You won't remember what happened to you here. But I will tell you what will come to be. You'll enjoy knowing this."

Bessus raised his gaze.

"I will return you to the time of Xerxes, and you will live out your days as is fated to be. The line of your son will gain your revenge one-hundred and fifty years after you are gone. A Greek King named Alexander will bring an army to conquer Persia. While you are allied with the Persian Royal Family, your grandson, many times over, will kill the Persian King, Darius."

Bessus bellowed the victory cry of the Bactrian homeland.

"Your outburst is too loud for this dome. I may need to drink the nectar to heal my ears."

"Then I will at least have that revenge?" Bessus asked.

"You will, and you served me well. You helped to keep many generations from slavery. Now you understand."

"Then the Sorceress shall live, and I will go home."

"You won't be whole until you get there, Bessus. Home will restore you."

The Dome lifted off and streaked westwards.

Apollo said, "I'll bring you to the mud hole, and it will be a long journey back from Greek lands. I will place you with Xerxes when he hastens his retreat after the great sea battle of Salamis. I regret that you must return to who you were. But, Bessus, you have had a taste of being your own man. I'm pleased you made this choice."

"You can stop flapping your lips now. Send me through the mud, and I will be home."

"I have gifts for you." Apollo handed Bessus his favorite double-bladed axe, lost within the long tunnel at Delphi.

Bessus's eyes flashed twice the size, and he screeched his pleasure. "It's mine again! My enemies will tremble at the sight of it."

"I have one more gift to you, worth more than all the gold in your kingdom, you once said." Apollo held a set of upper and lower dentures in his hand. "These are yours. When you are asleep while we travel, I will attach them to the metal studs in your jaws. You can take them on and off. They will hold firm, and you will be able to chew a steer if you like."

"Teeth? I can eat again?"

Apollo laughed heartily. "You may. I will not separate a giant from his appetite. You won't remember how you acquired them, but I will take that risk. You deserve these rewards."

When they reached Delphi, Apollo sent Bessus through the transit. "Farewell, Stinkpile. Remember to hold your breath."

69

San Diego, California

NEAR FUTURE

The news anchor repeated the instructions from Homeland Security.

"Stay in your homes. There's rioting and fires across the country, shortages of food, water, and medicine. Obey the instructions of law enforcement officers. Martial law has been declared. No one on the streets after 10 p.m. Looters will be dealt with harshly. Preserve energy as authorities restore power, water, and utilities. Call the police if you need to go to the hospital after 10 p.m. These attacks on our country have been devastating. We don't know if there will be more."

Zack wrapped his arm around Lauren. "It's bad, but it could have been far worse. At least, we have a future. I hope they give us more news from the capitol. Apollo didn't mention he knew what was occurring there."

The newsman returned on the screen.

"The provisional government of the United States has announced that the US armed forces have shot down a great number of missiles coming from Chinese nuclear submarines. While we are reeling after the attacks of the last couple of days, we have avoided annihilation."

Lauren kissed Zack on the cheek. "Did you get out your Star Wars shooter and splash them?"

"All Apollo, Honey. I wonder when he'll be back. We still must figure out what to do with Fung Junior in the bedroom."

From the TV, they heard the reporter say, "Take heart, America, that we have a second chance to rebuild our nation. Who will help to recover, mend and go forward is not yet clear. This just in: China has apologized and insists that the Chinese government did not sanction this attack. The nuclear attack submarines taken over by Neo-Maoist radicals have blown themselves up and lie on the bottom of the ocean. China announced that a cave complex in Chongqing was used as a base of operations. It has been destroyed by PRC troops. The Chinese government also stated that they look forward to working with the United States in building positive relations in the future."

"Even knowing ahead of time didn't help Apollo or us," Lauren said.

"I'm starting to crash, but there's so much to tell you about what I just saw happen."

The news ticker by scrolled by at the bottom of the screen. The battle for the Capitol Building is over. The President and Vice President are safe, as are all the elected representatives. Many policemen and SWAT team members sacrificed their lives. At this time, we have not identified the terrorists, and no group has claimed responsibility. Someone did help us to avoid further disaster. A caller, using an unregistered phone in Virginia tipped off the police with just enough time to save our leadership. This is often said, maybe without enough meaning, but everywhere in the country, we should all stop what we're doing and say, God Bless America. We have been in the belly of the beast, and we survived, somehow."

Zack relaxed against Lauren. "The caller must have been Sam Fung. He regretted the betrayal of everything he believed in. His whole plot came crashing down."

"Speaking of plots, does this mean the mind control drug has been confiscated?" Lauren said.

"We can only hope. If it proceeds as Apollo has said, then a lot of what we did here will be for nothing. That drug must be safe-guarded in the right hands. The promise of a cure for dementia is still valuable," Zack said. "Where are the kids?"

"Watching Fung."

Zack heard music. A stringed-instrument played. He grinned.

Lauren looked around. "Where's that coming from? It sounds like a plucked violin."

"Listen closely," Zack said. "The notes sound like George Harrison's song, "Here Comes the Sun"."

"What?" Lauren looked confused.

Zack grinned at her. "I forgot to tell you. Whenever I hear Beatles music, I know who it's coming from."

Apollo materialized in a swirl of blue energy.

"Apollo's back!" Lauren exclaimed loud enough to be heard a couple of houses away.

Demo and Cassandra ran into the family room. They attempted to hug Apollo, but his force-field blocked their approach them.

"Please. Alert me before you knock me over," Apollo said, grinning. "With our enemies defeated, perhaps I can now remove the shield and allow me to be as I am."

"What do you mean?" Demo asked.

"I declare to you that I am as mortal as you are." He saw the shocked faces of the kids. He illuminated the blue dome. He set aside down his lyre and shut off the field. "With my protective shield down, I am no more a god than you."

"You're freaking me out here," Demo said.

Apollo said, "I became an entity more powerful than you to lead and inspire you."

Demo poked Apollo with his finger. "Yep. Shield is down."

Lauren said, "After seeing holograms about your former life, we began to put two and two together, but we're still confused about how all this happened."

"So, when you brought me to meet Ben Franklin, Pericles, and Martin Luther King, that was all a representation? Not really them?" Zack asked.

"Disappointing, I know. All of the people you met were accurate holographic images I created for you."

"That must have been an interesting...conversation," Lauren said.

"All the training, all the…adventures…couldn't you have just done this all yourself?" Zack asked, tilting his head as he waited for an answer.

"Did you gain an appreciation for what you have, Traveler? You have a way of life to save…or to squander. While I trained you for war, I educated you for peace."

Cassandra saw the silver flask at Apollo's waist. "What's in the flask?"

Zack said, "He's given it to me before. It heals wounds quickly."

"There are three chambers within the flask," Apollo said. "One allows you to survive the transit of time. The second allows me to influence you. To have the dreams I sent you. This is a futuristic version of the medicine Fung began in this time. The third kind, as you know, heals wounds at a rapid rate. It has mended you, Traveler, and the Bactrian I just left."

Lauren folded her arms. "And what's the story with him. Do I still need my baseball bat by the door?"

"He's back in his time, Golden Hair. You are free of him. He chose a reunion with his son. And he said that he knew you were warrior who fought him and lived." He handed to Lauren the driver's license Bessus had kept in his waist pouch.

She smiled. "Thank you. It's great to be not wanted."

"Remember that he put himself at risk to preserve your country. He saw the wisdom of discarding his vehemence towards you. Do you want to be outdone in morality by a barbarian?"

"You're right. I'll work on it."

"Here, Golden Hair. This is the last of my flasks. I'll make more now that I'll have the time."

Lauren tried a sip. "I tasted something like this before."

"I put some in your hummus in Athens, so you would survive the transit. What you taste now is the medicine."

"You planned this from way back," Lauren said.

"Might you remember the young man who attacked you in the classroom? I compelled him with pulses of my medallion to challenge you. This was designed to test your toughness. A beginning to see if you had the fortitude to be the heroine I needed. You proved yourself in your struggles with Bessus. As did Cassandra." He smiled at the young Marine.

Demo said, "So, what now?" He took a sip of the drink and handed it to Cassandra.

"I tasted this, too. When you visited me back at my farm," Cassandra said.

"That is correct. Sit down, all of you. I want to speak of the future." Apollo put a finger to his lips. "I will help you to rebuild your nation. I will be Merlin to your Arthur and Guinevere."

Lauren asked, gesturing towards Zack, "So who's on top, me or him?"

Apollo laughed hard. The teenagers cringed.

"Golden Hair, you have proved yourself to be a hero of the highest caliber. You can lead if you so desire. You're every bit as capable as your husband. Maybe more. It's up to you." He grinned at Zack.

Taking no offense, Zack said, "So you'll guide the rebuilding of the nation?"

"You must do the hard work and make the difficult choices. Otherwise, all I have done is for naught" Apollo said. "I want you to know that we have saved more than people and nations."

"How so?" Demo asked.

Apollo said, "For so many thousands of years, priestesses worshipped the Earth Mother. The multiple nuclear detonations we just stopped would have created devastation that even a hundred and fifty years later, in my time, had yet to heal. We preserved Gaia, the Earth, and we must make accelerated efforts to do so as we go forward."

"Second freak out! That far ahead? Demo said. "No wonder. Wait. How did you get here…I mean…travel here in time? I wanna hear about how your scientists managed that and where the underground facility was in this country?"

"In the state called Utah, and we'll have plenty of time to discover that later, Demo. What about Fung?" Zack asked.

"Come, Traveler. Let us consult with him while your family relaxes."

Zack removed Fung's gag and sat on the edge of the bed.

Apollo said, "Your plot is undone. We destroyed the Chinese submarine ballistic missiles. While there's severe damage to the economy and our leadership, we will recover in time."

Fung screamed, "You'll never succeed in stopping us. Just because you…"

Zack interrupted, "But we have, and now I suggest we examine your thoughts again, Fung."

Perhaps there's more to tell us."

"No. Not again. My head can't take it."

Apollo's medallion made a whirring noise. "You don't understand, Fung. You have failed. The Chongqing Facility has been destroyed by the Chinese government. The Chinese submarines scuttled themselves and lie on the ocean floor."

"What about Lian? She was in Chongqing?"

"Whoever she is, she has either died in the siege or has been captured. The drug you created was militarized in the years ahead as you hoped. Nations and people ruled under the whip. I'm from that future. That medicine also allowed the slaughter of entire races." Apollo stood next to the bed. "I come from a time where freedom is unknown, never dreamed of. There were no thoughts of independence, because populations have been drugged."

"Do you have anything to say, Fung?" Zack asked. "Your diabolical vision is over."

Fung said, "If my wife dies, I'll make you pay. Your corrupt bankers know. Your government knows. Homeland Security knows. Do you think the world feels safe from you?"

After clearing his throat, Fung went on, "Your own institutions plot it, too. To dominate all of you. You've been sold out, manipulated, and you don't see it. My *Yie*, my father, knew."

"Your delusions nearly destroyed millions of lives," Zack said.

"Delusional. That describes all of you. Do you think the future I have in mind is worse than what's coming?" He stared at Apollo. "Master manipulator or quasi-god, whatever you are, you didn't calculate a different future, one where humankind is limited, even extinguished. I am saving the future, you idiots. On my terms for a select group, I admit. But rule of the best… and the brightest, and the strongest race."

"You don't know that's how the future will turn out," Zack said.

"I'm choosing human life over global chaos. Don't you get it?" He struggled with his restraints. "Machines process information at exponential speeds over humans. We can't efficiently halt its coming dominance without a select group of people, limiting its advance and quelling competitive wars among nations for domination of resources. Think about what I'm saying. That day will come. It's not that far away. I'm creating a cadre of superhumans to ensure the survival of the species…limit the populations of all races, control and coordinate their technological advances so there will be order. Stop me and you sentence humanity."

Fung's voice became weak. "I ensured the correct mix of people." His sneer returned. "And none of you were invited. You're all so naive."

"Your plan has failed, Fung," Apollo said. "We showed your father what you said about dominating the common people and populations. He knew you were a traitor to his cause. You want human robots, not people. He couldn't live with the shame. He informed the authorities in time to disrupt the attack on the Capitol… and I've been informed he blew himself up in his home."

Fung grimaced and shouted, "You unbelievable bastards!"

"We'll control the threat of the technological advances you describe. Nothing you're selling defends the execution of millions," Apollo said.

"You think you own the truth, Fung," Zack said. "You even betrayed your own father. You're power drunk."

Fung spat, "You'll fail. You have no discipline. No control over yourselves. You think we're beasts. Look at your…"

The round door handle twisted. The door flew open.

San Diego

NEAR FUTURE

Zack saw the pistol first.

Police? Swat team? Why the drawn gun?

"What the hell?" Zack said.

A man in black tactical clothing dashed into the room. No hood. An Asian-looking guy.

What?

Zack heard shouting coming from the living room.

Lauren? The kids?

Zack, seated on the edge of the bed beside Alfred, saw the intruder glance at him.

Shots and screams sounded from the front room.

Zack heard his named called twice. He needed to get to Lauren.

Aiming at Zack, the gunman fired in rapid succession.

Apollo leapt in front of the bullets.

Zack jumped off the bed and grabbed the hot muzzle of the gun.

Strongly built, the intruder wrestled Zack for control of the weapon. He tried a head-butt, but Zack spun out of the way. They both slammed against the wall. The man put all his strength behind turning the muzzle towards Zack.

Zack rotated sideways just as the gunman emptied the rest of the clip.

In the direction of the bed. Fung groaned.

Zack locked his leg under the assailant, shifted his weight and kicked at the Asian's kneecap. He heard a snap.

Learned that from Diomedes.

The intruder cried out. Zack fell atop him.

Air rushed from the man's lungs. He dropped the gun.

More shots in the chamber? Zack wondered. He couldn't count. His heart raced. Adrenaline. Electricity. Desperation. Animal. Like at Salamis. And Plataea.

Zack picked up the weapon and whacked it against the man's head until his skull cracked.

Screams sounded from the living room. Zack jumped to his feet and ran out the door.

71

San Diego

NEAR FUTURE

Lauren said, "Cassandra, could you put all these sneakers by the door? Getting a bit messy in here."

Three pairs of shoes in her hands, Cassandra walked to the front entrance. A man dressed in black clothing smashed open the door with a metal battering ram. He dropped it and raised a handgun.

Cassandra hurled the sneakers at him just as the guy fired.

Five pops. She heard swearing behind her. Cassandra slammed her fist into the guy's cheekbone.

Lauren screamed for Zack.

The intruder chopped at Cassandra's neck. He missed. She crashed the heel of her hand into his chin. He fell backwards, discharging his weapon.

The shot tore into her shoulder. She spun and fell against the wall.

The attacker moved forward, scanning the room.

Lauren picked up a vase and threw it at him. It missed, shattering against the fireplace.

Demo, standing in the kitchen, grabbed a knife and hurled it at the man, but it pin-wheeled past him.

The gunman fired again. Lauren saw Demo grab for his side. She ran to the kitchen and seized a ceramic pot.

The intruder reloaded.

Demo stumbled into the living room.

Lauren shouted, "Zack!"

The gunman followed her to the kitchen. She hurled a container of baking flour into his face. He sputtered and coughed.

Demo came from behind him and buried the Marathon sword in the attacker's neck. The guy gasped, twisted, gurgled and collapsed.

Zack ran into the room.

Lauren saw her daughter struggling to stand, her hand covering her bloody shoulder.

Grimacing, Cassandra said, "We have to wrap it and stop the bleeding. I think the bullet went clean through."

Demo glanced at the sword and then at the man scissor-kicking on the floor. Letting the weapon fall, he stared at the blood on his hand.

Zack checked Lauren. "The side of your head is bleeding." He glanced at the assailant, who now lay motionless on the floor.

She said, "I heard the shot go by. I just felt a sting."

He ripped a paper towel off the spool and set it against her earlobe.

Lauren looked past Zack. "Demo!"

The teenager's knees buckled.

"Call an ambulance," Lauren said, dashing to him. "He's bleeding from his stomach, or his side. I don't know which."

"Get me towel," Zack said. He ripped open Demo's shirt and saw a bullet entry wound to the right side of his stomach. He turned him over to check for an exit wound. "Call an ambulance. Hurry."

Demo groaned.

Lauren dialed the number on her cell phone. "Are they all dead, Zack? Are there any more of them? We're all shot up here."

"No more, so far," Zack answered.

"I'll be okay, Mom," Cassandra said. "Help Demo."

"Ambulance and police on the way," Lauren said. She ran to the laundry room and grabbed towels. She quick-wrapped Cassandra's wound with one of the towels and made a sling. "Go to him, Mom!"

Lauren kneeled and clasped Demo's face. "We're getting you help.

Breath slowly."

Demo sputtered blood. "Don't press so hard. It's starting to hurt."

Zack held a cloth over his son's wound. "Keep breathing."

"Where's Apollo?" Lauren asked.

Zack cried out, "Oh, no! Stay with Demo." He raced for the bedroom.

Everyone had seen the horrified expression on Zack's face.

Cassandra said to her mother, "Go. I'll stay with Demo."

Lauren bolted after Zack.

72

San Diego, California

NEAR FUTURE

Zack leapt over the gunman's body in the doorway.

He saw Fung, his eyes open and fixed.

He turned Apollo over onto his back.

An uneven circle of blood covered his chest.

And a head wound. Blood seeped from a ragged hole.

"He's been hit," Zack yelled. "It's serious."

Lauren ran into the room. "Please, no!"

Zack listened for a heartbeat. "Get his nectar," he said, seeing the shot into Apollo's temple.

She ran for the silver flask.

Putting his finger in the carotid notch of Apollo's neck, Zack reported, "It's weak. Hurry."

Lauren found Cassandra in the living room, pouring the last drips of nectar into Demo's mouth.

"None left, Mom," Cassandra said.

"It's gone?' Lauren said. "Let me have it. Apollo's in trouble." She dashed back to the bedroom.

Lauren wondered how someone with such god-like strength minutes ago, could be broken so fast. She tipped the flask. Nothing. "We drank most it before. We must do something, Zack."

Apollo opened his eyes a sliver. He strained to speak, coughed up blood and groaned.

Lauren held his face in her hands. "Tell us how to save you."

Weakly, Apollo said, "Yours…now. *Agape.*"

Accepting the gravity, Lauren said, "We love you, Apollo. Thank you for all you've done for us, for the nation, for the future."

Cassandra helped Demo into the room and down onto the floor beside Apollo. She said, "911 on the way."

Each held one of Apollo's hands.

Zack said, "Stay with us, Apollo. We need you."

A breath escaped him. He turned his head to one side.

Zack checked for a pulse. He gazed up at his family. He couldn't hold back his agony. Not any longer. None of them could. They all cradled his body and wept.

Rising finally, Zack said, "You must understand. There was no time to think. He reacted and sacrificed himself…for me. Dived into the path of the bullets."

Lauren stood. "He died for you." She sighed, then asked, "What do we do with him, Zack? How do we identify him to the police?"

"We can't. I still can't believe he's gone. There was so much more to know…to achieve."

Cassandra stayed nestled on Apollo's side. "We should secure the medallions and the flask.

No one will understand."

"We have to explain this to the police somehow," Zack said. "We'd better untie Fung. He's dead, but they attacked us. We defended ourselves. There's no way to explain everything. Police are overtasked now. They might be too busy with the riots and the desperation out there to investigate in depth. I'm just going to tell them the truth, except for who Apollo is."

"Should we let them have Apollo?" Lauren asked.

Zack had to think. *Better to keep his body, or give it up?*

"I think we should let them take him. Say we just met and don't know his name. With no ID, they'll declare him a 'John Doe'. But we'll volunteer to arrange and pay for the funeral."

"I can't believe he's gone. What do we do now?" Cassandra asked. "I feel sick."

Lauren said, "How are you doing, Demo?"

"It aches. Those last drips of his medicine must be helping, but that's not what's making me feel terrible."

They stared at Apollo's prone body until police sirens broke the silence in the room.

73

Tora Bora Mountains Afghan/ Pakistani Border

NEAR FUTURE

Six months later, Corporal Cassandra Fletcher pushed aside brush with the muzzle of her AR-15. She peered inside the cave opening. The last wisps of smoke from a grenade blast wafted past her. The Taliban fighters had escaped from other units.

But not from her.

She checked to see if her 9 mm pistol was fully loaded and a new magazine in her rifle. Using hand signals, Cassandra directed her squad to follow her into the cave.

A private whispered, "Didn't they bomb the shit out of this area with B-52s back in 2001?"

Cassandra put her finger to her lips and then motioned them to move forward. Around two corners and no sign of the fighters. With little light, they switched on their head lamps.

Crouching, she gestured for her team to do the same. "I'm turning mine off and going ahead. Keep your lights on but direct the beam towards rocks or off to the side. These Taliban are mine."

The Marine recon unit was undermanned now. A staff sergeant and the gunny sergeant had been killed earlier, which left Cassandra in charge.

Her first command.

She had shot the fighters who'd killed her leadership. She'd never heard much good about the Tora Bora. Black mountains, dirt, dust, and little else besides the goat turds beneath her booted feet.

Cassandra slung her rifle and crawled forward, her 9mm pistol at the ready.

She heard voices. She knew these caves served as hideouts, but they'd also had been used for burials in the distant past. Sacred ground, she'd been told. They shouldn't have hidden in here.

Muzzle flashes and bits of rock showered her. Good thing she was on the cave floor. The shots went high, but she knew their location now. She shot at the flashes. Two screams sounded, and the clang of weapons as they hit the rocks. Another man groaned and could be heard trying to flee. Lauren turned on her head lamp. A terrorist turned a corner. She followed him. Caves didn't bother her. She'd lived and played in one for a week at a time with her Uncle Nestor. Her lamp created shadows ahead, but she spotted a man as he scampered into a crevice.

Then, she heard a voice. She had her weapon ready. Whoever fired first would survive.

Turning the last corner, Cassandra saw the fighter on his knees kneeling with his back to her. He looked up at a small outcropping of rock, murmuring what sounded like prayers. Along the cave wall she saw a series of skulls lined up.

A graveyard? she wondered.

Cassandra saw that the terrorist had dropped his AK-47 and kneeled before a concavity. He turned suddenly. The flashlight revealed the terror in his eyes. Crazed, he pointed at a central skull and waved his arms.

Then, he drew a knife and lunged at her.

Cassandra fired. He crumbled to the tunnel floor. She kicked aside his knife.

Her head lamp illuminated the gravesite. How old could it be? Maybe generations of the locals. Some looked ancient. Right in front of her sat an enormous skull, surrounded by the tips of ivory tusks and colored beads.

A shrine of some kind...with elephant tusks?

She picked up the human skull and gasped. Large bony ridges over the eye sockets. All teeth missing, but...holy hell. False teeth? A denture with metals studs stuck into the jawbones.

Cassandra picked up the skull and looked at the upper denture, twirling it slowly until she saw writing on the outside flange. Hard to see in the dark. She used her flashlight to be sure.

Bessus.

What?

Only Apollo could have arranged this. Bessus had, in fact, returned to his time.

She would have smashed the skull to pieces if he hadn't helped to save the Homeland. She remembered when she'd stabbed him in the back and saved her mother.

I was tough for a young girl. Then again, I was bred an Athenian.

Cassandra detached the worn upper denture from the implant studs. She tucked the denture in her pocket. She carefully replaced the skull in the nook.

She smiled, thinking the denture would be a great White Elephant gift for her mom.

Lauren is going to screech when she sees this!

74

San Diego, California

NEAR FUTURE

The engineer held up three fingers and counted down. "On the air in 3.2.1." He pointed at Zack and Lauren, who sat across from a lady interviewer organizing her notes.

"Good morning. I'm Marianne Molak, and we welcome Professors Lauren and Zack Fletcher from San Diego State University to our studios. Your message to America has resonated loud and clear on your radio and television shows. But now, everyone wants to know the answer to one question: Are you going to enter politics?"

Zack cleared his throat. He opened his mouth to speak, but Lauren cut in.

"Entering politics may be a goal someday, but first we'd like to offer an educational series to all Americans. If it's true that a democracy, or a constitutional republic, survives with educated voters, then we'd like to be part of that effort."

"Well put, Lauren, and I'll add to that," Zack said. "The percentage of Americans proficient in the Humanities, and its relevance to our future, needs improvement. Is it only science and technology that are important?"

The interviewer said, "It's a function of the job market. Is anyone getting a job with a history degree?"

Lauren said, "You have a point there, but in the end, a well-rounded, informed individual will make better decisions on the advance of civilization. History, philosophy, and literature can help guide our leap forward in technology. One must wade through disinformation. An educated citizen, who can evaluate both sides of an argument, is more likely to discover and preserve the truth."

"She's just getting started," Zack said.

Lauren grinned. "Okay, I won't run on like that again, but let me finish. When the proper time is given to educate the public, then we might entertain a political path…"

Zack said, "She has me on board."

Marianne's eyes widened. "Back to the interview. Let's talk about heroism. Both of you are recognized for your selfless acts to defend us against the attacks the country suffered."

"Now that's a serious subject. But yes. We acted, and I would argue that Lauren here is just as much the hero as me, especially in my eyes."

Lauren gave Zack a surprised look. "How do you figure?"

"Because you saved me more than once-physically and psychologically. I owe you my life."

"My, we're getting syrupy here," Lauren said.

"You two are driving me crazy."

Lauren smiled at Zack.

"Let's get back to heroism," Marianne said.

"So much has been made of that already," said Zack. "Let's talk about something else."

"Like?"

"We want to be part of the rebuilding of this nation. The schism that plagues the nation must be mended. Good people across the country are volunteering to run for office. We need them as participants in our rebirth. You could call it a second revolution in the Martin Luther King style. Peaceful, deeply thoughtful, and determined."

"How will you do that?" Marianne leaned in.

"The corruption of money must be excised from our election process. We're fully aware it will be no small feat, but so much of what is wrong is related to the raising of contributions to gain and hold office. Technological and biological advances must be safeguarded to benefit the health of our citizens, the nation, and global community. Robotics, Artificial Intelligence—all this must be evaluated and equated for the good of humanity. It's time for soul searching before some giant leap leaves us no choices."

"That sounds like a campaign speech."

"On the surface. What Lauren and I intend to do is open an Academy to teach in the style of Aristotle, Socrates and Plato with a modernized, and innovative course of study. Of course, we'll bring in scientists, mathematicians and other professors to broaden the curriculum, but the goal will be to teach moderation, balance…the middle road. Be inclusive of all citizens. First, we want to begin a think-tank outside of political circles to discover what can be done going forward to avoid disasters like the one we just escaped. Safety is fleeting. We must find a way to rid ourselves of the corruption that rots our system from the inside. We want a national, and then an international panel, to rediscover the middle ground in the political debate. Where rule by the people began in ancient Athens, we want to reestablish that concept in our country where many feels that control is slipping to a perpetual aristocratic class."

"That's ambitious. Is this a doable goal?" Marianne asked.

"If many more are educated and involved. To govern, or *gubernare,* is a word with Latin roots, but it's derived from the ancient Greek word *kybernetes,* which means to steer a ship. We want to help steer the rebuilt ship of this country, to be pilots, or Kybernan."

"Stated just like a professor." Marianne laughed. "We need good people to move us forward. Anything else you want to say?"

"Yes, there is," Lauren said. "I will be happy to join him on the podium afterwards."

"After what?" The interviewer asked.

"I want to announce that we're pregnant." Lauren smiled. "Five months along, in fact."

Marianne tossed her interview papers in the air.

San Diego

NEAR FUTURE- FOUR MONTHS LATER

Zack took a swig from a water bottle as he left the hospital cafeteria. He realized he had not checked his email since arriving in the maternity ward with Lauren twelve hours earlier. Thumbing his cell phone keys, he saw a message from San Diego State.

A congratulatory notice from the Dean of Arts and Letters, announcing he had made tenure for his exceptional work in bringing the lost Minoan language back to life. A full professor.

He'd made it.

Lauren and him had traveled to Greece for the University after national and global uncertainties had calmed down. There he took her to all the places he'd visited on the journey from Santorini to Delphi in 1600 BC. Able to locate the obscure cave entrance and discovering it undisturbed, he found the skeletal remains of Mela and the other warriors who had perished in the battle on the coast of the Mani Peninsula.

And a skin upon which he had written, detailing the Minoan alphabet, a version of Linear A, and its translation into English.

Zack turned the corner and found a nurse waving at him from the delivery room.

"Be quick, Professor Fletcher. Baby is going to be born anytime now."

Zack sprinted. The nurse held open the door.

Lauren scrunched her eyes shut as Dr. Leslie, the obstetrician, said, "Push, push, push."

Zack grasped Lauren's hand. "I'm back, honey."

"And you're needed, why?"

He saw the exhaustion and pain of labor in her eyes.

Lauren said, "They must sell whiskey in that cafeteria. I need someth…." She cried out.

Dr. Leslie said, "I see the baby's head. All is going well. Now, Lauren, push as hard as you can."

Lauren dug her chin into her chest and gritted her teeth.

"That's good," the doctor said, adjusting her safety goggles. "Give me another big push."

A weary Lauren blew out a gust of air and looked at Zack. "And I asked for this."

Zack said, "You're doing great. Everything we ever asked for. Come on, honey, just a few more times."

"Apollo, help me!" Lauren shouted, grabbing the bed rails.

"Who?" the doctor asked. "Here we go. Turning this baby, now."

Zack peered at the workings of the obstetrician. He could see the babies emerging head. Lauren wailed.

The infant landed in the doctor's hands.

"It's a boy," Dr. Leslie declared. A nurse swaddled the infant in a cotton blanket. A tap on the rump, and the baby cried.

Lauren laughed. "A son…a son."

A speechless Zack peered into baby's face. A moment later, the little boy opened his eyes and looked at Zack and Lauren with the most quizzical expression.

"He's confused…takes after you." Lauren said, squeezing Zack's hand.

Dr. Leslie gently placed the infant into Lauren's arms. "He looks perfectly healthy. After you hold him for a while, we'll bring him over to the heated table and check him out more closely. Congratulations, both of you. I know how difficult this was and all you went through to get pregnant."

Lauren kissed his head, which was covered with a smattering of dark hair. "He's so beautiful. He's ours, Zack."

"I can't believe it. I just can't," Zack said. "Can I hold him?"

"Wait your turn. He's going to be a momma's boy for a while."

"Okay. You did all the hard work. Love you, honey." Zack slid into the bed beside them.

Dr. Leslie finished caring for Lauren. "And now that you know he's a boy, what shall we call this fine young man?"

Lauren and Zack looked at each other. Lauren touched their son's little nose. "I hereby name you … Nestor Apollo Leonidas Atlantea Fletcher."

Zack threw his head back and laughed. "Yes…yes, perfect." He smiled. "He'll be good at spelling with a name like that."

"The future is bright for this child," Dr. Leslie said. "It is for all of us, thanks to both of you."

A nurse carried Nestor over to a heated table. Lauren whispered into Zack's ear, "I'm so happy, so very happy. It's a miracle. I still don't know how."

Zack said into her ear, "Apollo gave you the last of the nectar. Somehow it must have…allowed you to get pregnant."

"We owe Apollo so much. I can't help seeing Persephone's face and Uncle Nestor's, too."

"Diomedes."

"Even Queen Io. We had an appointment with destiny that can't be explained. It's all good, Zack. I'm okay with everything. We're all together. Let's bring the kids in to meet their brother."

"I'll go get them."

"Make sure you come back."

"I will, and I'll never be away from you, honey. Never again."

Delphi, Greece

NEAR FUTURE- SIX MONTHS LATER

The family stood on the hillside beneath the famed twin peaks of Mount Parnassus.

Apollo's entrance to the tunnel remained covered with dirt and stone. A wind blew in from the Corinthian Gulf, and little Nestor cried.

Lauren pulled a blue blanket over the six-month-old, wondering if he might be hungry. It had been a strenuous hike to reach the site on which their lives had changed forever.

Demo and Zack took shovels from their backpacks. They dug square hole three feet deep, and then they lined it with stones.

Cassandra removed a small vase with red figures painted on a black background, like those made in ancient Athens. They'd had the vase custom made with scenes of Apollo's feats, especially his destruction of the missiles with his dome's laser. She kissed it and placed it into the grave.

"He'll always be here," Lauren said. "He'd be pleased. I'm glad we didn't disperse his ashes. This is …fitting."

"Shall I say a few words?" Zack asked.

"Yes," Lauren said. "Do the honors."

Zack nodded. "Here you began your odyssey. You helped us to defeat the enemies, and now you're home and whole again in Zeus's cosmos.

Rest well, Apollo."

No one spoke for a time.

Lauren broke the silence. "He made us a family. A family that, in ages past would have been a story around a campfire, or maybe in a fantasy movie. But we're here, and it all happened."

Everyone threw a handful of dirt onto the vase. As Lauren and the baby looked on, the rest covered it with rocks and soil. No stone would mark the site.

Cassandra slipped the two medallions out from under her jacket. "Wait, should these be buried with him?"

From one, the image of Tyche arose.

What came from the other medallion made them gasp.

Another of Apollo's holographic memories emerged.

Apollo remembered the first trip. Within the Blue Dome, with the hot mud burning in his belly, he'd landed in the time and at the place that Hera had arranged for him.

At Delphi. The ancient Oracle of Apollo. The god he had taken on as his personality.

He created a polarity out of a magnetized stone and set it on a hillside, just beyond the temples. He joined it to a long tunnel, which lead into the complex, to hide his comings and goings. The Blue Dome now served as his transportation. Another marvel devised by Hera and Hephaestus, channeling gravity into power and acceleration. He visited Athens and Sparta, marveling at the accuracy of the historical records.

Fascinated with the massive Persian army that marched towards Greece in 480 BCE, he listened to meetings of King Xerxes and his royalty, but his eyes were drawn to one warrior in particular-an enormous warlord from the eastern satrap of Bactria with massive biceps braced with bronze bands. With cruel eyes and a crooked scar on one side of his face, his manner betrayed impatience and even disgust for those whom he served.

Perhaps he might be useful, Apollo thought.

He met one other person back at Delphi. A girl of twelve with a gentle, yet courageous nature. She told him about working on the farm and defending the livestock against wild dogs. Much to his regret, he'd had to return to preparing the others for an exciting plan he had devised.

Stepping from the roiling tunnel matter that hardened behind him, Apollo saw his fellow gods lined up. He accepted their praise for his courage, but he didn't want to waste time. Once he had them all seated, he described his journey and what he had witnessed in ancient times. His fellow scientists barely breathed.

Then he told them of his plan to reverse the history of mankind from the early 21st century until their present time. Why should generations live in slavery?

Apollo said, "We've become enamored with the ancient Greeks, because of the gifts they brought to mankind. We have read Sophocles, the works of Socrates and Pythagoras, Sappho and Aeschylus. We know war among themselves and others is a stain on their memory, but they left us architecture, playwriting, athletics, drama, science, and, of course, the kernel of democracy. The arts flourish in modern times, taking their roots from the ancient world. We have all enjoyed discovering what they call Classical Music, as well as the advances that led to the music from the last half of the twentieth century."

"We all agree with your assessment," Ares said. "Can we all make the journey to the past now?"

"I don't know exactly when," Hera, the former Chin, said. "But soon."

A day later, Apollo recalled that Hephaestus had given them all powerful microprocessors shaped like large coins and bearing a symbol of their god-personality. On his, and recognizing the representation of Apollo's skill and influence, the embossed image of an archer and the sun.

But now, he made the case to the others that the people who lived in free countries should join in on the cause to stop the collapse of the West and the enslavement of the world. Each went to his or her respective stations and researched how the West had failed.

Reports came in fast. Overleveraged economies, a lack of concern for the growing corruption within the countries, discord and subterfuge by the political parties against each other, endless war and the constant threat of it.

Then, the attack that ended it all - an economic disaster, followed by foreign attacks on the US homeland, Europe, and Russia. But no more details. How had the economic disaster occurred, and who had been responsible? Who had initiated the nuclear weapon strikes? A report said from the Far East, but not which country.

The record halted on a single day.

Zeus agreed. "We will all transfer back and ensure that the cataclysm is stopped. We will train the people to change their ways and shun excess. We have made other technological advances to support our cause. An energy platform which materializes to enhance your transfer within the time transit, and for general travel, has been created. We each will have one, and the protective system that comes with it. I also recommended that it be armed."

Apollo labored at his monitor. He searched for 21st century men and women who might be candidates to build a new country. He filtered education, age, physical condition, family situation, and backgrounds. Many names displayed on the screen. Only one couple met all the parameters.

Researching further, he found they were teachers at a university. A picture of the male professor at a meeting cross-checked with a name mentioned in the Hall of Heroes back at Apollo's home school.

The name: Saabir. One of the lower races, but someone who had helped to facilitate the destruction of the enemy.

Somehow, the two were connected in the collapse and the attack. He had to know. The wife had honey-colored hair and reminded him of others he had seen in the lines ready to get their assignment when he was twelve. Many of the fair-haired girls became concubines.

He stared at the picture of the woman professor. *Such a shame. You must have died in the inferno that destroyed the United States?*

While he, Zeus and Hera prepared the computers and supplies for individual leaps, a commotion sounded from the main enclave.

Poseidon rushed in. "Mars and Athena have been arrested in the corridors. They sent us a garbled message. The Overseer has discovered us."

"How long before they penetrate Olympus?" Hera asked.

They heard explosions at the metallic door. Poseidon and Hephaestus ran towards it. Without any weapons, they had no chance of stopping the overseer and his guards. Nonetheless.

Zeus turned to Apollo. "Someone must go. You have the experience. Take up our cause. We'll hold them off."

Hera handed him two flasks of medicine. "They will heal you. I have adjusted the machine to also allow transit without the dome in case it malfunctions. You must ingest the tunnel material first, though. Three kinds of medication in three chambers within. One to heal, one to enable the transit, and a third to influence thoughts."

They heard the attackers cutting through the metallic vault door with lasers. Smoke began to fill the room.

"We will seal travel from this end. We cannot let them go back in time to stop you." Zeus held up an explosive cake. "I made it last week."

Apollo saw his colleagues striking the guards with clubs as they tried to push open the door.

Hera said, "Set for Delphi in the early 21st century just before they attack. You'll need time to plan…"

Screams at the doorway. Guards burst in over the crumbled bodies of Poseidon and Hephaestus.

Hera left Zeus with a smile, a touch of his hand, and she ran for the door to hold them off an instant more.

Exhaustion and misery evident in his eyes and in the lines of his face, Zeus said, "Go now, Arex, I mean Apollo. Change what happens." Zeus hung his head. "We're depending on you. I will destroy this end of the transit after I'm sure you've made it."

Hearing shots and a scream, an anguished Zeus said, "Hurry."

The bluish energy of the dome surrounded Apollo. He leapt into the swirling tunnel matter and disappeared.

He absorbed the velocity of the transit with his heart racing.

Apollo shouted within the swirls, "They sacrificed themselves for me, for every generation to come. I must succeed."

The image halted.

Zack kissed Nestor's head. Lauren smiled at Zack.

She said, "It's clear now. The gods sacrificed themselves for Apollo. He sacrificed himself for us. Unconditional love. The definition of *Agape*."

"It's truly up to us now," Zack said.

Lauren rocked the infant in her arms. "You saved us, Apollo. You gave us a second chance. Everything depends now on how well we rebuild. We'll have to define the soul of the country before we can move ahead."

"Remember when we thought he was a god? We believed in him, and yet he wasn't one."

"Nationalities and religions can live and work together. Bessus changed, and he helped to save us."

A wind whipped up the mountainside. Lauren covered baby Nestor with a blanket.

"I always imagined that Apollo would take us back someday to be with all the people we met," Zack said with a forlorn look.

"Uncle Nestor and Persephone," Lauren said, "even Diomedes, Io and the boy, Atlantea, Zack."

"And you never met the others I traveled with in Thera. Heebe, Talos and their twin sons."

"Would you have preferred to have never have been involved, Dad?" Cassandra asked.

Zack drew Cassandra into the crook of his arm. "We don't get those choices sometimes. Apollo told me once that Liberty called you to serve her. And we're all going to do that from here on. But most of all, we have you and Demo."

Lauren reached for her daughter's hand. "Did we learn anything, Zack? Yes, we held off disaster for now, but there has to be some greater lesson here beyond survival."

Leaves pirouetted on the breeze. Zack laid his hand on Lauren's back, ensuring a safe negotiation of the rugged path down. "Maybe, that so must had been sacrificed for, over so long, and not to take anything for granted. Anything." He returned Lauren's smile.

Demo flipped the medallions in his fingers. "Who knows, maybe someday we'll figure out how to use these."

"What?" Cassandra said. "And be like, Demo, the all-knowing deity for some future age?"

"You don't think I could be a god? Come on. I already know all the phrases. Behold. I am Demo, the powerful...Demo the magnificent..."

"The Magnificent? Sounds like a Vegas sidebar magician."

"Can you imagine the magic show I could do if got these medallions to work?"

"Can you take them away from him, Dad? God or magician. He's dangerous." Cassandra smacked Demo on the shoulder. He laughed and slipped the bronze medals under his shirt.

"Wait, "Zack said. "I have music to play." He tapped buttons on his cell. A searing guitar solo began. After the intro, the band sang about peaceful revolution.

Demo glanced at Cassandra. When it finished, he said, "Hey, that guy has a pretty good voice. What's his name?"

Zack smirked. "Lennon."

"Vladimir?"

"Not quite. He and his bandmates led a musical and cultural revolution. Kind of like what we're going to do, but we're going to take it even further."

"I think I know who you're talking about. Got any more of their songs?"

Zack nodded. "Sure, Demo. When we get back to the car. They have a couple of other good ones."

After a last goodbye to Apollo's unmarked resting place, they carefully made their way down the mountainside along Delphi's Sacred Way. Lauren, carrying Nestor in a front-loading baby harness and supported by Zack's firm hand, said, "Hey, kids. Professor Lisa is flying into Athens to meet us."

Cassandra smiled at Demo. "This is going to be fun."

Zack said, "Demo. Can you help your Mom for a second?"

Zack paused and turned for a last look at Apollo's resting place. His chest filled with angst. How do we leave him? he wondered. Why must life always involve so much tragedy?"

Lauren saw Zack staring back up to the grave. "We're mortals, Zack. Great promise, but limitations. We can't live forever. We must enjoy the days we have. He gave us that gift."

"Thanks, honey." Remembering words from some Irish poem, one he'd heard said about a president struck down too early, Zack said, "So long, Apollo. We hardly knew ye. You left us too soon."

After a steadying breath, Zack said, "You have a place in the setting you loved. Now, you can watch the turning of each day. We learned from you the need to be vigilant for what has already been earned for us, so that we, too, can enjoy many more peaceful sunsets."

THE END

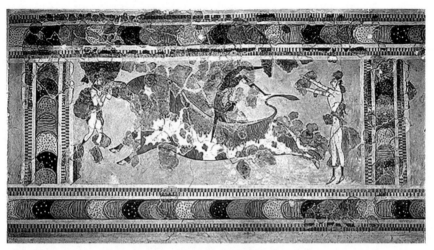

The *Bull-Leaping* Fresco from the Great Palace at Knossos, Crete

{{PD-US}} – published in the U.S. before 1923 and public domain in the U.S.

AUTHORS NOTE

Writers approach the task of writing a book, or a series of books, with ambition and trepidation, especially when blending history, philosophy, the promise and tragedies that hallmark human nature, and the innate desire to both entertain and inform their readers. While warfare portions of The Apollo Series might be considered somewhat graphic, those components of the story represent documented world history and present day geopolitical and cultural challenges. We cannot know the future, but we can project that barbarism and warfare will persist among humans, but so will inspirational acts of courage and compassion.

What began as my desire to bring attention to the Spartan stand at Thermopylae became a cautionary tale about a group of ordinary people swept up into extraordinary circumstances. Through these characters, we've experienced recorded ancient history in real-time, including emotions ranging from wonder and disappointment to greed, corruption, arrogance, sacrifice, and undaunted heroism.

At times in this trilogy, I have made changes to places and timelines in the ancient world. For example, Mycenae never recovered its former glory from the 1200 BCE period, but I recreated a fragment of the splendor that may been the Mycenean citadel during its glory days. As well, the ancient island of Santorini had to be imagined for the purposes of the story. What marvels they must have been before they were swept away by history! Shall we be cautioned to not endure the same fate.

We can only imagine the advancements that will occur in transportation, robotics, and weapons systems development. Progresses in science open the doors to the possibility of altering all that forms the essence of a human being. We're fast approaching a time when almost anything can be achieved with technology. The question arises: should we attempt to alter the human species and, if so, where do we draw the boundary lines on technological progress that will also protect and preserve humanity?

On a personal note, I want to express my deep respect for the medical research currently being undertaken on behalf of patients suffering from the tragic and debilitating disease of dementia. We all pray for rapid advancement in dementia research, and I hold the utmost regard for the patients, physicians, and researchers seeking medical solutions.

Lauren and Zack, Cassandra and Demo, Bessus, and, of course, Apollo have completed their journeys. Thank you for sharing it with them. Were Apollo here to bid you goodbye with a song, accompanied by his seven-stringed lyre, you could choose what he might play for you.

AK PATCH - 2018

Stay connected for future projects!
www.akpatchauthor.com
Facebook: Passage at Delphi- AK Patch Author
Twitter: @akpatchauthor

Thank you for all your attention and devotion to this saga. I would appreciate an extra step to help bring the story to others.

The best ways to show your regard for the series is to refer it to your friends and leave a review on Amazon. Reviews assist other readers in finding books to enjoy, and help authors gain traction on ratings.

Once again, Thank you so much.

CHARACTERS AND TECHNOLOGY

MAIN CHARACTERS

Professor Lauren Fletcher- Ph.D. in Ancient Languages at San Diego State University

Professor Zackary Fletcher- History Teacher at San Diego State University

Bessus- Warlord from the ancient province of Bactria

Apollo- Additionally identified as Calchas, a modern-day Athenian waiter and Scout, an ancient Persian warrior.

CHINESE

Alfred Fung- Ph.D. in Biochemistry/ MBA International Business

Sam Fung- Cybersecurity Specialist for Federal Reserve System

Lian- Laboratory Supervisor in the Chongqing Facility

Andrew Fung- Physician

Jean Fung- Wife of Andrew Fung

Borfan- Forensic Team Supervisor becomes Zeus

Chin- Forensic Team Supervisor becomes Hera

Hongwei- Forensic Team Overseer

PAKISTANI

Saabir-Conspirator in the Athens attack- killed by Zack in the attempt

FINANCIAL TEAM

Anthony Ladros- CEO of Steelburg Voleur

Philip Fischer-Homeland Security Officer

Deborah Hayworth- Chief Financial Officer Steelburg Voleur

Thomas Crevinski- Council Representative

SAN DIEGO

Professor Roberta Collins- Department Head African American Studies

MODERN DAY
Captain Philip Olinger- Commanding Officer of USS Port Royal CG-73

ANCIENT MINOAN AGE
Talos- Boat builder and Merchant in Thera/ Calliope
Heebe- Wife of Talos
Melos- Twin son of Talos and Heebe
Hippon- Twin Son of Talos and Heebe
Nia- Head Priestess on Calliope
Menes- Egyptian Ambassador
Krekrops- Delphi Captain

CIA/MILITARY
Top Gunnery Sergeant Morando- US Marine Corps
Agent Stone- Technical advisor
Agent Kinahan- Technical advisor
Agent Bichajian- Languages Specialist
Chief Truscott- Chief Corpsman- US Navy

MILITARY WEAPONS
SM-3 Bock IIA Interceptor- Land and Sea Defense Antimissile
    Interceptor currently in development
SM-6 Dual I - Antimissile for both terminal-phase ballistic missiles
    and cruise missiles
THAAD - Terminal High Altitude Area Defense- US Army land-
    based anti-ballistic missile system used against terminal phase
    attacks using a no-warhead kinetic kill technology
Patriot PAC-3 MSE - Land to Air missile defense with kinetic kill
    technology
Type 096 Chinese Ballistic
Missile Submarine - in development
JL-3 SLBM- - Chinese submarine-launched intercontinental ballistic
    missile. Each of 24. SLBM's can destroy 64 targets simultaneously.

ACKNOWLEDGMENTS

I've had to lean on the generous guidance of many to craft and deliver the three novels contained in the Apollo Series.

Their sage advice has helped me to think clearly as to how I wanted the story of Apollo, Lauren, Zack and Bessus to develop.

Advisors have been many.

I must thank Mike and Enriqueta Sullivan- been with me since the first undecipherable yellow pages.

Dr. Tony and Bobbi Marciante- brilliant conversations about the Classics, the challenges of the modern day and how each relate to the project.

Lawrence and Jean Patch, Philip Patch, Linda Sommers, Marianne Patch, Laurie Shay, Deborah Dugan, and Leslie O'Brien- lending critique on the adventure.

Prolific readers- Lisa Tabor Fleisher, Dr. Chuck Darzenta, Dr. Michael Strassberg, and Dr. Thomas Olinger- valuable advice on the story line of Journey from Delphi.

David and Betty Feldman- always there with editing, insight and encouragement.

Editor and author Laura Taylor- her expert guidance invaluable to the completion of this series.

Editors and advisors Matt Clement and Matthew Pallamary for their in-depth evaluations.

Publicity professionals- Strategies- Antoinette, Jared and Richard Kuritz. Gwyn Snider for her expert covers and formatting.

Dr. William Fischer for a memorable research trip to Greece.

Of course, I owe everything to my wife, Nancy, and children, Alexander and Lauren, for the many years of support as I pursued the dream of delivering this story.

CPSIA information can be obtained
at www.ICGtesting.com
Printed in the USA
FSHW01n1939080618
49126FS